# ELLA'S DOMINION

## BOOK ONE OF THE LOST WARRIORS

CHRISTINE PRIESTLY

To all the cats I've loved before.

And to Mr Lee, who allowed me to disappear into my creative void
(mostly so he could disappear into his).

# Author's Note

## To my esteemed purveyors of fantasy

**A note on language:**

As you embark on this magical journey, I invite you to embrace the spellings peculiar to the Australian (UK English) dialect of its author. Readers more used to US English spellings may be unaccustomed to the quirks of UK English, such as the additional 'u' in words like 'colour' and 'honour', but trust this will enrich your reading experience as you become immersed in the author's world.

**A note on content:**

Certain content contained within this novel may be sensitive to some readers. As specific content warnings are not spoiler-free (nor without their own perils), I invite readers seeking content advice to head to christinepriestly.com/content/ to learn more. Or to enjoy your read spoiler-free, simply begin your journey.

In magic and kinship,
Christine Priestly

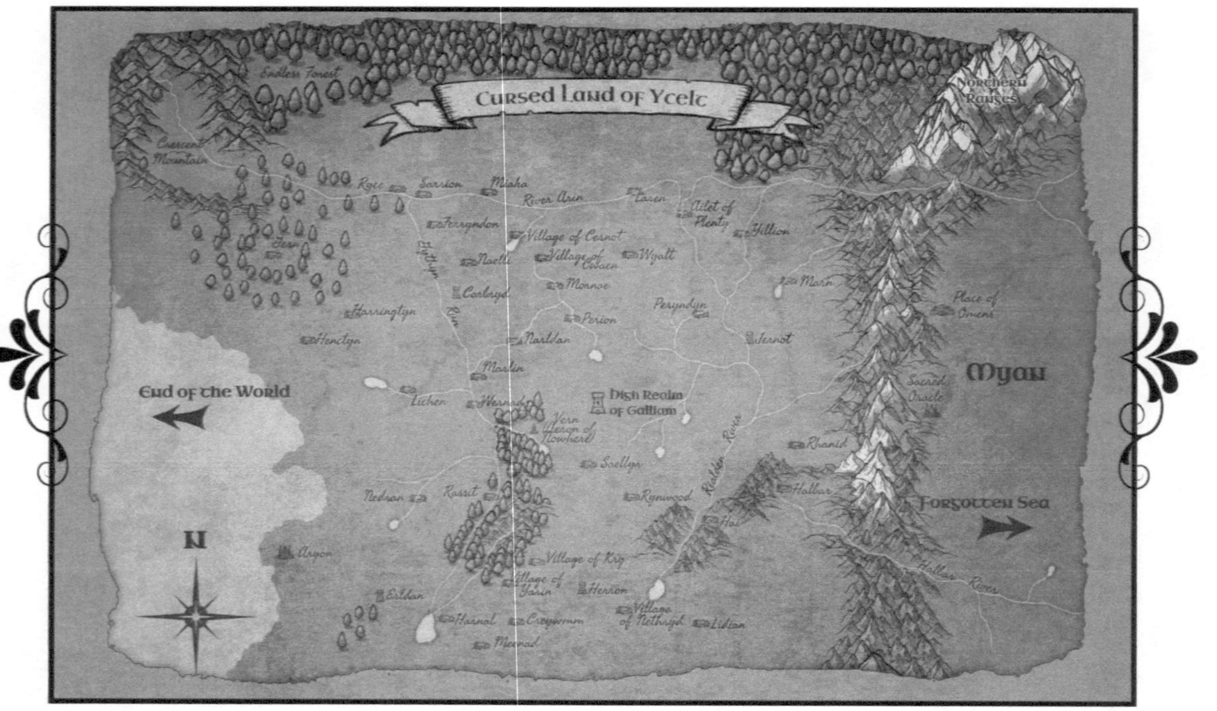

Cursed Land of Ycelc
Northern Ranges
Endless Forest
Crescent Mountain
Ryee
Sarrion
Miaka
River Arin
Taren
Ailet of Plenty
Yillion
Ferryndon
Village of Cernot
Village of Cosaen
Wyalt
Naelli
Marin
Place of Omens
Fern
Monnoe
Carlrye
Peryndyn
Harringtyn
Perion
Nernot
Henctyn
Narldan
Myan
Marlin
Sacred Oracle
Lichen
Wernad
High Realm of Galliam
End of the World
Vern Heron of Nowhere
Rhanid
Riddlen River
Saellyn
Nedran
Rassit
Rynwood
Hallar
Hoi
Forgotten Sea
Aryon
Village of Kiy
Village of Yarin
Herron
Esldan
Village of Nethryd
Lidian
Harnal
Creywrm
Meenad
Hallar River
N

# ELLA'S DOMINION

## Book One of The Lost Warriors

*Some men pray to the Sun and others worship the Moon. Some wear a ring or wield a sword and demand others kneel. But what is it that gives one man dominion over any other? Does Xenon not teach us that a man can only ever have dominion over himself?*

The Lost Warriors by Ynad of the Gern

# PART ONE: DOMINION

## The Kingdom of Erldan, Ycelt

**Year: 793 A.S.**

# ONE

'Gon! Give her to me.'

'Not until you show me.' Gohran picked Ella up and slung her over his shoulder. He balanced her between his arms and twirled her around.

Raven hair whipped across her face, blinding her, making her giddy. Ella loved that her older brother could still lift her with ease.

He set her down on the grass, her skirt billowing, then stood above her, hands on hips. 'I want to see her move, like before.'

Ella waited for her dizziness to pass. 'You must be seeing things, Gon. Nellie's just a doll. Shame they don't make daft men kings.'

'I am not daft. I saw it. You know what that means? You'll be packed off to live at Aryon with Aunt Bree.'

Ella inhaled sharply. *Aryon. Where witches lived.*

She launched herself at her brother, fists pounding. He caught her wrists, but she squirmed away. He gave her one of his commanding looks, eyebrow raised, towering over her. She let out a sigh and sagged beneath him. Though her body was warm, Ella shivered, hugging her knees to her chest. He would be her overlord in a few years.

'That's better,' he said. 'Wait here.' Gohran stomped across the leaf-littered glade to a lone elm tree, shooting suspicious glances over his shoulder to see if she'd stayed put. He kneeled at the base of the elm where the ground sank between knuckled roots and shifted the surrounding litter to reveal a hollow. He reached inside and pulled out a doll stitched together from scavenged rags. The doll was dressed in scraps of fabric, with matted tufts of spun wool for hair—the best Ella could manage after her sisters ruined every doll before it.

'You hid her!'

'I knew Raeyn and Jay would never look here.'

Ella thrust her arms about her brother's neck and squeezed, Nellie squished between them.

'You're too old for this, you know.' He drew her closer.

She looked up at him, hopeful. 'Can we make a daisy chain?'

Gohran grinned, and they fell back upon the grass, breathing blossom scent. He flipped over, sprawled on his stomach, and set about searching for long-stemmed daisies.

Beside him, Ella rolled onto her belly to watch his large hands at work—warrior's hands. She joined the search, grass tickling the underside of her arms, but she only found three daisies with long enough stems to Gohran's eight. After making slits along each stem, she passed them to her brother. Gohran took them and looped stem through slit until he had formed a chain. The final two stems he twisted together to make a circlet.

'A gift for Her Royal Highness.' With a bow, he slipped it over Ella's head, then rested his hands on her shoulders.

The chain dangled noose-like about her neck, his breath warm against her hair. She looked up to meet his mirror-blue eyes. *Why couldn't Gohran be like this all the time?*

He searched her face. 'You still haven't shown me.'

She shrugged his hands away. 'There's nothing to show.' She removed the daisy chain from her neck and circled it around her doll's. She wished he would leave it alone.

He grabbed her arms and tried to make her meet his eyes. 'Please, El. I know what I saw.'

She hated that hard line to his mouth. It meant he was closing off, shutting her out. Her stomach clenched. 'Promise you won't tell?'

He relaxed his grip, grinning, knowing he'd won. 'I swear it on the light of Elnora.'

The tension in her stomach eased. 'Very well,' she said. 'Just this once.'

Behind them, the shadows had lengthened, and Ella could smell crushed grass and hear herself breathe. Unused to doing this in front of anyone, she bit down on her lip and held Nellie with both hands out in front of her, roughly halfway between her and Gohran.

She closed her eyes and drew a deep breath, giving herself a moment to clear her mind and forget that Gohran was watching. As she exhaled, she pictured Nellie, not as cushioned rags, but as a living girl, a young woman. The girl-doll was milk-pale, with hair like the moon. Ella breathed in the verdant air and felt the shift of her mind switching from imagination to something more. Another moment passed, and she opened her eyes to see the world not as it was, but as she imagined Nellie would see it if the doll was alive.

She used this focus to peer around the glade. Light flecked through the vegetation, the earth, and the sky like tiny jewels. The nearby trees seemed to tower above, their dull-yellow leaves changing to bright gold and cinnabar. Even the tree hollow where Gohran had hidden Nellie appeared to stretch above her, dark and cavernous. Tinged with indigo and magenta, the grass rose as high as a horse's belly, while overhead the blue-grey sky appeared like running water, deep and frothy and green.

A cloud passed over the sun, and for a moment, the glade grew darker, bleaker. Ella shuddered.

A noise to her left. She turned. Nellie wasn't alone. Beside her stood a man Ella had never seen. His hair was darker than night against his ashen skin, his eyes bluer than her mother's sapphire ring. He smiled at her—or rather, at Nellie—and held Nellie's hands, which were cool and wax-like, not like real skin at all. He drew her close, and she imagined Nellie looking upward, waiting for his lips to meet hers.

'Ella! Gohran! Come inside, both of you!'

Nails dug into Ella's arms. She blinked, her mother's strident call bringing her back to her senses to see Gohran staring at Nellie, eyes ready to pop. She grimaced. His nails continued to dig into her flesh as he clutched her arms, head shaking back and forth.

'A trick,' he whispered. 'It has to be.'

Briefly, she saw what he had witnessed moments before—a forest that moved, a doll bloated to human-size, variegated light playing over the entire scene. She blinked again, and the light faded. She watched as Nellie shrank and fell to the earth, lifeless beneath the chain of daisies that still encircled her neck.

'Ella! Gohran! I will not call you again!'

Ella felt Gohran's grip loosen before he broke away and fled. She knelt to pick up her doll, trailing warily after, watching as Gohran sprinted off the green, up the pathway and towards the keep. He only slowed when he approached their mother, as though at that moment, he feared Ella more.

Queen Prya stood in the old stone archway that formed part of the city's inner walls. As Gohran neared, she leaned in to clasp his arms, stern-browed and ready to scold her only son.

Ella's stomach fell away. She couldn't hear what they were saying but she recognised her mother's look, knew the force of her grip. If he was telling her what he'd seen... Her cheeks tingled and flamed, and she felt a block in her throat that sat like wood.

The moment Prya looked Ella's way, Gohran slid out of his mother's grasp and darted towards the safety of the keep.

Ella edged closer, stopping when she reached the foot of the steps.

'Are you weeping, darling?' Prya's words were kind, but their tone was flat, empty.

Ella swiped at her cheeks, shaking her head.

'What happened? Why was Gohran so flustered?' Prya took Ella's hand in hers, stroked her hair with the other, but her action felt stilted.

*Gohran hadn't told her.* Ella exhaled with relief.

'Look at me, Ella.'

She had no choice. The power in that hold, in her mother's voice, was compelling. She looked up. 'Nothing happened. We were just playing.'

'Good. Just playing, and nothing happened.' It wasn't a question. Prya continued to stroke as she held Ella's gaze. The pressure was uncomfortable.

*Nothing happened. Nothing,* Ella repeated in her mind. So why the look on Gohran's face? That look! She wanted to take it back. She should never have shown him.

'You must stop these childish games, darling. Gohran, too. It is not fitting for a future king.'

'Then I'll have no one.' Ella's words sounded whiny, even to her, but they were true. Besides her brother, the youngest princess had no real playmates, let alone friends.

Prya's eyes snapped. 'You have your sisters. You'll be thirteen come summer solstice. High time you joined Raeyn and Jaydyn in the women's quarters.' Prya tucked a stray dark lock beneath her widow's cowl, then gripped Ella again. 'I travel to Harnal in the morning. While I'm away, I expect you to work with your sisters on the men's shirts and not distract your brother from his training. Will you do that?'

Ella sniffed and nodded.

'It is so important, darling. Gohran will be the master of this house. Do you understand what that means?'

*Master of me,* she thought, bitterly. 'I understand.'

'Good.' Prya let Ella go, and her entire body slackened. 'Now head inside. Lyrra will be up in a moment to help. You want to look your best for supper tonight. We have some important guests.'

All Ella could see as she trudged up the stairs was Nellie sprawled, lifeless upon the grass, the ring of daisies laid upon her like a wreath and Gohran's head shaking back and forth, his mouth forming one word over and over—*witch.*

# Two

The women's hall was spacious and warm, its stone walls covered with wine-coloured drapes, the thick carpets woven in royal hues of sapphire and emerald interlaced with gold. To Ella, however, they might have been beige and fawn. She hated sitting with her sisters, loathed their idiotic chatter, their squeals, and spats. Perched before the large hearth on their cushioned chairs, the women worked from the sewing baskets resting in their laps, cloth heaped before them. Erldan owed fresh shirts to every man in the royal service each year, as if sewing was all Ella and her sisters were good for!

That morning, Ella had watched her mother swish out of the room, so regal, so elegant, her back plank-straight, head held high. She called over her shoulder, 'Remember what I said. Raeyn and Jaydyn will keep an eye on you while I'm gone.'

She need not have worried. Ella had no reason to sneak out when Gohran seemed determined to avoid her. Did he despise her now, knowing what she was? *Nothing happened. We were just playing.* Tightness in her stomach and chest. She struggled to breathe. She leaned over towards the window and peered into the courtyard below. Gohran was down there with the fencing master, sparring.

Normally, Ella would have watched from the nearby grass, picturing the warriors' imaginary battles, observing their skilled movements—experiences she would never have. From here she could make out the arc of their swinging arms and hear the clang of metal on metal. She liked the way Gohran moved, as though he knew where the fencing master was going to strike before the master did. Not graceful, but fast and strong, whereas she was awkward and clumsy.

Gohran looked up. Sweat curled the ends of his hair. Despite the sun's reflection on the glass, Ella was certain he looked directly at her. After a moment, he turned away, his dampened back seeming a deliberate slight.

'By Our Lady, Ella, look what you've done to that shirt.'

Ella looked where Jaydyn pointed. She had stitched the yoke on back-to-front.

Raeyn peered down her nose. 'I hope that's not meant for our esteemed brother.'

'Can you imagine his face if he saw it?' Jaydyn nudged her older sister.

'Like when he caught Jay and a certain someone in the stables—'

'Raeyn!' Jaydyn slapped at her sister.

Jayden and Raeyn were sixteen and seventeen, respectively. Unlike Ella and Gohran, who shared their mother's unusual colouring, both had inherited their father's wiry copper curls and freckled pale skin, typical of the western provinces. It wasn't just in their looks that they differed from their younger siblings. They had almost nothing in common with Ella or their brother.

Ella concentrated on unpicking the yoke she had just sewn. She felt as though bugs crawled in her belly.

As soon as she could, she excused herself and ran upstairs. Just before the landing, she bumped into her brother. Gohran held his soaked shirt in one hand. Sweat dripped from the wispy dark hair on his chest. He seemed about to speak, but then pivoted and went downstairs. The bugs in Ella's stomach writhed and wriggled. She wanted to call after him, tell him he had imagined Nellie moving, that nothing had to change. She knew everything had changed.

The bustling town was alive for market day, carters dragging their wares, merchants haranguing, and peasants hurrying to get their trading done before sunset. Gohran pulled his damp shirt over his head and strode towards the town centre. He ignored the eyes that followed him, the tips of each hat, the bows, and curtsies of those he passed. All he could see was Ella's look of reproach, her open hurt.

Gohran expelled the image from his mind. He would not—*could not*—think about it, about what he'd seen, what had happened, what it would mean.

He stopped outside the temple of the goddess. The temple appeared small and dreary, even from the outside. Ivy clawed its way up the crumbling masonry, invading the cracks in the walls, and ravaging the last of the paint that peeled away from the oversized doors. Gohran stepped over the threshold, crossing three fingers along his forehead and then his heart in the sign of warding.

Inside, the floor lay cold and bare. Rows of scuffed and worn wooden benches latticed the room. Gohran made his way to the granite altar and knelt, eyes closed. He could still remember when father had first brought him here, a boy of perhaps five or six. When he had stepped through the imposing archway, he had been in awe of the temple's elevated windows and towering ceiling. Crisp white statues had observed his every move while the colourful tapestries danced along the walls.

The intervening years had turned the once stark white of the unearthly figures a dull grey, their coverings worn and pale. The thatch upon the roof could no longer keep the rain out, leaving a clinging damp that even the priest's incense could not disguise. It was Gohran's favourite place.

After a few moments, a comforting hand rested on Gohran's shoulder. It was Davith, Erldan's head priest. Davith had taken Gohran in when his father passed, had sat with him as the sun crawled across the sky, and allowed him to weep.

Gohran looked up with a wry smile, rising from his knees to perch on the nearby pew. Davith took a seat beside him, waiting patiently for the prince to speak.

Gohran cleared his throat. 'Is it possible for a man to see things that aren't there? A sane man, that is.'

'Certainly, when the mind is under great strain, or when a man is simply mistaken. What is it this man believes he has seen?'

Gohran kicked at the floor. An echo flashed behind his eyes. *Shadow and crystalline light, moonlit hair, skin like wax.* Then his mother's stern gaze, melting it all away. 'Nothing important.'

Davith rubbed his chin. 'The queen expects great things from her son. This kingdom will be yours to protect, Your Highness.' The wind scratched through the poorly thatched roof, like a beast clawing its way in. 'Be mindful that the priesthood serves the goddess, and therefore this kingdom, and therefore you. No one man can Cleanse the darkness.'

*Heresy.* Gohran ran his fingers through his hair. He had not meant to reveal so much. 'You have my thanks, Davith. I will remember your loyalty to the queen.'

'Save your words, Your Highness. Your good esteem is all I require.'

# THREE

'You took a great risk coming here.' Breeyan ushered her sister inside.

Prya followed her through Aryon's dark corridors. It wore the stains of ages and exhaled the odour of centuries. 'It was a risk, but I had no choice. This concerns our family.'

Breeyan paused, stiffened, and then continued into a tiny, shadowed room. She stood behind an oversized and elaborately carved desk and motioned for Prya to sit opposite. Like everything at Aryon, the room had an ancient feel, ornate and impractical.

Prya perched on the edge of the rigid, high-backed chair. *How many years had passed since their last encounter?* Breeyan had aged. Her skin was leathery and worn, and grey streaked her hair. They were born five summers apart, but time had etched itself onto her sister's body.

A young priestess with braids the colour of saffron brought in a steaming pot and two thimble-like cups atop a wooden slab. She eyed Prya with undisguised curiosity. With a bow, she set the slab down, backed out of the room, and closed the door.

It had been a risk, Prya thought. It had also been an ordeal. Not just for the unaccompanied journey, overnight and in disguise, but for what this place represented. Had the fates played a different hand, Breeyan's life might have been hers.

Prya sipped the bitter tea. Breeyan was watching her, waiting. She could sense her unspoken words, the question that hung unanswered between them. She put her tea down. 'He's fine.'

Breeyan let out her breath. 'Gohran.'

'I'm here because of Ella.' Prya clasped her sapphire ring between willowy fingers, twisting it around and around.

'Go on.'

'Gohran saw her using magic. They were playing together, and she made her doll move, animated, created an entire world from nothing. It was unlike anything I have seen.'

'You knew she had magic.'

'I did, but I thought if I didn't train her...' Prya slid her ring back and forth over her knuckle. 'Mother always said she trained me so I wouldn't lose my abilities. I assumed if I let Ella be...'

Breeyan shook her head. 'If she has tapped into her gifts...'

'What I saw—Bree, it was spectacular. But I'm sure Ella did not understand what she was doing.' Prya studied her sister's expression. She wore a look of practised sympathy. 'I wonder now if I made the wrong decision. Do you recall when mother took us aside and told us how we were different, and how she would send one of us here to Aryon?'

Breeyan's eyes narrowed. 'That as the youngest, *you* would be sent here, and as the Princess Elder, I would be made a match in Ycelt. How can I forget?'

Prya's fingers hugged her ring. 'When that did not happen—when I was the one who stayed—I hated having begun my training. Magic runs like a siphon. Once it flowed, I could not stop it. You are safe here. The treaty keeps you safe. I must hide what I am every day. From my friends, my family—I even had to hide from my husband.'

Breeyan released a slow, controlled breath. *Rohan.* 'Especially from the late king.'

'I thought if I told Ella nothing, taught her nothing, she would know nothing.'

'And therefore, have nothing to hide?' Breeyan hid a smirk.

'I don't expect you to pity me, Bree, but I expect your compassion. Not for me, but for the children. I don't want Ella to live as I have done.'

Breeyan's face mimicked sympathy, but it was tight, cold. She was staring at Prya's hands, watching her twist the ring—the ring which would have been hers. 'Bring Ella here. It should be her, anyway.' *She is the youngest.*

Breeyan slipped the thought into Prya's mind and Prya felt a cold creeping in her throat. 'It is too soon. Ella is just a child. Sixteen—marrying age, we said.'

'Then what do you want?'

Prya heard the catch in Breeyan's voice. Her eyes said, '*What more can you possibly want?*' Though she kept this thought to herself. 'I need one of your priestesses.'

A breeze caught the door, forcing it slightly ajar. Breeyan stood to close it tight. She paused before turning back around. 'Do you know what you're asking?'

'I do. I wouldn't ask if I believed there was any other option.'

'There must be.'

Prya shook her head. 'Believe me, there isn't. I have done everything in my power already. Ella needs to learn how to hide what she is. A priestess can easily pose as a tutor. The household pays little mind to servants, so will leave them alone. No one will even know what lessons are being taught. I would compensate you, of course.'

'Compensate me?' Breeyan shook her head in disbelief.

Prya would not beg, plead, or wheedle, as she had for that cursed sapphire ring, the ring that marked her queen. She hated what she was about to do, but she would not let Breeyan hold her accountable forever. Rohan had chosen her for his wife. Prya could not change that. 'It will only be for a short time. We owe each other nothing, sister. Not anymore.'

She saw Breeyan weigh her words. Would this be another injury, another guilt, to tangle their lives? Had the treaty not bound them, there were knots enough to see they were never free of each other.

Eventually, Breeyan sighed. 'As you wish. I will put it to the council, but it will be their decision, not mine.'

# FOUR

Prya stood outside Aryon's council chamber, waiting for the priestesses to call her. The saffron-haired novice who had brought them tea kept watch beside her. Prya sensed the girl's thoughts tucked around her. She did not venture her mind further. There was no point. Breeyan would have laid a seal over the entire room.

When they summoned her, Prya stepped inside, with her head held high. The chamber was bulbous and echoey, with its high ceiling and bare floors. Unlike many other rooms in the citadel that had been adapted and partitioned, the chamber stood almost unchanged from centuries before when Aryon had belonged not to priestesses but to kings.

'Queen Prya of Erldan,' Breeyan announced.

Prya took her place at the long table, studying the women's coarse faces. Many bore distinguishing features, moonbeam-pale and night-dark hair, violet, emerald and amber eyes, peach-warm cheeks, and cherry lips. Others had beaked noses, or flattened foreheads—marks that spoke of the gods.

The women on the council wore robes covered with sigils to mark them as Elder, Wise, or Veritatis, the soothsayers, as eminent here as nobles in Ycelt. She bowed her head, mindful of their rank. They stared back openly, unmindful of hers.

'I have explained your situation,' Breeyan said, 'but the council still has some concerns.'

She had not even settled in her seat when a woman with startling aqua eyes called, 'How can you expect one of us to return?'

'You are asking us to risk our lives,' hissed another.

Prya looked to her sister, expecting the women to be hushed for addressing her so, but Breeyan, too, awaited her response. So many eyes, their judgement seeping into her skin. She wanted to scrub them all away. She cleared her throat and stood to face them. 'What I am asking is that one of you returns—under my protection—to act as a tutor for my daughter, the princess of Erldan.'

'It is dangerous. Too, too dangerous. Have you no concern for our safety?'

'It is dangerous, but Erldan is not like the provinces further east. There are no henads, for one thing,' Prya said.

'The priests may not have formal spies, but they have ears and eyes.'

'We left Ycelt for a reason.'

Prya let out her breath. There was more going on beneath the surface, mind-to-mind. It was in the shift of their eyes, thoughts exchanged but unvoiced, like the background humming of a hive of bees. It prickled. 'Of course, they do, and of course you did, but now you have the training to hide from them. My daughter does not.'

'Why can't you train her?'

Prya was astounded. Did they not see how it would look for a queen to take a sudden interest in one daughter—her youngest daughter? 'I want suspicion cast away, not towards her.'

'You have managed.'

'Your mother managed,' said another.

'My mother was not a dowager. I have no time to train the princess. I have matters of state, subjects, a household, a court...' Blank faces stared back at her.

'We will train your daughter, Your Highness, but here, at Aryon,' said a quiet, dark-haired woman whose robe denoted an Elder.

'For which I am grateful, but at marrying age. Then our neighbours will assume we have made her a match elsewhere in Ycelt. If I send Princess Ella here now, people will ask questions.'

'What questions?' said the aqua-eyed woman.

She might as well have been arguing with a flock of ilaks. 'I came here to ask for help, to protect my child. My family owes Erldan one daughter—any daughter—would you rather I sent my second child, who has no magic at all?'

'You mock our treaty, Highness,' this from the Elder. 'It is in place to provide a haven for those of your line born with magic, not for you to be rid of an unwanted girl-child.'

'The treaty is in place to protect our two provinces, yours and mine.' She met and held each gaze. 'Erldan is the only province between Aryon and the rest of Ycelt. Without Erldan's protection, what is there to stop some zealot rekindling the ancient war?'

'We have the Curse,' called another priestess.

'Which forbids you from bearing arms,' Prya said.

'Which forbids anyone from bearing arms against us.'

Prya shook her head and took a deep breath. 'I thank you, sister, for hearing my case, but I see my daughter's life is of little consequence. Your people have skills and training to hide and to teach others to remain hidden, but they deny your own blood. Let them find Ella out, let the priests burn her, and then let their henads come scouring my kingdom. It won't be long before they find their way here.' She stood to leave.

'Wait,' said the aqua-eyed woman. 'Perhaps you are right. But what you ask, going back...'

'If one of us dies for you...' said another.

'Then we will all die soon enough. If you go back, trained, and armed against prying, you are in a much safer position, even than me. One of you can hide and help hide my daughter. It is safer for us all this way.'

Breeyan stood, and the women fell silent. 'Please leave us, sister. We will let you know what we decide.'

Prya stepped out into the hallway. The rush of her blood made her skin itch. She walked the length of the corridor, back and forth and back again. Had she made a mistake coming here? These women were beyond court life, beyond society. How could they understand? Inside she could hear their murmurs, the occasional raised voice, nothing to reassure her.

'Your Highness?' It was the saffron-haired girl back again. They must have summoned her. 'If you will follow me, we have a bed made up for you.'

'But I'm not—'

The girl looked at her with something resembling pity, an open, naïve sympathy.

'I take it there will be no decision today?'

'We usually eat in the refectory,' the girl said, 'but I can have some supper brought up to you.'

A flash in her mind, sudden and repugnant, of a crowd of women lining rows of long wooden benches, slurping at their bowls of gruel, like warriors in their mess. 'I think that is best.'

When she arrived upstairs and saw the tiny, partitioned cell, she almost regretted her decision. Covered with worn linens, the bedframe was narrow, the thin mattress overstuffed with compacted straw. The girl was watching her. She must know what Prya was thinking, though her expression showed nothing. 'What is your name, child?'

'Amber, Your Highness.'

'You are a novice here?'

Amber nodded. 'A refugee.'

This did not surprise her. The girl did not look like a typical pledge. She had intelligent eyes, the hawklike sharpness of someone who had seen more than they ought. 'If I know my sister, you will sit on that council one day.' A wry twist to Prya's lips. The poor girl didn't know how to respond. 'We shall see, I suppose.'

It was a full two days before the council pronounced their verdict, which Prya spent pottering in the library, reading from scriptures. If she had not been so anxious, she might have lost herself up there. As it was, she nearly wore a hole in a single page of one book. She hated that she had come begging for her sister's aid. She couldn't undo what had transpired between them, not even for her daughter's life. And if the priestesses refused her? Prya brushed the thought away.

When she entered the chamber, instead of fending off pairs of hostile eyes, many of the women refused to meet her gaze. Her throat hardened.

'Highness,' Breeyan nodded.

'Your Holiness, sister.' She nodded around the table. There was shifting and shuffling. Still, no one would look at her.

'I will not take any more of your time. Our council will satisfy your request.'

Tension eased out of her, but only for a moment. She sensed the silent mind-murmur of their underlying unease.

'One of our pledges, Sallyn, will accompany you back to Erldan.'

An ashen-haired girl with pale white skin made a gentle bow and then looked up. A fire-slap blotch covered one side of her face.

'May I?' Prya motioned for the girl to join her. Sallyn did as she asked. Prya placed both hands on her shoulders. The girl had white-blonde lashes and brows, her watery-blue eyes so pale they were almost colourless. It was a nothing face. Prya cast her eyes back around the circle. 'She has no magic.'

A unified gasp, unvoiced, travelled across the room.

The aqua-eyed woman hissed, 'Of course she has magic. Sallyn is a sworn priestess.'

'Not enough. Not nearly enough.' Prya turned to Breeyan. 'Sister, tell them how strong Ella is. Tell them she needs someone more, someone bright. Someone like the girl you left me with—Amber. I want Amber.'

'Sallyn is one of our most trusted tutors,' said the woman.

'If that were so, you would need her here.' With her minimal training, Prya had trampled Sallyn's mind like ilaks crossing a field of clover. If the priestesses had chosen her as someone expendable, they were not just ignorant, they were fools.

'You mock us, Your Highness.'

'And you insult me. I thought I had made myself clear. Princess Ella is not a commoner. All eyes are upon her, just as all eyes are upon me.' She turned again to Sallyn. 'You were raised here, at Aryon?'

Sallyn looked towards Breeyan. 'I was.'

Prya addressed the group. 'I have spent the last few days with your girl, Amber. In a plain smock, she will pass for one of my servants. I mean you no insult—Sallyn, is it? You're doubtless a talented and worthy tutor, but you will be noticed in my court.'

'Amber is a mere novice,' Breeyan said.

'Yet I have already observed how strong she is. She was a refugee, Bree. She knows Ycelt's ways. Amber is perfect.' Breeyan's jaw tightened. She knew Prya was right.

'Amber would have to agree, of course,' Breeyan's voice cut through the room before the council members could object. 'And it will only be for one cycle of the sun. Then she will return and bring Ella with her.'

'Thirty moons and not a day less,' Prya said. 'I cannot be seen to marry my daughter at fourteen summers.'

'And I cannot risk my priestess's life waiting until Ella turns sixteen.'

'It is the priests' law, sister, not mine. That has not changed.'

Breeyan exhaled through clenched teeth. 'Then it must be so.'

As the council dispersed, Breeyan caught Prya's arm. 'No more favours after this. No more lies. Ella comes here, and we are done.'

Breeyan summoned Amber with the news right away. 'Queen Prya has honoured you by offering this opportunity,' she said. 'Your sacrifice will honour the god and your sisters.'

The young priestess trembled, and her voice wavered as she nodded her assent.

Prya supposed her sister was not someone whose wishes the girl would dare frustrate.

She had Amber stow her belongings as though she were already her servant. The girl had nothing of her own to pack, save a handful of tomes.

'Put this on.' Prya handed her a simple day dress and underskirt. 'You'll have to leave that robe here.' She rested a steadying hand on Amber's shoulder. 'You'll need to untie those braids, too, but you can do that while we ride.' Then they set out for Erldan before Amber could bid farewell and change her mind.

On their journey, Prya explained Amber's role. 'Your primary responsibility will be to train the princess. She must learn to control and hide her talent. If you can, teach her to suppress what little she already knows. If anyone uncovers her abilities, it will mean her life and yours.'

They stopped for the night some distance outside Harnal, the closest village to the east of Erldan. 'I left my serving women at the inn,' Prya said. 'We shall meet up with them in the morning and head back to Erldan.' This meant camping on the side of the road, but Prya wanted no witnesses to their arrival.

Without prompting, Amber tethered both steeds where a large patch of grass surrounded the water's edge. Above them, the failing light set the clouds aflame. She laid out their blankets and lit a fire.

Later, in the dark, Amber's shoulders shuddered, her muffled tears carrying across the embers as she unravelled each strand of her sacred braids.

Prya rolled over to face the night. *Her sister would not betray her now, not over this. There was too much at stake for them all.*

# FIVE

Ella spent a tedious few days sewing shirts beside her sisters in the women's quarters. Mostly, she could tune out their constant prattle, getting lost in her thoughts.

'Imagine making love to Sheevan,' said Raeyn.

'Those eyes,' said one serving woman.

'That chest...' Another tittered.

'Girls, that's enough.' Their mother entered, and the room fell silent. Prya handed a bundle of fine white linen to one of the serving women. 'I just bought this in Harnal, so you need not bother unpicking that one.' She motioned to the shirt in Ella's lap.

Ella looked down. She had once again stitched an entire panel back-to-front.

'Use it to practise on wedding shirts for your dower chests.'

Raeyn and Jaydyn squeezed hands, grinning.

Prya ignored them. 'We have a guest arriving. Lord Venn of Nedran is visiting for some weeks.'

Raeyn rolled her eyes.

Prya peered down at her daughters. 'Venn is a well-respected lord from a wealthy city. Raeyn, you can forget about Sheevan or anyone else from Crey-wmm. It would be a crime to give your land and title away to anyone less worthy than a dryhten. In the meantime, girls, you had best hurry with these shirts.'

'If Ella would pay attention, it wouldn't take so long.'

'As of tomorrow, Ella will have even less time to help you. She will be study-ing.' Prya held up her hand before Ella or her sisters could speak. 'A tutor by the name of Amber was recommended to me in Harnal. I think she will do nicely for you, Ella. She begins in the morning.'

'She has a tutor all to herself?'

'Lyrra has all three of you to tend to and I see now it has been too much since losing your father. Ella, I have neglected your education for long enough. It is time you stopped grubbing around all day. You must learn to be a lady of the court.'

Ella felt her sisters smirking.

'We'll have to rearrange your bedchamber to make room for your study, but I'm sure it will suffice.'

Ella's stomach sank. Why not the library or some other room? Was this tutor a means for mother to keep her hidden and out of the way?

Once, Ella's room had been an attic in a remote tower. As a child, she'd loved to play up there, tucked so far from everything, rummaging through the old artworks, tapestries, and homeless furniture. It was much better than her old room above the kitchen, which wasn't much larger than a servant's cell.

Ella remembered pleading with her father, King Rohan, to make the room hers, smiling one of her special smiles, the kind that felt all warm and buttery but afterwards left her cold, as if by smiling she had sucked all the heat from the air. As always, her father surrendered. Out went the dreary furniture and in went a canopy bed, dresser, armchair, and carpet. Soon after, the hearth was widened and remodelled, purging the last of the gloom. Best of all was the large window that looked out over the entire western glade. Much better than her tiny cell, and better again than sharing with her sisters.

When Ella retired to her room that night, she found the servants had pushed the dresser against the wall and nearer to her bed, and they had removed the armchair altogether. In their place was a small desk covered with books, blank parchment, and writing tools.

Her bottom lip quivered. She wanted to weep. It was like someone had stolen the last precious moment she and her father shared. Meanwhile, mother, who never singled her out, was setting her apart in this peculiar way. Was this yet another thing to mark her?

When Ella's lessons began the next day, she couldn't believe how young Amber appeared. She must have been no older than sixteen, with gingery-blonde hair—almost the exact colour of the spice she'd seen the dyers trading in the marketplace—which she wore loose to her waist. She had a warm smile that made her eyes sparkle, yet she looked ill at ease. Her movements were stiff and awkward. She looked almost frightened—not like her mother's usual proficient hires.

At first, Amber paced, as if she didn't know where to begin. Then she stopped, turned, and took a deep breath, pulling at the edge of her bodice as though it squeezed. There was something about her, Ella thought, something familiar. Another breath and Amber placed a parchment on the dresser before her. It read *The Nine Points of Etiquette*, but when Amber spoke, it was not about manners or protocol.

'My Lady Princess, what do you know about Aryon, about the Order of the Black Moon?'

Ella felt a hundred beetles had crawled out of her stomach and were scrambling all over her limbs. She shook her head side-to-side as if she could deny what was coming.

'They must have taught you about the order of priestesses at Aryon?'

Ella frowned. 'What do I know about priestesses?'

'What do you understand about their magic?'

The bugs pinched. 'People who have magic are heretics, unsouled, and poisonous. They need to be Cleansed before they can taint everyone and everything around them.'

Amber shifted uncomfortably. 'And the Order? What have you been told about the people at Aryon?'

Ella looked out of the tower room window. The view on this side of the castle was unhampered by the eastward-sprawling farmlands that lay beyond the city walls. Even the marketplace and spattering of smaller shops within the city's heart were tucked away, out of sight. As far as Ella knew, Aryon was out there somewhere, beyond the western glade, beyond the wilderness, beyond the jurisdiction of the king of kings, the High King himself.

'It's where the priestesses live. Where my aunt lives.' People whispered that Aryon was full of witches and heretics, its inhabitants all peculiar, even deformed. Priestesses were exiled slaves to a heretical god, forced to live in a cursed place alongside other cursed souls. It was a story told to frighten—that she and her sisters used to frighten one another.

'Your Aunt Breeyan, do you think she is a heretic? Unsouled and poisonous?'

'Why are you asking me this? Who are you?'

'I live with your aunt. I'm from Aryon.'

The room was closing in around her. 'A witch...'

'Please—don't use that word. Magic is a gift. It's only the priests who worship Elnora who term it witchcraft.'

Images of fire flashed through Ella's mind, priests chanting, flames devouring. 'Get away from me. Get away!'

'Please—' Amber reached out to her.

'I will scream for mother. I will—'

Amber caught her wrists. Her hands were warm, too warm, and Ella's arms went limp. She had no control over them. She squealed and Amber clamped a hand over her mouth.

'Hush,' Amber said.

A sudden pinching at her mind, before soothing flooded her, forcing her to be still. Her panic leaked away. The surrounding air grew chill, as though someone had let a gust of wind into the room.

'That's better.' Amber took her hand away from Ella's mouth but kept hold of her wrists.

'I don't understand. Mother hired you—'

'Your mother hired me to train you.'

Ella shook her head back and forth.

'She wants me to help you hide your abilities.'

'This is a trick, a lie. I have no abilities. Are you a henad? Are you working for Elnora's priests?'

'Ella, look at me. Look into my eyes.'

Ella stared at the wall.

Amber reached out and turned her chin until they were face to face. 'Look into my eyes.'

A peculiar sensation crept through her. It was a need to share, to unburden, and it did not belong to her.

'You can feel it, can't you?'

Ella shook her head, though it was a lie. She could feel it. It churned around her, hot and cold at once. Amber's eyes glowed, shimmering, as though lit from within.

'Look again now.'

Amber's eyes were dull. There was no power in them. She might have been an ordinary young woman, after all.

'When I look at you, I see that glow. I'm going to teach you how to make it dull when you need, show you how to build a shield around your thoughts...'

'I don't know what you are talking about.' Yet Amber had used the very words that Ella had thought.

'Your mother says you can create images, that you can find your way in the dark when others stumble.'

'Lies! Mother would never say those things. Was it Gohran? Did my brother say something?'

Amber ignored her protests. 'Do you perceive things that others miss, and sometimes know what people are thinking, though they have not spoken? Have you dreamed a certain way, more vivid than an ordinary dream, where what you dreamed about has later occurred?'

'Why would you ask me this?'

'Because magic manifests differently in different people.' Amber wore a pained expression. Ella realised it was fear. Amber did not want to be here, did not want to say these things. Ella also realised she knew this only because Amber wanted her to know. The need to share, to unburden, was there again, stronger this time, more insistent.

Then a thought, clear as if Amber had spoken aloud, slipped into her mind. It was a memory of her mother whispering. *If anyone uncovers her abilities, it will mean her life and yours.*

Ella felt queasy. The bugs in her belly writhed and clawed, and she thought she might be sick.

'Let me tell you a story,' Amber said. 'It was a long time ago now, but I remember it vividly. I was just a girl and the village I grew up in was at war. My brother had gone off to fight. I cannot recall how or why, but I was staying with a neighbour. We were huddled around a brazier, and he was asking me questions. I remember thinking the fire was odd because it was the height of summer. In any case, the neighbour wanted me to stare into the flames and describe what I saw.'

'Stop! I don't want to hear.'

Amber stared at her, through her, cold and terrifying, and continued as though Ella had not spoken. 'I told him I could see my brother. There was fighting all around. Then he wanted to know what the people looked like, what colours they wore, what emblems marked their shields. I told him I could see a man wearing a green tunic with a red hawk on it. He kept getting closer and closer. His beard was mangy from a scar that crossed his chin. He raised his sword, swiping back and forth.' Amber motioned with her hands. 'He swiped again, and my brother doubled over, crumpling like a dry leaf. I felt his pain, and I screamed.' Amber shuddered. 'Mother came running, howling, and screeching. One moment she was weeping for Tanno, the next she was shrieking at the neighbour, at me. The neighbour swore he would tell no one, but mother wouldn't listen. She made me pack up all my belongings, and we rode west. I don't know how many days and nights we rode. The whole time, mother kept praying, first to Elnora, and then to Xenon. I didn't understand what was happening, or why she was so upset. I thought it was something I had done.'

'Why are you telling me this?'

'It is how I came to live at Aryon. Mother left me with the priestesses, with your aunt, and then she fled for her life. I have not seen her since.'

She let Ella see it then, the picture of Amber's mother with the same gingery-blonde hair, leaning down to kiss her daughter goodbye.

'For a long time after that, I hated her. Later, I realised she was trying to protect me. She lost both her children that night.' Amber looked away. 'I confess it was hard coming here. In the order, they teach us Ycelt is cursed, that the people hate us, fear us. Have you ever seen a Cleansing?'

Ella's throat tightened. She shook her head.

'I have. It was the summer before mother took me away. A girl from my village. People used to say we looked like sisters. I think she may have been a cousin, but I never had the chance to ask.'

Amber's pain flooded her, the memory still raw, unhealed. Ella wondered if this was the first time Amber had shared her tale. She frowned. No, not the first time. There was one other... 'Nykki,' she whispered. The name came to her, along with an image of a girl smiling. It was a sad smile, twisted with longing.

Amber startled. 'Did you say something?'

Uncertain, Ella shook her head.

Amber frowned. 'Your mother must care for you a great deal, Ella. She is risking much to keep you here.' Her tutor looked at her again with fire in her eyes. 'Do you understand why I am telling you this?'

Ella wanted to scream that she did not understand. That it explained nothing, that this had nothing to do with her. Mother was mistaken. Yet what had Amber said? Did she have dreams that later manifested? Could she move through the darkness, clumsy as she was? Did she sense what others did not and know what people thought when she could not possibly know? *That name. Those images.* Memories that did not belong to her, but to Amber. 'Goddess, no...'

Amber took Ella's hands and squeezed.

'Your mother hired me because it is not safe in Ycelt for people like us.' That glow... After a moment, Ella felt her eyes glow back in recognition, burning from within.

Burning. Ella felt the word open and swallow her. It was what they did to witches, to heretics. Cleansed them. Burned them alive.

# Six

When the bell rang for noon tea, Amber felt relieved. She had hoped to have the queen and Ella to confide in, but for some unfathomable reason, Prya had kept Amber's true purpose secret, even from her daughter.

Amber watched Ella leave for the dining hall and sank into the dressing chair. The princess could have been a walking portrait of her mother. Amber should not have felt surprised. The High Priestess was a handsome woman, but there was something about her sister and niece that was more than mere beauty. It was difficult to pinpoint, but when either of them stood before you, they seemed bigger than the ordinary world, so captivating you stopped noticing anyone or anything else around them.

She picked up Ella's hand-mirror. Her reflection was a grim mixture of weariness and fear. She was unused to seeing her hair loose about her shoulders and face. The ghosts of her childhood haunted her eyes, which she let go out of focus. She meant to picture Aryon, the Hall of Prayer, to offer her thoughts to Xenon. Instead, her mind wandered to her mother, her dead brother, and to the place that had been her home all those years ago. The image upon the mirror shuddered and stirred like the surface of a turbid lake but did not resolve into anything. Amber realised she was weeping. *Well, how could she not?*

She put the mirror aside, blew her nose into her handkerchief, and went to find the chamberlain.

The chamberlain was a crotchety old fellow with frog-skinny legs and hunched shoulders. He peered down at his wax tablet. 'You are on linens this afternoon. Alyss will show you.' He nodded towards a plump servant who eyed Amber warily, then moved on to speak to some others.

'This way,' Alyss called without introduction. Amber tried not to stare at the long winding corridors, the small high windows and ornate embellishments as Alyss led her to the main bedrooms and women's hall on the upper floors. Erldan was constructed more recently than Aryon, but apart from the exterior, there was a similarity in style between the layout and buildings.

They stepped into the first bedroom. This was no partitioned cell, but a proper chamber, with solid walls from floor to ceiling and furnishings that might have belonged to an order of high priestesses. Alyss began pulling down the bedclothes and motioned for Amber to help. 'Grab the other end, will you?'

Amber hesitated. What if she spoiled them somehow? These were not the worn linens she was used to.

'Where do you hail from?' Alyss tugged at the soiled sheet as though it wasn't woven from finely spun fibres.

Amber nearly blurted, *the west*, but caught herself. 'Southeast.' She grabbed the sack off Alyss, who stuffed the sheets inside.

'Near Herron?'

'A bit further than that. Perhaps you've heard of Lidian?'

'I have indeed. The farthest city east before the Halbar ranges. Quite a devout lot that way, by all accounts.'

Amber stiffened, clamping down on her thoughts. 'And you?'

'Harnal. Close enough that each day of the sun I head home to pay respects to Our Lady.' Alyss paused, frowning. 'They're not so religious round here. Well, except for the prince. The goddess has a temple in the town proper, though, just opposite the marketplace.'

Amber said nothing, willing Alyss to move on to some other topic as she drew upon her power to quiet her hammering heart and still her breath. She was thankful Erldan was a world apart from the village where she grew up, where the cult of the Dark Sun was on everybody's lips and behind everybody's eyes as they watched, waiting for someone to slip up. But then, in the cities further north and east, peace was the exception.

As far as Amber knew, peace had reigned in these parts for several generations. Though Erldan had greater defences than Aryon, Amber noticed much of the city sprawled beyond Erldan's high walls. In times of war, the inhabitants must take refuge within the main citadel. Not something they could tolerate often, or for long.

They continued working in silence, stripping bed after bed, then making them up again with fresh sheets until it was time for supper.

Amber followed Alyss back down the stairs and past the central courtyard, the library and the main doors that led out to the stables, barracks, and mess hall for the queen's men. When they reached the dining hall, they encountered another group of servants laying out linen and utensils and lighting candles. To one side, minstrels tuned their instruments, while a flurry of bodies carried platters piled with meats and tubers and dishes Amber could scarcely identify. There was enough food to feed three armies, their wives and children, and the cooks had sculpted the vegetables and stuffed the pastries until they resembled exotic birds and animals. Food that would not and could not be eaten, Amber was sure. Her stomach rumbled. The constant effort of keeping her surface thoughts neutral had left her ravenous.

'This way,' Alyss called. They kept walking, leaving the clamour behind until they reached a cramped, musty kitchen that smelled of lard and rotting vegetables, and out to a smaller, windowless room. Someone had placed a single lantern on a wooden table surrounded by benches rather than chairs. Amber scurried to take her place.

'So, you're the new tutor?' one servant asked.

Amber nodded.

Someone passed her a dish of boiled tubers. They were cold. She wanted to weep. 'If you're prepared to wait, there'll be plenty left over from in there,' the woman nodded back towards the dining hall. 'Once the dogs and warriors have had their fill.'

Someone else snorted.

At least they were speaking to her. Mostly they avoided her, looking at her dress, her feet, her hands, but never into her eyes. It reminded her of when she had been in Ycelt all those years before. People had looked around her, rather than at her, even crossing the street or turning aside so as not to pass her. As if they could sense that she was different—dangerous.

More servants appeared and took their places. Not one of them acknowledged her, and Amber had never felt so alone.

That night, Amber lay beside her new companion. Tired as she was, she could not sleep. Alyss snorted and snuffled, taking up most of the large mattress as she tossed and turned like a hog roasting on a spit. Ordinarily, Amber could have blocked it out, her mind trained to switch on and off, to keep focus, but not tonight.

Of all the priestesses, why had Queen Prya chosen her? She was a nobody, not even a great sorceress, just an ordinary girl from a nowhere town, and here was Ella, a princess with power beyond anything Amber had seen. She kept seeing Ella's eyes, the energy churning in and around them, as if caught in a whirlpool, sucking at everything around her, heard her whisper, *Nykki*. These were not Amber's surface thoughts Ella had read, but something much deeper, a desire Amber barely acknowledged to herself. Nykahlia, the one she had left behind. Amber's throat caught. She would not cry again. Not here, not now.

All she would acknowledge to herself was that if Ella's powers were beyond her, this task was more so.

# Seven

'I think the green one.'

Ella watched her eldest sister hold up a silk brocade dress. Raeyn turned this way and that before the mirror, one hand holding the gown against her, the other piling her hair atop her head.

'Then I shall keep the maroon.' Jaydyn stood beside her, wearing a dress she had long outgrown. It cinched her waist, forcing her breasts upwards until their tops pillowed over the edge.

Raeyn peered at her. 'Mother won't approve.'

Ella saw Jaydyn smirk as she resumed admiring her reflection. Jay was always lording her curves over her rake-thin older sister, whereas Raeyn held tight to her one advantage over her younger siblings. Gohran would inherit the throne, but as Princess Elder, Raeyn would carry a title and land of her own.

Footsteps interrupted Ella's musings, and she looked over to the door.

Prya strode into the room, surveying her daughters. 'Girls, make sure you help Ella. She'll be joining you this evening. And Jaydyn, you will need a shawl over that dress.'

Jaydyn pulled a face as Prya departed once more.

Ella ought to feel excited. Her first ball! Yet it all seemed so distant—banal. Images from her morning with Amber flashed through her mind. Something stirred that was not quite dormant, but not quite alive either—kindling finally receiving enough oxygen to blaze. There was a coldness, too, where she felt numb. Disconnected from her sisters, from the room, and from herself.

'Why are we bothering?' Jaydyn tugged at Ella's laces until they pinched her skin. 'It's not like you'll be marrying anyone,' she hissed into Ella's ear.

The pain drew Ella back to her surroundings.

'They'll ship you off to Aunt Bree with all the other oddities.' Raeyn nudged her sister.

'Odd little Ella.' Jaydyn sniggered.

Had their father lived, he would have arranged a good marriage for her, Ella was sure. And she wouldn't live with horrible uncertainty, wondering if they would one day uproot her, trade her off like a herd beast to the sisters of the Black Moon, and all for some ancient treaty no one cared about anymore.

The treaty was forged following the Great War when henads were purging and Cleansing heretics across Ycelt. Aryon stood as one of the last surviving havens for those who followed the old god, Xenon, Ella's ancestors among them. Back then, Ella's family had pledged one daughter from each generation to join the order at Aryon. Ella assumed this was repayment for some debt, or for some other reason that no one had adequately explained. It was how it had always been, and so it was now—she or one of her sisters had been promised before they were born.

She wanted to shout that her sisters were wrong. *She wasn't going anywhere!* But her protest caught in her throat...*Odd little Ella.*

She was odd. She had always felt like an outsider looking in, apart from her sisters. Apart from everyone. Not deformed or peculiar, just *different*. Something she had never encountered in anyone else until she experienced it that morning reflected in Amber's eyes. Once or twice, she had felt something akin to it with Gohran, but this was distinct. It was as if, for the first time, someone truly *saw* her.

Saw what? *That she was a witch?*

Hot and cold crept across her flesh. Bugs crawling. Ice and flame.

That meant mother saw it, too. That day in the glade—she knew. And she hadn't spoken to Ella about it! Nor had she outed her. Amber said her mother hired her to help Ella hide what she was. A ruse to be maintained, even between them.

She pushed the thoughts away and pulled herself back to the present, though the strange combination of heat and numbing cold remained.

As each guest arrived, Prya nodded in greeting, her daughters lined up beside her, nodding in turn, before being presented to Gohran, their future king.

'So lovely,' Ella heard one courtier whisper, admiring her mother, who wore a midnight blue dress, not quite black. Prya's hair was pinned back softly, a chain with an enormous sapphire showing off her graceful, willowy neck.

'One so young, so beautiful... wasted,' said another.

'A shame.' Brows furrowed with envy and pity.

The ball was in part to welcome Lord Venn of Nedran, who would visit for some weeks. It also offered Gohran an opportunity to assume his prospective duties, which their mother encouraged. After all, the throne would be his in just a few summers.

Tall, lithe, and bland, Lord Venn was the last to arrive. Though he was born only a few summers before her brother, his quiet poise made him seem older. Ella knew her mother hoped to make a match for one of her daughters with the dryhten, though neither of her sisters had shown the slightest interest in the unremarkable lord. Instead, they were vying for Sheevan of Creywmm, a cocksure minor lord with hair the colour of hallit in the afternoon sun and a strong, broad nose.

Ella had met both men before, but nobody had presented her. Though she was not yet of marriageable age, that she was joining her sisters alongside the potential suitors came as a relief. If she was being introduced at court, it meant there was still hope for her future, no matter what her sisters said. It occurred to Ella then that Amber's presence was also a sign of hope. Why would Prya invest in her education otherwise?

In the luminous main hall, a group of minstrels played upon a dais. Around Ella, conversation thronged like cicadas. She couldn't catch hold of any one thread. Rather impressions, hints of mood, of intent, shifted into focus, then drifted away.

Her sisters hovered around Sheevan. A hand resting upon a shoulder. The press of bare flesh. A coy smile. A whisper. This was a familiar game they played. Tonight, Jaydyn took the lead. With an arm threaded through Sheevan's elbow, she turned towards one or another of the men in their circle of acquaintance. With her free hand, she touched an arm here, a shoulder there, then let it drift back to the blush of her neckline, lingering. The next time it would settle on a twist of hair, twirled between her fingers. She switched her attention back and forth between the man of her interest and one or another whose interest she tried to engage. Her shawl had long since slipped away, the corners draped through each elbow as she worked the room. Gazes fell on her exposed skin, her hair, her lips. Sheevan leaned close to whisper in her ear, and she pressed herself closer. Ella sensed rather than saw his body respond. A heat between them. Jaydyn turned away, her attention on a couple of older lords. Flushed, one asked her to dance. Jaydyn shrugged at Sheevan and went with the lord, peering back over her shoulder as they made their way to the dance floor.

Ella watched her sister repeat this sequence, always circling back to Sheevan, making sure his eyes remained on her. Meanwhile, Raeyn's expression soured. A few guests spoke dutifully to her, but she barely acknowledged them. Instead, her eyes, too, were on her sister.

With a slow, even breath, Prya crossed the room to join her daughters. 'Raeyn, I'm sure Lord Harrys here would be delighted to accompany you for the next dance.' The lord in question nodded eagerly and held out his arm.

Prya offered him a gracious smile and her daughter a firm nudge, and motioned for Raeyn to take it. She headed towards her second daughter, who was now surrounded by several suitors. She drew Jaydyn aside and whispered in her ear.

A flush spread across Jaydyn's chest and set her cheeks on fire. She drew her shawl back up and around her bare skin, curtsied, then stomped back to the table, and slumped into her chair, sulking. She stayed that way until her mother's attention was elsewhere. Then she stood to cross the floor, tugging at Sheevan's sleeve, beckoning him towards the balcony.

Ella watched them leave and tried to spot Gohran. She saw him standing with Raeyn and Lord Venn. She wished he would come to find her. They could steal into a quiet corner and poke fun at their sisters like old times. As though she'd spoken aloud, he looked her way. She smiled and waved, but before he could respond, a blonde lass moved between them, beaming up at her brother. Gohran flashed the girl one of his rare smiles and turned towards her, his back to Ella. Ella imagined shoving the girl aside. The girl stumbled, her face reddening. Ella stared after. Had she caused that stumble, just by willing it so? Heart thudding, her breath came thick and fast. Amber's words echoed in her mind. *It is not safe in Ycelt for people like us.*

'That's not the lovely smile you wore when last we met, Your Highness.' It was Lord Venn.

'Oh!'

'My apologies. I startled you.'

Ella wrenched herself back to the here and now and forced a smile.

Venn grinned in return, warm and sincere, and her forced smile soon became genuine.

'Now that is the look I long to see.' Venn held out his elbow. 'May I?'

No one had asked Ella to dance before. She hooked her arm through his, and they stepped onto the dance floor. Where his hands slipped around her, she quivered. His body felt different to her dance instructor, different even to Gohran's. He was taller, sinewy. As she relaxed into Venn's lead, her awkward and uncertain movements flowed, becoming comfortable and smooth. He was a wonderful dancer, graceful and strong.

The minstrels played a traditional lament for love lost and then found, as the couples circled. Ella imagined Venn's arms sliding around her waist as Sheevan's hand had slid around Jaydyn's. Unlike Sheevan, Venn kept a modest distance between them.

'May I say you look exceptionally well?' he said.

'Only if I may say you look very fine yourself.' Ella made a show of looking him up and down. 'A little more tanned, in fact.'

He grinned. 'The seasons will turn a pale man ruddy and back again soon enough.'

'They will indeed, when your days take you out of doors. I envy you,' she pouted mockingly.

'Oh? Have they been locking you inside?'

'Sadly, yes. I'm studying to become a fine lady of the court.'

'You don't look happy about it.' He chuckled, and she blushed. 'Well, tan or no, it suits you well.'

'My thanks.' Heat made its way down her chest and into the pit of her belly.

'We must arrange a few outings while I'm staying,' he said.

Heat quivered through her as she imagined strolling beside him in her favourite glade, arm in arm, fingers entwined. He would slip his hands around her waist, pull her in tight... She closed her eyes, imagining the warming pressure of his lips...

He twirled her under his arm in sync with the music. When they came back together, he said, 'It's not good for you and your sisters to be always indoors. I will have a word to the prince—see if we can't persuade him to release you.'

Cold, empty air between them. Her brother. Not her mother. That's how it was going to be more and more. She shuddered inwardly. 'You have my heartfelt thanks.'

Almost as though he heard his name, Gohran appeared beside them. Venn turned and made a bow. The prince whispered something in his ear, glancing to the side. Ella caught sight of Raeyn watching them with a sour twist to her thin lips.

As soon as the dance ended, Venn bowed and made his way over to her sister. Raeyn's face lit up as the two of them danced.

Ella's stomach sank and she searched the room. Where was Gohran now? Not dancing but mingling, that same blonde lass smiling up at him with wide blue eyes.

It was a relief when a cadence signalled the end of that set, and the main course was served. Ella tiptoed over to the honour table and took her place beside Raeyn and Jaydyn. As usual, they huddled together, watching the crowd, whispering. At the opposite end of the table, in her father's old chair, sat her brother. He was talking animatedly to some guests, facing slightly away. Ordinarily, he would have looked over and smiled or waved, though not tonight. Their mother sat to his left as she had once sat beside King Rohan. As dowager queen and regent, Prya had every right to sit at the table's head. However, tonight she gave this honour to her son as the Marked Prince. Along the table's length sat their relations and other courtiers, while the lesser nobles sat at the tables below. Trenchers piled with roasted ilak and root vegetables were passed around, topped with blood gravy. Around her, the guests were chatting, cutlery and crockery chinking.

'His Highness has grown so handsome!' said an older woman to her mother.

'He will make a fine young ruler,' said another.

'You must be so proud, Your Highness.'

Prya's mouth tightened. It was the slightest movement, yet Ella perceived the shift in her mood.

*Sycophants.* She'd heard their priest, Davith, use the word, and it came to her now as these women sought to ingratiate themselves to the dowager and king-to-be alike. *Not her thought.* Her insides roiled. She feared she might be sick.

Ella pushed her plate of moated morsels aside and excused herself, making her way to the balcony. She needed air.

The evening breeze cooled her flaming skin. She willed her breath to slow and deepen, forcing her attention back on what was happening inside the main hall, and away from what was happening within her.

The servants cleared tables, and the minstrels switched to a well-known ballad so the dancing could resume. Through the arched doorway, she caught sight of her sisters. Raeyn had shoved her way over to Sheevan, leaving Jaydyn pouting in the corner. Several guests approached the younger princess, only to be chased away with scowls and the whip of her tongue. Gohran had settled into a game of tiles with Venn and several of the husbands, all of them drinking and gambling for tokens. The abandoned women, Ella's mother among them, stood to one side and gossiped.

'Raeyn is a stately girl, isn't she?' said the woman closest to the queen. 'An excellent quality in a Princess Elder.'

'And the men all appear to admire Jaydyn,' said another. 'You are lucky, Your Highness, to have such elegant daughters.'

'Pity your youngest isn't dancing more. She'll have suitors flocking when she is of age. It is never too early to cultivate relationships, I always say. If you don't show her off now, how will the right families know to keep her in mind for their younger sons?'

Prya's smile hardened. 'You have my heartfelt thanks, Esmay.'

Ella shifted uncomfortably and moved to where she could see the game of tiles. She peeked between a burly pair of spectators and spied six men seated at the round table, though only two were left in the game, Venn and Gohran. It was a game Ella knew well. The object was to build suits, with players exchanging tiles or drawing from the discard pile. By now, the men's wagers were heaped in the centre of the table.

Venn frowned, concentrating. It was his last move. After this, they would show their tiles. The crowd leaned in, waiting. Venn's fingers moved back and forth between two tiles. He discarded one and waited for Gohran's response. Gohran reached forward and selected a tile. A slow smirk spread across his face. Venn let out a small, disappointed sigh and laid his tiles down, face-up—a broken suit, with the neophyte as his highest tile. Gohran laid his tiles down one at a time, from the warrior up to the king. Even with two tiles of a different suit, the run of ordered tiles from the king down made his hand the stronger. Without knowing how, Ella was certain Venn's last move had been false. He had just let her brother win.

'Congratulations, Your Highness.' The spectators nodded and clapped as Gohran collected his winnings with an open grin.

Ella searched the room. Now the game was over, Venn might return for another dance.

The blonde lass who had stood with her brother earlier appeared beside Gohran and Venn. 'Most superbly played, Your Highness. May I?' She leaned in to pour Gohran's wine, then smiled just as eagerly at Venn and moved to pour his wine as well.

Ella wanted to slap her stupid hands away, make her spill the jug all over her pretty dress. The girl's hand trembled. She gripped it with both hands until the whites of her knuckles showed. A splash of dark liquid escaped the jug's lip and fell upon her hands. Ella stifled a cry. Was that her magic, too? She scanned the room. All attention was elsewhere. She exhaled. Then, despite herself, she smirked.

'Oh! My apologies,' said the girl.

Venn leaned across and took the jug, holding it steady. 'See the effect you have on women, Your Highness?'

The men laughed, while the lass looked mortified.

Gohran took her wrist, his grip lax, yet insistent. 'Lady Vera of Lichen, isn't it? Please—stay.'

She beamed.

'Let us see if you can't bring me luck again this round.'

The servants poured the remaining drinks as Gohran started dealing a fresh hand.

Venn stood before Gohran could deal him in. 'Please excuse me, Your Highness. I promised your sisters another dance.'

Ella saw Venn spot her on the balcony and make his way towards her. She forgot about her magic. All she could think was how her skin still tingled from where he had held her, how she couldn't help smiling whenever he smiled at her. How had she ever thought him bland?

She was about to step forward to meet him when she heard, 'Pardon, Your Highness.' She turned to see Lord Kerr of Rynwood, just about kneeling at her feet. 'May I have this dance?'

She wanted to scream at him to get away, to take Raeyn's hand, or Jaydyn's, or the hand of that blonde lass, and leave her to dance with Venn, but Venn had moved aside and was now headed over towards Raeyn. She stayed silent and let Lord Kerr lead her to the dance floor to circle with the other couples. He was a short, stocky fellow, though beyond that Ella couldn't say what he looked like. All she saw was Venn's head bent near Raeyn's, and Raeyn with her mouth covered to hide a laugh as Venn whispered in her ear. A knot moved from Ella's stomach to her chest.

Lord Kerr insisted on dancing the next with Ella, and then a few of the other men danced with her as well. Not that she remembered any of them. For the rest of the evening, Venn stood with Raeyn.

# Eight

The following day, as Ella and Amber settled into their schooling, Ella barely heard a thing. She was remembering the ball, seeing Venn with her sister, and before that, the moment she realised she could *will* a girl's wine to spill. In her mind, she heard a whispered hiss—*witch*.

'Princess, are you listening?'

'Of course. My apologies.' Ella sat to attention, trying to calm her belly, to concentrate on her lesson in magic. *Magic.* Not some abstract thing invented by the priests to frighten, but something real, something that belonged to her. And now here was someone to teach her to hide it. To hide what she was.

Amber was still speaking. Ella pinched the back of her hand, trying to stay focused.

'We can't make something from nothing,' Amber said. 'So, we draw fuel from the air, the earth—any of the elements. Anything containing living energy. Sorcery uses an element beyond all known elements. It is other than fire, water, air, or earth, and yet it is all these things, too. Those blessed, like us, can draw upon it to manifest changes in the world. Like an ordinary person might draw upon fire to warm or water to cool. If there is no fuel to draw upon, we use the energy stored inside our bodies, at least as much as we can. This can be dangerous, though. There's only so much available.'

Ella shuddered.

'It wasn't always this way. Once, the Sacred Stone of the East provided all the power we could ever need.' Amber paused. 'Did they teach you about the stone here in Ycelt?'

Ella nodded, recalling Davith's dreary sermons. 'Before the Great War, the High King had the stone embedded in his sword so he could wield its power as a weapon.'

'Yes. And all those in Ycelt could draw upon it, some with much strength and others with only a little.'

'Is it true that back then the god Xenon walked the earth with men?' Ella asked.

'That's what the priests teach, yes.'

'And that's what started the Great War? Men feeling threatened by earthly gods?'

'So we're told. The High King sought the help of the Goddess Elnora to defeat Xenon and banish him from the earthly realm. Then, at the end of the war, Xenon shattered the sword and took the stone away, laying His Curse upon Ycelt.'

The Curse of War and the Curse of Death, it was called, cursing the men of Ycelt to be forever at war, and bringing death to those who defied His will. To the people of Ycelt who worshipped Elnora, it was Xenon's people who brought the Curse. Heretics. Witches. *People like her and Amber.*

'And then the people couldn't use magic anymore?' Ella asked.

'Only those touched by the god, like the priestesses of the Black Moon.'

*Touched by the god. Touched and stained and cursed,* Ella thought.

'Touched and *blessed.*' Amber pushed her parchments aside. 'Those who worship Elnora believe we are cursed because we *bring* the Curse. That's the real reason they fear us. That, and our magic, which they can no longer access.'

Ella frowned. 'But Xenon took the Sacred Stone with him when he retreated to the heavens...?' Hearing Amber describe the lore was like believing your entire life that the sky is blue, only for someone to say it just *looks* that way. It is actually green. You've just been calling 'green' blue.

'To the Afterworld, yes. And though we don't have the Stone anymore, we can still draw energy and manipulate it. In serving Xenon, we learned to draw power from the elements. For example, we can concentrate power into something tangible, like a ball of light, or use it to influence or persuade, to channel thoughts, and so on.' She stood, fidgeting. 'Once you can visualise the energy—that's probably not the right word... It's more like a feeling, like sensing the vibrations all around you. Some objects sort of pulse, lifelike, while others feel cold and dead.'

Amber continued describing various forms of energy, and Ella let her eyes go out of focus. She pictured her doll Nellie coming to life, felt her mind opening, the shift to seeing through Nellie's eyes, recollecting the cold and the warmth in her surrounds. She recalled some pockets of heat, but at first, it felt no different from the natural shift of temperature. Focus still soft, she transferred her attention to the room around her. Then she sensed it... A kind of vibration in the surrounding objects and in the air between them. Pockets of heat throbbed, enveloped by vacuums of cold where everything was still. Not an arm's length in front of her, Amber's body blazed white hot. It was the feeling she got just before building Nellie a grown body. She could feel it!

Amber was right. Magic *was* unlike anything else, yet it was also no different to seeing, hearing, smelling, or perhaps more like digging and lifting, because it left her feeling sore and tired. Was that because she was drawing upon the energy inside her?

'Over time, you will learn to scoop up energy like handfuls of soil or snow.'

Ella imagined reaching and grasping at the vibrations, but her hands slipped through the air, and the heat dispersed. She was trying too hard. When she played with magic, it was just *play*. She let her focus drift once more, the tension easing from her body. She pictured snow instead, imagined scooping a handful of energy into a snowball of light. Ella let out her breath and her muscles relaxed. This time, her hands found something to hold on to. She grabbed at it, pulling and moulding, forcing the substance into a tight, but invisible, ball.

Amber was still talking. 'And later, once we start practising, I will show you how to control it, building and dispersing energy at will...'

Ella sensed the power altering, as though it were melting. The sphere of force hung in mid-air, glowing as brightly as a lantern. Eyes wide, now focused, it was there, in front of her. She let out a cry.

Amber inhaled sharply.

She must see it, too!

Ella's tutor exhaled slowly, and said with an even command, 'Stop drawing now. Release the energy. Let the light go until it disappears.'

But it grew larger, more solid, flowing through her.

'Let go, Ella.' Amber's voice was firm. 'Princess! Let—it—go!'

A deep breath in. Ella imagined the light bleeding out, breaking into tiny star-like points, scattering, and then dwindling like sparks from flint and steel being struck together, leaving an empty darkness.

The room was ice cold.

Amber was stricken.

'What's wrong?' Ella asked.

'Nothing. It's fine. I just didn't expect—' Amber coughed, then cleared her throat. 'Well done. You have discovered how to manipulate energy.'

Amber's voice sounded light, yet Ella felt certain she was afraid. She hugged her arms across her chest.

'You feel the chill in the air? That's from where you drew the energy. You've taken some warmth out of the room, and now the surrounding air is cold.'

Yet the sudden chill that moved through Ella came from an altogether different place.

Amber went on. 'If there's not enough energy to draw upon, we need to find or create some. We can build a fire, for instance, or draw from the forces that occur in nature. Living creatures also store energy in their blood.'

Ella remembered the white heat coming from Amber. 'Even people?'

Amber fidgeted with her parchments. 'Yes, even humans, but we never use this source.'

Ella frowned. 'Why wouldn't we?' The echo of that heat was tantalising just to think about.

'The Curse will fall upon any who do. It is one of Xenon's forbidden things, like a sworn priestess using violence, or acting out a lust. And Ella, the Curse hurts not only the violator—it touches those around them. It's said to bring horror thrice over.'

The crawling feeling was back, sharp, and tight. Ella thought she might be sick.

'Ella, you look unwell.'

She shook her head. 'I'm fine.'

All her life, people had warned Ella about the Curse, but it had always seemed like some faraway thing, something that fell on other people. Suddenly it seemed very real, and very close.

# NINE

Ella was becoming accustomed to her new routine. Lessons each morning with Amber, broken by the noon tea, and then the afternoons spent with her sisters. Since Ella had inadvertently created a ball of light, her lessons had consisted entirely of history and lore.

Ella groaned. 'By Our Lady, there are so many rules. Give me three score shirts to sew, but spare me!'

Amber shifted in her seat. 'I know this seems tedious, Princess, but I promise the more you understand the lore, the safer you will be.'

Ella couldn't imagine how all these tenets and rules could change anything.

'Think of it this way,' Amber said, though Ella hadn't spoken. 'In your world, the secular world, a minor slip in the way you address a great lord can cause harm, damaging relations. It's the same in my world. What if you were to intone the wrong chant, or invoke the wrong sigil? You might lose control of your power and hurt someone. Or worse, what if you were to break one of Xenon's commands and inadvertently summon the Curse?'

A shudder. There it was again, the Curse.

Amber leaned back in her chair, her forehead creased in thought. After a moment, she perched forward decisively. 'Perhaps we could look at how the mind stores energy. A bit more practical knowledge couldn't hurt, I suppose.'

Amber shuffled over to the hearth and knelt. She motioned for Ella to join her. With a flat palm, she smudged a section of floor with cinders, then drew a large ring in the ashes. 'Imagine this circle holds all the different parts of your mind.' Inside the ring, she drew a series of smaller circles, some overlapping.

'One like this holds all your memories. Another creates dreams. See where they overlap? Then again, with this one, which stores energy.' She drew another series of circles. 'These control your body and everything you sense and do.'

Ella pictured a sphere of energy pulsing inside her mind.

'Once you learn to identify the different sections, you'll feel the various parts working. Each one vibrates differently.'

Ella tried to imagine the circles within her mind, matching the ones Amber had drawn, but it was like something grinding inside her head. None of the shapes would fit.

Ella's face scrunched. 'Why does it hurt? The circles—they hurt!'

'Ella, what are you doing?' Amber grasped her hands. 'Your skin is icy!'

'Picturing the circles...'

'Ella, stop! Let the image go.'

Ella exhaled, released the vision, and opened her eyes, frowning. 'Why did it hurt?'

Amber pointed to her drawing. 'Were you imagining this?'

Ella nodded, chewing on her bottom lip. 'I was trying to fit your picture into my mind.'

'Ella, this is just an illustration, an example.' Amber sat back on her heels, her brow crinkled. 'You weren't supposed to put your power behind the exercise. It's dangerous to try things you don't yet understand.'

'I didn't mean to...' That fear again. Ella withdrew, turning her back to look out of the window, her shoulders trembling.

'You're cold... Let me fetch a blanket...'

Ella swiped at her cheeks where tears had formed. Not just a witch, but a broken one. Even Amber feared her!

The warm weight of a blanket wrapped around her. Amber drew her close. Ella wanted to push her away, to scream that it wasn't her fault, that it wasn't fair! Why couldn't she be like everybody else?

Amber held on more tightly, and Ella felt waves of soothing warmth circling around and then through her. Tension eased. She sagged against Amber's solid frame, weeping.

All will be well. We'll work it out. We're in this together.

The thoughts dropped into her mind. But there was another layer of thought not meant for her. Amber was comforting herself as much as Ella.

That afternoon, Amber sought the chamberlain. The chill that gripped the room from Ella's unintended working had seeped into her bones, a creeping cold that prickled and ached. Ella had a raw talent unlike anything Amber had encountered, which should have made their lessons easy, and yet she drew power with such intensity, without even meaning to, that Amber shied away from the practical lessons she needed to tame her magic.

Amber found the chamberlain peering over the shoulder of the kitchen maids, *tut-tutting* and occasionally slapping his displeasure. She hovered nearby until he noticed her.

'What, what?' He brushed his hands on his trousers and scowled at her.

'I need to speak with Her Royal Highness. It's about the princess.'

He waved the other servants away and drew Amber aside, gripping her arm. She winced.

'I oversee all household matters. So, what is the matter?'

'I beg your pardon, but I believe Queen Prya would—'

'Would, what?' Fingers pinching. 'Speak or it will be twenty lashes.'

Amber's eyes watered. Behind them flashed a memory. *Soldiers screaming, threatening...* She steadied her breath, looked straight at the chamberlain, caught his gaze, and held it. His anger had generated heat... It might be enough. She pictured the heat as if it were solid, imagined scooping it up in handfuls, weaving it around him, a soothing warmth. She watched the tension ease from his shoulders. His jaw slackened. 'I need to speak with Her Royal Highness.' Slow and deliberate—yet almost melodious, as if unimportant—her words landed. 'I will be in my room for the rest of the day.' He nodded, releasing his grip on her arm as she released hers upon him.

Amber shivered with cold. She needed warmth and sustenance before her knees buckled under her. The other servants had busied themselves the moment the chamberlain's attention was away from them, and she saw no signs of them noticing anything was amiss. She wanted to be certain, but there was nothing left to draw upon. She hurried away, trying not to stumble.

It wasn't until after supper that a servant summoned Amber. She had slumbered most of the day. She knew the chamberlain would not bother her. Still weak, she dragged herself upright and followed the servant to the queen's chamber and waited to be announced.

When Queen Prya saw her, she narrowed her eyes. Amber had not dressed nor combed her hair. She stood with a blanket wrapped around her nightdress, her eyelids heavy.

'Leave us,' Prya commanded. The servant curtsied and closed the door behind them. Prya turned back to Amber and motioned for her to sit.

Amber could feel the sharpness of the queen's displeasure. Disapproval, even disgust playing behind those flawless features, before Prya shut her out, like a curtain drawn around her mind. A mask of perfection.

A sharp breath and a sharper tongue. 'Never persuade in the open like that again. Not ever. Do you understand?'

So much unspoken between them, understood. Yet not understood at all. Amber had no words to describe her terror, Ella's untamed strength. She was a mere novice, unsupported, under constant threat of discovery. This arrangement was not safe. She was not safe.

She opened her mind to the queen, everything laid bare, not trusting herself to speak.

Amber recalled Prya's steadying hand upon her shoulder that first night as they had ridden away from Aryon—her haven, her home. She reached for that camaraderie and understanding, but there was no compassion there now. No sympathy. The queen was hardened, cold. What should have been a sharing was a violation. Amber shuddered and shuttered her mind closed.

'Taking Ella with you is out of the question.'

Amber had not asked, had not even recognised her own request, yet it was the only way. She found her voice, a whisper. A hiss. 'It is not safe here. I cannot keep her safe.' She wrapped her mind up even tighter.

'You can, and you will.' Prya might as well have slapped her like one of the chamberlain's maids. 'You do not know your own competence. This task is well within your capability.' Prya waved a dismissing hand. 'And if you want to see your home again, you will make certain that it is.'

Prya slipped instructions directly into Amber's naked mind, and with them, newfound confidence. She was capable. If it was not true, Amber would make it so. Ella's survival depended on it. *Her survival.*

A flash of anger quickly suppressed. Not quickly enough.

'I take responsibility for today. You had no way to reach me. An oversight on my part.' *But do not do it again.* 'I have taken care of the other servants. They won't recall a thing.' She reached into her purse and pulled out a small hand mirror. 'If you need to contact me in future, use this—only in the evenings after your bedfellows are asleep.'

Amber would have access to the queen from now on, even if she was sleeping. Prya now knew the pattern of her mind. Amber had just shown her, though she wished she hadn't. It was naïve. The queen was not her ally, and certainly not her friend.

Yet from that day, something shifted between Amber and her pupil, as though a wall between them had crumbled. Amber felt she understood Ella a little better, and though she feared Ella's wild talent, she knew they were in this together. They would make it work because they had no choice.

Amber did not mention what transpired when Ella inadvertently used her magic, so neither did Ella. Instead, Amber taught her how to visualise the different parts of her mind without Amber's clumsy representation. Ella learned how to recognise which segment did what, how to isolate individual parts, and how to build a shield around them to hide certain thoughts. Amber showed her how to pour energy into a shield to block off only those thoughts she wanted to hide.

'If you do it correctly, all your other thoughts, your surface thoughts, will still be there, so you can answer questions normally,' Amber explained. This was in case a priest, henad, or layperson ever questioned her.

'Come, sit by the hearth,' Amber said. The season had cooled enough that they could build a fire during the day without arousing suspicion. 'Today I'm going to show you another foundational skill.'

Ella sat cross-legged before the flames.

'This is called scrying. You can scry using fire, water, mirrors, crystals, or anything with a reflective or energy-charged surface. Fire is the easiest because you can draw upon the heat as you work, which is what we're going to do now.' Amber motioned for Ella to stare into the flames, slow her breathing, and let her eyes go out of focus.

Ella forced her shoulders to relax and let her expression slacken.

'As you watch the flames, think of a place you know well or a person you like.'

Ella thought of Venn, his warm eyes watching her, a slight smile playing at the corners of his mouth. Soon she pictured him as though he stood before her. The vision widened, and she saw the surrounding room as well. He was with her brother in his study. After a moment, Gohran turned and looked her way, as though he could see her watching him. 'Ella?'

Startled, Ella lost the vision, seeing only the flames of the hearth. Cold shivered through her. Amber wrapped a blanket around her shoulders—it was never far away these days.

'Like using any magic, visions can leave us drained,' Amber said. 'When getting warm isn't enough, food and drink can help. Wait here. I'll fetch some.'

But Ella knew no amount of food or drink could take away her chill.

# TEN

Venn's visit lasted some weeks. Dedicated as he was to entertaining the princesses and their mother, most often he hunted or sparred with the prince. Venn first saw courting Gohran as a duty he owed to his city and its people, but he soon discovered he and the prince had a great deal in common. In fact, he was coming to enjoy Gohran's company as much, if not more, than that of any other acquaintance.

On that morning, the pair headed out of the city on horseback towards Gohran's hunting preserve, followed at a distance by a pair of footmen lugging their gear. They meandered along the deer trails that would lead to the thick of the forest, and Venn steered the conversation around to business. 'Jaydyn seems to get along well with Sheevan of Creywmm. Are you looking to arrange a match between them?'

'I have had thoughts along those lines.'

'And once you have settled her, I assume you will want to find suitors for the other princesses.'

'For Raeyn, certainly.'

Venn paused. 'And your youngest sister?'

Gohran's jaw clenched tight.

'I don't mean to be presumptuous, Your Highness, but I assumed you would want to settle all the princesses. Of course, Princess Ella is still young... Though I don't envy you your position in the next year or two. She'll be fighting suitors off.' Venn paused, trying to gauge Gohran's reaction. He sensed no encouragement, but no resistance either, and continued. 'Some men would argue that's to your advantage, however...' Venn let his voice trail off.

'You think otherwise?'

'All that conniving and politicking? Having to dance around so no one takes offence when you make your choice, compensating the losers and so forth...' Venn mimed a shudder. 'Greater men have forged enemies over less. Of course, it would be different if an agreement was already in place.'

'My current priority is finding a match for Raeyn,' the prince replied, not taking his eyes from the bushes.

'Which is why a pre-betrothal contract—'

'I can't simply throw Raeyn's estate and title away.'

'Of course not, Your Highness.'

'As much as the match will be political, I'd like to see her betrothed to someone I can trust—a friend.' He looked up, catching and holding Venn's gaze. 'And what about you—when were you planning on securing some heirs for Nedran?'

Venn tried to look away but couldn't. 'I'll be honest. I'm eager to settle my sister Lynden first, much as I assume you are doing.'

Gohran raised his eyebrow but said nothing, releasing Venn's gaze and turning back to study the vegetation. A moment later, he held his palm out for silence. Venn halted his steed and froze. They sat in utter silence. Venn could neither see nor hear anything.

With a sudden jerk, Gohran drew his bow and loosed an arrow with terrifying precision. The arrow whirred, slicing through the underbrush, and struck a boar in its side. The beast squealed, squirming and writhing. Gohran followed up his arrow with a clean toss of his javelin, skewering the beast a second time. The boar stumbled, then thudded to the ground. 'That was over a lot more quickly than I expected. Hardly any sport at all.' Gohran slipped his bow back into his saddlebag and dismounted.

Venn followed, sliding off his steed. 'You must have the most finely tuned senses in all Ycelt, Your Highness. I didn't sense a stir nor snuffle.'

'I've always been a hunter at heart.'

Gohran's grin caused Venn to shudder.

The footmen collected Gohran's kill, but rather than heft the beast onto their packhorse, they dragged it out to a bare patch of grass and then stood back as their prince strode towards it. Gohran drew his dagger and held the blade two-handed above his head. He let out a war-cry before slicing through the carcass's belly, squelching through guts, and cracking through bone. Gohran knelt and, with bare hands, tugged at the organs and entrails. Eyes half-closed, he breathed in the beast's vitality and spread the innards along the forest floor. Fresh blood soaked into the earth—an offering to the gods. Satisfied, Gohran beckoned for Venn to join him. Venn trod over, taking in the pitiful boar, its eyes staring into a strange vacuum.

'Can you feel the life spill out onto the earth?' Gohran asked him, breathing hard, eyes flashing.

The prince's smile penetrated Venn's very soul and in that instant, Venn felt it—at least, he thought he did. Like heat from the sun wrapping around him and pulsing through his veins, only the sun was Prince Gohran.

Gohran took Venn's hand in his now-bloodied ones, and drew the lord towards the gash in the boar's side, guiding his hand to sift through wet-warm flesh. Venn took his dagger, severed the arteries, and retrieved its heart. He held it up and met his friend's eyes, now intense and dark.

'A life for new life.' Gohran gripped Venn's hand and squeezed the last of the blood out of the dismembered heart.

'To the goddess.' Venn's voice trembled.

'The goddess and trusted friendship.'

'Our friendship.' Venn's words reverberated around the forest.

From up in the segregated women's hall, the three girls and their mother peered through the high window, watching eagerly as Venn and Gohran returned. The men were laughing, patting one another on the back.

'Lord Venn must be keen to form a bond with this family,' Prya said.

'I do hope so.' Raeyn sighed.

Prya eyed her eldest daughter. 'You should wear your hair down today. I'll have Lyrra style it for you.'

'You can borrow my earrings, the pair that belonged to Grandmother,' Jaydyn said.

'You have my thanks, Jay. They will suit my new dress.'

They both looked expectantly at Ella, who had inherited the matching brooch. Ella pretended to remove a thread from her bodice.

Lyrra arrived a short time later, tooled with combs and pins. She set her wares alongside a ceramic bowl of water and fragrant oils. Taming and moulding Raeyn's hair was no simple task. Both Ella and Jaydyn helped hold their sister's hair in place as the afternoon crawled by.

'Lord Venn is sure to be smitten when he sees you tonight, Miss Raeyn.' Lyrra secured yet another twist of hair with a pair of pins.

Jaydyn groaned, making a show of shaking out her cramped fingers. 'By the goddess, he'd want to.'

'Do you think so?' Raeyn's hope was pitiable.

'Undoubtedly,' Lyrra assured.

'Can you imagine if he—?'

Ella's grip tightened, tugging on her sister's hair. Raeyn shrieked.

'Oh! My apologies.' Ella released her grip, letting the air inflate her chest as Amber had taught to slow and calm. She would have to pay more attention to the task at hand and less to the churning in her belly.

The night began almost as though scripted by her family. When Venn first arrived, he sought Raeyn and made a show of kissing her hand. The girls' earlier efforts bore fruit, and for once, the Princess Elder looked quite pretty, made more so by the glow Venn's attentions brought to her cheeks. All night she smiled and laughed, flirted even, and Ella felt her innards sinking through the floor as if they might never come back.

At dinner, Ella sat beside Jaydyn and dutifully responded that yes, Sheevan was the most handsome man she had ever seen, and yes, she was sure he liked her, and yes, Jaydyn was to be envied by all the women in greater Erldan, while Gohran and Prya discussed politics and the lucrative hallit trade. After a while, Ella drifted into her thoughts, watching Venn and Raeyn out of the corner of her eye. Raeyn was telling an involved story, tracing a diagram on the table with her fingers. Venn made a show of intent listening, but while Raeyn was looking down, his focus slipped towards Ella. At one point, she risked meeting that gaze. His smile touched hers, and she thought her heart would burst through her chest. She soon noticed her brother watching them, scowling. Venn noticed, too, and fixed his attention back on her sister.

The crawling feeling returned, and Ella felt hot and cold in equal measure. As soon as she could, she excused herself and retreated upstairs to her room. With a sigh, she flopped onto her bed. What good would it do to get her hopes up?

Still, when she closed her eyes and remembered Venn's smile, she caught herself pouring energy into the vision. She pictured them dancing as they had the very first time. She replicated Venn's graceful movements and affectionate eyes, flooding the image with warmth until she could see him, feel him, just as she had once done with her dolls. But it wasn't the same anymore. She now knew the body she created was made of an ethereal substance, cold and hollow, and her enchantment held no charm.

Her eyelids grew heavy in want of sleep, the air chill around her—side-effects of sorcery.

No mystique at all.

Bitterness in her stomach. She stoked the fire and crawled under her blankets, trying not to weep as sleep hovered, always out of reach.

# ELEVEN

After the noon tea, Venn offered to accompany all three princesses on a walk through the glade while Gohran tended to business. The sun was shining when the four of them set out, though a crisp breeze spurred them to walk at a brisk pace. Along the way, they passed one of the formal gardens and Venn bent to pick a posy of marigolds, handing a flower to each of the girls, starting with Raeyn. When he reached Ella, his hands circled her wrists. He squeezed, then let go.

Raeyn wasn't happy. Ella felt, rather than saw it, a painful pinching of the air between them. She reached across to tuck her flower in Raeyn's hair. 'There,' she said. 'You look so lovely, Ren.' The pinching eased. Yet when Ella glanced Venn's way, he was looking at her, rather than her sister.

They strolled for some time, the leaves rustling around them. Whenever the wind stilled, the sun's rays warmed Ella's arms and cheeks, and she yawned. It was true, she thought. Using magic was draining.

'Princess Ella, do you need us to stop?' Venn asked.

'I need to sit for a moment, but you go on ahead.'

Venn frowned. 'We shouldn't leave you on your own.'

'You can wait with her, can't you, Jay?' Raeyn looked hopefully at her sister.

Jaydyn rolled her eyes but tugged Ella by the wrists towards a nearby thicket. The pair settled on the grass as Venn and Raeyn walked on alone. Ella hugged her knees to her chest, allowed her eyes to close and practised segregating her thoughts. Beneath the surface, she thought of Venn with Raeyn, while above, she concentrated on Jaydyn's prattle.

Jaydyn sprawled on her stomach, ankles crossed, and rested her chin on her clasped fingers. 'Do you suppose Creywmm is much like any other village? It seems so far away, almost as far as Herron...' She was already talking like Sheevan's future wife.

Ella focused on the sound of her drawn-out breaths, almost a snore, until she heard nothing at all.

The surrounding air grew chill. Thick shadows moved along the grass, against the trees, making shapes caused by nothing visible. The leaves shifted of their own accord, lifting into the air as though caught on the wind, yet no natural wind could make them hover and skip as they were doing. The air itself seemed to thicken and glow, the greens, reds and browns of the forest appearing crystalline, like a lantern burned within them.

Jaydyn jerked upright and let out a squeal. She shook her sister.

Ella opened her eyes, and saw the colours and shadows vanish, leaving Jaydyn pointing at the empty air.

The others heard Jaydyn's cry and came rushing back.

'What is it?' Raeyn panted.

Jaydyn shook her head back and forth.

'Bandits?' Venn perched like a hunter.

Ella tried to still her thudding chest, to gulp down her panicked tears. Venn was so concerned, but she couldn't look at him. She didn't want him to see her like this, to suspect. His arms wrapped around her, drew her face to his chest, and smoothed her hair.

'Hush now,' he whispered. 'You're safe.'

Ella pushed herself free and brushed the grass off her skirt. 'No bandits. Nothing like that. A sleep terror, that's all.'

'But I wasn't—' Jaydyn's voice wavered, her cheeks aflame.

Ella caught her hands and squeezed, eyes pleading.

Jaydyn abruptly yawned, then frowned as though the yawn surprised her. 'El's right. I must have fallen asleep.'

The four of them headed back to the main keep in near silence. When they arrived, Venn excused himself to prepare for supper.

All three girls trailed after, Ella a short way behind her sisters. Gohran passed them on the landing. He let the elder girls through, but caught Ella's wrist.

She looked away, trying to hide her puffy eyes.

'You look tired. Why don't I have your supper brought up?'

'My thanks.' She heard the catch in her voice. Ella slithered out of her brother's grip and hurried past.

A short while later, there was a knock at her door.

'El, it's me. Open up.'

Gohran. She flinched. Already in her nightdress, she grabbed a shawl and pulled it around her before unbarring the door. Gohran stepped inside, put her supper tray down, and motioned for Ella to sit. Perched opposite, he clasped her arms in his large hands, calm yet firm.

'What happened today?' Ice-blue eyes framed by dark brows. It was the first time he'd visited her since the incident in the glade. The most he'd spoken to her.

Head shaking. 'It was all so daft. A nightmare, nothing more.' Ella saw the ridges of his jaw clenching. He knew. He must know.

Gohran leaned in and stroked Ella's cheek, thumbs resting for a moment. He ran his fingers through the ends of her hair as he'd done when they were children, then pulled her near and held her there.

Ella had longed for them to be close again, but this felt odd. The hot-cold queasiness was there again. She felt his heartbeat through his shirt.

Abruptly, he let her go.

Ella watched him retreat. She couldn't stop trembling.

Later, as she recounted her day's events with Amber, she didn't mention Gohran's visit.

The next morning at breakfast, Ella found both Venn and her brother gone. Raeyn and Jaydyn bickered, and Prya had no patience for anyone.

A servant approached with a jug of milk. Prya knocked it out of her hands. The jug cracked on the floor, spluttering frothy white liquid everywhere. 'Look at that filth!' Ella looked where her mother pointed. Among the mess was a curved sliver of black—a solitary hair. 'Clean this up.'

Ella shrank into her chair. Her mother's gaze caught and pierced her, anger flaring. Just as quickly, it was replaced with some other emotion Ella couldn't quite place. Not fear, exactly.

She didn't dare ask after either of the men. Instead, as soon as was polite, she fled to her room and her studies.

# TWELVE

The moon sat bloated on the horizon when Gohran ordered his armed escort of twenty men to stop for the night. Making camp involved erecting a large canvas tent for the prince, and laying out the puddle of bedrolls that would do for his men. Two of the soldiers set about carving up the remains of the spit-roasted boar they'd speared the previous day, while Gohran led prayers for those squatting around the fire. They passed ale along to accompany the meat. Tonight, they could finish it, for they would arrive at Creywmm in the morning.

The men talked about the coming summer, but Gohran barely heard them as he stared into the flames. Venn's sudden departure bothered him. Urgent business to tend to in Nedran, he had said, but Gohran suspected the departure related to his sisters and whatever mishap had spoiled their outing. If it was anything like what he had seen... Gohran shuddered. No, Venn suspected nothing, just as Raeyn and Jaydyn suspected nothing. It was too improbable, implausible, to make the connection. If Venn had left on purpose, it was more likely a reflection of his desire for a marriage being at odds with the prince.

The skin of ale had made its way back around. Gohran took it, shook out the last few mouthfuls, and tossed the empty skin into the fire. He felt the men's eyes upon him. Why did Venn have to want Ella? Her dowry was pitiful compared with Raeyn's, and he'd have to wait another year or two before the priests would make a ruling. Sixteen summers was considered the earliest marrying age for girls, though the betrothal could be in place from fifteen. Gohran knew of priests who would seal men to girls as young as twelve, but it was frowned upon, and no doubt cost the bridegroom's family a considerable sum.

'Are you worried about the coming summer, Your Highness?' a tall, greying man named Tarraen asked, retrieving the smoking skin from the fire with a stick.

'Why do you ask?'

'The crease etching its way along your forehead.' Tarraen chuckled under his breath. 'It's like the crackle of static in the air before a storm, isn't it?'

Gohran looked up sharply.

Tarraen caught the prince's gaze and smiled disarmingly. 'Perhaps I just have the blood-scent of a vulture after all these years.' He scratched his beard.

'I suppose you're wondering why Creywmm?'

'As always, you see through me. It's not an alliance to fill Erldan's coffers, so it must be one to secure her borders.'

A familiar shiver tingled through the base of Gohran's spine. 'A prince should always tend to his borders, Tar.' An alliance with Creywmm offered Erldan a stronghold close to the nearest rival kingdom in Herron.

Gohran felt Tarraen's eyes upon his back as he walked away. He was weary and needed to be alone. Tucked inside his tent he could hear the men's bawdy banter, the intent clear though the words themselves were indistinct. Was Tarraen right? Would there be war? If not this summer, then soon?

The constantly shifting alliances within Ycelt were a source of consternation for any ruler, but Gohran felt a pressing need to shore up Erldan's allies, though he couldn't quite pinpoint the cause. It almost felt inevitable that trouble would erupt after so many generations of peace, as though Erldan couldn't remain immune to Xenon's Curse indefinitely.

An icy quiver across his flesh. What would become of his family? His sisters? He thought again of Ella. Something in him stirred. She had been the one to befriend him when no one else would. Mother had told him it was hard on the other lads, who saw the Marked Prince as different. Untouchable. It was a difference that seemed to mar his very core. Yet he never felt that way with Ella. With her, he was naked, vulnerable, safe. She was like him.

Unlike him, however, Ella was adored. Their father doted on her, and the servants rushed to do her bidding. He, too, longed to give her everything she could want, and then some. The fire that lit her eyes when she smiled infused his senses like mead. Is that what Venn saw in her, what he felt when their eyes met, when he held her?

Gohran craved the night air against his skin. With the back of his hand, he felt his forehead. Fever. Outside, the men's chatter had died down. Now he heard only the rhythmic snuffling of sleep-breathing. He threw off his bedclothes and untied the tent flaps, heading to the now-empty campfire which had reduced to a pile of glowing embers. As he neared, it rekindled briefly, sending sparks into the indigo sky. With his back to the fire, he waited for his eyes to adjust to the darkness.

Gohran abandoned the grey camp and strode sure-footed towards the nearby stream. He took one look back to the sleeping camp and stripped off his clothes. Memory flared in his mind. Things that moved in stillness, thoughts heard, shared. He pictured Ella's tear-stained cheeks. It was only a matter of time before someone put the pieces together.

The night air carried the fire of the sun against his skin. He plunged into the icy-cold water. The murky surface surged outwards in a series of rings. Ducking beneath, he grabbed hold of a rock wedged along the river's bottom and slowly emptied his lungs. He cupped a handful of gravel from the sludgy depths and began scouring at his skin, the gravel's edges biting. He kept going, letting the stones slice and cut. Pain like fire, but also release. A soothing calm. His lungs ached. They might rupture down here. Still, he fought the urge to surface. Finally, he let go, floating back to the top. He burst out above the water, gasping for air. Cold struck wet skin.

'Highness!' It was Tarraen. He had stripped down to his smalls and was about to jump in.

'Throw me my shirt, will you?' Gohran climbed out onto the grassy bank.

Tarraen tossed the nearby shirt to the prince. Gohran's shins were bleeding. Rather than pull the shirt on, he used it to soak up the blood.

'I'll fetch another, Your Highness.'

'Leave it, Tar. I'm going back to my tent.' Now that the panic had left him, Gohran was weary. All he could think about was crawling beneath his blankets, sleep wrapping around him. His negotiations on the morrow must go as planned. It was the only way to keep Ella safe.

Ella found out soon enough why her brother had ventured so far from home.

'A betrothal? It should be me first!' Raeyn's freckles faded into the rage of pink that covered her cheeks. Gohran had sent word by speeded courier that Neryda and Samwwl of Creywmm had eagerly accepted the offer of marriage for their son, and while Jaydyn was smugly moon-bright, Raeyn was ready to cast every possible storm cloud over her joy.

'How many times have we been over this? Sheevan is a minor lord. Not a dryhten. Not a prince. And Neryda and Samwwl are very keen to form a connection with this family. I agree, I would have preferred to make you a match first, but here we are.'

Ella sensed her mother's displeasure was less about the order in which her daughters would be married, and more to do with Gohran usurping her authority. She continued measuring out lengths of cloth as the girls cut out various sections. They still had dozens of shirts to sew before they could start on the dresses, and now they would need to make wedding clothes, too. Jaydyn kept glancing her sister's way.

'You can take that self-satisfied smirk off your face, Jay—Sheevan wants this alliance, not you.'

For the rest of the afternoon, Jaydyn had the serving women in a flurry, trying to find the exact coloured thread she wanted to use on the wedding shirt. Her enthusiasm was contagious, eroding Raeyn's resentment.

Ella told herself she was pleased for Jay. But what would it mean for her? Lord Venn also wished to form a connection with Erldan. That much was clear. If Gohran had secured an alliance for Jaydyn, rather than Raeyn, it must mean he was saving Raeyn for something—or someone—more. A dryhten. The surrounding air thickened and she struggled to breathe. She ran outside before they saw her tears.

Not long after Gohran's return, he gravitated towards the comfort of the temple. As always, Davith appeared almost immediately, as though he had nothing better to do than await the prince.

'I have arranged a marriage for one of my sisters,' he said.

'Princess Jaydyn. I heard.'

'I suspect it was against the wishes of the queen.'

'Is that what she said?'

'Not in as many words.' Stubble tickled the top of Gohran's lip. He scratched his forefinger along it, trying to relax his clenched jaw. 'An act of defiance—or so she assumes.'

'Do you have reason to doubt your motives, Your Highness?' Davith's tone remained steady, but Gohran saw his eyes narrow.

'Not at all. I did it for Erldan. Mother herself said we couldn't allow Raeyn to marry someone of such low standing and I had to secure that alliance. I had to...' Gohran's voice trailed off.

Evenly, Davith said, 'You know Your Highness, it is of considerable benefit for you to strengthen your kingdom's position. I can see no sound reason anyone would object to your decision. Quite the contrary. It shows great foresight on your part.'

'You see trouble afoot.'

A pause. 'Not specifically. It's just—' Davith glanced around. 'Well, Your Highness, ordinarily I wouldn't give credit to idle gossip, but I have now heard this concern expressed in more than one quarter.'

With a gesture, Gohran hurried Davith along.

'There has been some consternation over the youngest princess's new tutor.' Gohran looked up sharply.

'Some villagers wonder that your mother would take someone into such a trusted position when so little is known about her. She hails from the east, or so she claims. A woman in the Harnal baths your mother frequents vouched for her, yet no one in that village seems to know of her.'

'But why would mother...?' An ugly suspicion formed. Gohran had barely paid attention when his mother hired Amber—it was a women's matter.

'As I said, ordinarily I wouldn't give it a second thought. But tongues are wagging, as they say, and now that your family has chosen to ally with a family so far to the east...' Davith looked down his nose at the prince.

'I trust you have assured those with impure and suspicious minds that the queen loves Erldan more than her own life.'

'Of course, Your Highness. No one would ever suspect the queen of *knowingly* placing Erldan in danger.'

So, Gohran thought, they suspected Ella's tutor was a spy.

Gohran caught Davith's gaze square on and for a moment the priest couldn't look away. When Gohran eventually released him, Davith's voice was barely a whisper. 'I will do everything in my power to stamp out these rumours, Your Highness. I swear it on the honour of Our Lady of the Dark Sun.'

'Then your loyalty will be remembered, Your Holiness.' Gohran stood to leave. He would have to speak to mother, and soon.

# Thirteen

For Ella, the next few moons dragged. Other than her studies, her only entertainment was helping prepare for Jaydyn's wedding. Whenever her mother inquired about her schooling, both she and Amber reported they were going well. Ella still couldn't quite believe she was studying magic, of all things. Magic! Between her and Amber it became as ordinary as learning to crochet or memorising lore, but when every moment was cloaked in secrecy and voiced in code, she sometimes wondered if it was even real. Other times, she would notice a curious glance cast her way, or overhear a hushed whisper, and fear would paralyse her.

Ella's only other worry was her brother. Now and then she caught Gohran watching her and at odd moments she sensed his thoughts upon her, though she couldn't read them. Was he looking for signs of her magic? Much as she hated to, she used her newfound knowledge to build a shield to bury her thoughts from him, but it was like closing off a part of her childhood, a part of herself.

With Venn gone, Raeyn kept to her rooms, only joining the others at mealtimes, and then making a show of snivelling, giving curt responses to questions when prodded. Her stamina for sulking eventually ran out, and she allowed herself to be coaxed back into joining her sisters in the women's hall.

Jaydyn immediately boasted of her letters from Sheevan, which were over-stuffed with accounts of his military prowess. 'Strong *and* handsome!' She sighed, glancing towards Raeyn to gauge her reaction.

Even the resumption of her sisters' bickering couldn't distract Ella for long. Instead, she stared down into the courtyard below where her brother was sparring. After a time, he wiped his forehead and glanced up. Their eyes met, and Ella's stomach churned. Although he looked away almost immediately, Ella couldn't shake the feeling he was still thinking about her.

When evening came and Ella retired to her room, she lit her fire and drew a blanket around her shoulders as she sat cross-legged and watched the flames dance, sipping a cup of warmed ilak's milk. As she peered into the flames, she could have sworn Gohran stared straight back. She tried to blink, to turn away, but his gaze held her. Finally, he turned, moving back from the fire and she realised she was seeing him through the flames, having just lit a fire himself. As he withdrew, she could make out the surrounding study. Prya sat at a nearby desk, watching as her son paced back and forth.

'I don't understand why you won't take this seriously,' Gohran said.

'And I don't understand why you won't let it be,' Prya responded with a dismissive shrug, though Ella could see the whites of Prya's knuckles as the queen fidgeted with her sapphire ring.

'When left unchecked, idle gossip can swell into serious discontent—there's more than one way to overthrow a monarchy.'

'Now you're being dramatic. If Davith has nothing better to do than fill his days fuelling these kinds of rumours, then perhaps it is time he considered whether he wishes to remain the head priest for this family.'

Gohran stopped pacing and perched on the stool opposite Prya. 'Consider that at present, people only suspect political spies. Do you want them to take a closer look at this household?'

'Why shouldn't they?'

Gohran's ice-blue eyes challenged his mother's. 'I'm not a fool. I know what that supposed tutor is doing here. It won't work. She'll have to go to Aryon. It's time you faced up to it.'

'Gods, she's still practically a child!'

'She's almost fifteen. Moons have passed since Lord Venn was last here. What do you think scared him off? Jaydyn still goes on about how she saw something moving in the forest that day. If it was anything like what I saw...'

'What nonsense. Lord Venn wasn't "scared off." He had his city to think of. Once Neryda and Samwwl finalise the deeds, they will settle Jaydyn near Creywmm, where she can fuss over nothing all she likes. Ella has been making excellent progress in her studies. Imagine the match she will make for Erldan when—'

'Match? Ha! What about the treaty?'

'I have three daughters. Only one is currently betrothed.'

Gohran slammed his fist on the table. 'We've been through this, mother. You said yourself we couldn't make a match for Raeyn with a lesser noble. And we need that alliance. If I hadn't acted then, Sheevan would have set his sights elsewhere.'

'I might have persuaded him to wait a few years.'

Gohran pushed back against the table to stand his full six feet. Ella hadn't realised how much he had grown. 'How could you have even considered risking a stronghold so close to Herron?'

'With Ella as the inducement?'

Ella saw Gohran's jaw muscles bulge.

Prya rose and rested her hand upon her son's shoulder. 'Venn will be back. He's not looking to marry for a few seasons. By then Ella will almost be of age. We still have time to make this work.'

'And the treaty?'

'Let me worry about Breeyan.'

Ella saw something strange then. As her mother's eyes sought Gohran's, a beam of blue light travelled from Prya towards her son. As the blue light flowed, it shimmered like heat coming off summer roof tiles. The beam thickened as it neared the prince, circling, wrapping around him.

Gohran's eyes went out of focus, and his jaw slackened. 'Of course, mother. You're right. We'll wait.'

With that, Ella saw only waning flames before her. Shivering, she stoked the fire and clutched her blanket, gulping down the rest of her milk, trying not to choke. *By every god and demon. Mother has magic, too.*

That night, Gohran had no desire to be on his own. Instead, he took refuge in the barracks with his men. Seated beside Tarraen and Ganno, he watched some of the other lads engage in a drunken match of tiles and downed a steady stream. He signalled to be dealt in the next hand and played until the early hours. For some reason he couldn't quite pin down, his mother had just persuaded him to do something against his better judgement, or at least, against his wishes. It hovered at the edge of his mind, but he could never quite grasp it. In the end, it was more frustrating to try to catch the thought than let it slip into inebriated oblivion.

Prya sat atop her bed, watching her trembling reflection in the dresser mirror. Her room was large, with rich coloured carpets and wall coverings. The tapestries showed scenes from the old war, with some fantasy thrown in, such as the mythical dragons circling the mountain ranges. The dresser was ornately carved and embellished with gold leaf detail. She ran her fingers along the furls. Curse Gohran for circumventing her and going straight to Creywmm. How could he be so determined to hide his sister away? It made no sense. The match Ella could make would profit him more than Prya. Erldan would ultimately be his kingdom. And it wasn't just that Ella's beauty would attract a powerful suitor. Her abilities could be used to influence those around her. But how could she explain without giving herself away? What little influence she'd exerted over him just now wouldn't last—it never did. She did not have the training to control him completely. While Gohran had inherited his looks from her side of the family, he'd inherited his father's stubbornness and strength of will.

With a sigh, she lay back on top of her coverlet. If only her mother had shown her more than a handful of mind tricks. She wanted to consult Amber, or even Bree. She couldn't, of course. It was too risky. She didn't even dare share her intent with Ella. What if she raised her daughter's hopes, and it all came to naught? How bitter a lifetime of servitude would be, knowing the alternative had been within her grasp!

Among the handful of charms her mother had taught her was a nerve calmer, a trick to help expel her emotions. She called upon it now, inhaling and closing her eyes. She let her breath come in slow, steady beats. In her mind's eye, she saw a point in the air a few feet above her and four points around her body, one at each of her outstretched arms, feet, and head. She then drew a line with her mind to connect the points, forming a pyramid, her body along its base. The pyramid glowed, charged with energy. Then, like a siphon, the peak drew out her bad thoughts—much like a poultice will calm an inflamed wound. With an exhale, she released the points at the pyramid's base. The vortex sucked at the edges, drawing them in until a lone ball of power hovered above her. With a wave of her hand, she banished the force. The blue light dissipated into darkness.

Composed, Prya sat up. She straightened her coverlet and dress and smoothed her hair. The mirror reflected her serenity—no forehead crinkles, a slight curve of the lips, neck muscles relaxed, jaw soft. She decided then and there that if Ella was to stay in Ycelt, she would teach this one thing to her.

A gust of wind crept along her neck, sending a shudder along her shoulder blades and down the length of her spine. With sudden certainty, she knew she would never have the chance.

# Fourteen

Spring was slow in coming that year. It was almost the equinox before the snowmelt eased enough to let travellers through. Eventually, the roads became passable and Sheevan arrived with the draft betrothal contract, which kept the women entertained for several days until he returned home again.

Raeyn and Ella barely saw Jaydyn or Sheevan for the entire time the lord was visiting. When they did, the couple appeared permanently entwined like a pair of courting snakes, which set Raeyn off on another sulk.

All that remained to finalise the betrothal was the deed of settlement for Sheevan's property. When Ella saw the date upon it, she realised Amber had been at Erldan for over twenty moons, which meant she had been studying sorcery that long. Even now, she had to remind herself it was real, a secret hugged to her chest, encased in the wall she had built and solidified within her mind. She smiled, feeling her mental muscles had grown stronger, more powerful, like a warrior's hardened body.

On this day, the daughters of Erldan huddled in the women's hall, decorating candles. Prya had just joined them, servants flurrying behind.

'Ella darling, it will be your birthday soon. Gohran has agreed to host a party. He also agreed you shall have a new dress.' Prya looked her up and down. 'In fact, it was his suggestion.' Ella squirmed. At almost fifteen summers, her girlish dresses had become ill-fitting. 'I saw some lovely gold cloth I thought would be perfect for you.' Prya described the fabric and cut she had in mind. Before her elder daughters could grumble, she said, 'Jaydyn, you'll need a wedding dress soon, and Raeyn, you shall have a new dress then.'

Ella tried to muster some enthusiasm as she helped her sisters prepare the guest list and plan the menu and decorations. Her skin prickled with unease. The surrounding air seemed to grow thicker, heavier. Muffled voices—her sisters reciting names—drifted by as if from another room.

Jaydyn fossicked through her needlework basket and held up strips of fabric to show her sisters.

'Ugh, you can't use *that* blue with *that* green, Jay!' Raeyn snatched the strips from her.

Jaydyn snatched them right back. 'I'm putting the gold between them. See? It will look perfect. Won't it, El?'

Jaydyn's elbow prodded her. 'It will be lovely, Jay.'

'You could at least look at it.'

'Sorry.' Ella made a show of taking in her sister's handiwork—sapphire and emerald-coloured fabric inlaid with gold. The gold blazed as though alight. All around her, the air felt dense as smoke. Ella coughed, tears stinging her eyes.

'Stop sputtering all over the silk!'

Ella swallowed, blinking to force the vision to disappear, clutching her hand to her throat. 'I need some air.' She left her sisters and hurried outside.

Out in the open, Ella leaned against the castle wall, inhaling, palms flat against cool stone.

'Ella?' It was Amber, carrying a basket of flowers towards the main keep.

Ella struggled to shield her thoughts.

Amber frowned. 'Something's happened.'

Ella shook her head and forced a thin smile. 'I just needed some air...'

Amber's eyes narrowed. She was about to say more when she heard the chamberlain's voice from inside the keep. 'We'll talk about this tomorrow.' She hefted her basket back up and hurried inside.

That night, Ella dreamed she was dancing with Venn at her birthday ball. So comfortable in his embrace, so easy. Movements flowing, they circled smoothly until another man cut in and whisked her away. Her new partner's arms slid around her waist, firm where he caught and held her. Ella wanted to slither away until he smiled down at her. Her breath caught just to look at him. Heat where his skin touched hers. Aflush, she could barely breathe, his smile turning her knees to water. But then—across the room, Venn was kissing her sister. She had to stop them! She pushed her partner's arms away, thrashing, but he was too strong.

'Do you smell something burning?'

Wispy mist wound around them, long arms of white, thickening into smoke, filling her throat, and settling upon her lungs. She struggled to get enough air. Where was Venn? The smoke was too thick to see through. She had to reach him! Her dance partner tugged at her waist, dragging her outside. Over his shoulder, she spied her brother watching them from the doorway, his lip curled in a sneer.

Ella sat up, wide awake and gasping, staring into the cool dark.

The next morning, Ella relayed the story to Amber. Her tutor frowned, sucking in her cheeks. 'You say the visions began during the day before I saw you outside?' Ella nodded. 'And you saw them again in your dreams? That bodes ill.' An abrupt exhale, cheeks puffed, 'I suppose now is as good a time as any to learn about omens.'

'As in portents?'

Amber nodded. 'Just that. Those who are god-touched are sometimes sent omens of what is to come. They can appear as dreams and visions, or as earthly signs. I even read of some causing the earth itself to shudder.'

Ella shuddered in response.

'A raven's caw, a star falling, a clap of thunder—any of these can signify a god-sent foreshadowing, but an omen is more about the unease than the sign itself.'

Another shudder. Unease was an understatement. Ella's vision had practically choked her! 'But what does it mean?'

Amber shrugged. 'Sometimes we can meditate to uncover the meaning... Sometimes not.'

Ella felt like weeping. 'I just want the feeling to go away...'

'I know.' Amber squeezed her hands. 'Come, lie beside me. Let's see what we can uncover.' She motioned for Ella to lie on the carpet. Then she stood and retrieved a couple of brass censers. 'I don't dare light a fire, but we can use smoke for the working.' She opened a censer and lit the incense within.

Perfumed wood filled Ella's nostrils.

'Meditation only works when Xenon has sent a true sign. You can't just pick at the future unbidden, like a shaman in the marketplace,' Amber said, lighting more incense. 'It's forbidden to search for omens not freely revealed.'

A chill travelled down Ella's spine.

'Now, close your eyes and slow your breath,' Amber instructed. 'That's it. Slow, steady breaths. Let your limbs relax... Imagine your entire body sinking into the floor... Then, concentrate on the uneasy feeling...'

Ella couldn't help but feel it—an icy hand gripping her, creeping its way towards her throat.

'Clear your mind of everything else.' Amber's voice sounded distant, distorted, as though she stood on the other side of a thick wall. 'Imagine speaking to the god. Ask about the omen...'

Smoke, thick and grey, filled Ella's lungs. Not from the censers, but heavy, as in her dream, as if fire surrounded her. Heat blazed all around. The hand-like presence squeezed her throat. She gasped for air, wheezing and sputtering once again. She kept trying to do as Amber asked, but it was getting harder to breathe. In the distance, she heard Amber's muffled voice, but couldn't make out her words, as they drifted further and further away. Smoke clouded her vision, and she struggled to grasp a single thought as her mind wavered, dreamlike, until there was only darkness, and then nothing at all.

Amber gaped at her pupil. Ella's face was ashen, her lips tinged with blue. 'By the gods! Ella, stop it, stop thinking about it.' Amber shook her. Ella's skin was burning! Amber snatched her hands away. She needed to banish the working before Ella drew more power. She stubbed out the incense and waved her hands to clear the air. Every surface she touched was sleet cold as Ella continued to draw.

Amber's limbs ached, and she shivered, teeth chattering. She was competing for every iota of energy inside the room. There was nothing left to help her shut the working down. Her eyelids felt so heavy... Her heartbeat, slowing... She just wanted to lie down, close her eyes, and slip away...

A slap. Her hand jolted her awake. Again. And again. Slap! Slap!

Amber shook her body and stamped her feet, blinking. She looked for something—anything—to stop the working, to stop Ella from drawing more power than her life, their lives, could sustain. But there was nothing... Except...

*Ella herself.*

Forbidden.

Amber's own words came back to her. *We never use this energy... The Curse will fall upon any who do...* Amber's breath came in foggy puffs. 'Xenon, help me,' she murmured. Her legs buckled. She slid to the floor. Another glance around the room. She saw nothing else she could use to draw upon. Amber struggled to sit upright as she placed her hands upon the princess. Still hot. Hot and yet icy cold. She wasn't breathing. Ella wasn't breathing!

*It's said to bring horror thrice over...* 'Forgive me, Xenon. Forgive me....' Amber whispered over and over. What choice did she have? If she didn't draw the power away, Ella could drain them both.

She let her eyes drift out of focus until she saw the white-hot energy flowing through Ella, power coursing through her like river rapids. She clawed at the energy, scooping it towards herself. Heat surged. Her entire body crackled, a sizzling tremor through every inch of her. Her senses heightened. She could hear the faintest gasp, and smell the very earth trapped between the stone of the walls. The fabric of her dress sent a thrill through her skin, while around her the room appeared as shards of crystal so bright she had to shield her eyes. Exhilaration unlike anything she had ever experienced—pure power.

Frantic, she shot the excess force through her fingertips. Shafts of blue flashed like lightning. Bolts of energy burst against the walls, scattering power, restoring the room's warmth. She fired more bolts until the colours dimmed, returning to their usual opaque dullness, her senses restored to their natural muted state. She only stopped once the last of the tingling sensation abandoned her, spent.

Lying unconscious on the floor, Ella's taut muscles eased. Colour returned to her cheeks. Her breath came in juddering gasps, but at least she was breathing. Amber drew her close and held her until her breath relaxed into the slow steady beats of natural sleep.

Amber felt wrung out. She regained her ordinary senses, but a leaden ache lingered deep in her bones.

She watched Ella sleep. So beautiful—so vulnerable. Her body yearned, ached, to draw still more power, to feel that electric thrill once more. A wave of nausea.

She scrambled to her feet and away from Ella. She needed clean, natural energy, free from impure temptation. A fire would take too long and draw too much suspicion. Food. She needed to eat.

Amber left Ella sleeping to source something from the kitchens, all the while praying under her breath for forgiveness. She'd had no choice. No choice at all.

Later that night, Amber set the queen's hand mirror beneath her lantern. Faint and steady snuffles indicated her bedfellow was deep in slumber. She ought to reach out to Queen Prya, yet she hesitated. Instead, she found her thoughts drifting back to Aryon. She pictured her beloved Nykahlia, imagined she could smell Nykki's hair, the skin of her neck... How she longed to hold her, to be held. *Too risky.* She shook the image away. *Breathe. Focus.* If she was going to contact anyone at Aryon, it ought to be the High Priestess. And say what? That Ella's meditation had almost smothered them both? Or worse, that Amber had to resort to the most unclean of magic to stop what she had inadvertently started? *No.* She couldn't. Not to Breeyan.

A tug at her mind. Breeyan's image appeared before her in the reflection. The High Priestess must have sensed her.

Amber turned the mirror over, breaking the connection. She couldn't do it. Whatever had happened today, it must stay between her and Ella. She licked a thumb and forefinger to smother the lantern's light before crawling back to her shared bed.

# FIFTEEN

In the weeks that followed, the preparations for Ella's birthday celebration consumed her. By the time her birthday arrived, eager anticipation filled her, the working and omen that preceded it, a faint memory. The last thing she recalled was lying down to meditate, and then falling through some dark, dreamlike chasm, to wake hours later, wrapped in blankets.

'I shouldn't have allowed you to perform that working,' Amber had said the next day. 'I blame myself—you weren't ready.'

Amber explained her magic had almost suffocated her, yet Ella had no real recollection of it. It was as though whatever Amber had done to shut the working down, she had taken the ominous feeling and memory with it.

And now, as she looked down at her finished dress, Ella smiled, pleased with the flattering but modest fitted bodice and high waist. The delicate gold thread embroidered over the heavy silk shimmered as it caught the light of the gold leaf candelabra.

Jaydyn's decorations adorned the entire hall, amidst the tables set with crisp linen and fine silver. 'See?' Jaydyn gestured around the room to showcase her work. 'Didn't I say the colours would work well? And these are the *original* colours of our dynasty.'

For once, she earned her brother's admiration, as Gohran took in her preparations with a satisfied nod. 'I'm not sure these shades are quite true to the original, but it looks very striking, Jay.'

Ella squeezed her sister's arm. 'I think it looks *just* like the colours on Grandfather's old genealogy map.'

Prya interrupted, placing her hands on her middle daughter's shoulders. 'How are you feeling now, Jaydyn?'

'Much better, my thanks.' Jaydyn had complained about feeling sick every morning for almost a week. She had even vomited for good measure. But that afternoon she looked surprisingly well.

'Doubtless.' Prya peered down her nose at her daughter. It wouldn't have been the first time Jaydyn had cried off sick to avoid the tedious preparations, only to recover miraculously when the event arrived.

As the minstrels warmed up, the family took their places to greet the arriving guests. They had invited most of the neighbouring nobility, along with some important families from further afield. One of the first to enter, Sheevan sought Jaydyn's company right away. When Venn appeared soon afterwards, he introduced his brother Jonas to the royal family.

Jonas stepped forward, bowing low to catch Ella's hand in both of his. He looked up, eyebrow raised, lip curled, teasing. 'Your Highness.' His velvet voice sent a twinge through her belly, down to her groin and up to her breasts. His lips found her hand, his kiss lingering. 'I hope to have the genuine pleasure of dancing with you this evening.' A blush crept upwards from her chest and neck until she thought her cheeks might burst into flame. She was both relieved and disappointed when he sauntered on.

The introductions continued for some time. *Had there always been so many unwed lords surrounding Erldan?* She responded dutifully to their compliments, the tall, the short, wide, and lean, many old, some young, all the while keeping an eye out for Venn. When she spotted him, she saw him standing beside his brother. Jonas caught her eyes and smiled. A tingle of anticipation and trepidation fluttered through her.

When the dancing began, for once, Jaydyn seemed content to sit beside her betrothed. 'You don't wish to dance, my love?' Jaydyn shook her head. 'Not right now. I feel so weary!'

Ella had little time to ponder her sister's odd behaviour, as lord after lord requested a dance, including Venn's brother Jonas, but not the dryhten himself. Between times, guests flocked around her, like ilaks to fresh grass after the winter snow. She supposed they must wish to ingratiate themselves to such a powerful dynasty. At each dance's close, she waited, hopeful for Venn to join her. She caught sight of him dancing several times with Raeyn before he approached with a gentle bow. He offered her his outstretched arm, and she accompanied him onto the dance floor.

'We meet again, Your Highness,' he said as they fell into step.

'We do, my lord.'

'And how do you like your ball so far?'

'It has been most enjoyable, my thanks.'

'I see you have had the pleasure of dancing with my brother.'

Venn's voice caught, and Ella tried to read his thoughts. His mouth was tight.

'You look puzzled, Your Highness. Was it not enjoyable?'

Ella frowned. How should she respond? 'As enjoyable as any other dance I have had tonight before this one.'

'No one could fault your politeness.'

'Perhaps not, if my words were mere flattery.'

Venn's tight smile gave way to a genuine grin. He twirled and caught her, arms looping around her comfortably. Ella wanted to stay in this moment forever. Venn paused, and she looked up, expectant, but his head wasn't bending to meet hers. Instead, he stared across the hall. Ella followed his gaze to where Raeyn and Gohran huddled together, Raeyn scowling. Enthusiasm leaked out of Venn's movements. Raeyn lowered her face as Gohran gestured their way. 'Forgive me, Your Highness. I had best tend to the prince.'

He strode away, leaving Ella standing with the empty air, bitter cold in her belly. She felt a tap on her shoulder. Jonas.

'May I?'

Ella found it hard to swallow but nodded her assent.

Jonas slipped his arms around her waist. The familial resemblance between him and his brother was slight. His hair was a lighter shade, and his olive skin brought out the flecks of green in his hazel eyes. While he wasn't as tall as Venn, he was broader. He held her close. Uncomfortably so. She could feel the line of his muscles—a warrior in training. His breath was warm in her ear. 'You are *most* beautiful, Your Highness.'

Her cheeks and throat burned crimson.

'There's no need to be modest. Your beauty will surpass your mother's, I am sure. And in a few years, they'll be marrying you off like Jaydyn.'

Ella gasped. Over the music and the crowd, doubtless only she could hear. Even so, how dare he be so candid?

He lifted his hand to brush her hair and stroke her cheek, his hand trailing down along the vulnerable skin at her throat.

'I want you to ponder that. You will be married to someone old and ugly, for power, for wealth, and you'll get no say in it. He might be cruel, and it won't matter. Your beauty will be a prize for him, not you.'

Jonas's breath was hot now, and she felt a thrill of excitement and dread. He was right, of course, but why speak so?

'You've only a few years of freedom left.' One hand slid along her cheek, the other gripped her waist. He must sense what he was doing to her heartbeat.

The song ended, and Ella excused herself, fleeing to the night air of the balcony. She leaned back against the uneven stones and let the air cool her skin. She watched the stars wink in and out from behind a scatter of clouds. The crescent moon hung in the sky like a sinister smile. She shivered. If her family intended Raeyn to marry Venn, there would be no benefit from a liaison between her and Jonas. Jonas would see that as clearly as she did. So, what did he want from her?

A screech from inside the hall.

Ella rushed back in. Silence cloaked the room. The minstrels' instruments dangled, lax. Everyone seemed to stare towards the honour table. Ella followed their collective gaze. The crowd had created a wide berth around it and Ella saw Gohran stood with one arm raised, backhanded, above his middle sister. Jaydyn clutched her cheek while Sheevan stood beside her, frozen.

'You couldn't have waited another few months to spread your legs,' Gohran spat. He towered over the couple, eyes hard, nostrils flared. 'So much for your precious genealogy—what does any of that matter when you shame yourself like a commoner? I couldn't blame Sheevan's family if they broke off your betrothal now. Why would they want to taint their bloodlines?'

Tears streamed down Jaydyn's cheeks. She shook her head wordlessly, tugging on Sheevan's sleeve. 'Tell him. Tell him we'll still marry.' She clung to him, positioning him between her and Gohran. She trembled, but so did he. '*Sheevan!*'

Eventually, Sheevan stepped forward, his legs leaden as if pulled by a puppeteer. When he spoke, his voice was oddly flat. His shoulders still shook. 'We—we wanted to start a family straight away. It's not Jaydyn's fault. It's mine.'

For some reason she couldn't explain, Ella found her attention being drawn to the other side of the room. *Mother.*

Across the hall, Queen Prya stood eerily still, eyes half closed. For the barest moment, Ella could have sworn she saw a distinct beam of blue light flowing from her mother. The light crossed the hall and wrapped around Sheevan in shimmering waves. It was just as she had seen that time through the fire when mother had used her magic to influence Gohran. *No—It couldn't be.* Ella shuddered. A puppeteer, indeed! Sheevan would have turned and fled if he could, Ella was sure of it.

Ella searched the faces of the other guests. They appeared unaware of anything amiss beyond the physical commotion right in front of them. If Sheevan seemed reluctant to speak up, well, why wouldn't he be? Who in their right mind would want to cross the prince in a rage?

Gohran studied his brother-in-law-to-be, almost as though he were trying to read Sheevan's thoughts. Bit by bit he relaxed, letting both hands come to rest upon his hips. 'Well then. If you'll still have her. I'd hardly...' His voice trailed off. Head cocked, tense like a strung bow.

Ella followed his gaze as it travelled the length of the room, just as hers had done moments before. She could not deny he focused on the same blue line of force. *He could see it!* That could only mean one thing. He must have magic, too!

When his gaze landed on Prya, Ella covered her mouth with both hands to stifle a squeal and clamped down on her thoughts.

Eyes narrowed, Gohran picked up his goblet, gulped its entire contents, and then slammed the empty vessel down. The entire bench shuddered. He turned to face their mother and strode towards her, slow and purposeful. The crowd parted to let him through. The hall had never seemed so long. Prya sucked in her breath. The silence in the room grew so thick Ella thought she would choke on it. Everyone watched them. One of Prya's nearby acquaintances clutched her throat, her face pallid as she slinked away.

Finally, son and mother faced one another square on, eyes locked.

'It's you—You're controlling him.' Gohran's voice was like ice.

Prya's eyes narrowed, her smile constricted.

Ella sensed Gohran's coldness clawing at some place in Prya that Ella had never witnessed.

Sheevan, who had stood as though strung up on wires, stumbled, slumping into his chair. His terror now showed plainly on his face. Shameless, he clung to his betrothed.

For an agonising moment, Prya stood tall and proud. 'What are you talking about, my *son*? Are you quite well? You look feverish...'

An undercurrent pulsed between them that Ella didn't understand. Her mother, beseeching, soothing. Her brother, defending, vying.

Gohran didn't waver. 'I'm perfectly well.' The chill in Gohran's voice was like an icy hand down Ella's back.

'You're flushed.' Prya's voice faltered, and she reached out, as though to put her arm around Gohran's shoulder, taking him under her wing. He raised his arm to block her, twisting to grip her extended wrist. She tried to hide her flinch, but Ella saw. That same taut smile as Prya tried to laugh it off. 'Gohran, my son, I command you, go—sit back down.' With her free hand, she signalled to a nearby servant. 'Bring some wine, will you? You can see the prince is unwell.'

The servant bowed and fled.

Prya tried to squirm away while maintaining her poise for the audience.

Gohran pulled her in close and hissed, 'You have left me no choice.'

Ella saw something in her mother break. 'No Gohran…' Prya's face turned grey, and she shook her head feebly. Her hand picked a meandering path towards her neck.

The servant arrived back and knelt to present a filled goblet. Gohran broke away from his mother and knocked the vessel out of the boy's hand. It clanged upon the wooden floor, wine splattering across his trousers. The boy clutched his wrist, grabbed the cup, and scrambled out of the prince's reach. Gohran ignored him and turned to face the stunned crowd, arms spread wide.

'Friends and allies,' he boomed across the dense air, each word landing like stones tossed into a deep well. 'Your queen, the woman who bore me, who gave me my blood and flesh, has shown herself to be a loathsome sorcerer, a practitioner of heresy, an abomination in the eyes of Our Lady of the Dark Sun.'

'Darling, *please…*'

'No, mother, it must be done. The people must know their queen is nothing more than a witch.' He turned back to the crowd. 'Did you all hear? Queen Prya is a witch!'

The entire room gasped in unison. Some wept. Others drew three fingers across their foreheads and then their hearts, the sign to ward off witchcraft.

Ella felt she'd stepped into a pool of melted snow. *This couldn't be happening. Gohran couldn't be doing this. It was another nightmare. It had to be.* Yet there stood her sisters, shedding silent tears. Around her, the crowd murmured like leaves rustling in a storm. Bodies shifted and shuffled.

'Guards! In the name of Our Lady of the Dark Sun, I command you. Arrest the queen.'

For a moment, no one moved.

'Guards!'

Still the hesitation, guards looking back and forth at one another until one stepped forward, a tall lanky lad whose eyes never left the ground. 'Your Highness, the queen, she is—'

'*She* is a witch. Arrest her.' Gohran towered over them wearing his murderous face. 'Unless, of course, you choose to defy the will of the goddess?'

'Never, Your Highness.'

'Good. I trust you have no desire to share her fate.'

Instead of heading for the queen, however, the guard made his way to Sheevan. He hovered for a moment. 'By your leave, Your Highness, the priests demand the victim confirm the allegation.'

Gohran's lips formed a grim line, but he nodded.

The guard whispered something to Sheevan. After some back and forth, Sheevan nodded, eyes lowered. Jaydyn's cheeks burned. She glowered at him. The guard signalled to his men, who stepped through the parting crowd towards their queen. Embarrassed and horrified mutterings seemed to leak from the walls as guests avoided meeting each other's eyes, and more particularly, Gohran's accusatory glare.

Ella heard someone nearby whisper, 'By the goddess, if I hadn't seen the change in Sheevan with my own eyes, I never would have believed it.'

Somehow, Prya remained almost unnaturally calm. *It must be her magic*, Ella thought, *keeping her so*.

When the guards reached the queen, she spoke again. 'I will stand trial as the priests demand, but I refute the charge of heresy, for what crime is it to revere all gods equally?' Prya shrugged the guards away and strode out of the room, chin raised, leaving them to trail behind.

Ella's tears were like fire upon her cheeks. She ran towards the guards, uselessly beating at them. She wanted to shout, to cry out, but her words stuck in her throat.

Prya didn't turn back. Coldly, quietly, she said, 'Leave them be, Ella. This is not their doing.'

Ella swiped at her tears, and turned to see her brother's stony expression, his hands folded coolly over his chest. She let the guards go and flung herself at him, beating her fists upon his chest, clawing at his arms.

He caught her small wrists with ease. 'Ella, you need to stay calm,' he whispered. '*Please.*'

She grew limp in his deadlocked grip.

Louder, he said, 'I'll not have you disrespect the goddess.'

He drew her towards Raeyn, who had taken refuge with Venn, his arm encircling her shoulders. 'Take her...'

Raeyn's quaking arms wrapped around her and pulled her close.

Once Prya was out of sight, Gohran again addressed the crowd. 'Friends, I feel this loss more keenly than you could know. However, we must not let our emotions cloud our judgment. The laws of the priests are the laws of the goddess, and the laws state we must not tolerate heretics under any circumstance. They must be Cleansed if they are to be saved—if we are to be saved from them. I cannot risk our souls or hers.'

Several members of the audience gasped. Cleansings were almost unheard of in this part of Ycelt.

Ella's entire body was numb. She felt apart from her flesh, as though she were scrying the event or dreaming, rather than living it.

Though Gohran invited their guests to stay and enjoy the rest of the evening, most made excuses to flee back to the quiet of their homes and territories, even if it meant travelling through the night.

Sheevan bid Jaydyn a perfunctory farewell.

'Take me with you,' she begged. 'I'm carrying our child now.'

He shook his head. 'I would if I could...'

Jaydyn's sobs faded into the night as he rode away.

Venn remained at Erldan, though he sent Jonas back to Nedran on horseback to watch over their sister. 'I shall stay as long as I'm required,' he offered. Raeyn wept against his chest, one hand still clutching Ella.

'Venn, would you find Lyrra and escort Raeyn to her quarters?'

Raeyn released her sister's hand and let Venn lead her out of the hall.

Gohran watched them leave and then turned to face Ella. She trembled.

'Leave us,' he ordered the last of the servants. As soon as they were alone, he bent down and pulled Ella towards him, gripping her shoulders.

She refused to look at him, turning her head away.

'I had no choice. Surely you can see that?' His voice set her teeth on edge. He let go of her shoulders and held her cheeks between his palms, forcing her to meet his gaze, his eyes so like her own. 'I did it for Erldan, to protect our sisters. To protect you.'

Ella pictured her mother's head held high as her only son betrayed her. The room swam. Ella thought she might faint.

Gohran pulled her close. She didn't struggle, but his warm body might have been made of lead. After a moment, he pulled his arms away as though her flesh pained him. 'Your tutor won't be safe when the priests arrive for the trial. They'll doubtless bring henads.' He turned his back and paced. Helpless, Ella watched. 'When Venn leaves for Nedran, I want you to go with him.'

'I won't leave our mother. I can't—'

Gohran spun around. 'You can, and you will. Just until things have settled back down.' Ella saw the creases in his forehead. 'You shouldn't have to witness mother's trial. Not at your age.' His voice was thoughtful, scheming.

'But Ren and Jay?'

'Your sisters will stay here. They will be safe enough.' His unspoken words hung between them.

Venn appeared in the doorway and cleared his throat. 'Lyrra has given Raeyn some herbs to help her rest. I assume Jaydyn was already sleeping.'

'You have my thanks.' Gohran didn't take his eyes off Ella. 'Try to get some sleep, El. You can see mother in the morning.'

Ella retreated to the safety of her small tower room and the comfort of her sole ally. But when she arrived, she saw Amber's parchments were already gone, and presumably, Amber with them. She threw herself down onto her bed and howled.

# Sixteen

As she often did, Amber watched the party through the fire. Almost immediately, she knew something was amiss.

While Ella was busy with Jonas, Jaydyn had been just as busy whining. 'Things had better liven up soon, otherwise, I might fall asleep right here at the table!' And when the servants placed trenchers of meat upon the tables, she wrinkled her nose as if they contained rancid fowl instead of fresh roasted game. 'By the goddess, what horrors has the cook prepared? That stench is enough to make me quite ill!'

At that, Gohran paused, studying his sister for a long moment, though he said nothing.

It was only when Jaydyn later begged to be excused to lie down that the prince asked her outright if she might be with child. Before she could reply, Sheevan leapt to her defence, but Jaydyn cut him off. 'Sheevan has bed me several times and there is nothing you can do about it!' It was then that Gohran struck her, and she screamed. From there, Amber saw the entire mess unfold.

The moment Gohran had denounced the queen, Amber banished the vision. There was no path forward from here. She barely had time to collect her few belongings and scrawl a message for Ella. What food she could find, she shoved into a small sack, before sneaking out to the stables. Thankfully, the scene inside the great hall preoccupied the other servants, so no one noticed her leave. Once in the stables, she took care to saddle up a steed that belonged to the royal family. The last thing she wanted was some visiting lord hunting her down over a stolen horse. She pushed up her sleeves and hitched her skirt up to mount. Then, muttering a prayer beneath her breath, she kicked the steed to a gallop and rode west towards the crescent moon.

To Amber, the passing pastures and farmsteads appeared lit up as though the moon was as fat and round as a wheel of cheese, instead of a mere sliver in the sky. She realised it must be her power, drawn from the churning excess of panic, casting a glow through the darkness wherever she focused. All at once she felt she was a girl once more, fleeing for her life but not knowing why. Yet this time, she knew the reason all too well. She kept expecting to see her mother riding beside her, only to remember she was utterly alone.

Hours passed and the dull ache in her limbs evolved into a deep burning like fire, her stomach muscles clenching till she thought she would be sick. She rode on. To spare her wearying steed, she slowed from time to time, then kicked him into another burst of speed. By the time she arrived at Aryon, the sun was creeping into the sky. She dismounted and staggered towards Breeyan, who stood waiting.

'Thank the gods you made it back.' The High Priestess took the horse's reigns. 'Where is Ella?'

Amber shook her head. 'My apologies, Your Holiness. It wasn't safe to wait for her.'

Breeyan's expression was cold. 'You did what you could.'

Ella woke to the sound of someone pounding on her door. A moment later it creaked open and her brother stepped inside, a washbasin in hand. She sat up, reaching for her covers to find she had slept atop them.

'How do you fare?' He set the basin down on her dresser.

'What does it matter?' Ella threw her legs over the side of her bed and edged forward, pushing her fingers through her tangled hair.

'Look at your new dress, El. It's all crumpled.'

Ella looked away.

'I thought you might like to tidy up before you visit mother.' He waited a moment for her to respond. 'When you are ready, she is in the holding cell. The guards are expecting to let you in.' She said nothing. He hovered over her a moment, then reached out to wipe the leftover scatter of tears from her cheeks. She flinched. 'I'd best see to your sisters.'

Ella remained stubborn, staring at the wall until she heard the door shut behind him. She hurried after to slam the bar over her door. The gods knew how much she longed to scream at him, to claw out his eyes, to collapse back onto her bed and bawl, and yet those parts were now buried beneath a numbness that was almost more painful.

She practically tore off her gown, then stood hesitant before the washbasin. In the still water, her reflection showed eyes cold with determination, a grim line for a mouth, and hair as wild as a peasant's. She punctured the water's smooth surface, scooping handfuls of cold liquid to splash upon her face. The shock against her flesh was oddly soothing. She scrubbed until her skin was pink and raw, a camouflage for her tears. She wiped her face and hands on her petticoat, then took to her rat's nest hair with a comb, smoothing and fastening it at the base of her neck with a bone clasp. Then she picked up a mirror to examine her reflection—cheeks now a healthy pink blush, eyes clear, hair tidy. As an afterthought, she picked her dress back up and laid it flat on her bed.

Like a citrus squeezed with cut fingers, Ella had to admit that Gohran was right. She wanted to look respectable for her mother's sake and felt better for it. She would not admit he was right about anything else. Last, she pulled her day dress over her petticoat, took a deep breath, and lifted the bar from her door.

The holding cell was one of several chambers dug out beneath the castle keep. At the foot of worn slab steps, a barred door set into a wall of mud bricks separated it from the root cellar. The cool air smelled of damp earth and rot, and further along, the lingering stink of a disused privy. Ella noticed someone had laid down thick, clean straw, and a laundered blanket. That same someone had also hung dried flowers and strewn herbs about to provide some relief from the stench. When she reached the bars, Ella hesitated. To see her mother, always dignified and commanding, reduced so, was like some festival prank gone horribly wrong. She pushed the invisible creases out of her skirt, smoothed down her already-impeccable hair, and stepped forward.

'Darling.' Unfamiliar affection filled Prya's greeting.

Relieved, Ella responded with more warmth than she felt, the coldness clinging to her heart. Somehow, her mother had lost none of her stateliness. She might have been conducting a council in the great hall for all her hauteur. Perhaps she was a touch paler, but that was all. Ella again wondered if she was using magic to keep herself so.

'Darling, listen carefully,' Prya whispered. 'Tomorrow, the priests will come. Where is Amber?'

'She left last night.'

'Then I'll thank the gods for that.' Prya's eyes sought her daughter's, and Ella caught the barest touch of uncertainty, nervousness, and even fear there. 'Ella, my sweet, you must use everything Amber taught you to protect yourself. Use every tool at your disposal—regardless of the cost. Promise me.'

'What will happen to you now?'

Prya shook her head. 'You are not a child anymore, so I will not lie. The priests will find me guilty and then they will burn me alive.'

Ella stifled a scream. 'They won't—they can't!'

A wry smile played at the corner of Prya's lips. 'They can and they will.'

'But you are their queen!'

'Precisely. There hasn't been a Cleansing in these parts for many generations now. Don't you think the priests will itch to get their claws into the people here? Oh darling, even if the priests were to let me go, how long would it be before people wondered at the lack of convicted heretics in Erldan? Once the doubt sets in, it will grow like a cancer, consuming Erldan's very soul. I love my kingdom too much to see that happen.'

Ella couldn't believe her ears. Her mother, not just giving in, but giving up. And all because of a tiny blue line of force that no one without magic could see. Only her—and... 'What about Gohran? Won't people ask—?' Did her mother realise Gohran had magic, too? Did he?

Prya held up a hand to silence Ella, her brow raising, lip curled. 'Your brother has much more cunning than I ever credited him.'

Before Ella could respond, Prya said firmly, 'Once all this is over, you must go to live with your aunt. You will be safe there.'

'Gohran's already sending me away. To Nedran.'

Prya looked as though Ella's words had slapped her. 'Is he?' Her eyes narrowed.

'He thinks it will be safest for me there.'

'He's right. It will be. For now.'

Ella had never seen her mother look so cold.

'Just remember what I've said. Promise me, darling.'

Ella nodded, but she couldn't bring herself to speak. Prya reached between the bars to take Ella's hands. After a long moment, she whispered, 'Goodbye, my love.'

Though the queen lived still, the household was already in mourning. Silent servants shuffled with their heads bowed. Gohran paced, barking out orders, running hands through his hair. None dared speak to him, but hurried to do his bidding. A dark cloud settled over him, extinguishing the brief tenderness he had shown the previous night.

It was Venn who came to find Ella to let her know Jaydyn had run away. 'She must have left last night.'

Raeyn slumped in her chair, despondent and exhausted. The herbs helped her sleep, but they couldn't erase what was happening.

Venn slipped a comforting arm around Ella's shoulders. 'We should pack your belongings.'

So, Gohran's plan was going ahead. Too numb to feel anymore, she let Venn walk her up to her room, where he left her to gather her effects. Lyrra soon arrived with a large trunk. *How long was she to be kept away?* No doubt Gohran would want to be rid of her for as long as possible. After all, she was a witch, like their mother. *Like him.*

Lyrra reached a tentative hand out to squeeze Ella's arm. 'I am sorry, Your Highness.'

How Ella despised that pity. She had to stop herself from lashing out. Everywhere she went, she felt it upon her until she thought she would drown of it. What good was their sympathy? If they wanted to feel something, why couldn't it be anger?

With a toss of her head, she bundled up a handful of dresses and underclothes and stuffed them into the trunk. None of them fit her properly, anyway. Atop her bed, her precious gold dress mocked her. She snatched it up, tossed it on the ground, and kicked it beneath the bed. As she cleared the items from her writing table, she saw the book Amber had left behind: *The Lost Warriors*. And wasn't that what she was now, a warrior unable to fight, to be free? As much a marionette as poor Sheevan, and all for being born with a gift she never wanted. Ella flicked through the illuminated pages. The movement caused Amber's scribbled note to fall to the floor.

*Dearest Ella,*

*Please understand why I had to leave. As soon as it is safe, you should follow. Until then, you know you can reach me. I am truly sorry.*

*Love always, Amber.*

Ella understood all too well. She couldn't be here when the henads arrived. There was no question of that. But if she followed Amber to Aryon now, they might catch her on the roads trying to flee. And if by some miracle she reached the order alive, what chance was there of coming back? Once sworn into the order, her sisters always said there was no way out. You belonged to Xenon. Even if her sisters were wrong and the priestesses let her go, people would question where she had been. She would never be safe.

So.

Her mother was right. Gohran had seen how this would play out. She would be safest at Nedran, for now. An exile, maybe, but the alternative was to spend the rest of her life as a prisoner of the god, unable to return.

At least this way she would have time. Time to find a way out. For how long would it be before Gohran packed her off to Aryon anyway to keep his throne secure? How long before he forced her to live the life he chose? The memory of Jonas's words sliced through her very soul. *You've only a few years of freedom left.*

# PART TWO: MACHINATIONS

## NEDRAN PROVINCE, YCELT

**Year: 795 A.S.**

# Seventeen

Death knell stares followed Ella as she prepared to leave for Nedran the next day. She sensed Raeyn's reproach as Venn's footmen lugged her trunk down the stairs and hefted it onto the carriage. There was no sign of Jaydyn. Ella supposed she had gone after Sheevan. Bile rose in her throat. Was she any better? Once, she would have given anything for this chance to be with Venn. But not now, like this. Worse were Gohran's unbearable attempts at tenderness, as if he had any right to offer her sympathy. Mostly, she hated the relief that washed over her as she climbed into the carriage, about to venture further from home than she had ever been.

A trip such as this would once have excited her. Instead, she felt numb. She sank back into the cushioned bench, staring out of the carriage window as they passed endless pastures divided into a patchwork of farms along the north-running road, a major thoroughfare for the towns of Harnal and Rassit. The latter town sat directly upon the Gythyn Run, which carried barges north and south across Ycelt. Nedran itself was situated on one of its tributaries. Here and there, untidy woodlands grew wild. It was like looking at a puzzle board. The tiny farmers closest to the road hauled sacks of grain and tilled soil. When they nodded or bowed to the passing lord, Ella pictured game-pieces in play. She envied them, beneath notice, living simple lives that left room for little else.

Venn took Ella's hands in his. He, too, looked at her as if her mother was already condemned. She closed her eyes, willing reality to disappear into the darkness. Haltingly, he reached for her. She flinched at first, then relaxed against him. Sinking into the comfort of his body, she inhaled. He smelled of sweat and sandalwood. Exhaling, the rhythm of her breath soon matched his.

'Why would Gohran do this? His own mother! Our mother!' She sobbed into his shirt.

Venn stroked her hair. 'The queen herself is suspected of heresy. Regardless of any truth to that suspicion, it casts doubt upon the entire kingdom, especially those closest to her—the prince, your sisters, even you.' He sighed. 'If Gohran shows leniency, how will that look to the priests? We should pity him that burden.'

Ice upon her heart and fire in her stomach. She wanted to curse, to scream, to cry. How could he not see what was so plain to her? And yet she knew he was right. If a queen was not safe from the priests, then nobody was. Her mother had seen that and allowed herself to become a sacrifice.

Hours dragged, and eventually, Ella slept. The sun was ambling towards the horizon when she jolted back awake, still nestled against Venn's shirt, now crusted with snot and tears.

'Welcome to Nedran,' Venn said with pride.

Ella sat up and stretched, cat-like. She peered out of the small window. The carriage bumped its way towards an iron gate embedded in an enormous stone wall that curved out of sight around a steep valley. 'It's so vast...'

Venn perched forward. 'No larger than Erldan. It's just that the outer walls surround most of the town, not just the keep.'

Outside, the streets were abuzz. Everyone they passed nodded or waved. The carriage continued through the inner walls and the guards drew back the gates to let them in. The main keep proudly bore Nedran's emblem at each of the corner towers. Even the crenulated walls were dressed finely with broad banners. Parts of the inner structure looked new, the stones pale and even.

Venn helped Ella out of the carriage and led her inside while servants tended to their belongings. Ella stared at the high vaulted ceilings. The main passage gave way to a central courtyard bordered by arches, and Ella heard what sounded like a brook.

'That's the water garden through there.' Venn pointed. 'Beyond is the main hall. Come and I'll introduce you.'

Once inside the large chamber, Venn's brother Jonas greeted her, his charming features now tender with concern. Beside him stood a tall, slender girl of perhaps sixteen summers. She was as captivating as Jonas, sharing his ruddy complexion and light brown hair. Dark lashes framed her hazel eyes, and her lips wore the same sumptuous smile.

'Princess Ella, may I present my sister, Lady Lynden?'

Lynden took Ella's hands in hers. 'Princess Ella, how I've longed to meet you. If only it wasn't under such circumstances.'

Beside her, key personnel had formed a line. Venn motioned to a tall, slim man who appeared to be a good decade older than he. 'This is Mykan, my steward.' The steward stepped forward and bowed. 'And this is—'

'Venn, let the poor girl get settled! There will be plenty of time for introductions.' To Ella, Lynden whispered, 'I don't imagine you'll remember anyone's names, anyway.' Then loudly, 'Let's get you to your room.' She looped her arm through Ella's elbow and steered her towards the stairs.

Ella followed, relieved.

'Jonas explained what happened.' Lynden squeezed her arm. 'Losing your mother... I'm so sorry. Were you close?'

*Were*, Ella noted, a weight settling upon her throat. She considered the question. Had they been close? Those last moments of tenderness seemed so remote, so alien, and yet there were occasions—glimpses of consideration if not affection... She cleared her throat, her answer measured. 'As much as a queen can be to her daughters.'

Lynden's eyes were soft, kind. 'I wouldn't know,' she said wryly. 'I never really knew mine.'

'Oh. I'm sorry...'

Lynden waved her sympathy away, but Ella sensed a more recent pain beneath the surface—the loss of Lynden's father, and a thought, unvoiced, *I suppose we're all orphans, now.*

Ella winced. *No. Not yet.*

The stairs took a sharp turn, then opened into a wide corridor. It had none of the dark foreboding Ella was used to. 'This is your room.' First on the left, the chamber was modern and airy, though not furnished as finely as her old tower room. 'Mine is just up the hall. I'll show you the women's quarters in the morning. You won't have to worry about a thing while you're here. I've promised to take the best care of you. Let's fix you up, and then we'd best get to the dining hall.' She let Lynden comb her hair, fastening some of it back and releasing the rest to fall over her shoulders. 'There! You're just as adorable as Jonas described.' Another squeeze.

Such warmth! Like rain upon parched earth, Ella longed to soak up that tenderness, yet it ran over her, as though her heart were a desert, crusted over.

'Come, and we'll take our supper,' Lynden said. 'Cook will have made something lavish, I expect, with royalty in our midst.'

Yet Ella barely ate. Her chewed food stuck to the roof of her mouth, and she forced it down with wine until her head spun. Conversation droned around her. When prompted, she responded with one- and two-word answers. Mercifully, Jonas and Lynden monopolised the conversation, and Ella could slip into the background. Afterwards, she escaped to her room, relieved to be alone at last.

She sagged upon the unfamiliar bed. Around her, the room whirled, until she fell into a kind of restless unconsciousness that was not true sleep at all. The last thought to enter her mind before the spinning eased into blackness was that Gohran should have denounced her, too.

# Eighteen

The next few days whirred by. Lynden tried to distract Ella by showing her around the keep, taking her to the marketplace, and introducing her to all and sundry. 'I have so much to show you. I promise you won't have time to dwell.'

The entire time, Ella longed to be alone with her grief, yet the first day they left her on her own, she craved company and distraction.

'I feel terrible leaving you,' Lynden said. 'I promise I'll be back before supper. Bess will get you anything you need, and I'll leave out some parchment in case you want to write home.'

'Honestly, Lynden, I'll be fine.' Ella forced a smile. But once Lynden was gone, Ella was at a loss.

Downstairs she could hear the recognisable bustle of servants, but up in the women's quarters, the quiet seemed oppressive. She pottered around, studying the wall hangings and ornamental sconces, anything to divert from the weight of her thoughts pressing in, threatening to swallow her in darkness. Instead of the overly-elaborate interlace patterns and flood of too-rich colours that gave Erldan's halls an almost crowded feel, the style of everything at Nedran was neat and uncomplicated. Ella could tell the choice was deliberate, cool blue and matte-silver trimmings giving the whole an open, fresh feel, as though to defy the shadows of her heart.

She settled into one of the cushioned chairs and picked up a waiting tapestry. Someone had already chalked out the design, so all Ella had to do was stitch coloured thread over the existing lines. She completed a few ungainly rows using a pre-threaded needle, but when she needed to change colours, she couldn't do it. Her hands shook too much to thread a new needle. She put the job aside and tried to compose a letter to Gohran. After several failed attempts, she put that aside, too. Next, she tried reading, but her mind skipped across the words, taking nothing in. She shut the book with a thud and headed towards the door.

Bess stood in the corridor. She dropped into a curtsy. 'Princess Ella, can I get you something?' Bess was a slight girl of around eighteen summers, with pale skin and watery eyes, sweet-natured and unassuming.

Ella faltered. 'I was hoping to walk around the grounds.'

'Oh no, Your Highness, I don't think that's a good idea. Lady Lynden never goes out alone.'

'Is there no one who can accompany me?'

'I'm afraid not, Your Highness, not today.'

Bess looked stricken. She wasn't used to waiting upon royalty, Ella supposed. Ella considered heading out on her own, but a cold ripple across her flesh changed her mind. 'In that case, would you mind fetching me something to eat?' she said. 'I might retire to my room.'

She watched Bess disappear down the corridor, then headed to her chamber. By the time Bess arrived with a tray of oven-warm bread, cheese, fruit, and milk, Ella was shivering. It wasn't from cold, but she asked Bess to light a fire, anyway. Alone, she barred her door and knelt before the hearth, watching the fire catch and grow. Random images threatened to show themselves midst the flickering light, but Ella refused to let her mind fix on any one thing, instead concentrating on steadying her breath.

*There was still a chance*, she thought. *Prya was their queen. They might let her go.*

Blood thrummed through her veins. Her heart thudded and her stomach lurched with the now-familiar sensation of bugs crawling. She tore her eyes away from the fire and jumped to her feet, pacing the length of the room. She clenched her hands then shook them out, peering back at the hearth. *She would not use her magic. Could not—*

Yet when she inhaled, soothing calm from the fire flowed from her torso through to her limbs. With a long exhale, she closed her eyes, drinking in the feeling. *Just enough to soothe my nerves,* she told herself. *Just enough—*

The buzz of energy steeled into a kind of bleak fortitude. Another breath. Ella opened her eyes and crouched before the hearth. *It's only flames jumping, that's all.* She remembered her mother as she'd last seen her, in the holding cell, whispering goodbye. A cold tug at her mind. She shoved it away. The flames before her blurred and shifted out of focus, only to resolve once more. Her body tensed. An electric thrill ran through her. She tried to ignore it.

Smoke billowed around her, but not from her tiny hearth. It was like she stood amid a haze. The smoke ought to be stinging her eyes, but it wasn't. It just blocked her view of whatever lay beyond. Ella's pulse quickened. She needed to see through the haze. Yet part of her needed the truth to remain hidden.

Another deep breath. Another flood of soothing warmth. She couldn't look away. After a long, torturous moment, the smoke cleared.

There she hung, Queen Prya, bound to a stake like a stuck animal, still burning.

*By the gods,* Ella thought, *they had gone through with it. Gohran had gone through with it.*

Ella felt the heat from the blaze, smelled charred flesh... She choked and sputtered, banishing the image with arms waving to clear the smoke and push the horror away. Quaking and sweating, she gagged and grasped for her chamber pot. Her guts seized, and she vomited until there was nothing left to purge.

She crumpled to the floor, so spent she couldn't even weep. She wanted to feel something, anything. And yet she felt so numb, so hollow, it was almost painful. Trembling, she crawled onto her bed, staring into a void.

How could this have happened? How could Gohran let it happen? She had seen him through the fire, standing, watching. A twist like a knife. Her old Gon, her only childhood companion, had grown not just into a stranger these past moons, but into a monster.

After what seemed an eternity and no time at all, Ella was called to supper. The fire had dwindled to a handful of embers. With a cold wrench of will, she stood. She needed to tidy herself before anyone saw her. Her dress was a soggy, wrinkled mess. With a deep breath, she smoothed out the creases, then splashed her face with cold water, scrubbed at her skin, and pressed a cool damp cloth against her cheeks until they returned to a natural pink glow. She combed out her hair, pinning it in place and checked her reflection. The face that stared back could have belonged to a stranger.

At supper, Ella sat between Jonas and Lynden, but she could have been at another table altogether. Their chatter passed over and around her, as though she were peering down from some faraway place. She kept seeing flames, smoke, and charred remains.

'What are you going to do when old Borsyn finds out about you and his daughter Kerryn?' Lynden asked Jonas, peering archly over her wine glass.

'He won't find out because there's nothing *to* find out.' Jonas cast an anxious eye Ella's way.

'That's not what I heard,' said Lynden.

'From Vera of Lichen, I suppose,' said Jonas. 'Come on, Lyn, it wouldn't be the first time she's chased the wrong ilak from its fold.'

'Only where you're concerned.'

A page approached, interrupting them. 'My lord.' The boy dropped to kneel at Venn's feet. In his trembling hand, he presented a scroll bearing the blue and green seal of Erldan.

Ella froze, her fork halfway to her mouth.

Jonas and Lynden fell silent as Venn took the parchment and waved the page away. He unrolled the message and read, his expression betraying nothing. After a long pause, he cleared his throat. When he spoke, his voice was stiff.

'The Marked Prince Gohran of Erldan has requested a representative from Nedran attend upon him three days hence.'

Ella's cutlery clanged onto her plate. 'Gohran's coronation.'

Venn reached across the table and squeezed Ella's hand. 'I'm so sorry, Your Highness.'

Ella's grip remained lax. 'I didn't truly hold out any hope for the trial, my lord.' It didn't seem real. It couldn't be real. Yet she knew, had seen...

Lynden's arm rested upon her shoulder. 'Oh, Ella...'

'It is as the gods would have it, and no one can argue with the gods.' Ella hated the dispassion she heard in her voice. She was distantly aware of their sympathy as she sat staring stonily at her barely touched plate.

'Shall I have Bess help Ella pack after supper?' Lynden asked.

'That won't be necessary,' said Venn. Then, to Ella, 'Your brother thinks it best if you stay here.'

'But mother's funeral...' Ella's voice trailed off as she realised that, as a convicted heretic, the priests would deny her mother their last rites. Instead, they would scatter her ashes on unhallowed ground. And now Gohran wanted to keep Ella away even longer. She swallowed the charcoal lump in her throat. 'Did he say why, my lord?'

'Doubtless, he feels you will receive better care here, while he is occupied with his duties.'

Better care, indeed! Ella couldn't help thinking it was for Gohran's sake and not hers that he kept her away. After all, he couldn't hide what Ella was, not from the henads, and he wouldn't dare risk any more scandal for his precious kingdom, not when he was so close to having his ambition realised. Ella felt bitter bile rising. This was to be his reward for betraying their mother, for her torturous death. She wondered if she had ever truly known Gohran.

'Custom dictates Nedran's overlord attend upon the new king, but as Gohran placed Ella in my care...'

Jonas shifted in his chair. 'I suppose I'll be going.'

'You have my thanks, Jonas. Gohran was clear that I should prioritise his sister's welfare, so I dare not leave Ella.'

'If you'll excuse me, my lord?' Ella said. 'I need to lie down.'

Alone in her room, Ella flitted in and out of consciousness. She kept seeing her mother's body, imagined Gohran smirk as he watched her burn. She wanted to scream, to shout, but she couldn't move. Ella knew it was a dream, yet she couldn't wake.

When she finally roused, she found herself drenched in sweat, bedclothes scattered across the floor. Ghostly images danced before her until she pulled herself together enough to banish them. Shivering, she relit her fire and tried to calm herself, drawing on the heat to dispel the echo of her visions. At last, she could breathe normally.

After this, she never wanted to use her magic again. For all that Gohran wanted to spare her the horror of witnessing Prya's death, it had done her no good. Amber had called her gifts a blessing, but to Ella, they would always seem a curse.

With that thought, Ella felt an anxious tug at her mind. Amber. She shook the sensation aside. Somehow her tutor's image had become tangled up with that of her mother's burning body, and all at once she realised it was simple fear that made her shy away. Amber would tell her the only place she could be safe was at Aryon—and she would be right. Ella didn't trust her own resolve not to flee to the safety that could be her enslavement.

# Nineteen

'**E**lla—what are you doing up and about?' Venn looked up when Ella entered the dining hall.

Despite having barely slept, Ella forced herself to attend breakfast, where Venn and Lynden talked in hushed whispers.

'I can have your breakfast brought up to you,' Venn said.

'I'd like to eat here, if I may.' The scant pastel furnishings and soft linens adorning the table helped the room appear open and airy—more relaxed and intimate than any room at Erldan. And more welcoming than sitting alone in her guest room.

'Of course, but then you should rest.' He jumped up to pull out Ella's chair.

'Fresh air is all I need, my lord. There's no point dwelling indoors.'

Ella took her seat. Venn looked at her as though she were a helpless child. She wanted to shove his pity away. She sat up, pushed her hair from her face, and served herself breakfast from the array of pastries, smoked cheeses and dried fruits laid out on wooden trenchers, willing him to act normally.

Lynden took her cue and said with forced brightness, 'Bess mentioned you wanted to see the grounds, Ella. Venn, perhaps the two of you could go riding?'

Ella nodded. 'I'd like that very much.'

After breakfast, Venn had one of the stable hands saddle their horses and together they rode across the city, leaving the bustle behind as they passed through the outer walls.

'This is the way I used to ride as a boy,' Venn said. A little way along, they dismounted and continued on foot. 'My men will take care of our steeds.'

Ella looked back and noticed a pair of guards some distance behind them. Venn slipped his fingers around hers and led her off the main track, down an overgrown trail that followed the tributary. Straw-like grass brushed their legs and Ella smelled dry, cracked dirt where the summer sun had baked the earth. Venn squeezed her hand.

Ella treasured the warmth in his touch. 'It's kind of you to take the time to distract me, my lord. I can't bear to be trapped indoors.' *Trapped with those memories*. Venn had a way of looking at her that made everything else seem far away, and in that moment, she could push her thoughts into a distant chamber at the back of her mind.

'I'm at your disposal, Your Highness.' His smile was almost shy. 'Your brother placed you in my care, after all.'

A cloud cast a shadow over them.

'Only so I'm not underfoot while he takes mother's throne.'

Venn rested a hand upon her shoulder, his eyes soft. 'Try not to be too hard on him, Ella. A king doesn't have the luxury of showing pain.'

Ella turned away, sliding out from under Venn's grip. She stared at the water trickling past.

'I know it feels like you're alone in your grief, but I promise you, I understand the pain of losing a parent—the anger when someone takes them from you.' Venn's voice cracked.

'Your mother?'

He nodded. 'Mother used to love to ride out here. Once she had Lyn, her nursemaid would accompany her, but she refused to be guarded. One of my last memories of her is insisting to father that she was not a prisoner, and so he let her go out alone. And then one day, she didn't come home.'

Ella turned back to meet Venn's gaze, reached out her hand to him.

He took it and squeezed. 'Father sent the entire army out combing the woods. They found Lyn still in her pannier, screaming, but mother was nowhere to be seen. It was a few days before they found the maidservant's body—what remained of it.'

'Venn, I'm so sorry. I knew you had lost your mother, but I didn't realise the circumstances.' Ella recalled Bess's alarm when she had asked to tour the grounds. 'Is that why the guards follow you?'

'They follow *us*. We haven't seen bandits around Nedran for many years, but it pays to be cautious. I swore to your brother I'd protect you, and I meant it.' Venn pulled her close. 'My apologies, I shouldn't trouble you with my old grief.'

'Not at all. I want to know. If you're comfortable sharing.' Ella felt old tension easing from his muscles like water topping a dam wall and flowing freely. She looked up at him. 'What happened after that?'

'Mykan, my steward, told me my father spent seasons hunting for the culprits. Outlaws, thieves, poachers—anyone where they ought not to be—were captured or slaughtered. Father was thorough and merciless.' Eyes narrowed, teeth grinding, as though he pictured his father's vengeance.

'But they never found your mother?' Ella asked.

Venn shook his head, voice cracking. 'No.' His arms drew her tighter to him. 'And after that, father never spoke about her. I remember him withdrawing from us, throwing himself into his duties. For a time, we hardly saw him, and when we did, he would choke up and hurry away. Back then, I didn't understand. I thought he blamed us. Blamed me, somehow. It was only later I came to understand that seeing us must remind him of her.'

Venn took a deep breath. 'We might as well have lost both our parents that day. Lyn and Jonas were both so young and so I needed to help raise them—especially Jonas, though he's always resented me for it. Mostly I felt alone, like no one could know what it was like, not truly.'

'Venn, I'm so sorry.' Venn's breath felt warm against her hair, and she smelled the sandalwood of his neck and chest, felt the prickle of his stubbled chin. She sensed the guards nearby, knew she should feel wary, but with Venn's arms around her, it seemed nothing could ever harm her. She tilted her face up towards him expectantly.

Yearning, his eyes searched hers, but when he brought his lips towards her, they brushed her forehead. 'I don't want you to have to feel alone in your grief like I did.'

She recalled seeing that blue line of force when only she and Gohran could. Her brother's horror, his accusations, their mother struggling to remain dignified, imprisoned in her city by her own men. And then her charred remains as her people burned her. Her own son! When he and Ella were the same as her. What of that could she ever share with Venn, with anyone?

She squirmed out of Venn's embrace, and they continued in silence. The river snaked in and out of the grassy bank, gated here and there with piles of jagged rocks. To one side, the valley fell away. To the other, the earth rose in a series of grassy mounds, as it did in patches throughout Ycelt.

'Fairy mounds,' Venn said, pointing.

Ella's eyes followed his aim. 'Tombs for the Ancients,' she sighed.

'Lyn's friends used to scare themselves silly running widdershins around those things.'

'Looking for goblins and girraweens. Gohran and I did that, too.' Her voice caught. The wind pushed at the grass, causing it to slant. 'They don't look like they were dug by human hands. By the gods, perhaps.'

'It's the way the trees don't grow on or around them.'

Ella shuddered. She had heard the story of how some children at play discovered the first graves as they dug around in the dirt. Instead of soil, the children uncovered a cavern piled with bones and grave goods. A better grave than her mother would have, she thought. Not even an unmarked mound to house her ashes.

The trail took them across a stone bridge and past an old weeping willow, its tendrils trailing along the river's edge. Ella wanted to see the beauty in the gold-shimmering sun, but it barely warmed her skin.

When they reached a rocky outcropping by the water's edge, Venn halted. 'We should head back. I have business that needs tending, but perhaps we could ride again soon?'

Ella nodded hopefully and even managed a weak smile. 'I'd like that.'

When they arrived back at the main keep, Ella excused herself and retreated to her room.

Within minutes came a knock at the door. 'It's me, Lynden.' Lynden bustled past, carrying food, writing implements, and a couple of dresses slung over one arm. She set the tray down. 'In case you find your appetite. And these are so you can write to the new king.' She motioned to the parchment, quills, and ink.

The thought of having to congratulate Gohran on his coronation, as custom demanded, was like vinegar on Ella's tongue.

Lynden frowned. 'Or I can have the scribe draft something?'

Ella's voice caught. 'My thanks. I'd like that.'

Lynden took the dresses from her arm and held them up alongside Ella one at a time. Next to her plain linen dress, Lynden's looked so elegant. Even her day dresses were made from fine silk brocade. 'These should fit you nicely once we take them in a touch and adjust the hem.' Their height difference was considerable.

Ella felt her cheeks burn. 'I couldn't possibly...' Yet the only dress that truly fit her was her gold birthday gown. Why hadn't she borrowed something from her sisters?

'Please, I'd like you to have them. I was going to give them to Bess to repurpose anyway,' Lynden said. 'I've never had a sister to share anything with.'

Lynden left her alone to rest, and Ella hugged the dresses to her chest. Such a minor gesture, yet one so foreign to her. Why had the queen allowed her daughter to roam around in clothing she'd long outgrown, when here was a virtual stranger noticing and attending to her needs?

At the thought of her mother, Ella wanted to scream, to sob, to howl. She realised it was less at the loss of her mother and more the grief that she had never felt loved by her the way she should, the way she longed to be. It was a selfish grief. An anger, a resentment. As though Prya had chosen to abandon her, even while she was alive. Ella couldn't help thinking there must have been something more Prya could have done to stop Gohran from denouncing her. And once again, she cursed her brother for betraying them all.

# TWENTY

Jonas's ride to Erldan took longer than it should because Jonas never rode in a straight line anywhere. Instead of travelling directly to the neighbouring kingdom, he headed towards the town of Rassit to the east along the Gythyn Run. Rassit was a thriving town, alive with the wealth of fertile soil and excellent craftsmen, but more notably, as a key stop on the north-south trade route, Rassit harboured fat merchants and fatter publicans.

As he rode, he pictured Ella. There was just *something*. The way her dark hair fell across her shoulders, eyes he could drown in... He longed to taste those lips, slip his arms around her waist, and press her to him... He'd wanted nothing so badly in all his life. The timing was all wrong now, of course. Worse, it was clear as clear the princess adored Venn. Boring, bland, lacklustre Venn.

Jonas had to laugh at himself. Why should he care? Ella was pretty, but she wasn't the only woman in Ycelt.

He made his way along Rassit's cobbled streets to The Riverside Tavern, one of the cleaner, more respectable inns in the town. He stabled his steed before sauntering into the bar. The bell above the door tinkled to announce his arrival.

'Jonas!' Grall, the tavern-owner, called out over the haze-filled hall. 'We haven't seen you in these parts for a while.' Grall was a beefy fellow, gruff but friendly, if he took a liking to you.

The place was almost empty, with just a handful of merchants and mercenaries on their way north or south, stopping off for a drink and a bite to eat, and some who had only just roused themselves from their drunken stupor of the previous night.

'How are things up north?' Grall said, pouring ale for another patron.

'Good, good.' Jonas took a seat at the bar. 'I can smell Leesa's cooking. I don't suppose there's anything ready yet?'

'Doubtless she can throw something together for you.' Without waiting to be asked, Grall handed Jonas some ale and then headed towards the kitchen. The door opened with a creak, then banged shut.

After a moment, he returned, trailed by his young wife Leesa, who carried a steaming bowl of stewed meat with barley. Leesa was surprisingly attractive, with honey-coloured hair and skin and dark eyes. Her father had arranged the position for her at the tavern, but when she arrived, she discovered part of the bargain had been her betrothal to its burly owner.

Leesa leaned across the bench to hand Jonas his meal, smiling coyly. Jonas maintained a bored veneer, pretending to ignore her curves.

As Leesa retreated to the kitchen, Grall smacked her buttocks and chuckled. 'She's something, isn't she?' Grall turned to Jonas. 'I suppose you're headed to Erldan?'

Jonas nodded, blowing on a spoonful of stew to cool it.

'Terrible times, just terrible.' Grall shook his head. 'Where's your brother?'

Jonas swallowed. 'At home. I'll be Nedran's representative at the coronation.'

'No offence, but won't the new king take it amiss?'

'Venn says not. He's taking care of Prince Gohran's youngest sister while all this is going on, you see.'

Grall lowered his voice and leaned into Jonas conspiratorially. 'I wouldn't say this to anyone else, and I'll thank you for keeping it to yourself, but I've always thought Prince Gohran was a strange lad. I'd have picked him for a witch before his mother. He's such a handsome fellow, and yet he's never been one for the ladies, nor the lads. And now what does he do? Denounce his own mother.'

'I'm certainly not looking forward to seeing the royal ring on his hand.' Jonas took a long swig of ale.

'Looks to me like Venn feels the same way. It's not like he couldn't leave you in charge for a few days, is it?'

Jonas's grip tightened around his drink. 'Ella of Erldan is a younger version of her mother, only lovelier if you can imagine that.'

'I see,' Grall chuckled, patting Jonas on the back. 'A wise man, your brother.' The tavern-owner left Jonas to his meal.

Jonas continued to drink as the tavern filled with customers, including several locals. Leesa had dished out the last of the supper and Grall was serving ale when she dropped by and offered to show Jonas to his room.

'You look like you've had enough for today.' She slid his drink from his hand and led him towards the rickety stairs. Grall's drunken belly laugh sounded below. He'd be going for hours yet. Leesa slipped into Jonas's room behind him and shut the door. She leaned back against her hands.

Jonas slid his arms around behind her, catching her wrists. His breath was hot against her neck. He pinned her against the door and kissed her, hard.

'One of these days he's going to realise,' she whispered as Jonas's lips trailed along her neck and his body pressed hers against the door.

'Then we'll just have to be careful,' he said, lifting her skirts.

The next morning, Jonas slipped out before breakfast. As his horse picked its way along the worn road to Erldan, instead of remembering Leesa, he kept wondering what it would have been like with Ella. He cursed himself for being a fool twice over and kicked his steed onwards.

Beyond the town proper, Jonas encountered more and more travellers. By the time he arrived at Erldan and stabled his horse, the crowds were almost unbearable. Peasants and nobles alike had crammed into the city walls, awaiting the ceremony's commencement, the air thick with their stench.

A dais draped with gold silk and bearing Erldan's emblem had been erected just outside the walls of the main keep. It struck Jonas that this was most likely the very spot where the queen had been tried and executed only days earlier. He supposed instating the new king so soon afterwards was a necessity. The consequences for a province left too long without a sanctioned ruler weren't pleasant. Conquest was one thing, but in Erldan's case, they also had the church to fear. The robes would no doubt be hedging to take hold of lands made forfeit through heresy.

Sure enough, when Jonas scanned the crowd, he noticed several henads dotted here and there, milling among the people. Though they bore no physical marks of their occupation, there was something about the religious spies that set them apart.

In contrast, Elnora's priests flaunted their elaborate ceremonial garb as the people flocked around them, eager for their piety to be noticed. The robes might not have got their hands on Erldan yet, but Jonas guessed Gohran's instatement had come at a cost.

A series of horns sounded, and the crowd fell silent, poised as the priests ushered Gohran onto the dais, ready to begin. Gohran wore the royal livery, complete with a draping cape in rich sapphire and emerald hues. In one hand, he held a gilded staff. Jonas stifled a yawn as the priests droned on in an ancient tongue that only they understood. Solemn, Gohran knelt before them and swore to protect the kingdom and its people, to fight for the goddess Elnora. Jonas could hear the tremor in Gohran's voice.

When the head priest placed the sapphire ring of the monarch upon Gohran's finger, the crowd cheered. Gohran stood to face his subjects. Jonas raised his arm alongside his companions but remained silent. Members of the nobility approached the dais to swear their continued fealty to Erldan's new ruler. Jonas knew any such oath made, even before the priests, was tenuous. At the first sign of trouble, the lords might switch their allegiance. After all, no one from Creywmm had shown up today.

Once the swearing-in was complete, Jonas fell into line with those of the nobility who were there to congratulate the new king, rather than reaffirm fealty. On the dais, he knelt as custom demanded. Gohran stood with the arrogance due to a king. But the moment before he bowed his head, Jonas could have sworn he saw fear behind that front.

At the ceremony's close, Jonas joined several of the other lords and ladies in the dining hall where a sumptuous feast was served. A lesser banquet was provided for the peasants outside, who gorged on spit-roasted meat and scooped mugs of ale from a row of open barrels.

Raeyn sat to her brother's right, looking sullen. Atypically subdued, Jaydyn sat beside her, shrinking away from the crowd where once she would have basked in the attention.

'Can you believe she's here alone, after everything?' Jonas heard one lady at his table sneer. 'Those dresses won't hide her swelling belly forever.'

'I heard when she went to Creywmm, Sheevan refused to see her,' said her companion. 'I wouldn't show my face again at such a public event.'

'Yes, but you would never be in that situation.'

Jonas wondered what Gohran would make of his sister being the object of such derision.

Between courses, several lords and ladies crowded around the newly crowned king, vying for his attention. For Venn's sake, Jonas ambled his way through the mob to offer his congratulations.

When he reached Gohran, he made a gentle bow. 'Lord Venn would have come himself, Your Highness, but having given you his personal assurance to look after Princess Ella, he felt it prudent to stay with her at Nedran.'

'Of course...' Gohran took Jonas's arm and led him aside until they were out of earshot of the milling crowd. 'How does she fare?'

Jonas found his intense gaze disquieting. 'She's well, Your Highness, though she would have liked to be here.'

Gohran's eyes narrowed, but he didn't respond.

'I see the elder princesses are here,' Jonas continued. 'I admire your mettle for allowing Princess Jaydyn at the table of honour. Royal scandals provide far too much fodder for some of these nobles. Anyone would think they hadn't concerns enough of their own, the way they home in on other people's misfortunes.'

'I've no time to concern myself over idle gossip.'

'Wise to think so, Your Highness.' Jonas cleared his throat. 'I will let Ella know both her sisters are well.'

'Most kind.'

'You must place a great deal of trust in my brother. I can't say I'd like for Lady Lynden to be left alone with two hot-blooded males watching over her.' Jonas watched as Gohran's face turned red, then almost purple.

'If you dare lay a finger on her...' Gohran's voice was like a blade slipping.

'I wouldn't dream of it, Your Highness.'

# TWENTY-ONE

The next morning at breakfast, Ella found herself alone with Lynden. 'Is Venn not eating with us?' She had hoped he would take her riding again. 'He took the men out at first light for some practice manoeuvres.'

Ella sipped her tea, hiding her dismay. She couldn't bear spending the day cooped up in the women's hall. 'Do you think I could head out to watch them? I used to watch my brother with his men sometimes.'

Lynden looked puzzled, but shrugged. 'I don't see why not.'

As soon as she'd finished eating, Ella headed out to the paddock where Venn drilled his men. From a safe distance, she watched him pace, instructing his warriors. Now and then, he demonstrated a sword stroke or movement, either on foot or on horseback. His fluid motions were mesmerising. Compared with Gohran, Venn's gliding strokes seemed like dancing rather than fighting. She hadn't realised swordcraft could be so graceful.

Though still low in the sky, the sun had some kick to it. Venn's hair was damp, clinging to his forehead. The fine lines of his abdomen were visible through his now-wet shirt as he twisted, drawing his sword in swift arcs. Ella imagined what it would be like to run her hands along those lines, across his chest, down to his waist. Venn wiped his forehead and caught her watching him. Ella flushed and shifted uncomfortably until she saw him grinning. Relaxing, she returned his smile.

Ella spent several days in this manner, watching the men in the mornings, and then keeping company with Lynden in the afternoons. Without the constant banter between Jonas and Lynden, mealtimes were oddly quiet, just the three of them chatting politely.

When Jonas finally reappeared, the family had retired to the drawing room for the evening. He looked fresh-faced, like he'd already washed away the dirt from the road.

'Princess Ella, will you honour me with your company in the gardens?'

A flutter in her chest. Perhaps he had news of her family. 'I'd like that very much. Lynden, you'll join us, won't you?'

'I won't, but my thanks. I was just on my way to bed.' Lynden punctuated her excuse with a yawn.

Ella tried to get Venn's attention, but he was involved in an intense discussion with his steward and didn't look up.

'Looks like it's just the two of us.' He watched her in a way that flooded the pit of her belly as it had on the night they met.

They headed towards the water garden, a secluded inner courtyard, elaborately landscaped. A series of sconces lined the walls, their light reflecting off the running water. The air was crisp, and Ella shivered.

Jonas removed his cloak and draped it over her shoulders. His fiery breath against her neck and the brush of his hands along her arms sent a thrill through her entire body. *Why did he have this effect on her?*

Ella tried to keep from thinking about how close he was. 'Do you have news of my family? How is Gohran? Did you see my sisters?'

'The princesses were well, all things considered.'

'And my brother?'

'The newly instated monarch was as you would expect.'

'Did he send anything back for me?'

Jonas shook his head. 'Were you expecting something?'

'I thought he or my sisters might have given you a letter, at least... I suppose everyone was a little preoccupied.'

'Doubtless.'

Ella sat on a nearby bench and pretended to study the moss growing upon a rock bed. Jonas took a seat beside her. His thigh brushed against hers, causing liquid heat to pulse through her.

'Your brother is very protective of you, isn't he?'

Ella stiffened. What if Gohran's concern for her was causing more suspicion, not less? 'I suppose he feels he must be now. This is all new to him.' She hated defending him, but what choice did she have? No one could suspect the truth.

Jonas cocked his eyebrow and said, 'I suppose it is.'

Something in his tone gave Ella pause. She searched his expression.

With a wry smile, he shrugged. 'It didn't have to be, did it?'

Ella sat, stunned.

'It can't be undone now, though, can it?' His eyes softened. 'I feel for you and your sisters.' His fingers brushed her cheek.

She thought she might weep.

'Come, let's get you inside. It's getting late.'

The next day, Lynden begged Ella to spend the day with her in town. 'I have to choose some cloth for a new dress,' she said. 'We'll no doubt find something for you, too. And we'll look at jewels and haberdashery. You must come, Ella. It will be a wonderful diversion.'

An image of stinking bodies pressing in and around her flashed behind Ella's eyes. She could almost hear the stall holders hollering, rabble-like. A sour twist to her mouth. Yet the alternative was being abandoned with her crowded memories. Ella smiled weakly. 'That sounds lovely.'

Lynden hooked her elbow through Ella's and gave her a delighted squeeze. 'Hopefully, we can stitch something together before Cousin Moyra visits. She always turns up eventually, and she's quite forthcoming with her opinions.'

Lynden invited Bess to join in, while a silent guard stood by, watching.

'What do you think of this?' Lynden held up a sample of deep turquoise cloth.

'Oh Lynden, it's lovely,' Ella said.

'Not too bright?'

'Not at all. Where did it come from?'

'All our stock is dyed in far eastern Myan, honoured ladies,' the mercer boasted. 'I assure you we sell only the finest cloth using dye chosen by the guild master himself.'

Ella nodded approvingly.

Lynden made a show of scrutinising the weave, running her fingers along the surface, and tugging the corners to see how it withstood the tension. 'I wouldn't want to rely on this to keep my laces tight,' she whispered over-loudly to Ella. 'And you see that?' She pointed to a section of the fabric that, to Ella's eyes, was indistinguishable from any other. 'If the rest of the spool is as patchy as this, I'd need to buy a third again as much, just so I can place the panels to hide the imperfections.'

Lips pursed, the mercer busied himself with sorting and arranging fabrics.

Ella shifted uncomfortably. He must be hearing every word.

'What do you think, Bess?' Lynden asked.

'It is pretty,' she offered cautiously, 'but I'm not sure it's worth the asking price.'

'No, it's not, is it?' Lynden grabbed her companions' arms and shuffled them along to the next stall.

Lynden repeated the charade, this time picking out fabric for Ella. Awkwardly, Ella played along, just to avoid drawing attention to herself. Lynden's critiques set her cheeks aflame, and she longed to merge into the crowd and slip away. Finally, Lynden declared they would find nothing suitable, and they headed back home. The tension eased from Ella's body.

On the journey back, it occurred to Ella that even if Lynden had loved the wares as much as her, Ella didn't have a silver to spend. Had Gohran thought to provide an allowance for her while she was living on the charity of others? Already she'd appropriated several of Lynden's old dresses. If she stayed much longer at Nedran, she wasn't sure what she would do. She was loath to write to her brother and beg, but what choice did she have? A forgotten princess without a coin to her name!

Up in the women's quarters that afternoon, Ella said, 'Can you honestly tell me you didn't like a single thing you saw today? I saw more things that I liked than I could ever want or need.'

'Surely you didn't mean what you said about the blue-green cloth?' said Bess. 'It so suited your complexion.'

'It did, didn't it?' Lynden responded, arching her brow in the same manner as Jonas.

'Well, my lady? Will you go back and buy it next market-day?'

'If it's still there,' Ella said.

'Don't fret, ladies.' Lynden held up her palms. 'It will all work out. You'll see.'

Sure enough, not three days later, a courier arrived with a package—a polished oak box, addressed, *To the illustrious Lady Lynden, with humble compliments.* It was signed by the head of the mercer's guild in nearby Rassit.

Ella and Bess huddled around as Lynden opened it. Inside, they found a generous length of turquoise fabric, even finer than the sample they'd viewed in the marketplace. Beneath it was another, smaller parcel—a cloth bag containing a scroll, a handful of glass beads, and a short reel of dyed thread. Lynden unrolled the parchment and read. 'It says that the cloth is a gift, and the rest is a sample of some of their other wares.' She clasped her hands together.

'They're just giving it away?' Ella asked.

'Not exactly. They know I'll need thread and trimming, you see, and that I'll be stupidly generous about it. They also saw that we were looking to buy for you, and a princess would never be so shabby.'

'You've done this before?'

'Don't look at me like that, Ella, my sweet. I'm shocked that you haven't.'

For the next few days, the girls set about designing Lynden's gown. They ordered beads and cloth at lavish expense, and the three of them began cutting out a pattern. In all the fuss, Ella's spirits were high—it had proved a diversion after all.

# Twenty-Two

'I hope it doesn't rain, or this will be a short outing,' Ella said, looking up at the ominous grey sky.

'Goddess willing,' Venn replied, frowning as the wind stirred. For the past few weeks, his training and duties had consumed him, leaving no time for his unexpected guest. Now, when he had finally got away, the weather threatened to steal that opportunity, too.

Venn pressed on, leading them to a place called the Leaping Lake, a river broken by a series of stepped rocks to form a succession of gentle waterfalls. After dismounting, they strolled alongside the dancing water that collected here and there in shallow pockets before flowing onwards. He offered Ella the crook of his arm. She threaded her elbow through his, resting her free hand upon his arm as they fell into step.

'I only wish I had more time to tend to you, Your Highness,' Venn said, his smile infused with longing.

Heat flooded the pit of Ella's abdomen and her cheeks reddened.

'My men and I need to make the most of the warmer months to keep in form.'

'Of course,' Ella said. 'Are you expecting fighting soon?'

Venn shrugged. 'It pays to be ready for any eventuality.'

'Well, I have enjoyed watching you train, my lord. You move beautifully.' She tucked her hair behind her ear and glanced up at him through dark lashes.

Now it was Venn's turn to blush. 'I'll have more free time once the weather changes.'

'And will I still be here, then?' It felt strange to be away from home for so long, mourning alone. She felt a pang of guilt, knowing part of her was grateful to be here. With Venn by her side, she could almost forget what she left behind.

'I've heard nothing to the contrary.' Venn pulled her close.

She could feel his heart beating as fast as hers, longed to wrap her arms around his neck, taste his lips on hers...

A rustle in the nearby bushes. Ella startled. 'What was that?'

A clang, and then a squeal, raw and piercing.

Venn held up his hand, stepping away. 'Wait here.' He strode towards the bushes. The squeal sounded again, followed by a whimper, hoarse like an animal. The whimpering continued. Venn cursed under his breath.

Ella dared not turn around, instead watching the water's surface. A dragonfly skimmed across a pool, ducking down to forage for larvae, its frantic wings beating so that it seemed to dart, then hover, then dart once more, as if it sensed danger in staying in one place too long. The water's surface shifted and blurred. The wobbled reflection of upside-down trees transformed, tanned bark becoming fawn and fur-like, shuddering. A creature wriggling.

Ella blinked, trying to restore the image of the water. It was no good. Huge brown eyes stared back at her. A trap snared the creature between metal jaws. Venn knelt over it and rested a calming hand upon its flank. 'Hush,' he soothed. The animal's shaking subsided. Venn pulled his hand away, covered with blood. With his other hand, he sought the mechanism's clasp. It sprang open. The animal screamed again, blood oozing. Its body convulsed, then went limp. Through her vision, Ella saw the rise and fall of its laboured breaths. Venn lifted it gingerly, arms closing in. Everything went black.

Screams—human this time. Ella's. She was crying, shaking.

*He killed it. Venn had killed it.*

Venn stood by the river, blood on his shirt, on his hands, everywhere. He pulled his shirt off, dunked it in the river, and squeezed. Then he rinsed his hands and wiped them on his trousers. He stepped back from the water's edge and headed towards her. Cool hands rested on her shoulders. Arms wrapped around her, rocking her back and forth as she wept against his clammy skin.

'I'm so sorry—I didn't mean for you to hear...'

'I—I saw. I—' Her voice choked off. *Had he noticed her slip?*

'Hush,' he whispered, as he'd done to the creature, holding her against his thudding chest.

*Nothing was amiss.* She relaxed against him.

Pulsing heat throbbed around his body. Remnants of the creature's blood, its vitality, soaked into her, through her, awakening her senses. Lightning forked the sky. An electric thrill travelled from her fingertips to her toes and her breath caught in her throat. Thunder rumbled as the dark clouds that had been hovering over them came good on their threat of rain and let loose.

Venn scooped Ella up and carried her over to her steed. His touch surged through her. Eyes half closed, she drank him in.

He helped her mount and slapped the horse forward, then mounted and kicked his steed into a gallop behind her.

By the time they reached the stables, the rain had soaked their clothes through, the electric thrill now dulled. Venn helped Ella dismount, and they hurried back to the main keep. Once indoors, Venn wrapped his cloak around her and squeezed. 'I am sorry you had to witness that. I haven't seen a poacher's trap in these parts for years. When animals get caught like that, there's no hope for them.'

'I know, my lord.' She shuddered, thanking every god and goddess she hadn't given herself away.

'You must be freezing,' Venn said. 'I'll order you a hot bath.'

Grateful, she nodded.

Later, as she soaked alone in the hot soapy water, Ella felt she was scrubbing away more than the day's dirt, warming more than her chilled flesh. The white-hot thrill of animal blood upon Venn's clothes, his body, still echoed within her flesh. She slid her hands along her arms, her legs, her torso, felt the tender yielding of her maturing body. Energy pulsed and throbbed. She sought the moist heat between her thighs and closed her eyes, riding the waves of pleasure that shuddered through her. At least expelling energy through her physical body felt safe. Clean. A natural way to placate and soothe.

Afterwards, the emptiness returned. She hadn't wanted to use her magic, yet it continued to flow around and through her. There must be a way to shut it down. She hoped against hope that the little she used to keep herself hidden would do just that.

# Twenty-Three

Venn had watched Ella head upstairs, still panting from the ride back. Though the air was crisp, heat surged through his body as sweat mingled with rainwater to drip from his hair, his shirt, his trousers. Usually, after putting an animal to rest like that, he would feel a mixture of sorrow and disgust, but on this day, he had never felt so alive. And then when he found Ella weeping, he had wanted to scoop her up, hold and comfort her, but when she looked at him, he could think of nothing but the touch of her body against his. He wanted to drown in those eyes, lose himself in the smell of her.

What kind of base man was he, lusting after his honoured friend's sister? He was supposed to be watching over her, not acting like some debauchee. He was as bad as Jonas! Once a suitable period had elapsed, he would approach Gohran again about a marriage. With Jaydyn's betrothal dissolved and Gohran instated as monarch, the new king might reconsider the matches he would make for his sisters. In the meantime, Venn needed to focus on his duties, not his loins!

For instance, why were poachers encroaching on his land? It did not bode well. He'd heard recent reports of thieving, and even one story of kidnapping, but this was the first material evidence he'd encountered. In his experience, this type of crime increased whenever warfare or soaring taxes stripped villagers and townsfolk of their livelihoods. However, there had been no fighting in the region, and Venn had not raised Nedran's taxes. Though perhaps some neighbouring lord had.

Venn knew for certain something was amiss when that evening one of his patrol teams returned with news of an unsanctioned encampment in the forest on the other side of the Gythyn Run between the township of Rassit and the village of Kry. He ordered a small contingent of his men to accompany him to investigate the following morning.

The men set out before dawn, riding hard towards Rassit where they camped for the night, before heading east and south across the Run. The terrain in this part of Ycelt was a mix of rocky outcroppings, hills, and woodlands. Not much in the way of arable land, but plenty of places to hide in between raids on nearby farms and village homesteads, which is how the outlaws had evaded capture until now.

Venn's scouts had stumbled upon the shoddy campsite during a routine patrol. The outlaws had erected a lean-to covered over with canvas, which was well-camouflaged, but the smoke from their campfire had given them away.

The scouts led Venn's men to the now abandoned lean-to. Ashes of a recent campfire smouldered, so Venn surmised its inhabitants would return. 'Let's spread out on foot and see if we can locate their usual tracks, so we know what direction to expect them from. We'll leave the horses back at that farm we passed, and then circle back. See if we can catch them unawares at nightfall.'

Sure enough, when night came, the bandits returned, laden with sacks of grain and slaughtered fowl. When Venn saw them, his heart near broke. A couple of lads no older than he, and a girl who couldn't have been over fourteen summers. They trudged barefoot towards their camp, wearing torn, muddy clothing.

The girl's white-blonde hair peeked out from behind a scruffy shawl as her bright aqua eyes scanned the terrain. When she spotted Venn's party, she shrieked, and Venn signalled for his men to descend. They encircled the camp, surrounding the trio, who dropped their wares but froze, as if unable to decide whether to fight or flee.

One lad wielded a small carving knife, while the girl held out her arm as if to stay the lads. She stared at Venn, her gaze so intense he thought she might read his very soul.

'It's all well, Gareth, they don't want to hurt us,' the girl said to her companions.

'That's right, we don't,' Venn said, moving closer, arms outstretched to show he was unarmed, while his men remained on guard, surrounding the camp. Something about her reminded him of Ella. 'We want to know what you're doing out here, however, and why you're thieving from honest men?'

'Honest? Hah!' the lad called Gareth snorted.

'Good sir, we just want what's owed us,' the girl said.

Up close, Venn saw bony arms, visible jawlines, and sunken eyes. 'Owed you?' He wondered how long they'd been living out here like this. 'If someone has wronged you, it is your right to seek justice. Who is your overlord?'

'You're Lord Venn of Nedran, aren't you?' said the other lad, eyeing their blue and silver livery.

'I am. And what is your name?'

'Hush! Say nothing!' Gareth hissed.

Venn turned to the first lad. 'You're Gareth?' Gareth didn't respond. 'Who is your overlord, Gareth?'

Arms crossed. 'I don't have to answer to you.'

'Perhaps not, but you have to answer to the folk whose goods you've stolen.'

Silence. The three of them looked back and forth.

It was the girl who finally spoke, pulling her shawl around her hair and shading her peculiar eyes. 'My lord, we just need enough to feed ourselves, that's all. We don't mean any harm.'

'Then you should go to your overlord. Ask for work or for charity. It is a lord's responsibility to keep his people fed and clothed. Or go to your local temple. The priests can provide shelter.'

The girl looked stricken.

Panicked, the other lad interjected. 'It's not safe. They—they—'

'Hush!' Gareth yanked the lad's arm to silence him.

The girl met Venn's gaze once more. 'We had to flee, my lord.'

For a moment, he couldn't look away. He felt light-headed as the world lilted. Her fear was palpable. Had some predatory overlord or priest hurt them? When he spoke again, his tongue felt thick and gluggy. 'I am sorry you have not felt able to seek refuge. If you're willing to make amends, I will make sure you have a haven in my city.'

'My lord,' one of his men whispered. 'You're going to welcome thieves into Nedran?'

Venn knew it was a risk to take them in, but what else could he do? They must be desperate to see living like this as their only option. 'Not without proper restitution,' he said. 'I will harbour any who seek refuge, but I expect my citizens to abide by the laws and act justly.'

To the trio, he said, 'We will guard your camp tonight, and, in the morning, you can either ride with us back to Nedran or we will escort you to your local lord and you can face his judgement.'

'Are we to be your bondsmen, then?' Gareth said.

'Not at all, I assure you.'

'Yet you won't set us free.' It was not a question.

'You are free to choose my protection or that of your local lord, but you are not free to steal or break your lord's laws.'

Venn half expected them to flee during the night, so supervised their fire-building and meal preparation from the slaughtered fowl before commandeering their knives. The grain he confiscated to return to its owner. He offered them clean blankets, then directed his men to unroll their swags and take turns keeping watch.

He caught the girl watching him, that same sensation as though she were trying to read him from the inside out. *Well, let her,* he thought. He had nothing to hide.

Something about her, about this situation, troubled him. He didn't believe any of the neighbouring lords would be so cruel as to let their citizens starve, nor let their overlords starve their workers. Not intentionally.

Come morning, the sullen lads looked towards the girl to decide their fate. She nodded her assent, and the trio allowed themselves to be escorted begrudgingly back to the farm where Venn and his men had stabled their horses. Venn thought about binding their hands but worried this would only confirm their fears that he was taking them captive to be enslaved, rather than harbouring them as refugees.

It turned out the stolen goods had come from this very farm, so Venn returned the grain and offered coin for the stolen fowl and for stabling his horses. He had the trio apologise and made assurances they would remain under Venn's protection and not trouble him again.

'I dare say there's not a lord so honourable in all Ycelt,' the farmer said. 'Any other nobleman would have cut off your hands, if not your heads.'

# TWENTY-FOUR

The morning after their walk, Ella arrived at breakfast to find Venn's place empty.

'There's been some trouble along the eastern border,' Lynden told her. 'Venn's taken some men to sort it out.'

Had Lynden and Jonas not acted so casually, Ella might have felt more concerned. Meanwhile, Jonas seemed uncommonly conscientious about his warrior's training, leaving the two women to spend the next little while working on Lynden's dress.

Lynden surveyed their progress. 'We'll be finished soon. Then we can make a start on something new for you.'

How did Ella tell Lynden she had no money for fabric or trimmings? Gohran still had not written or sent her any kind of allowance.

Lynden studied her expression. 'Or we could rework my old cream dress, make it look like new?'

Ella wanted to weep. 'You have my heartfelt thanks.'

When a few days passed with no sign of Venn's return, Ella grew concerned.

'Ella, my sweet, boring a hole in his empty chair with that worried stare won't bring him back any sooner,' Lynden teased over supper that night.

'Perhaps a walk in the night air will work the creases out of that lovely forehead, Your Highness,' Jonas said.

Ella turned to Lynden. 'You'll come, won't you? It's early yet.'

The three of them stood to head outside, but stopped as they reached the doorway. Muddied and out of breath, Torr, one of Venn's riders, entered the hall and knelt, his head bowed.

'Forgive my intrusion, but his lordship sent me to tell you he's been summoned to wait upon King Gohran of Erldan.'

'Did something happen at the border?' Jonas asked. Ella had never seen him look so concerned.

'No, my lord. We settled everything as planned. We were just heading back when the king's messenger intercepted us. His lordship sent all but a small escort home while he attends upon the king.'

At the mention of her brother, a sense of urgency gripped Ella. With it came a kind of knowing, like someone had implanted a notion into the core of her being. *If she didn't move quickly, she would lose Venn, and with him, her one chance at freedom.*

She desperately wanted to use her magic to scry, to learn what the portent might mean, to find out why Gohran had summoned Venn now. But at the thought of using her magic, terror churned her stomach and flooded her veins. She shoved the impulse away. Besides, the thought of seeing Venn with her brother was like swallowing a bowl of lemon rinds. She would not give in to temptation. She had to block off her magic or she would never be safe. Never be free.

The days grew shorter as the seasons changed, and it was almost sundown when Venn and his riders reached the village of Rassit. Venn had directed the men to set up camp when a courier found him, carrying a letter from Erldan that requested he attend upon the king. He would have to let his men escort the trio back to Nedran in the morning while he ventured south to see Gohran. He wondered what was so urgent that the king would have him leave Ella and come alone.

Gohran's summons tugged at Venn like a lodestone at iron filings and when he arrived in Gohran's private study the following day, Gohran's greeting felt like sun warming bare skin after the chill of winter. Like home.

The king stood and grinned when he saw Venn enter. He clasped Venn's hands in his.

'Your Highness,' Venn bowed. 'Let me offer my heartfelt congratulations and deepest condolences.'

Gohran opened his arms and pulled Venn into a hug, clapping his hand on Venn's back. 'Be at your ease, my friend.'

It felt so good to be in Gohran's company again.

The pair settled into their usual conversation, as strange as it was to see the monarch's ring on Gohran's finger instead of his mother's. Venn caught an occasional moment of disquiet in his friend, a shadow passing over his features, and he knew his mother's death affected Gohran more deeply than he would ever admit.

The following afternoon, Gohran arranged a hunt for them, and they set out on horseback. As they neared the hunting preserve, they tethered their steeds and proceeded on foot. The ground had hardened over the summer, and insects droned in Venn's ears as they slowed, walking shoulder to shoulder.

'When your man found me,' Venn said, 'I was on my way back from investigating reports of thieves hiding in the woodlands between Rassit and Kry.'

'Oh?'

'Have you come across any thieves or poachers?'

'I haven't,' Gohran said. 'Though I have heard rumours.'

'Do you have any idea why there would be more around than usual?'

Gohran's eyes narrowed, mouth tight. 'Were you aware that until mother, Erldan had not seen a Cleansing for generations?'

Venn shook his head.

'I believe recent events have certain people frightened.' Quickly he added, 'But perhaps they ought to be. Who knows how many heretics have been hiding among us all this while?'

Venn pictured the outlaws, that peculiar lass, how afraid they seemed. Had he taken in a witch?

Gohran was still speaking. 'In any case, it's better to flush them out one way or another.'

There was something Gohran wasn't saying. 'I suppose you're right,' Venn said, frowning. *Was it better?*

After a time, Gohran steered the conversation to his true purpose in requesting Venn's attendance—binding their two provinces through marriage.

'So soon? Are your sisters not still in mourning?' Venn said, his throat dry. The usual period was twelve moons.

'They are. However, it was you who once told me how beneficial a pre-contract can be.'

Gohran seemed irritated. Sweat prickled Venn's skin, an anxious patter in his chest. 'Indeed, I did.'

'I'd like to set out the terms of that contract,' Gohran said. 'But we can look the details over with Davith and my steward once we're done with our sport.' Gohran held up his hand for silence and cocked his head toward a deer that had ventured into the clearing.

At dinner that evening, Venn sat beside Raeyn. She smiled coyly, poured his wine, and rested a hand upon his arm. Venn offered his condolences, spoke of the weather, and asked after her health, all the while aware of Gohran watching them. He attended equally to Jaydyn, but it was a delicate balance. He needed to show enough interest and consideration to satisfy the king, without giving either sister false hope for a marriage he did not want.

The situation would be so easy if he could be content with Raeyn. He always expected to marry for duty, after all. But just as the thought of displeasing Gohran gnawed at him, the thought of losing Ella ground at his very soul. All he could hope for was time. Time to talk the king around, for Gohran to see the benefit of a match with his youngest sister, rather than the elder. Time to persuade him that Venn choosing Ella freed Raeyn's land and title for Gohran to make another advantageous match for Erldan.

Yet whenever he thought about broaching the possibility with Gohran, it was like something pinched at his mind. His heart raced and his stomach churned, and he felt he might be sick. The unpleasant sensations would not subside until he let the thought go, yielding to Gohran's will. After all, Gohran knew what was best for their provinces. He should trust the king.

With that resolution, Venn felt calm once more, mind quiet, his stomach stilled. In that moment, the notion of a marriage with Ella seemed like a childish fantasy.

It stayed that way until he neared Nedran once more, when he pictured Ella's azure eyes, her midnight hair. Venn imagined he could smell her, feel her against his chest, circling his arms around her to draw her into him, where he longed to keep her forever. He choked back his longing and steeled himself. He had to do what was right for Nedran.

# TWENTY-FIVE

A full week passed before Venn returned home. It was after supper, and Ella and Lynden were deep in a game of tiles. Jonas and Venn's steward, Mykan, had engaged in a weighty discussion across the other side of the room when Ella heard Venn's graceful stride. Warmth flooded her. She sought Venn's gaze, feeling her heart might burst in her chest.

Venn's face broke into a smile. As he neared, that smile grew tight.

'My lord.'

Venn bowed. 'Princess Ella, I trust you've been well?' A shadow played over his eyes.

Ella nodded.

'I was hoping we could ride in the morning,' he said.

There was a catch in his voice that Ella didn't understand. 'I'd like that, my lord.'

Venn nodded, turned, and summoned his brother and Mykan to join him. Ella sank into her chair as she watched the three of them leave in an intense huddle.

'Ella, my sweet, it's your turn,' Lynden prompted.

'Of course, my apologies.' Ella discarded a random tile from her pile, which in the end cost her that game.

U p in Venn's private chambers, the two brothers and Mykan hovered around a yellowing map that showed the territories along the length of the Gythyn Run, from Harnal in the south to far north Sarrion-Ryce. Venn pointed to the stretch of land that marked the border between Erldan and Nedran.

'The charter King Gohran proposed would include free trade access right along the road into Rassit,' Venn said.

Jonas popped a date into his mouth. 'What if Gohran encroaches on our share of the hallit market?'

Venn shook his head. 'I think there's more to be gained from the alliance than the potential loss of income.'

'May I interject, my lords?' Mykan waited for Venn's nod of approval. 'I think given the recent situation with old Borsyn's daughter—Kerryn, is it?—that it would be prudent to give more consideration to Nedran's financial position.'

'Go on,' said Venn.

'I understand you've offered to make provision for Kerryn now that she's claimed your brother as the babe's father.' Mykan's voice wavered as he caught sight of Jonas, who picked up another date and tossed it into the air, catching it in his mouth. 'I just worry about the financial repercussions...' His voice trailed off.

Jonas chomped down, imagining it was Mykan's throat.

Venn took a slow, deep breath. Mostly he tried to ignore his brother's meandering loins, but at times like this, he wondered if Jonas played the rogue to vex him. 'I take your point, Mykan, and you have my thanks as always for bringing your concerns to my attention, but I believe we have reached a satisfactory resolution.' Eyes on his brother, he said to Mykan, 'Perhaps you could fetch us some more wine?'

With a sideways glance at Jonas, Mykan picked up the empty carafe and excused himself.

The door banged shut and Jonas faced his brother. 'You know Kerryn's only pointed the finger at me for the coin.'

Venn sighed. 'Well, I'd be a poor overlord indeed if I let her father throw her out onto the streets.'

'And I'd never wish that upon Kerryn, but Venn, Mykan's right to be concerned. If you pay her out, how long will it be before every coin-hungry craftsman or farmhand comes forward claiming I've sired a bastard on his daughter?'

'What choice do I have, Jonas?' Through gritted teeth, 'The reputation you've so painstakingly earned for yourself doesn't help matters.'

Jonas crossed his arms over his chest and let out a forced sigh.

Venn ignored his brother's sulk. 'I've already decided I won't be handing over any money, at least not to Borsyn.'

Jonas raised a curious eyebrow. He picked up the last of his sweet wine to wash down the dates and waited for his brother to continue.

'I'm going to offer Kerryn a position at court.'

Jonas spat out his wine.

'Put yourself at ease. I've no intention of having her stay here. I've already written to Cousin Heathmott in Mornae, and he's agreed to take the girl in. It's got to be better than slaving away on Borsyn's farm. And then she'll have the other serving women to help when the babe comes.' Venn held his hand up before Jonas could protest, peering down his nose at his brother. 'I've half a mind to make you deliver the news to her and her father yourself.'

Jonas paled.

'Lucky for you, I don't want this getting out, so I've told Heathmott, and I'll tell anyone else who asks, that the father is one of my riders. But Jonas, it would help if just once I could trust you to keep your trousers fastened.'

Mykan returned carrying a full carafe, which he placed atop Venn's desk. For a moment he hovered, watching the siblings glare at one another.

After an awkward pause, Venn found his voice. 'Thank you, Mykan. I think we'd best finish this discussion in the morning. I'm overtired tonight.'

'Of course, my lord.' Mykan bowed again and retreated.

Jonas followed but paused when he reached the door. 'Venn? Though I swear to you the child's not mine, I'd hate to see Kerryn ruined, so you have my thanks—for everything.' He headed towards the barracks where he could nurse his wounded pride in the company of other men and a good quantity of ale.

The sun was high above them when Ella and Venn set out the next day. A gentle breeze kept them cool as they walked along the riverbank. From time to time, Ella sensed Venn's thoughts upon her, the same flood of warmth she felt when she thought of him. Occasionally, she caught some other emotion, too, as she'd felt when he entered the hall the previous night. An ache quickly suppressed.

They stopped to rest and sat for a long moment in silence. Once or twice, Venn cleared his throat as though to speak, but then seemed to change his mind. He reached his arm around Ella's shoulders and pulled her close. He breathed in her skin, her hair, his exhale a sigh tinged with sadness.

'What is it, my lord?' Ella turned to face him, but Venn refused to meet her gaze, instead studying the grass.

With his free hand, he tugged out a few tufts and tossed them aside before continuing. 'I wasn't sure whether to tell you, as it seems Gohran hasn't mentioned anything.'

Her stomach clenched. 'Mentioned what, my lord?'

'Now that your brother is king, he is keen to formalise my betrothal to Princess Raeyn.'

Her heart plummeted.

'I told him it's not timely at present.'

Ella let out a slow breath.

'After all, you're all still in mourning. I will have to do something about it eventually, though. It's my duty to Nedran.'

Her voice caught in her throat. 'Of course, my lord.'

She wanted to scream, to cry. *His duty to Nedran.* Surely, a betrothal to any of the princesses would seal the alliance between their two provinces. Why did it have to be Raeyn? Yes, she had land and a title, but Nedran was already prosperous, and unless Ella had completely misread Venn, there wasn't an avaricious bone in the lord's body.

She closed her eyes and steadied her breath, fighting back tears. What if it wasn't Raeyn's land he wanted at all, but Gohran's goodwill? After all, the king had honoured him by offering the Princess Elder. Perhaps it would be an insult to bargain for Ella's hand instead. But that didn't explain why Gohran was insisting it be Raeyn.

*Unless Gohran intended to send her to Aryon to satisfy the treaty after all.*

Was that the sense of urgency Ella had felt the other eve? Panic rose in her throat. *Aryon. Where witches lived.* A life sequestered away, no better than a bondswoman, enslaved to the god of heretics, forbidden to love, to marry, to do anything but work and worship. There must be something she could do to avoid that fate.

The return journey was strained. Ella couldn't keep the ice out of her clipped replies. Eventually, Venn gave up on trying to maintain the conversation. Once they reached the castle keep, he muttered something about having unfinished business with his steward, bowed stiffly and strode away. Rather than gaze after him like some pathetic lovelorn lass, Ella turned and entered the keep just as purposefully. *By every god, how did he expect her to react?* Should she have thrown her arms around him gratefully for offering her a few meagre months of his companionship after telling her she was losing him forever?

# TWENTY-SIX

When Amber had re-entered the citadel at Aryon, a gaggle of curious priestesses greeted her, Nykahlia among them. Years earlier, she and Nykki had each arrived at Aryon as refugees. They stumbled upon one another, recognising they were kindred souls. Their friendship grew with an intimacy they could never act upon, forbidden by the laws of the god that were supposed to protect them.

Amber's face lit up when she saw Nykki. She fell into Nykki's embrace, drank in her scent, soaked up the comfort of her body, the stroke of her mind, tears welling. Before they drew suspicion, Amber pulled away, choking back her tears. She hugged the others and tried to answer their questions. *Why was she back already? Where was the princess? What had happened?*

The holy citadel should have been a haven, but Amber never found it so, not completely. Breeyan ruled with a harshness she had seen mirrored in her younger sister. She wondered what had made them both so. Most of the other women at Aryon were gentle, with artless warmth and naivety, until you got to the inner conclave, where political undercurrents writhed beneath every interaction.

After resting from her ride in her old familiar bed, Amber slipped back into her former duties at Aryon almost as though she had never left. But while everyone and everything around her seemed unchanged, she felt a world apart from this life. It wasn't like when she had first arrived from Ycelt, when the environment and its inhabitants were novel, because now they felt like home, but a home she had outgrown. The only noticeable difference was Breeyan's coldness towards her. Amber felt her disapproval for leaving Ella behind as an icy whip across her psyche.

The other priestesses seemed oblivious. All except her beloved Nykahlia.

Silently, privately, Amber confided in Nykki about the details of her stay at Erldan, depicting the queen's steely rule, her daughter's incredible power, and her son's betrayal. The one thing she dared not share was the time she had drawn power directly from her pupil. It had been to stop Ella's untamed magic from draining and possibly killing them both. But it had forced her to draw power from a forbidden source—a secret she would carry to the Afterworld.

In the weeks following her return, Amber tried to reach out to Ella, but Ella consistently shut her out, as though she now feared Amber. *Well, why wouldn't she?* Amber represented the very thing that cost Ella's mother her life. Amber knew that fear all too well.

While Amber never felt entirely at ease at Aryon, she cherished the safety it offered from priests and their henads, from suspicious eyes, and that knife's edge of always fearing someone might *notice*. She wished she could offer that to Ella if only Ella would let her.

She wondered how the princess fared. Rather than try to force contact again, Amber decided she would scry her out as soon as she was able. She needed to know if Ella was safe.

Amber was on laundry duty that morning with Sallyn, the priestess who had almost gone to Erldan in her stead. The women had hitched up their robes and stood in the cool stream where they could rinse away the soap made from ilak fat and wood ash. They used the rocky banks to beat the cloth, then wrung the fabric out before laying it flat upon the nearby grass to dry.

They were elbow-deep in suds when Sallyn announced she needed to fetch more soap. 'I'll be right back,' she said, rinsing off. She patted down her arms and legs and headed back towards the citadel, leaving Amber unobserved.

Amber would have a brief window before Sallyn returned. She directed her attention to the play of light across the running water and let her eyes go slightly out of focus. She pictured Ella, the pattern of her mind, and drew breath, sucking up the latent energy in the water's momentum, which chilled against her ankles.

After a few moments, Ella's image came into focus. She was beside Lord Venn, the dryhten from Nedran who Ella had been fond of. They weren't anywhere Amber recognised. Amber widened the vision and saw them walking in a meadow beside a stream. They had tethered their steeds nearby, tended by a pair of guards bearing a blue and silver insignia that presumably belonged to their lord. Were they at Nedran?

As the couple walked side by side, a gentle rhythm of longing passed between them that was almost tangible through the god-sight. Azure light, the colour of Ella's eyes, emanated from the princess in gentle waves. Unlike a line of influence, it was some imperceptible current that seemed to flow on and around her, as if it wasn't anything Ella was doing, but something about her. Is that what Amber sensed when she looked at Ella? That utterly captivating *something?* She hadn't noticed it through the fire when she was at Erldan. What was strengthening it now?

Venn looked at Ella with a beguiled yearning that was near painful. Something in Amber's memory of the lore nagged at her. She could sense him wanting to give in to that longing but holding back. Almost like there was another desire just as strong, getting in the way.

Thumping footfalls approached. Amber blinked and turned away from the water.

'Found some!' Sallyn puffed. 'We must be due to make more soon.'

Amber focused back on scrubbing, beating, rinsing, and wringing, until her limbs and back ached. She needed to ponder what she had seen, but at least if Ella was at Nedran, she was safe for now.

# Twenty-Seven

'Ella, my sweet, I want your honest opinion. You can't possibly admire this gaudy thing.' Lynden held up a huge chunk of emerald embedded in a claw of garish gold.

'My apologies. My mind was elsewhere.'

'That's an understatement if I ever heard one.' Lynden handed the gem back to the affronted jeweller.

In the weeks that followed Venn's return from Erldan, he had been more distant than ever. Duty was his priority, and it felt like his mistress. So, when Lynden suggested a ride into town to look for a gift to commemorate the equinox and her sixteenth birthday, Ella eagerly agreed. She could always count on Lynden to lift her spirits.

All afternoon Lynden fussed over various coloured gems and different settings of silver and gold. She held up this brooch or that necklace for Ella to examine. 'When you have to rely on men's choices, you learn how to steer them in the right direction,' Lynden had said.

Now, as Ella dutifully nodded her approval at anything Lynden showed her, Lynden's eyes narrowed. She stepped out of the doorway onto the crowded street, hooked her arm through Ella's, and led them towards a quiet alleyway. Bess and the footman trailed after. When they reached a small wooden door marked with a red rose, Lynden motioned for the servants to stay outside.

There was no bell to announce their entrance, so it took a while for the keeper to notice them. It looked unlike any shop Ella had seen. The interior was luscious, with velvet cushions heaped upon a carpeted floor in semi-circles. It reminded Ella of both a tavern and a reception parlour. Dark wood panelling lined the walls, save for a stone recess where an elaborately modelled hearth lay waiting for winter or an evening chill.

Ella wondered what kind of shop it was, when a finely dressed gentleman appeared carrying a tray of titbits and wine. Ella followed Lynden's example and sank into a cushion as the handsome attendant placed the tray down in front of them. Without a word, he bowed, took their outdoor cloaks, and then left them alone.

'At this time of day, the Red Rose is always nice and quiet, though it'll be full by sundown.'

'Where are we, exactly?'

'Ella, my sweet, we are in what I like to call a ladies' haven. It's just a fancy tavern, really. A very exclusive tavern, mind you. Most of the clients are merchant's wives and noblewomen—a women's hall away from home.' She handed Ella a goblet.

Ella realised the only other patrons were women, and wealthy ones at that. Some were being tended to by pretty serving girls who polished their nails or styled their hair, while the male attendants shepherded drinks around. She took a tentative sip. Warmth flowed through her.

'It's good, isn't it?' Lynden said, smiling. 'There's no point wasting it on the men in the shoddy inns, is there?' After a few appreciative mouthfuls, Lynden got to the point. 'Now, are you going to tell me why you've been moping around like you've eaten a bowl full of lemons, rind and all?'

Lynden looked at her friend with such concern Ella was tempted to blurt out the truth. She took another sip and settled on a plausible reply. 'I just don't know what will happen to me now. I mean, Gohran has been crowned, mother is gone...'

'And you're still here?' Lynden finished.

'I don't mean to seem ungrateful, it's just—'

'You want to know what your future holds?'

Ella looked down, hiding her face.

'Ella, my sweet, I promise you there's not a woman in the entire High Realm who doesn't share your exact fear. I mean, it's different for the men, isn't it? They simply need to secure a place in someone's service, whether as a fighter, in a trade, or as a farmer. Most often, even that's already decided by birthright. Finding a wife is a secondary concern. Whereas our fates lie entirely in the hands of men. They decide who we marry, if we marry, whether we can have a craft of our own—not that I'm telling you anything you don't already know.'

When Lynden paused expectantly, Ella stuffed her mouth with a dried fig to avoid responding.

'I wasn't planning anything special for my birthday, but what if we hold a dinner and invite some of the neighbouring lords and I can introduce you around? I'm sure we could convince Venn. If nothing else, it will be a fun diversion.'

Ella mustered a weak smile, simply because she could see how much Lynden wanted her to.

'What's all this I hear about a party?' Jonas blustered in that evening, tossed his coat to one side, and plonked down beside his sister. 'Lynden hasn't been scheming, has she?'

'As a matter of fact, oh lord-of-laziness, it's a dinner, and while it will be for my birthday, it's for the benefit of our honoured guest.'

Jonas grinned cheekily at Ella. 'In other words, it'll be a whole lot of work for the rest of us, simply to show off whatever elegant trinkets my ostentatious sister receives to celebrate her miraculous birth.'

Venn raised a palm. 'I haven't agreed to anything yet. Having said that, I think it's a lovely thought for Ella's sake.' Eyes cast Ella's way.

Ella realised they were waiting for her. She sensed how badly each of them wanted her to want this, and she summoned a shy smile. 'Lynden, it's a sweet thought. Thank you.'

'That's settled then,' Venn said. 'Lynden, I'll let Mykan know he is at your disposal, but by the goddess, keep your plans in check, would you? We can't go frittering away every coin in our reserves.'

Lynden squeezed Ella's hands in eager anticipation. 'You won't forget this night, I promise!'

When Lynden's birthday arrived, the celebrations began over breakfast. Venn greeted his sister with a kiss on her cheek, while Jonas scooped her up in a big bear hug.

'You'll notice we don't do anything for my birthday.' Jonas looked over Lynden's shoulder towards Ella. 'But such is the way with younger sons...'

Lynden play-punched her brother's arm.

Ella leaned over to squeeze Lynden's hand and passed her a small pouch.

Lynden beamed, already wearing her birthday necklace, the exact one she and Ella had settled on during their scouting mission—a less gaudy emerald set in a sedate droplet of silver to complement her new dress.

Lynden opened the pouch and pulled out a pair of matching earrings. She squealed with delight and slipped them on. 'Oh Ella, they're lovely!'

Ella smiled shyly. It seemed a pitiful token considering all the family had done for her. But Ella had traded her only brooch—the sapphire she inherited from her grandmother—to afford even that.

After breakfast, Jonas helped Ella and Lynden finalise the arrangements for dinner. Ella discovered that while Lynden was adept at coming up with expansive plans, she was less so at executing them.

Although Lynden had invited Ella's family, Gohran sent an apology, stating that the duties of the realm prevented their attendance. Ella wasn't surprised. They were still in mourning, after all. The idea of a party should have felt at odds with all Ella had left behind. Yet her home felt so far away. As if by immersing herself in her new surroundings, she had stepped into another world, one where the worst thing imaginable was not having a pretty dress to wear!

Ella checked the rest of the guest list and noted neither Sheevan of Creywmm nor Lynden's childhood friend Vera of Lichen was attending.

Lynden shrugged it off. 'It was all quite hurried. I didn't expect everyone to attend.'

Later, as Jonas and Ella checked over the place settings, Ella pressed him for an explanation.

'Ah, the politicking of the Cursed realm,' he mocked, resting his hand upon hers.

'Jonas, I'm serious. It's because of me, isn't it?' She slipped her hand out from under his and crossed both arms over her chest. She turned to face him. 'Please tell me.'

Jonas heaved an exaggerated sigh. 'In Sheevan's case, it is most assuredly owing to your presence in our humble abode. For it would cause him great pain to feast his eyes upon your beauty, knowing you only have eyes for me.'

Ella raised an eyebrow.

'Fine, I'll be serious—serious and utterly boring. Sheevan wouldn't dare show his face around anyone from Erldan. As for Vera, until Creywmm's fealty is resolved, Lichen would as soon not draw attention to itself.'

'So, it's because of me on both counts.'

'I wouldn't trouble yourself over it. I have a plan to smooth things over with Sheevan, and as for Vera, she can never resist my charms for long.' He grinned, a glint in his hazel eyes.

When the guests arrived that evening, Ella saw Jonas's cockiness was justified. There wasn't a woman in the room who didn't melt when he smiled her way. Meanwhile, Ella did her best to keep out of the way. She would have succeeded, too, if Lynden hadn't been determined to introduce her to all and sundry. Before long, she was fighting off admirers of her own.

'See?' Lynden whispered. 'You needn't be so concerned about your future.'

Hopeful, Ella looked towards Venn, but he was deep in conversation with some guests.

'You appear in want of a dance partner, Your Highness.' Jonas dropped her a mock bow.

She glanced back at Venn. There was no sign of him dancing soon. She took Jonas's outstretched hand, and he led her to the dance floor, circling his arms around her. He smelled faintly of cloves. She tried to remain formal and distant, but he kept making her laugh, disarming her, and she relaxed against him. The music slowed, and he ran his hand through her hair. His fingers found their way to the back of her neck, brushing her cheek, and travelling along her throat. His other hand gripped her waist. Her skin quivered. Head tilted, Jonas leaned in close, until their noses almost touched. Her entire body turned molten.

Across the room, Ella caught sight of Venn. She might have trodden on him for the wounded expression he wore.

As soon as she could, Ella broke free of Jonas and sat down, awash with guilt. *Why did her body respond to Jonas that way?*

She had barely warmed her seat when Lord Kerr of Rynwood found her and requested her hand. She forced a smile and returned to the dance floor. His pawing hands and simpering smile were just as eager as when she had danced with him at Erldan. Clearly, her family's scandal had done nothing to deter his interest in her.

For the rest of the evening, Ella danced with anyone who asked, but she might have been watching herself from the sidelines, as she had once observed her sisters. Lynden was right when she said Ella wasn't lacking in suitors. But what good did that do her when the man she truly desired was out of reach?

# Twenty-Eight

Over the next few months, Ella savoured what little time she had with Venn, who grew more and more preoccupied with training his men. Though she had balked at surviving on the meagre rations of his limited affection, she was now keenly aware it might be all she ever got.

The rest of her time she spent with Lynden and occasionally Jonas, who had more time to spare than his brother. They played tiles, strolled through the grounds, and visited the marketplace. Lynden taught her some new games, and she finessed her skills with a needle and thread, which she'd always loathed before. For the first time in her life, Ella felt included. Wanted.

Ella wrote to her sisters often, but only received occasional correspondence in return, mostly from Gohran, whose letters were formal and brief. She recalled one such letter arriving on a chilly evening. She swallowed, tore the letter's seal open, and read.

*Dearest Ella,*

*My sincere thanks for your letter and humble apologies for the delay in responding. As I'm sure you'll understand, I have very little time at my disposal.*

*Our Lady of the Dark Sun's servants continue to take a keen interest in our kingdom. As Erldan's monarch, I am honoured to collaborate with Davith, my personal advisor and priest, on Her rites. Where once our kingdom was lax in Her worship, our souls allowed to grow fetid and corrupt, Elnora's temple now overflows with devout followers.*

*Your sisters are well. They appreciate your frequent correspondence, particularly Jaydyn, who doesn't have the benefit of an avid suitor to cheer her spirits as Raeyn has found in Venn.*

*I trust you are being well looked after—more so than I could offer you here.*

*My warmest wishes, Gohran.*

Still no word of her return. Was it Gohran's fear of the priests and their henads that kept her away? And what of Venn and Raeyn—could it be true that Venn was ardently courting her sister? She choked back her tears and threw the letter into the fireplace, watching it crinkle and blaze to blackened dust.

She wrote back, once more mentioning her reliance on Lynden's charity for suitable dresses, hoping it would shame him into sending her money or at least some cloth. The rest of his letter she ignored.

Then, on a morning when the trees were shedding their leaves, Venn took Ella aside to tell her he and some of his men were setting out on a longer expedition, leaving Jonas to watch over her and Lynden.

'My apologies, Ella, but I can't put this business off. I expect to be gone at least one full turning of the moon, perhaps more. If there is anything you need, please ask Lyn or Jonas. I've instructed them to care for you while I'm away.' He squeezed her hands in his, then pulled her against his chest, arms circling. He inhaled as though he could absorb her into him, kissed her forehead, then released her.

Ella wanted to weep. But perhaps it was better this way. If she couldn't have him, it might be easier if he wasn't right in front of her, yet always out of reach.

For the first few weeks while Venn was away, Jonas mostly left the women to amuse themselves, overseeing hearings and drilling the men Venn had left behind. Occasionally Ella watched them training as she had watched Venn. The rest of the time she spent with Lynden or reading in the study.

One overcast day, as she and Lynden worked on a larger tapestry with Bess and some serving women, Jonas arrived in the women's hall, sweat dripping from his hair. He had removed his shirt, scrunched it, and pressed it to his side. The surrounding muscles were taut, and his breathing laboured.

'Jonas! You can't be in here,' Lynden said.

Jonas was shorter and stockier than his brother, but lean and toned rather than bulky. His ruddy skin glowed from recent exertion and Ella felt heat rising as she studied the lines and shadows of his back, his torso, his chest.

He pulled the shirt away from his side to reveal a long gash.

'Ouch!' Lynden cried in sympathy. She put her needlework aside and rushed over to him. She took the shirt and staunched it back against the wound.

'Let's get this cleaned up and bandaged.' She ushered her brother to a stool and sat him down, motioning to Bess to fetch some alcohol. 'What happened?'

'Just me being cocky.' Jonas grimaced. 'I thought we would be fine working with steel instead of our wooden swords, but I forewent armour like a fool.'

'Fool is right. What were you thinking?'

Jonas winced as Lynden pressed down.

Bess arrived back with a skin of liquor in hand. Lynden took it and removed the shirt to expose Jonas's cut. 'Ready?'

Jonas grabbed the skin, took a swig, wiped his mouth on the back of his hand, and passed it back to his sister. 'Now I am.' He nodded, face scrunched in anticipation.

Lynden poured the liquor over the wound and Jonas inhaled sharply. His muscles clenched, and he breathed through gritted teeth. The smell of alcohol wafted across the room. A few more pours and Lynden dried and covered the cut with clean strips of cloth, which she secured around Jonas's torso.

'You're going to hate this part more, Lyn. I've ruined my favourite shirt.'

She rolled her eyes.

'But don't trouble yourself. I'll mend it myself.'

'You'll do what?'

'I'll mend it. It was my mistake. I'll fix it.'

Lynden snorted. 'How?'

'Well, I thought you could show me...'

Eyes to the gods.

'Why not?'

Lynden studied his expression. 'You're in earnest, aren't you?'

'Completely,' he said.

Lynden looked to the women. 'What say you, ladies? Shall we show my fool of a brother how it's done?'

The women snickered, peering at one another with reddened faces.

'How about this?' Jonas said. 'I'll offer an exchange. One of you can teach me how to sew, and I'll teach you how to fight.'

'The man who came in here wounded wants to teach one of us how to fight?' Incredulous.

'Now that hurts, Lyn,' Jonas mocked. 'Consider if you will that I have learnt a valuable lesson today, ready to impart on a willing pupil.'

'You hear that, ladies? My brother has lost his mind. Are you sure someone didn't poison that blade?'

As Ella watched this exchange, excitement rippled through her. 'I'll do it,' she said. All eyes upon her. 'I've always wanted to learn blade craft.'

Lynden frowned. She had never understood Ella's fascination with watching the men train. 'Truly?'

Ella nodded. 'Please, Lynden. I'd like to.'

Jonas looked Ella's way and grinned. She returned his smile with a quiver behind her ribs.

Lynden sighed. 'Very well. But it's on both your heads if anything goes wrong. I'm not facing your brother or mine, so by every god and demon, be careful, both of you!'

'Good day, ladies.' Jonas arrived in the women's hall the following afternoon, his laundered and torn shirt in hand. The faded shirt he wore in its stead was untucked, but he still appeared his charming self. He bowed to the women, eyes teasing, dropping an extra bow towards Ella. 'Princess.'

'How fares your wound, my lord?' Ella asked.

'Thanks to Lyn, it will heal in no time.'

'Thanks to me, and no thanks to you.' Lynden rolled her eyes, head shaking. 'It should never have happened, Jonas.' Concern played behind her mockery.

He sighed. 'Tell me something I've not already told myself three score times.'

'Fine—You still shouldn't be in here.' Lynden stood, picked up a sewing basket, and ushered her brother outside. She nodded to Ella. 'You two can set up in the study. I'll come see how you're progressing once I've finished this section.'

Jonas hooked the basket over one arm and held out the other to Ella. 'Your Highness.'

She grinned and slid her arm through his elbow, and they made their way down the hall.

'I have never understood why you women stay sequestered away,' he said as they walked. 'We poor men aren't monsters.'

'Are you sure about that?' Ella asked, dubious.

'Well. Some of us can be roguish, I suppose.'

'Some of you?' Eyebrows raised.

Jonas frowned, rubbing his chin as though he'd not truly thought this through before. His expression now solemn, he said, 'I suppose if I were a woman, I would want a haven.'

One thing Ella liked about Jonas was his willingness to consider different points of view. She recalled her father, stubborn and proud, while Gohran was more so. Both would churn their wheels on a matter like a carriage bogged in the mud.

Once inside the study, Jonas motioned to the longer lounge where they could work side-by-side. Ella positioned a nearby lantern where it would cast the greatest amount of light over them and took a seat. He handed her the basket and sat, running his hands through his thick hair, which fell over his forehead, curling around his hazel eyes.

'My esteemed brother would have much to say about the state of me,' he said. 'I need to repair this shirt and cut my hair. What a wretch I've become in his absence.'

Ella laughed. 'It's shocking.'

'What was he thinking, leaving me in charge?'

'You seem perfectly capable to me,' Ella said with a sly grin.

'Tell that to my esteemed brother. Venn did not prepare me for the absolute tedium of all this overlord business. I tell you, there is so much to do.'

'It's a wonder you would take the time to mend your shirt,' Ella said as she set out all they would need to teach Jonas how to sew.

Jonas shrugged. 'I prefer to clean up my own messes. When my brother lets me!'

# TWENTY-NINE

Venn wanted to get this excursion to Mornae out of the way before the winter snows set in. Foremost, he needed to ensure Jonas's illegitimate child received due care. If there was one thing Venn had learned from his shrewd tutors about succession in the Cursed land, it was that an heir was an heir, no matter how dubiously begotten.

The cover story of the babe's parentage wasn't only to protect Jonas's honour and Nedran from unscrupulous men's hunger, but to protect the babe. Usurpers vying for power had kidnapped and groomed bastard children as figureheads for rebellions and insurrections before. Others were legitimised to keep lines of succession alive. Venn wanted to protect any potential heir, raise them with honour, and give them an appropriate education, a task he didn't dare entrust to anyone else.

His secondary motive was to scout out suitable matches for his siblings, particularly Lynden, now that her sixteenth birthday had passed. An alliance between Erldan and Nedran seemed all but certain, so it made sense to settle her elsewhere in the High Realm. Mornae lay halfway between Galliarn itself and the River Arin in the far north, which cut right through the Northern Ranges into Myan. An alliance in this region might offer another lucrative trade agreement and a stronghold near the High King.

Venn would have liked to make the trip sooner and get Kerryn settled, but when he first arranged for Heathmott to take the lass in, he was still anxious about leaving Ella. He had been expecting word from Gohran of her return, but it seemed the king had no intention of Ella leaving Nedran before the end of her mourning period. Venn realised if he didn't leave now, there was no way he would make it back before the roads became impassable. He couldn't afford to wait out the winter—Kerryn's belly was already swelling. His concern for Ella had not abated, but between Lynden and Jonas, she seemed quite settled at Nedran, so he entrusted her care to them and left while he still could.

Venn mapped out their path and his servants provisioned the trip for himself, Kerryn, and their small escort. Once they reached the township of Marlin along the Gythyn Run, they had intended to follow the northeast tributary towards Mornae. However, they didn't make it that far. Upon arriving in Wernad, the innkeeper suggested they revise their plans.

'There's been fighting in Marlin,' he said, with a phlegmy snort, serving their ale from an open barrel. He was helping pour drinks in the unseasonably crowded bar while his serving women tended to the hungry patrons.

'At this time of year?' Venn asked, trying to keep his face neutral as the innkeeper spat on the floor.

'Old Lord Varos passed of a fever just before the equinox and his descendants are still battling it out.'

'Poor Varos. I hadn't heard. Did he not have a successor?'

'He did. But there have always been rumours about Lady Keena. I never paid them much mind, but there is enough doubt about Lord Marnos' legitimacy to send the vultures circling.' The innkeeper set out their drinks and wiped his hands on his apron. 'With plenty of folk keeping away from Marlin until this skirmish gets sorted, all our regular beds are full, so when you're done, I'll have my lass show you to the loft.'

Venn looked to Kerryn apologetically. The chill in the air already carried the promise of an early winter.

'I'll be fine, my lord. My thanks again.' It was better than the straw covered slats she slept on at her father's farm.

They settled in for the night, and Venn pulled out his map to consider alternative routes. If they were camping, it would have been easier, but he wanted to make sure Kerryn had proper shelter each night. Ordinarily, he would have veered west and stayed at Lichen, where he and his siblings spent much of their childhoods, but he didn't fancy answering questions about Kerryn. They couldn't head east, or they would end up in Galliarn itself, and Venn preferred to avoid the High King's realm unless by invitation.

Venn decided they would travel west along the main road, but turn north before they reached Lichen. Depending on where the fighting centred and how far it had spread, they could venture further west, or ride due north. He only hoped the roads off the major trade route were well-maintained. Otherwise, they would have to abandon their carriage and proceed on horseback. Which was not ideal for Kerryn or the unborn babe. Venn cursed Jonas under his breath, finished his ale, and retired to the loft.

The sewing lessons were haphazard around Jonas's other duties. When he had time to spare, he fetched Ella, and they settled into work. With Jonas sidled in beside her, Ella could sense the heat of his thighs touching hers, feel the ripple of his arms as she wrapped her hands around his to guide his fingers. It felt strangely intimate.

Ella demonstrated different stitches, showing Jonas the back and front of her fabric as she went, so he could understand each. Then she instructed him to copy. Ella assumed the lessons would take an afternoon—two at most. But Jonas found manoeuvring his less-than-nimble fingers to thread his needle challenging and struggled to keep his stitches in a straight line.

'I don't want to touch my torn shirt until I know I can get it right,' he said. 'If it were any other garment, I wouldn't care. But mother made this for my father.'

Ella heard the catch in his voice, so out of character for Jonas. She rested a comforting hand on his, the other on his shoulder, and he caught her gaze with a wry smile, the scar near his eye twitching.

The door creaked open, and Lynden popped her head into the study. Ella startled and pulled her hands away as though Lynden had caught them doing something forbidden.

'Are you two finished yet?' Lynden asked.

'So little patience,' Jonas scoffed.

'We're all just eager to see the result,' she retorted. 'And to see what you do with our poor sweet Ella, turning her into a hardened warrior.'

'Trust me, it'll be worth the wait,' he said.

'No doubt.' Lynden snickered, leaving them alone once more.

Eventually, Jonas expressed satisfaction with his stitching, and he replicated the result on his father's shirt. His handiwork was almost invisible from the outside.

Jonas removed his worn shirt to slip it on. His wound had scabbed over and was healing nicely.

Ella ran her fingers over it. 'Does it still hurt?'

He feigned a wince. Then smiled, teasing. 'Not at all.'

'Are you ever serious?'

'Serious is for bores.'

'Well, I hope you can find it in yourself to be boring enough to teach me your craft with all due care.'

He grinned. 'Of course. Unlike life, fighting is a true art and deserves respect.'

She returned his smile, watching him study the wound.

'Do you think you could cover that over before I wear my shirt again? It shouldn't bleed now, but I'd rather not take that risk. I did not enjoy scrubbing the blood out the first time.'

'Oh? I assumed you would have given it to a maid.' Ella rummaged in her basket for some clean strips of cloth. She wound the fabric around Jonas's chest. The feel of his warm silken skin sent a quiver into the small of her belly. She tied the strips off and stepped back, fussing over the remaining fabric, hoping he wouldn't notice her blush.

He pulled on his mended shirt, not bothering to turn away, as though daring her to keep watching. 'How does it look?' He ran his hands along the sides of his waist, a spark in those hazel eyes.

She cleared her throat. 'You did a great job, in the end...'

'Humph! Well, you have my thanks. I was taught by the best.'

'Now that's a lie.'

'You call it a lie—I call it a kindness.'

She grinned. 'Fair is fair, I suppose, if I'm going to learn to hold a blade from you.' She motioned to his bandaged side.

'Between you and Lyn, it's a wonder I feel worth a tarnished copper!'

# Thirty

Wind whipped through bare branches, boring into their bones as rain and snow formed sleet to dampen their horses, leaving the ground sodden. Venn had been right when he thought winter was coming early. Their detour had taken them as far west as Harringtyn, where the forest terrain continued into the mountains, before circling north to avoid the king in Corbryd, finally arriving in Cernot, which would be their second to last stop before Mornae.

Like most of the settlements near the River Yarin, Cernot was a mercantile village, with traders bustling year-round. Cernot's overlord had constructed oversized marquees to keep the worst of the rain and snow off its lakeside marketplace. But while the marquees protected wares transported over water, they did nothing to improve the state of the roads which grew icy.

As their carriage pulled up, Venn cast an anxious glance at Kerryn, and reached for an additional blanket to offer her.

She shook her head. 'There's no need for that, my lord. The babe keeps me warm enough.'

He could see her flushed skin beneath her hooded cloak, her green eyes framed by ginger lashes. She ran a hand along her swollen belly. He looked up at the sleet-grey sky that threatened a blizzard. They were running out of time.

'How would you fare if instead of stopping here tonight we continued on horseback?'

A wry smile. 'Forgive my saying, but are your noble women so delicate they can't ride a horse? I'm with child, my lord. I'm not made of glass.'

'You're also in my care, and I would hate for anything to happen to you or your babe.'

'I've endured worse, my lord, yet here I am.' She gestured to her robust figure.

She was right, of course. Kerryn was a farmer's daughter. Back home, she would have tilled soil and milked ilaks until the moment of her birthing, no matter the weather.

'If you're certain?'

Kerryn nodded. 'Better than being caught here for the entire winter, my lord.'

Venn breathed his relief and directed his men to unhitch the carriage. If they left right away, they might beat the blizzard all the way to Mornae. They could retrieve the carriage once the weather eased. Meanwhile, Venn sent word to Jonas that it was unlikely he would be back before the spring.

'T his garb feels so peculiar!' Jonas had loaned Ella an old pair of trousers and a loose shirt, which she tucked in and fastened with a rope around her waist.

'You need to move freely while you learn,' Jonas said when Ella wrinkled her nose.

A week had passed since they finished mending Jonas's shirt. The lord arrived to fulfil his half of the exchange and led Ella to a grass-covered field where he often trained. Winter hadn't yet settled in this far south, but the days grew colder, and Ella was eager to warm her limbs.

She ran her hands along her torso and down to where the fabric of her trousers hugged her thighs. 'I don't see how you can call these free moving, but I take your point.'

'Trust me, you'll move more easily than in those heavy dresses. Eventually, I want you to practice in your usual attire, though. Realistically, that's how you would be dressed,' he said.

She hadn't considered ever needing to fight. It was mere curiosity that spurred her to volunteer—the thrill of learning something new. That and wanting a distraction while she awaited Venn's return.

Jonas began by teaching her how to grasp and wield various-sized blades. 'You'll want to be familiar with whatever you have to hand,' he said.

She shuddered. He was treating this as though one day she might have to defend herself without warning.

Jonas stood behind her, circled his arms to encase her, and placed his hands over hers. His breath was hot against her neck, and she felt his muscles tense as he drew her wrists in slow arcs, blade in one hand, then the other, then both. 'Feel the motion as you observe your opponent's movements. Try to anticipate where they're going next.'

Ella relaxed into Jonas's lead. His movements were steady and rhythmic, and she fell into step with him, almost as though they were dancing. She pictured Venn's graceful movements, wishing it were him holding her, even as warmth flooded the pit of her belly and heat coursed through her veins. She was thankful Jonas couldn't see the fire that spread across her chest, her neck, her cheeks.

In the days that followed, Jonas suggested Ella also learn to wrestle. 'You won't always have a weapon to hand. And you don't have size on your side, so you'll need to rely on speed and agility. In truth, you'll spend more time slipping away than in any kind of combat.'

He was still talking as though Ella might one day have to use these skills. It was almost enough to extinguish the fire being so close to him ignited within her. 'Does Lynden know how to do any of this?'

'Of course. Father insisted she learn at least some techniques to defend herself, but you won't catch her practising. She groaned about her training the entire time until the weapons master was ready to slice off his own ears.'

'That's a horrid thought.'

'It was a horrid time for us all!'

They spent the next while rehearsing different stances, grips, and flips. Jonas taught Ella how to anticipate typical attacks and how to avoid and deflect them.

He was strong and nimble, frequently grasping her arms or her waist, turning her around, and pinning her down.

'Go again,' he would say, and they would reset their mock skirmish.

Out of breath, Ella's muscles burned, but she did as he asked, over and again. At first, he let her best him, just to understand the strategies and movements, but soon he was testing her, and she struggled against him until they fell about panting and laughing.

That day, she lay upon the grass, and he knelt over her, his arms pinning her down. They were both breathing hard. She waited until he was about to release her. The moment his grip grew lax, she twisted out from under him, dug her elbow into his ribs and wriggled away. He clutched at his side, and she used the distraction to push him down. She knelt atop him, legs astride his hips, and circled his wrists with her hands.

'That's more like it.' Jonas slipped his hands out from beneath her, clasped her thighs, rolled her over, and pinned her back down. 'Better to run away at that point, though.'

Her chest rose and fell as he held her gaze. He released her wrists, eyes soft as he ran one hand along the tender skin of the inside of her arm. His touch shivered through her. With the other hand, he brushed her hair from her forehead and cheeks. His fingers trailed the length of her neck, her chest, tracing the arc of her breast to the side of her waist. Her entire body liquefied as she felt him growing hard against her.

Footfalls thudding. 'My lord!' A rider approached.

'What is it, Torr?' Jonas stood, brushed himself down and then held out both hands to help Ella up off the grass.

Torr bowed. 'A message just arrived, my lord.'

Jonas turned to Ella. 'My apologies. I'd best see to this.'

'Of course.' Ella straightened her shirt, brushed the grass and dirt from her trousers, and scurried inside.

Up in her chamber, Ella lay back atop her covers. Eyes closed, she sank into her mattress. The memory of Jonas's lingering touch trembled through her. Liquid heat throbbed between her thighs. If that rider hadn't interrupted, if she had stayed a moment more... She untied the rope around her trousers and loosened them enough to slide her hand inside. Fingertips found the moist heat between her thighs. Her other hand cupped her breast beneath her shirt, circling her hard nipple as she took pleasure in the sensations her touch evoked. Her muscles tensed as pressure pulsed from her core, radiating outwards, thundering through her limbs and torso as she rode the shuddering waves of her release.

Afterwards, she let the tears flow. She hated that Jonas had this effect on her. But more, she hated that part of her wanted him to.

Jonas took the letter from Torr and wiped his forehead on his sleeve, breathing hard as he watched Ella run back towards the keep. He loved the way she moved. Loved watching her legs stride away, but more, feeling them astride him. Heat thudded like an echo through his body of every place she'd touched. He pictured the way her hair fell forward, biting her lip in concentration as she tried to best him. He'd never met a woman who left him feeling so alive.

Only once Ella had retreated inside did he turn his attention to the letter. With an exhale, he broke its seal, and read. Jonas swore under his breath. Venn's trip was taking longer than expected, and the northern snows had already begun. He and his men might not make it back now until the spring.

Jonas felt a pang of guilt. It was his fault Venn was making the trip at all. He thought of Kerryn. Her auburn hair, fiery against her creamy complexion and green eyes, always smelling faintly of earth and straw, being shipped so far from home. So far from him. He knew she didn't love him any more than he loved her, and that he wasn't the only man to have taken a tumble with her, a fact he admired about her. Like him, she took her pleasures where she could.

He would have felt sorry for her, but part of him wondered if she wasn't exactly where she wanted to be. Her father, Borsyn, wasn't a cruel man, but it was a cruel life for them on that farm. She would be working for him now if Venn hadn't found her a post elsewhere. She had sworn to Jonas she had taken every precaution, and he'd spilled his seed on the straw beside them, just to be sure. Yet here she was, belly swollen, claiming him as the father. Had he been fooled?

He and Venn.

Jonas reminded himself that this trip was Venn's idea, and it was Venn's decision to wait so long before leaving. He wouldn't let his brother put that on him as well. He groaned. Another few moons as Nedran's caretaker. He didn't know how Venn did it. Between the politicking and arbitrating the woes of ordinary folk, ruling a city was tedious in the extreme. He supposed taking on this responsibility was the price he paid for letting his loins rule him.

His thoughts veered back to Ella, as they always seemed to. Though he loathed the thought of acting as Nedran's lord through the dark of winter, at least he would have the princess nearby to light up the hours.

'That's a long time for him to be away,' Lynden said when Jonas shared the news at dinner that night. One hand fidgeted with her emerald necklace.

Ella reached across and squeezed her arm. As much as the news was sour, she was thankful to have something other than Jonas to focus on. She struggled to meet his gaze without recalling the heat of his body pressed against hers, the warmth of her thighs wrapped around his.

'At least he'll be well cared for,' Jonas said. 'Heathmott would adopt our esteemed brother if he could. In fact, he might get such a warm welcome he never returns.'

'No doubt Venn has a ready welcome wherever he lands,' Ella said, trying to sound detached.

'Truer words have never been spoken. Our Venn is loved by all.' A catch in his voice as he glanced Ella's way.

'Good thing you keep us entertained, Jonas,' Lynden said.

Jonas nodded in a mock bow. 'A marvellous caretaker, indeed.'

'What will he do all that while?' Lynden asked.

Jonas rolled his eyes. 'Probably find spouses for us all.'

'That's an unpleasant thought.' Lynden frowned. 'I have no desire to be shipped off so far from home. Will I even get to spend time with my future husband before I'm married off?'

'Venn is shrewd, Lyn, but he's not cruel. I can't imagine he would choose someone you wouldn't like.'

'It still irks.'

'I may be wrong, of course. Venn might take the time to enjoy a wondrous winter sojourn away from his bratty siblings and brattier subjects.'

Despite his front, Ella could sense Jonas's uneasiness as keenly as his sister's, an undercurrent of trepidation passing between them. Venn had been on long trips before, but none so far away, nor while the roads were impassable. She recalled Lynden's unspoken thought when Ella first arrived at Nedran, that they were all orphans now. Yet Jonas and Lynden had always had Venn. When Ella lost her father, Gohran had been the one to watch over her. He was her Venn. But now, she didn't know who he was. And here they all were, feeling orphaned thrice over.

She swallowed the hardness in her throat and excused herself. She needed to be alone.

J onas tried to ignore the disappointment so evident on Ella's face as she left the dining hall. He saw the way her body responded to his—to him—yet he would never be a match for his brother in her eyes. He ran his fingers through his hair and let out a slow breath. Normally he would take his frustration and escape to Leesa at The Riverside Tavern in Rassit, to Kerryn on old Borsyn's farm, or to any other warm bed that welcomed him—and they always did. But with Venn away, he couldn't leave his post. Ella may not love him, but she undoubtedly desired him, and perhaps that could be enough.

'I think I'll bunk in with the riders tonight,' he told Lynden. 'Shall I send Bess to check in on you in a bit?'

'I'd like that, my thanks.'

Neither of them needed to explain why they didn't want to be alone.

# Thirty-One

Venn's party barely made it to Mornae before the snows cut off the roads to the south, hemming them in. The men dismounted, and Venn helped Kerryn off her steed, holding up his cloak to shield her from the blizzard. A couple of servants led their horses to the stables while a page ushered the arrivals inside and out of the cold.

The main keep at Mornae was an odd conglomeration of old and new structures. Different rulers had added and removed sections, hodgepodge, according to their whims. Its interior was no different, with furnishings and tapestries of differing styles and eras all jumbled together.

Inside the main hall, which was blessedly dry and warm, Venn's cousin Heathmott welcomed them with a huge grin and open arms. He'd always had a soft spot for Venn, who reminded him of Venn's mother, Lynett, his favourite aunt.

Heathmott was a good score of years older than his cousin, which showed in the lines etched into his rough pink skin and wiry grey beard. Near-sighted, his squint formed deeper creases around his eyes and mouth. He was forever asking for things to be brought closer, including Kerryn.

'Lord Heathmott.' Kerryn dropped as deep a curtsy as she could manage and still balance her swelling belly.

Heathmott peeled Kerryn's hood back, and peered up and down, taking in her wavy auburn hair, clear eyes, and strong nose. His gaze lingered on her swollen breasts before settling back on his cousin. 'I can see how your rider got himself into trouble.'

Kerryn straightened up, eyes narrowing.

Venn rested a hand on her shoulder and gave a reassuring squeeze. 'Kerryn is a hard worker and will make a valuable addition to your household. I'm trusting you with her care, Heath.'

Heathmott chuckled as though to dismiss the implied threat. 'Don't fret, cousin. Mother watches over all the serving women.'

Venn felt a cold dread creeping into his belly at the thought that she should have to. Had he miscalculated?

Heathmott looked up. 'Speaking of which, here she is.'

An elderly woman strode into the hall. Though her shoulders hunched, Lady Servan carried herself with the air of someone half her age.

Venn startled. He'd almost forgotten how much his aunt resembled her sister. This could be an older version of his mother Lynett standing before him.

Servan squinted Venn's way, then smiled with recognition, pulling him into an embrace. 'Look how you've grown! Your mother would have been so proud,' she said, holding his cheeks between her warm palms. Servan had grown thicker and cuddly where the years padded her once-lithe figure.

Even now, thinking of his mother brought a hardness to Venn's throat and tears to his eyes. He swallowed. 'It's good to see you, Aunt.'

'Is this Kerryn?' Servan examined the length of her.

'My lady,' Kerryn curtsied.

'Well mannered, and a pretty young thing, aren't you? You'll do nicely as a lady's maid. And you won't have to worry about the babe. I've already hired a wetnurse and nursemaid to tend to such matters.' She waved her hand as if shooing a fly.

Kerryn looked stricken. Venn gave her another squeeze and a warning glance. 'My thanks, my lady,' she said, jaw clenched.

Later, once they had settled into their quarters, Kerryn caught Venn's attention on the way to the dining hall.

'My lord, I don't mean to sound ungrateful, but I would prefer to nurse and raise the babe myself. I mean, additional hands are always welcome, but I can't bear the thought of another woman nursing in my stead.' Her palms rose absently to her breasts.

Venn paused. 'I hear you, but there's nothing to be done about it. A lady's maid can't have a babe at her breast day and night.'

Kerryn looked as though she might weep. It was a hard thing to witness her hardy features contorting. A moment later, she restored her composure, the creases of her face ironing out.

'I see, my lord.' Head bowed. 'A lady's maid is an honourable post, for which I am thankful,' she said, but her tone was flat.

'Your babe will be in excellent hands, I promise you,' Venn said weakly. It was all he could offer, hoping it was true.

Jonas's duties soon took up most of his time as it once had Venn's, even after the cold of winter drove everyone indoors. At first, Ella was relieved. Given what had almost transpired between them, she wasn't sure she could trust herself around him. But when he invited her to walk with him one evening after supper, she realised she had missed his company. Besides, he wasn't about to dishonour them under his brother's roof. Ella took his outstretched arm and let him lead her outside.

'I think I prefer you in trousers than in all this puffy garb,' he teased, slipping her winter cloak around her shoulders. *Though I'd prefer you more in nothing at all.*

His underthought slid into her mind and pulsed through her molten core. Her grip on her magic must have loosened. With a breath, she reined it back in, inhaling the heady scent of winter pine. The crisp air cooled her fiery skin. 'It looks like it will be some time before I'm out of these dresses again,' she said pointedly.

'That's a shame,' he said, eyes narrowed, lips curving.

Away from the lights of the main keep, they paused. Moonlight played over the snow-covered grass and distant rooftops.

'Did you mean what you said about Venn seeking spouses for you and Lynden?' she asked.

'It's what I would do in his position.'

'It all seems so calculated.'

'It's supposed to be.' Jonas drew her to him and motioned for her to look up. Stars winked against the violet night. 'We are but pawns in this life. As insignificant as each star in the night sky.' She leaned back into his warmth as his arm circled her waist. 'And that is why I make the most of every moment.' His other hand brushed her hair from her neck. He inhaled, eyes half closed. 'You smell of jasmine.'

Ella felt his muscles tense against her, his breath moist. She closed her eyes as he turned her towards him. Head tilted, his lips pressed down.

Startled, she pulled away. Hurt and confusion played upon his face.

She cursed herself under her breath. *What did she expect was going to happen?* She closed her eyes, remembering the warmth of his lips, her body aflame. *What part of her ached to happen...*

Ella pulled herself together and took Jonas's hands firmly in hers. 'My thanks for showing me the stars, but it's getting late.'

She was angry, she realised. Not at herself, at her brother, or even at Jonas, but at Venn. Why had he chosen to leave her now? He must have known there was a risk of being kept away. What business couldn't wait until the spring? He could have been here, with her, for this entire winter. They could have been walking together by moonlight. It could have been his lips on hers... Why didn't he want to make the most of every moment?

# Thirty-Two

Winter in Mornae dragged excruciatingly. Venn welcomed the opportunity to reconnect with his cousin and his aunt, whom he hadn't seen since his father's burial rite, but his cousin's bawdy nature grew vexing. Each evening, he would down quarts of ale or mulled wine, his face flushing a grotesque crimson, as his words sloshed over one another. Venn took to making excuses to exit his company as soon after the evening meal as was polite.

'He didn't always drink so much,' Servan said one evening, once she and Venn had retired to the parlour. They sat before a blazing hearth in adjacent mismatching chairs. Servan's grandchildren played with a pair of dolls at their feet. 'It's only been since losing Emmy and the babe.'

Venn held out his palms to soak up the generous heat. 'I'm sorry to hear that, Aunt.'

'Poor Heath hasn't been the same.' Servan kissed her two grandchildren's foreheads and sent them to bed. Aged five and seven, Heathmott's surviving children were sweet-natured and well-mannered, and quite attached to their gran, who coddled and disciplined them in equal measure.

'Reminds me sometimes of your father after our Lynny went missing,' Servan said. Venn stiffened, and she reached out her hand to pat his arm. 'Apologies for mentioning it.'

Venn swallowed the hardness that formed in his throat. 'I miss her every single day,' he said, voice cracking.

'As do I.' Servan exhaled a rusty sigh. 'Bandits were a constant problem back then. It's different now, thanks to your father—may Our Lady rest his soul.'

'Do you know why there were so many?' Venn realised he'd never asked about that period before.

'Bandits? Only from what your uncle speculated.' Servan sipped a distilled spirit from a stout glass. 'If I recall rightly, there was some kind of rift between your father and the priests.'

Venn frowned. 'The priests?'

'Your uncle always said it meant trouble when a priest thought he should be the people's overlord, or a lord thought he should speak for the gods.'

'But father wasn't particularly devout, was he?'

'He wasn't. And that was the problem.' Servan raised her eyebrows meaningfully.

Venn rubbed his chin. 'I don't understand...'

'Neither did your father. Your uncle believed they took your mother for a ransom, but then she never turned up, did she? So, we assumed her death was an accident. A bumbled kidnapping.'

'By whom? The priests?'

'Hush!' She peered down her nose. 'Of course, not the *priests*.'

*Not the priests,* Venn thought, *but people working in their stead.* He sank back into his chair. With both hands, he picked up his glass and stared at the play of firelight on the surface as the liquid swirled.

Servan put her now empty glass aside. 'Please excuse me. I should get an early night to be up for the morning worship.'

Venn downed his drink and stood, head bowed. 'Of course, Aunt. I should do likewise.'

Servan strode away. Venn had never seen his aunt look so agitated. That the priests might have had something to do with his mother's disappearance was almost unthinkable. It was certainly unspeakable.

He thought of his recent encounters with poachers and outlaws, and the increasing presence of priests and henads in and around Erldan. Gohran had supposed the outlaws were heretics gone into exile, fleeing for their lives. It made sense, but what could be done about it?

Like his father, Venn had never been devout, but he honoured the goddess. He also understood it was necessary to balance taxes and tithes and to keep to your domain, earthly or sacred. Was that balance tipping?

Venn had never questioned Gohran's devotion to the goddess, seeing the comfort it brought him, and the guidance he took from Erldan's priests. He imagined how wrenching it must be to discover your mother was a witch, a heretic, loathed and feared by the goddess you honoured above all else. What did that do to a person? It wasn't Venn's place to advise the king on his dominion, but perhaps he should mention this discovery to Gohran when next they met.

In the lonely evenings that followed, Ella took the occasional stroll with Jonas. Since she had broken away from his kiss, he was more reserved, yet she felt fire behind every touch, his eyes soft with longing whenever she caught him watching her. Anytime he slipped her cloak on or off, the backs of his fingers would caress the edges of her arms, find her waist, linger at her neck. She leaned into him, aching for his lips to find hers, for him to slip his hands around her body, to cup her breasts and rub his thumbs over her nipples.

She told herself what was happening between them was perfectly natural. Venn had made his choice and his intentions clear. They owed each other nothing. And she would not pine after him hopelessly when he had abandoned her like this.

It also occurred to Ella that though neither she nor Jonas had estates in their names, her future could be just as secure with him as with Venn. With her dowry, and the provision Venn was likely to make for his brother, the match was not an unreasonable prospect. It was better than becoming a celibate priestess or being married off to some horrible lord of Gohran's choosing.

Besides, the hunger Jonas awakened in her was raw and carnal, and she doubted she could have stayed away from him even if she wanted to.

But one afternoon, as she and Lynden hunkered down together in the women's hall, Lynden forced Ella to take stock.

Once they were alone, Lynden leaned over and whispered conspiratorially, 'Ella, my sweet, I'm worried about you and my brother.'

Ella's face flushed crimson.

'I think you need to be realistic about your chances. Not that he's not keen on you. It's just that if Venn marries your sister, I can't see either Venn or Gohran seeing any benefit in the match.'

Ella froze. 'Wait—are you talking about Jonas?'

'Of course. Who else would I mean?' Lynden studied her friend's expression. 'By the goddess, Ella, if you're holding onto hope for Venn, that's even more futile! Besides, I've seen the way you and Jonas are with each other.'

Ella didn't know what to say.

Lynden leaned back, arms resting in her lap as she watched her companion. After a moment, she shook her head and resumed working in silence.

Ella wanted to weep. Part of her knew Lynden was right, yet she didn't want to believe it. She was a princess of royal descent down both lines of her ancestry, yet she was as much her brother's chattel as a farmed herd beast!

She closed her eyes, imagining she stood beneath the naked sky, a wild woman of the Ancients, taking her freedom and her pleasures under the moon. Back then she could have loved and lusted without censure, without consequence. What she could do if she were free! Free to choose. Free to be her true self. Her entire self. Not this stifled half-creature, always afraid. A pawn at the mercy of the whims of others, just like Jonas had described.

She would not give in, give up. Unless and until her sister and Venn signed a betrothal contract, there was hope. And as for Jonas, if he courted her, he must see some merit in the match. What had she to lose by keeping her options open?

# THIRTY-THREE

Now that Kerryn had settled into her new post, Venn turned his attention to suitors for Lynden. Over the remaining stretch of his stay at Mornae, he kept his eyes and ears open, learning what he could of the local nobility. He did not want to entrust his sister to some boorish lech, but the outlook appeared grim. From drunks and debauchees to unscrupulous gamblers and cheats, it seemed respectable men who considered the welfare of others were as rare as twin-headed ilaks. Is this what Gohran faced when choosing suitors for his sisters?

'There must be someone you can recommend, Aunt?' Venn said as they sat in their usual places in the parlour after dinner. Servan had taught him better than to rely solely on the way a gentleman presented himself to his peers. He should listen to and observe the reactions and opinions of those a lord might consider beneath his notice—particularly the women.

That evening, Heathmott joined them. His glassy eyes peered over the rim of his mulled wine, his surrounding skin reddened from collar to hairline. 'What about old Lord Argon's son?' Through his drunken drawl, it sounded more like 'old Lord Argonshon'.

'From Peryndyn?' Servan asked.

'The very same,' Heathmott replied. 'Peryndyn would give Nedran a stronghold near the High Realm and within reach of Myan.'

Servan wrinkled her nose. 'Strategically, Peryndyn would be a marvellous choice, but by all accounts, the lord beats his servants to within an inch of their lives at the least provocation.'

'What about Yillion's youngest? The handsome one, Lord What's-His-Name.'

'Handsome?' Servan nearly spat out her drink.

'That's what the men call him.'

'A troupe of jesters, all of them,' Servan rolled her eyes. 'That poor lad looks like someone chewed him up and spat him out twice over!'

'Lyn's not completely shallow, but that might be beyond her capacity for charity,' Venn said.

The trio continued to toss names into the air between them. It was a pity Venn was here over winter when he couldn't sight these gentlemen. But if he learned of some decent prospects, he could arrange for Lynden to visit over the warmer months when Servan and Heathmott could introduce her.

Once they had settled on some names, Venn checked in with Kerryn.

'Servants are best placed to learn the uncensored truths of those they serve,' his aunt had instructed.

He found Kerryn perched at a workbench, polishing a set of tarnished ear-rings, laying them alongside a now-gleaming hand mirror and comb. 'I haven't heard of them, my lord,' Kerryn said, putting her task aside to rub the small of her back. 'But I will ask around and keep my ears open.'

Venn's eyes narrowed as Kerryn stifled a grimace and picked her work back up. 'I'll have the chambermaid bring you a stool.' He paused, rubbing his chin. 'Also, some cushions and a heated hallit sack.'

'That's kind of you, my lord.'

'You must be almost ready to settle in for your confinement,' he said.

'Oh no, my lord. I've told Lady Servan I'm happy to keep working. I can't bear the thought of lying in a dark room for weeks together.'

Venn frowned. 'Ordinarily, I would respect your will on the matter. However, that babe could one day be in the line of succession.'

Kerryn startled, stammering, 'I—I hadn't really looked at it that way, my lord.'

'Why else do you think I've made provision for you and the babe here?'

In the end, Kerryn agreed to lie in for the remainder of her pregnancy, and he left her to her duties. However, their conversation left a sour taste in Venn's mouth. He recalled Jonas insisting the babe wasn't his, though he didn't deny taking Kerryn to bed. She wouldn't lie about something so significant, surely? Venn pushed the thought away. All this talk of dubious men had him questioning everything. Of course he could trust Kerryn.

Venn resolved to leave the search for viable male suitors in the hands of the women, and turned his attention to prospects for Jonas, who was forever avoiding the topic of marriage. Venn preferred not to force his brother's hand, but would do so if it meant choosing between his brother's wishes and the security and prosperity of Nedran.

He pulled out his well-worn map of Ycelt and flattened out the creases with the outside edge of each palm. The intricate alliances that existed across the realm had shifted and morphed since the Ancients first settled in Ycelt. Their migration had disrupted the entire hierarchical structure of the old land. Shortly after the first king arrived, several of his vassals campaigned for independence and migrated away from the original settlement land to set up their own fiefdoms. Some even named themselves kings, including three of the king's younger sons—he had five sons and one daughter in all. To regain some semblance of control, the king offered his younger sons formal titles. These lesser kings were ultimately under their father's rule, now the High King. Venn knew Gohran and his sisters were direct descendants of the king who had settled in Erldan in the southwest. The other kings settled in Jernot to the northeast and Corbryd in the northwest.

Over the years, this pattern continued whenever some dryhten or prince decided he wanted more wealth, more power, or a greater title. Often the outcome depended on whether the High King of the time believed he could succeed should the claim come to battle. Other times prudence won, and the High King offered the counterclaimant a title in the hopes this would satisfy. Once ordained and blessed by the priests, a new local king owed direct fealty to the High Realm while keeping the bulk of the taxes from his vassals.

Venn saw the constantly shifting ties between various kings and lords as a tangled ball of wool. As soon as you pulled a thread free at one end, you created a series of knots in the other. The priests claimed these shifting alliances were all part of Xenon's Curse, which deemed Ycelt should be always at war.

Where Venn's primary concern for Lynden was her comfort and happiness, for Jonas, it was strategy. As he looked at the map and current web of alliances, it occurred to Venn that an ideal match for Jonas might lie closer to home.

Venn and his siblings spent much of their childhoods in neighbouring Lichen, which owed direct fealty to the High King in Galliarn. A match between Vera of Lichen and Jonas was perfect. Proximity and familiarity aligned their families, and he knew Vera adored Jonas. She always had. If Venn then married one of Gohran's sisters, Nedran would lose some of its independence, but it would gain through connection to Erldan and Galliarn, creating a military and strategic stronghold across the entire southwest of Ycelt. However, if Vera married someone allied to a rival kingdom, the match would have momentous political consequences for the entire region.

Venn ran his hands through his hair, tugging at the ends. The air was already growing milder than in the preceding weeks, hinting that travel might soon be possible. Perhaps he ought to stop by Lichen on his return journey and commence negotiations with Vera's parents, regardless of whether Jonas was ready to settle down. He did not expect a love match for Jonas, any more than he had for himself before he met Ella.

*Ella.*

The princess's memory infused his senses. He closed his eyes, inhaling, almost as though he could smell her, feel her here with him. He wondered how she fared back at Nedran. Pictured her alongside him, imagined taking her in his arms, his lips finding hers, pressing her into the soft grass...

Another breath as heat surged through his limbs. He stuffed the images down and focused on the task at hand.

But alone in his room that night, Venn continued the fantasy. He allowed himself the animalistic pleasure of grasping her to him in his mind. Loosening his trousers, he imagined unlacing her bodice and cupping her breasts, lifting her skirts, turning her over, and with his hands gripping her hips, thrusting himself inside her.

Afterwards, his seed spilled, he stared at the ceiling, sweat and tears mingling. Was he as lecherous in his heart as the men he despised? Perhaps it was better to be away from Ella this winter. Easier than having her so close, yet forbidden.

Before rolling onto his side to sleep, he told himself again that he would raise the question of a marriage to Ella with Gohran. And perhaps while he scouted out suitors for Lyn, he could keep his eyes and ears open for matches for Gohran's older sisters, too. Anything to help further his case.

As he turned the prospect over in his mind, he finally kept hold of the notion that seemed to slip like liquid through his consciousness whenever he approached the king. He pictured obtaining Gohran's blessing and taking Ella to his bed legally, honourably. With that image gripped tight, he drifted to sleep.

# THIRTY-FOUR

Ella had her first indication the snows up north had melted when one evening during supper, Bess arrived carrying a letter. A quiver ran through every part of her.

'Is that from Venn?' Lynden's face lit up. 'He must be on his way home. What wonderful news!'

Across the table, Jonas watched Ella with narrowed eyes. For the barest moment, a shadow passed over his features. Then, with a twist to his mouth, he let out an exaggerated sigh. 'Thank the gods for that. My perfect brother can have his precious province back.' He took a swig of ale. 'My thanks, Bess.' Jonas took the letter and opened it, reading silently. 'Seems he's had a steady run south and west this time, and his carriage has already landed in Lichen. More good news for you, Lyn. When he leaves Lichen, he plans to bring Vera with him to visit for the spring.'

The politicking that had interfered with Lynden's birthday dinner must have resolved if her presence was no longer a deterrent, Ella thought.

Lynden jumped up and hugged her brother as if it were his doing that was bringing Venn and her childhood friend home to her.

After supper, Ella waited for Jonas to ask her to walk with him, but as soon as he finished eating, he headed out to the barracks to drink with his men, while Lynden excused herself to write letters.

Ella watched on with a peculiar sensation, like they were all slipping away from her.

Alone in her room, she let herself fantasise about Venn's return. She would hear his carriage pull up and run to him. The carriage door would swing open, and his eyes would lock upon hers. He would scoop her up and sweep her into his arms, and everything else would disappear…

Yet when Venn's carriage pulled up a week later, Ella felt unprepared. She and Lynden were up in the women's quarters when they heard it. Lynden cast her work aside, her features animated, as she tidied herself, ready to greet them. Ella wanted to join her, to rush to the carriage, throw her arms around Venn and never let him go, yet she felt weighted to her seat, frozen. It was only when Lynden prodded her she felt able to move once more, like she had broken an immobilising spell.

'Isn't this wonderful?' Lynden gushed, hooking her arm through Ella's. 'Let's go meet them!'

The leaden feeling stayed with Ella as they made their way to the foyer and awaited Venn and Vera.

When Venn entered, he held Vera's arm and hand in his. Vera was around the same age as Lynden, dressed as elegantly, but not as tall, pretty with her flaxen hair and wide blue eyes. She smiled with warmth and curtsied as she saw them.

Lynden rushed to clasp Vera's hands and hugged each of them.

'Easy, Lyn!' Venn extricated himself and turned towards Ella.

Her breath caught as their eyes met. It was as though time itself had ceased. For that moment, all the resentment she had harboured at his leaving her melted away.

'My lord,' she bowed.

He took her hands in his and she saw her joy reflected in him.

Just then, Jonas arrived. He made a mock bow, stepping between them to hug Venn. 'Welcome back, my esteemed brother.' He released Venn and turned to wink at Vera. Bowing deeper still, he brought his lips to her outstretched hand. 'Welcome, my sweet Lady Vee.'

Vera blushed.

Ella stood watching the four of them catch up, sharing a casual intimacy that predated and excluded her.

Eventually, Venn remembered he hadn't introduced Ella and Vera. 'Princess Ella, may I present Lady Vera of Lichen?'

Vera gave a gentle nod and held out her hand to Ella. 'Actually, we've met before—at Erldan.'

'Oh. I'm sorry, I...'

'I can hardly fault you for not remembering me.' Vera's smile was almost teasing, and she still had Ella's hand in hers. 'I recall thinking you were a little *young* to be out yet in company. It was at a ball your late mother hosted in Lord Venn's honour.'

Ella's cheeks burned. Vera let go of her hand and turned her attention back to Lynden and her brothers. Grateful, Ella faded into the background as she cast her mind's eye back to the night Vera said they had met. Ella pictured her—the pretty blonde lass who had been fawning over Venn and her brother. The one she feared she had unleashed her magic upon, causing her to almost spill her drink. Ella drew her breath and clamped down on her thoughts. The surrounding air cooled.

No matter how hard Ella wanted to forget what she was, it seemed the gods had a way of reminding her.

Lynden took Vera upstairs to get settled in, and Venn excused himself to clean up from the road, leaving Ella and Jonas awkwardly poised.

Jonas sighed and ran his hands through his hair. 'I guess that's my time over.'

'You must be relieved to be handing over responsibility,' Ella said.

A wry twist to his mouth. 'Something like that,' he said, his voice catching.

Ella felt an overwhelming urge to reach for him—to do what? Comfort him? Reassure him?

In his usual droll style, he said, 'I should probably go see Mykan and make sure all is where it ought to be before my esteemed brother can point out everything I've done wrong in his absence.'

Ella watched him leave. The leaden feeling had settled into her limbs and torso. She thought about walking it off in the grounds, but there was no one to accompany her. She looked around. No one was watching. No one was paying her any mind at all.

Though she knew she shouldn't wander the grounds alone, she slipped outside and headed towards the western meadow, increasing her pace, breathing hard, trying to shift that horrid heaviness. She pictured Venn's eyes lighting up when he saw her, the eagerness she felt in his touch, but then the moment was over, and his focus was on their pretty guest. Why did he have to bring Vera here now? Was he trying to put distance between them? And why did he rush off to bathe like that when he could have spent this time alone with her? He could reek of a demon's dung heap for all she cared. She just wanted to be with him.

Energy pulsed around her. She closed her eyes, letting her shoulders drop and the tension ease from her belly. The wind picked up and crisp air prickled her skin. She inhaled, drawing power from its movement, then let out a slow breath. And again. Time itself seemed to settle and slow. Another breath. Her heart quietened and her breathing stilled. With calmness came clarity. Ella was a guest here. Venn did not owe her anything. None of them did. They each had priorities other than her, and Venn was likely tired from his travels, about to be thrust back into his role as lord and ruler, wanting to take a moment for himself. It was a childish fantasy to imagine he would have been able to scoop her into his arms and take her anywhere.

For the first time in a long time, she thought of Amber, and almost wished she had her studies to distract her, to immerse herself in. Something that was hers.

Overhead, a raven cawed. She looked up. Clouds gathered, and she could feel the electric thrum of a storm brewing. Another caw. Her vision blurred as a sudden knowledge gripped her. With uncanny certainty, she knew she would need an emotional fortress around her to get through this visit.

# THIRTY-FIVE

When the family appeared at supper that evening, everyone looked refreshed. Vera, Jonas, and Lynden chatted nonstop, and Ella felt that same sensation of them all slipping away until she caught Venn's eyes upon her from across the table. She smiled, biting her bottom lip. She longed to reach for him, for everyone else to disappear, and for a moment in her mind, as Venn returned her smile, they almost seemed to.

Then, like a harsh intrusion, she heard, 'Shall we all ride together in the morning?' Vera's wide blue eyes smiled.

Ella's stomach sank.

'What a lovely idea, Vee!' Lynden said. 'I have business here, but you should all go. We'll have plenty of time to catch up later.'

'Jonas?' Vera asked, her coy smile mirroring Ella's of only moments before.

'I wish I could, my lady. However, my esteemed brother has asked me to tidy a few matters up before I hand over the reins of his province.'

'It's true. I'm an exacting taskmaster,' Venn said. 'But we three can go.' He smiled at Ella. 'It will give you two a chance to get to know one another.'

A tightness crawled across Ella's flesh, pinching at her mind as she willed herself to remain calm. She couldn't risk a repeat of her emotions running away from her as they had at Erldan. Not with Vera's keen eyes watching her like a hawk scouting for prey.

When the trio set out after breakfast the next morning, Venn selected their steeds for them. 'You take Charis,' he said to Ella, motioning to a bay steed. 'He knows you, and you ride him well.' He picked out a tamer palfrey for Vera, fussing over the bridle, then lifting her onto the saddle and helping her into the stirrups. Ella never recalled him taking such care of her.

The sun was still low in the sky but promised a mild day. 'Shall we head to the Leaping Lake?' Ella said. 'The snowmelt should be fast flowing by now.' Part of her didn't want to share this or any of their usual spots with their attractive guest, but another part pressed her to take the lead, as though she could lay prior claim.

Venn nodded, and she urged Charis forward, falling into an easy rhythm with his gait. Venn and Vera lagged, followed at a distance by Venn's ever-present guards. Once Ella reached the start of the walking trail, she slowed, coming to a halt where she and Venn usually tethered their steeds. She dismounted, patting Charis down as she waited for the others to catch up.

Eventually, they joined her, ambling side by side, heads together. Vera laughed at some jest Venn had uttered that Ella couldn't hear, eyes bright as Venn helped steady her palfrey. He dismounted and held out the reins to Ella. 'Would you mind...?'

Jaw clenching, Ella forced a smile. 'Happy to help, my lord.'

Venn smiled at her fondly. 'My thanks.'

She took the reins while Venn crouched to ease Vera's feet out of the stirrups, then stood to lift her off her saddle. Once Vera stood on firm ground, she brushed out her skirts. By then, Venn's guards had caught up with them and were standing by to take the reins and keep watch.

Wind whispered through the trees, carrying blossom scent. Vera inhaled. 'Isn't this place a delight?' she babbled, palms pressed together. 'I've so missed riding, my lord.' She turned to Ella. 'Back home, I seldom get near the stables, let alone atop a beautiful palfrey like this. But Venn always looks after me when I visit.' She beamed up at him.

Ella's smile was tight. 'It's so like Lord Venn to tend to those under his care.'

They set off along the trail, Venn in the lead, the women side by side behind him. They could already hear the water rushing across the rocks, forming swollen pools.

Vera looped her arm through Ella's the way Lynden often did, yet Ella couldn't relax against her touch in the same way. Her very presence prickled Ella's skin, like the uncomfortable tingling that preceded a sweat.

Vera leaned in and lowered her voice. 'In some ways, my father is so old-fashioned. He thinks women shouldn't ride. That it's no good for our wombs.' She rolled her eyes. 'Because of course, our only value as noblewomen is as broodmares!'

'Sometimes you exaggerate as much as my brother, Vee,' Venn said.

'Hush! You weren't supposed to be listening. This is our time to talk,' she said, winking at Ella. 'It's a shame Lyn couldn't join us, though this way I have you all to myself.'

'You and Lynden seem fast friends,' Ella said, trying to ignore the prickling sensation creeping along her arm.

'Lyn spent many seasons with my family growing up.' Vera smiled, reminiscing. 'Too many males around here, I suppose. We had my mother and aunts for company at Lichen.'

Venn heaved a mock sigh. 'I made for sorry company.'

Vera laughed. 'Not at all. You and Jonas were excellent company... For a couple of lads,' Vera said, winking at Ella once more, as she slid her arm out from Ella's and looped it through Venn's instead.

Panic rose in Ella's throat. That pinching feeling was back, sharp, and insistent. She imagined Vera tripping up, falling flat on that pretty face. Tension built behind her eyes. She tried to shove the image away, to stuff it down, yet it grew stronger.

A moment later, Vera stumbled.

Ella froze. *Had she done that? It couldn't be a coincidence again.* A sharp inhale. Bugs crawling.

Venn caught Vera and slipped his arms around her waist to steady her. He turned to meet her gaze, brows together, lips pursed. 'Are you hurt?'

Vera waved Venn's concern away, her cheeks aflame. 'Not at all, my lord,' she said, brushing her flaxen hair back from her face. 'My legs are unused to riding. I think they forgot how to walk for a moment!'

Another breath, slow and deliberate. Ella cleared her throat. 'The path can be uneven along this stretch, my lady.' She stepped forward to loop her arm back through Vera's. 'I'm forever losing my footing.'

For a moment, Venn looked as though he might speak, then changed his mind.

'So... What can you tell me about Lichen?' Ella said. 'I've never been there.' With the additional heat from their bodies in proximity, Ella hoped against hope that neither Venn nor Vera would notice the sudden chill in the air surrounding them as she continued to ask about their history together, about their provinces, anything she could think of to distract them.

That evening, when Bess arrived to help Ella dress for supper, she took particular care with her appearance. After their lacklustre greeting and group outing, she wanted Venn's attention solely on her. Wanted him to want her, to want to remove any obstacles, to be with her, just the two of them.

She selected one of Lynden's old dresses that they had altered, so the creamy fabric cinched in her waist and pillowed her breasts, the skirts trimmed and hemmed to just touch the floor. The gold-trimmed neckline was lower than her other dresses, but still modest, with sheer sleeves falling loosely along her delicate arms. Bess laced her in tight, then helped style her hair, weaving and pinning dried daisies around the crown of her head. She left a few curled tendrils of raven hair to grace her neck, as willowy as her mother's had once been. Then Bess lightly rouged Ella's cheekbones and subtly tinted her lips, using the barest kohl shading to accentuate the blue of her eyes.

Once Bess was done, Ella admired her reflection. For the briefest moment, she saw her mother's image staring back. A ghostly reminder. She had to get her emotions under control. Her life depended on it.

She put her mirror down, took another soothing breath, and headed downstairs.

Ella arrived to find Vera and Lynden already seated, Vera in Ella's usual place.

'Oh! Ella, you look lovely.' Lynden's face lit up, admiring.

'Yes, you do, Your Highness,' said Vera, her tone flat.

'My thanks,' Ella said. For a moment she hovered until Lynden motioned for her to take the seat next to Vera, further away from Venn's position at the head of the table. She slipped into place, biting her lip.

Ella fidgeted with her cutlery, eyeing the door. The servants poured wine and brought out trenchers laden with roasted ilak, tubers, and preserved vegetables.

Eventually, she heard footfalls, and the door swung open. It was Jonas. He heaved an obvious sigh of relief and plonked himself down at the table's head. 'Thank the gods our esteemed dryhten is back in residence!' He piled his dish high. 'Speaking of, dearest ladies, Venn sends his sincere apologies. It seems the mighty dryhten cannot spare even a moment to dine with such handsome company as this.' He made a sweeping motion to indicate the women, his gaze lingering on Ella. 'Which just leaves me to feast upon all this beauty alone.'

Ella felt her stomach sink through the floor. Was she not even to see Venn at mealtimes? She hid her face in her wine glass, pretending to focus on her meal as she slowed her breathing.

Vera nattered away to Lynden and Jonas as if she had never been away from them. On occasion, Jonas interjected to offer Ella some background and context to the ongoing conversation, but it felt like a token effort. Even Lynden seemed to have forgotten she was there. Ella might as well have stayed in her room.

She excused herself and slipped away, ignoring the confusion on their faces. If Venn wouldn't come to her, she would go to him. She almost ran through the corridors towards Venn's study, but when she reached his door, she hesitated. She could hear muffled voices on the other side. Footsteps approached. A moment later, the door opened.

'Ella?' It was Venn. He appeared weary, his hair mussed, his forehead creased. 'What are you doing here? Is something awry?'

'You weren't at supper, and I just wondered—'

'My lord?' Another voice intruded. Mykan, Venn's steward. 'We need to give them an answer. The courier is waiting.'

'My apologies, Your Highness. I need to get back to work.'

*Your Highness.* His formal address landed like ice on her heart.

'Of course, my lord.' She dropped a curtsy and retreated.

Alone in her room, she tugged at the laces of her dress, peeled it off and tossed it aside. She pulled on her nightgown and sat at her dresser, peering into the mirror. All that effort, wasted. She set the mirror aside, dipped a cloth into her washbasin and scrubbed at her makeup until her skin was pink and raw.

A knock at the door. She paused, damp cloth halfway to her face.

'El, it's me.' Jonas.

A sharp inhale. 'What is it? I'm not dressed,' she called back.

'You seemed quiet at dinner and then ran off. Are you unwell?'

Exhaling. 'I'm fine,' she called. 'Just tired.'

'You're sure?'

'I'm sure.'

An audible sigh. 'Very well. But let me or Lyn know if you need anything.'

'I will. You have my thanks, Jonas.'

She heard his footsteps retreat and pressed the washcloth against her face once more. Her shoulders shuddered, and she realised she was weeping. Jonas, not Venn, checked on her. All her resentment, all her anger, came crashing back over her in a wave. How many ways did Venn have to dismiss her before she gave up on him entirely?

**U**pon his return, Venn scrambled to familiarise himself with all that had transpired in his absence, wishing he had made contingency for the possibility of his being gone so long from home. He could see right away that Jonas had been ill-prepared. While his brother attended to straightforward matters, more complex grievances and rulings, he deferred. Between holding additional hearings to catch up on postponed matters, and arranging a tour of his fiefdoms, Venn had almost no time to entertain his guests.

He told himself it was for the best. For when he stepped out of his carriage and saw Ella that first day, it was as though she reignited a fire within him. He burned to be near her, yearned to hold her to him, but he resisted. Watching her ride, sitting tall with her thighs astride her steed, hair whipping through the wind, he didn't trust the animal part of him that craved taking her in the most savage way. He was grateful to have Vera's presence and his duties to hide behind.

Occasionally, he allowed himself to live out that fantasy in his mind, to stave off his lustful yearning and calm the fire—for a time. He told himself once he had seen to his province, he would see to himself, and approach the king about a betrothal. He had gone this long without her—he could wait a little longer. And perhaps the wait would make their reunion all the sweeter.

# Thirty-Six

As the weeks passed, Ella resigned herself to Venn's absence from her side. Occasionally, he joined the family at mealtimes, but the two of them still had not shared a moment entirely alone. Here and there he offered her a yearning smile across the table, resting a hand upon her back as they passed, squeezing her hand in his, but she felt her heart hardening.

The rest of the time, the women entertained themselves, often joined by Jonas. He was back training now that the equinox approached, bringing longer, warmer days, but whenever he could get away, he was by their sides.

It seemed his earlier boasts of Vera's fondness for him were well-founded. Ella noticed it whenever she caught the two of them together, laughing and flirting, shoulder to shoulder, or skin to skin. Jonas was this way with most people, but the way Vera beamed back at him, skin flushed, biting her lip, prickled the hair at Ella's nape.

One afternoon, while having tea in the women's quarters, Vera and Lynden confirmed Ella's suspicion.

'Jonas seems awfully fond of you, Vee,' said Lynden, grinning over the lip of her cup.

'I know my parents had hoped for an alliance in this region, but could I possibly be that lucky? And Lyn—imagine—we could truly be sisters!'

Ella's breath caught. *Of course,* she thought. *Vera wasn't here for Venn. She was here for Jonas.* A sharp twinge in her belly and a hardness in her throat.

Gods, why should she even care? She had no claim on Jonas, didn't even love him—at least, not the way she loved Venn. Yet seeing him with Vera, just *thinking* about her with either of them...

Another twinge, sharp and insistent.

Lynden leaned in close and said with a sly smile, 'Perhaps we can arrange a little outing for the two of you? See if we can't get a declaration out of him...' She and Vera shared a grin.

Ella blew cool air over her steaming cup, which was still too hot to drink, and imagined throwing it in Vera's face. The prickling sensation intensified, like water simmering, about to boil. Tension built behind her eyes as she tried to fight it.

It was no good.

Vera's fingers trembled, her teacup halfway to her mouth. Hot liquid splashed over the lip of her cup and down her front.

'Ow!' she cried, jumping up. The fabric of her bodice darkened with expanding moisture and the exposed skin across her chest turned blotchy and red.

Lynden took the cup from Vera, placed it on the side table, and used her hands to fan Vera's skin. 'Bess, quickly, fetch a cool cloth.'

Ella sat, stunned. *Again. It had happened again.* Flames pirouetted behind her eyes and bugs crawled in her belly. She drew power and slowed her breathing, encasing her thoughts.

'It must be nerves,' Vera said, joining Lynden in using her hands as a fan. 'I'm not usually this clumsy!'

Bess arrived back with a cool, damp cloth, which Vera used to pat herself down.

'Are you hurt, my lady?' Bess asked.

'I'm well, thank you, Bess.' The blotches were already fading as Ella's magic sucked the excess heat from the air. 'I don't think I've done any lasting damage. It startled me more than anything.'

Ella exhaled, relieved. No one had even glanced her way. But by every god and demon, she had to get this under control.

At supper that night, Lynden and Vera exchanged knowing glances as Lynden suggested Jonas take Vera out the next day. 'Vee hardly ever gets to ride, and I know you haven't had time to take her, Venn, but Jonas, maybe you could give Vee a few pointers?' She looked from Venn to Jonas, hopeful. 'That will also give me and Ella a chance to go into town. I've asked Ella to help me plan Vera's birthday surprise.'

'It's hardly a surprise if you announce it in advance, Lyn,' Jonas said.

She humphed. 'You know what I mean.'

'I think it's a lovely idea, Lyn,' Venn said.

'See?' Lynden squeezed Vera's hand.

'Only if you don't mind taking me, my lord?' she said to Jonas, peering through her wispy lashes.

'Not at all,' he grinned. 'How could I mind spending time in such exquisite company? I'll be up first thing to get our steeds ready.' For the rest of the meal, Jonas was more attentive to Vera than ever, pouring her wine and serving her from the laid-out trenchers.

The unpleasant sensation resurged, nagging as it pulsed through Ella's core, building to a frantic crescendo. She struggled to clamp down and control it, and she saw Vera's hands shake.

Ella stood, her chair dragging.

'Ella, are you unwell? You look pale,' Lynden said, concerned.

'I should lie down for a bit. Excuse me.'

Ella struggled to sleep that night as the prickling sensation crawled across her entire body. She couldn't stop picturing the way Vera smiled at Jonas, and how he smiled back. She knew how that smile felt, what it did to her, how easy it was to lose herself whenever she was alone with him... Only this time, it would be Vera alone with him.

Flitting in and out of sleep, Ella imagined them. Jonas running his fingers along Vera's arms, slipping them around her waist, his lips pressing down. Beside them, caught like an animal in a cage, she was forced to watch. She could feel his every caress as though it were happening to her. Only it wasn't. She reached between the bars of her cage and tried to claw Vera away from him, grasping at her pale silken hair, her nails leaving ugly red welts across that flawless face.

Eventually, her dreams left her in darkness. When she woke again, Elnora hadn't yet crested the horizon. She stared out her window at the false light that preceded daybreak. *Uhtan,* the priests called it. The light before dawn.

She rose, scrubbed her face and body with cold water from the previous day's washbasin, and dressed as finely as she could without Bess to help her. Under Lynden and Bess's guidance, she had grown more adept at applying makeup, styling her hair, and choosing dresses to flatter. Satisfied with her reflection, she headed out to the stables.

Sure enough, Jonas was there, brushing down the same palfrey Vera had last ridden. Ella watched his muscles work, his hair curled across his forehead, as the dawn sun caught the green of his hazel eyes.

Jonas turned to face her. 'Ella! Are you feeling well? You're looking well.' Those eyes drinking her in.

She chewed her bottom lip. 'Yes, my lord.'

'Then what brings you to see me at this hour?' Brow arched, lips teasing.

Ella paused. What did she want? She couldn't tell Jonas she wanted him to stop courting Vera when he was not bound to her, or anyone. In truth, a match with Vera was a much better prospect for Jonas than one with her. Politics aside, from what Vera had said, her future husband would be settled on a large estate near Lichen as part of her dowry—an attractive outlook for any man. And what could Ella offer? At best, a pitiful few warhorses and a handful of silver. She sighed. Why should she care? It's not as though she loved him. What was she thinking?

The truth was, she wasn't thinking.

She stepped forward, drew him to her, and kissed him. She felt his body respond, hungry for her. Felt the heat of his lips on hers, his arms insistent around her. The yielding of her soft breasts against his broad chest, the power of his thighs touching hers...

Jonas slid one hand around her neck as his fingers gripped her hair. The other slid down her cheek, across the arc of her breasts and along her waist, slipping around behind her to draw her to him until she could feel every part of him.

He breathed as hard and fast as she, his pulse quickening to match hers. His lips found her neck as his hands cupped her breasts. She could feel his arousal hardening against her. She ached for him to lift her skirts, to feel him even closer... She ran her hands across his chest, through his hair, down his back.

He closed his eyes and inhaled, catching her wrists. He brought them to rest together on his chest. Opened his eyes. Took another breath. 'Not now. Not like this,' he whispered.

Until Jonas uttered those words, Ella hadn't considered he would think to bed her here and now. All she knew was that in that moment, her body craved his so much she could barely breathe.

'I—I didn't mean...' She struggled to find her voice. 'I'm sorry, I don't know what I was thinking...'

'No, I'm sorry.' He squeezed her hands. 'I thought this is what you wanted.' Concern in his eyes.

She looked down at the ground, didn't want him to see her face.

'El...' He lifted her chin. 'Look at me...' Eyes gentle. 'We don't have to do anything you don't want to. Not ever,' he said. 'I have to go on this cursed ride, but we can meet again tonight if you like?'

She nodded, not trusting herself to speak.

He kissed her hand and let her go.

# Thirty-Seven

One of the first visits Venn made upon his return to Nedran was to Borsyn's farm. He wanted to reassure Borsyn that he'd settled his daughter Kerryn at Mornae, and to check on the refugees he had placed in Borsyn's care. This had been his steward Mykan's suggestion.

'If you offer Borsyn a trio of hands in Kerryn's stead and provide an income for them—at least while they're learning—Borsyn is less likely to begrudge you for depriving him of his only daughter,' Mykan had said. It also solved the matter of where to place the refugees. It was genius.

'With the coin going to the workers, not Borsyn, the refugees will know they are not bondsmen. And by giving the coin to them rather than Borsyn, you are not creating an incentive for other coin-hungry vassals to lay false claims against your wayward brother.'

*Wayward* was a mild way of putting it, Venn thought, exhaling. Mykan was right, however. With Kerryn gone, Borsyn would be grateful for whatever help he could get. The death of Borsyn's wife from a wasting sickness a few summers back left only Kerryn to work the farm alongside her father. Borsyn's two sons had left the farm years earlier, the eldest to join Elnora's priesthood, and the youngest to enlist with a troupe of warriors.

As Venn neared the farm, the alarmingly overgrown fields came into view. In the distance, Borsyn's flock of ilaks bleated uncomfortably. There was no sign of another soul. Perhaps they were all indoors, avoiding the hottest part of the day, given Elnora was almost at her zenith.

When Venn and his escort pulled up, Borsyn took Venn's reins. 'My lord,' he knelt. Dirt-covered and hunched, Borsyn appeared a score of summers older than his actual age of forty-five.

Venn dismounted and signalled for his men to do likewise. 'Borsyn,' he nodded, offering his hand to help the farmer up.

Borsyn groaned as he struggled to his feet. 'I would offer you refreshments, my lord, but I haven't had a moment to prepare aught.'

Venn frowned, puzzled. 'Where are your workers?'

'Gone, my lord.'

'Gone?'

Borsyn nodded, hand raised to shield his eyes from Elnora's rays. 'I did my best, my lord, but...'

'Come, let us sit indoors and away from this heat.' Venn ushered Borsyn towards the farmstead and waved his men to follow. 'Tell me once we've had something to quench our thirst.'

The party headed into the rickety building. The light streaming through gaps in the worn thatch roof made the un-swept floors more obvious.

'See if you can source us some ale or mead, will you?' Venn said to his rider, Torr. Venn perched on a stool set at the only table and invited the others to join him, including Borsyn, who slumped in his chair, wiping sweat and dirt from his hairline.

After some rustling and clanging, Torr reappeared carrying a pitcher of dark ale. 'Shall we share this? I couldn't find any clean cups.'

Venn nodded. 'Of course. My thanks.' Venn offered the pitcher around, taking his share last. 'Fetch us another round, will you, Torr?' Venn passed the empty pitcher across, then turned to face Borsyn. 'So, tell me, what happened to the refugees?'

Borsyn shrugged, shaking his head. 'They were hardy workers, my lord. Fast learners, too, especially that lass. Though she had a way of looking through a man that would make your skin pucker like a featherless fowl. Not like my Kerryn...' Borsyn's voice choked off.

'Kerryn is well, by the way,' Venn said. 'I should have informed you right away. She's settled into her new post as a lady's maid, and she'll have plenty of help once the babe comes. I assure you she's in excellent hands.'

Borsyn nodded, his mouth crumpling as though he didn't dare speak.

Venn rested a hand upon Borsyn's shoulder.

Torr returned with a fresh round of ale, and Borsyn took a few mouthfuls before continuing. 'Thank you, my lord.' He wiped his mouth on his sleeve. 'She'll be better off there with your lot, I'm sure.' He eyed the shambles surrounding them.

Venn cast an anxious glance around. 'I can see we need to get you some help here, and as a matter of some urgency.' If Borsyn didn't harvest his crops and get those ilaks birthed, milked, and shorn, he wouldn't be able to pay his taxes, and all Nedran would suffer.

Relief washed across Borsyn's face.

'You started to tell me what happened...?' Venn prompted.

'Yes, my lord. As I said, the young'uns you placed here started well enough. They got most of the hallit seeds planted before the frosts, and the ilaks herded to their feed. Around the farmstead, they kept to themselves, which suited me. I'm used to being on my own. But when it came to the Sun-day worship, they refused to attend. At first, I think it's a little odd, but then I say, "What's it to me?" and let them be, and head to the temple alone. I figure they can get more done around here while I'm gone.'

Borsyn took another sip of ale. Venn could see his men growing restless, shifting in their seats.

'But then my eldest, Morgan, comes home to visit as he often does over the winter. Well, my Morgan takes his priesthood to heart. Has ever since he swore himself to Elnora all those summers ago. He was insistent. Said if my workers won't attend the worship, he will take the matter to the High Priest. All three of them insist they aren't heretics. That lass, Kiara, her name was. She was adamant. Said it's not right to force people to worship any god or goddess. I have to say, my lord, I agree with her. But my Morgan wouldn't hear of it. And then, when we get home from the next service, they're gone.'

Venn's eyes narrowed.

Borsyn shook his head and shrugged again. 'Anyway, Morgan does like he said he would, and reports them. The priests sent their people searching, but there's not a trace of them to be found, my lord.'

Venn let out a slow breath.

'I let your brother know, but the young lord said he'd have to wait for your say-so before he could send out a search party.'

'You did the right thing, Borsyn. My thanks.' Venn ran his fingers through his hair, then wiped his hands along his trousers. He had never enforced religious worship on his subjects, and it did not thrill him to discover there were priests out there attempting to. Moreover, Morgan's priesthood was outside Venn's jurisdiction, which meant the priests' men had either trespassed on Venn's lands to conduct their search or co-opted local priests to help them. Either way, it wasn't their place.

Venn stood, patting Borsyn's shoulder. 'Leave this with me. I'll see if I can recruit you some hands to get those crops harvested and ilaks ready for birthing, at least for this season. And I will send word when Kerryn's babe comes.'

Borsyn bowed his head, grasped Venn's hand in his, and kissed it. 'My lord,' he said, tears in his eyes. 'May every god bless and keep you safe...'

# THIRTY-EIGHT

After her tryst with Jonas, Ella retreated to her room. She couldn't bear to face anyone. What had come over her? Was she the sort of person who would sneak around after a man like this? After Jonas?

She sent word that she had a headache and wouldn't be coming out today. Bess brought her breakfast up to her, but she couldn't eat. She paced the floor, clenched and released her fists, trying to calm her nerves. Eventually, she gave up and threw herself face-down on her bed. Lynden had tried to tell her not to get her hopes up about either of her brothers. What, by every god and demon, was she doing?

A knock at her door. 'Ella, my sweet. It's me, Lynden. Can I come in?'

Ella rolled onto her back and forced herself to sit up. 'Yes, of course.'

The door creaked open, and Lynden made her way over to Ella's bed, her brow creased with concern. 'How do you fare?' She perched atop the coverlet beside Ella, the backs of her fingers trailing Ella's cheek. *Like Jonas.*

Ella smiled softly. 'A little better, my thanks.'

Lynden's eyes fell upon Ella's untouched meal. 'You haven't eaten your breakfast. Do you want me to have the cook heat it back up for you? Or I can bring you something fresh?'

Lynden's eyes were so kind that Ella wanted to weep. She shook her head. 'I'm fine, my thanks. If I find my appetite, I'll eat it cold.'

'My apologies for being so caught up with Vee. I feel I've neglected you.'

Ella picked at the embroidery of her coverlet.

'I was looking forward to our outing today.' Lynden took Ella's hands and squeezed.

Ella looked up, meeting Lynden's gaze. 'I didn't mean to let you down.'

'You haven't. I mean, I'm disappointed, of course, but mostly worried...'

'Please don't be. This will pass.' Ella smiled weakly.

Another squeeze. 'If there's anything you need...'

'Just some quiet, my thanks,' Ella said.

'Of course.' Lynden stood. 'I'd best check on Vee next.'

'I thought she was out riding with Jonas?'

'They didn't go in the end. Vee had a terrible night's sleep. A night-terror, apparently. She woke up with these awful welts across her face, with clumps of hair pulled out beside her, but she can't recall doing any of it.'

Ella felt as though all the air had been sucked out of the room.

'It's dreadful. I've never seen Vee like this. She says it's nerves. I mean, she's always been so keen on Jonas. But you know Jonas. It's hard to know how he truly feels about anyone. He'd bed half the women in Ycelt if he could. Probably the men, too.'

Ella shifted uncomfortably.

'My apologies. I shouldn't jest. I know you're fond of him.'

Ella swallowed, but said nothing.

'Anyway, I'll leave you to get some rest. And then, Ella, my sweet, please eat something. You're awfully pale.'

Ella hid in her room for the rest of that day. What if her dream had caused Vera actual harm? She didn't know what to do or how to stop it. It was as though the more she tried to suppress her magic, the more it leaked out and spilled onto those around her. She couldn't end up like her mother.

When Bess checked in on her some hours later, Ella asked for more wood. The only thing she could think of to soothe and quiet her magic was to draw on her stoked fire.

Ella settled into the comfort of her solitude, and picked up the book Amber had left behind when she fled, the one with her scrawled note tucked inside. She opened the cover and ran her fingers along the yellowing pages. The volume recounted tales from the old war, when the god Xenon walked the earthly plane alongside his followers, whose magic the people deemed heretical, even then. They fought for their freedom and his, persecuted by the men who worshipped Elnora. *Then as now*, Ella thought.

Ella wondered why Xenon's followers were nearly all women. Surely it wasn't only females who had magic. Gohran had at least some magic, she was sure, even if he denied it. How else to explain the way he had seen their mother's magic? Yet it seemed much rarer among males. Then, as now, the men wielded earthly power and spiritual power, as kings, lords, and priests. According to lore, back then, anyone could draw upon the Sacred Stone as a source of magic, yet nothing in these annals indicated that was true. Women, yes. But already the men were fighting with might and the rule of law, rather than magic.

At some point, Ella's supper arrived. She still hadn't touched her breakfast. The maid cleared her dishes and closed the door behind her, and Ella continued reading, rising occasionally to tend to her fire.

Ella didn't know how long she had been sitting there reading when she heard another knock at her door. Already in her nightgown, her hair was loose about her shoulders. She put her book aside and opened the door.

There Jonas stood, hair tousled, his bare chest visible through his half-open shirt. He must be on his way to bed.

Her breath caught.

'I promised to meet you tonight, so here I am.' Eyes teasing. Lip curled.

Ella crossed her arms over her chest, half hiding behind her bedchamber door. She cleared her throat. 'How's Vera?'

'Poor Vee gave herself a fright,' Jonas said. 'The welts have gone down now, though, so that's something.'

'It's just awful,' Ella's voice caught.

'El...' Jonas reached for her. 'I've been worried about you. When you didn't show at breakfast or dinner...' He slid his fingertips along her forearms.

Eyes cast downward, Ella had to fight every instinct not to draw him into her room or slam the door shut and bar it between them.

'There's no shame in following your desires, El.'

'Perhaps not for you,' she said.

His expression was earnest. 'Not for anyone.'

She chewed on her bottom lip, studying the weave of her nightdress.

He lifted her chin until she faced him. 'If you're feeling better tomorrow, take a walk with me after supper.'

She bit her lip. 'What about Vera?' *That cursed smile...*

He took Ella's hand in his and brought her fingers to his lips, eyes upon hers the entire time. 'What about Vera?' He released her hand and sauntered away.

When Venn arrived back from Borsyn's farm, it was long after supper and everyone had retired for the evening, but he sent Mykan to fetch Jonas, anyway. He paced the length of his study, running his fingers through his hair. How had his brother let this happen?

He heard Jonas's swaggering footsteps approach. A moment later, he burst through the door, looking dishevelled, rubbing his eyes, and yawning as though he had just woken.

'You sent for me, my esteemed lord?' A mock bow.

'And you took your sweet time getting here.' Venn had no patience for his brother's drollness. Not tonight.

Jonas saw his brother's sober expression and braced himself.

'I went to see Borsyn today,' Venn said.

'Oh?' Jonas stood tall, arms folded across his chest.

'He says he came to see you while I was away. To tell you his workers had abandoned his farm, and that you did nothing about it. He told me you deferred the matter. Along with all these matters.' Venn slammed his fist atop a stack of parchments he had been working through since his return.

Jonas took a step back as though that fist had slammed into him.

'Now thanks to you, Borsyn has no workers, and we risk losing his harvest. And with no one to assist their birthing, his ilak flock, too.'

Jonas kept his breathing steady, his expression neutral, almost bored.

'Then Borsyn tells me his eldest lad sent priests out searching on Nedran's lands!' Venn was ready to explode. 'And the gods only know what other catastrophes I have waiting for me among all this.' Venn motioned to the pile of parchments. 'These matters have ramifications for us all, Jonas. It's fine for you to flit through the hours indulging your whims, but you have responsibilities, just as I do. You may not be the dryhten, but you're still a lord here.'

With fists clenched, Venn resumed pacing. 'It's not as though you're a fool. Far from it. You're one of the most intelligent people I know. So why can't you use that intellect on something important? Take some initiative. I know you have no interest in politics, in ruling, but by the gods, why can't you be trusted to take your duties seriously?'

Jaw set tight, voice quiet, Jonas said, 'Are you finished?'

Venn stopped pacing and turned towards his brother.

Jonas collected the parchments from Venn's desk, took a step closer and faced him square-on. 'You're right, brother. I have no love for leadership. But you can't leave me in charge with the barest training in matters of state, with explicit instructions to defer all complex business, and then blame me when I do exactly as you ask. You didn't have to take Kerryn to Mornae yourself. Gods, you have men enough for that. I used to think you didn't ask me to take on more because you didn't believe I was capable, but now I know it's not that you don't trust me. It's that you don't trust anyone. If you want me to deal with these, I'll do it, gladly.' Jonas held the stack of parchments out in front of him. 'But you need to let me. Give me the tools and the know-how, and then actually—' He flung the parchments into the air—'Let go.'

Venn saw his brother's face then. Truly saw him. Saw the anger, the resentment, but mostly his hurt. He watched the parchments scatter and fall to the floor between them as Jonas strode away and slammed the door shut behind him.

# Thirty-Nine

'It was the strangest thing,' Vera said to Ella at breakfast the following day. Ella had forced herself to attend and was relieved when neither brother joined them. 'I haven't had night terrors since I was a girl, and they were never quite like this.' Vera looked paler than usual. Her powdered skin bore the scantest hint of the scratches that had marred her, while Bess had done her best to disguise the bare patches of her scalp, strategically positioning and pinning dried cornflowers through twisted strands of hair.

Ella steeled herself. 'How awful. You must have been so frightened.' She hoped her voice didn't sound as wooden as it felt.

'And then Lyn said you were unwell, too, Your Highness. Are you feeling better?'

'Yes, my thanks. It was just a headache.'

Vera turned to Lynden. 'It must have been quiet around here all day, Lyn.'

'It would have been, but Jonas ended up taking me into town. Which means, Vee, I have your surprise.'

Vera raised one eyebrow at her friend.

'I wanted to ask if I could give it to you before your actual birthday so you can wear it on your ride with Jonas. Assuming you're still going at some point...' Lynden looked around. 'Where's Bess, I wonder? When she returns, I'm going to ask her what's going on with my brothers. They were both stomping around earlier and then they disappeared with Mykan.'

'So, the gift is something I can wear?' Vera asked, steering Lynden's attention back.

'Yes!' Lynden looked sly. 'Do you want it now?'

'Stop teasing. Of course, I do.'

Lynden clasped her hands together and jumped up. 'Wait here.'

'As if I'm going anywhere.' Vera rolled her eyes towards Ella, who forced a shy smile and continued to eat her breakfast. After an awkward silence, Vera cleared her throat. 'Have you received word from Erldan recently, Your Highness?' Her tone was syrupy.

'My brother the king wrote to me less than a week ago. Why do you ask?'

Still focused on her breakfast, Vera replied, an edge to her voice. 'I'm surprised King Gohran would keep you away for so long. You were always so *close*.'

Ella frowned. 'We used to play together as children, as siblings often do.'

'Yet not with your sisters...?'

*What was she getting at?* 'Gohran and I enjoyed the grounds, our sisters less so.'

'I don't suppose King Gohran mentioned Lord Kerr of Rynwood to you?'

'Actually, he didn't.'

'And has the lord declared himself to you?'

'Not at all.'

'That surprises me. From all accounts, he is keen to form an alliance. I assumed he had already approached you.'

Ella watched her rival coolly, but said nothing.

'Perhaps the alarming tale I heard was true after all...'

'And what would that be?'

'That when the lord approached your brother, King Gohran drew his sword, vowing that he'd slit the next man's throat who asked for your hand. At the time, I dismissed the report as vicious gossip.'

'That was doubtless wise,' Ella responded evenly.

'And what about the king himself? Is he planning to wed soon? He's already refused Lady Clarynda of Meenad. I heard that when her father rode to Erldan on her behalf, the king refused to discuss the matter.'

'You hear quite a lot, my lady.'

Vera looked as though she might say more, but at that moment, Lynden returned carrying a small wooden box. She grinned, pausing a moment to build suspense, then handed it to Vera.

Vera opened it and gasped. 'By the goddess, this looks like something out of a royal collection. Wherever did you find it?'

'Do you like it?'

'As if you even have to ask!' Vera threw her arms around her friend.

Ella wanted to slip away. It felt like she was intruding. Especially after Vera's barbed remarks. She wished she had her mother's fortitude and grace to banish idle rumours from her mind. What was it to Vera if she and her brother were close? If he chose to marry or not? Weren't all brothers protective of their sisters?

Ella stiffened. What if people thought Gohran was too protective of her? Might they think of her mother and wonder why?

'Ella, would you like to see?' Lynden prompted, as if she just remembered Ella was there.

Vera held the box open. Inside, a sapphire brooch sparkled. Ella's breath caught. Her old one, she was sure, the one she had traded in the marketplace. The setting had been replaced from gold into a more modern silver, but the stone was unmistakable.

'Shall I pin it on for you?' Lynden didn't wait for a response to attach it to Vera's bodice.

The irony of seeing her old brooch pinned to Vera's dress did not escape Ella.

'You still haven't told me where you found it, Lyn.'

Lynden mimed sewing her lips together.

'Fine, keep your secret. I love it, thank you.'

This time, Ella left the two women to share their special moment.

Mykan summoned Jonas shortly after dawn. Jonas had barely slept but pushed through. This was important. When he arrived back at Venn's study, Venn stood and stepped forward to meet him. He saw Venn had collected and tidied the strewn parchments from the night before.

'I thought about what you said, Jonas, and you were right. I didn't equip you as I should have. And I shouldn't have blamed you. As you said, you did exactly as I asked. I think sometimes I resent being born first. Having to take on all this responsibility...'

'Which you also love,' Jonas interjected.

Venn peered down his nose at him.

Jonas sobered. 'You have my thanks for saying so, Venn. I know I don't always make things easy.'

Venn rested his hand on Jonas's shoulder. 'Will you help me and Mykan work through these outstanding matters?'

It was as much of an apology as Jonas would ever get. He dragged a chair beside his brother's, and they set to work.

Venn took the time to break down each item and explain the surrounding context and factors they needed to consider making each decision. Jonas surprised them both with how much he already knew. The only thing stopping him from acting on that knowledge had been a lack of confidence and a lack of Venn's confidence in him.

Eventually, Venn steered the conversation around to Vera. 'How are you getting along with our guest?'

'You know I'm fond of her,' Jonas said, noncommittally.

'As she is of you.'

Jonas shrugged. 'What else is there to say?'

'That alliance is paramount to Nedran, Jonas.'

'And entirely dependent on an alliance between Nedran and Erldan,' he threw back.

'Which I'm working on,' Venn said slowly. 'It hasn't been timely while the family is in mourning, but that period is almost up. Speaking of, we should step up the training regime with summer approaching.'

Jonas sighed. Yet another thing to tend to.

Venn turned to his brother. 'Jonas, you have my heartfelt thanks. For everything.'

After supper that night, Jonas and the women retired to the drawing room. Jonas was back to being his usual playful self and the four of them settled into a game of tiles. Ella sat opposite him, with Lynden and Vera on either side between them. Ella sensed his attention on her, though he doted on Vera, pouring her wine, and helping her choose her tiles whenever she encountered a tricky play once he was out of a game.

Though Ella had always made a point of *not* tuning into her magic while in play, she found she could anticipate what each player was about to do, knowing instinctively whether someone had a favourable or poor hand. To begin with, she won round after round, not aware of her advantage until Jonas said, 'The gods are certainly on your side tonight, El.'

'Yes, Ella, are you sure you can't see our tiles reflected on something back there?' Lynden peered behind her, looking for a mirrored surface.

'I promise you, it's just luck,' Ella said, flushing.

She had never experienced this before. It was as if her magic had reached some tipping point where it flowed and wouldn't turn off, a constant hum through her body and mind that never died down.

After that, Ella threw as many rounds as she won, though it felt unnatural to do so. Thrice, she noticed Jonas watching her with his eyebrow cocked as she made her choices. Meanwhile, Jonas played terribly. Even when he had a useless hand, he persisted, never discarding and redrawing, as each player could opt to do once per round, which cost him several games in a row.

When he revealed his most pitiful hand yet, a spattering of unordered faceless tiles of varying suits, Ella said, 'Why, by every god, didn't you redraw that hand?'

'You know me, El. I always play the hand that's dealt me.'

'And here I thought it was because you enjoyed playing the fool,' Lynden teased. 'Who wants more wine?' She signalled to a nearby servant.

Jonas raised his palms. 'None for me, my thanks. I'm out after that abysmal effort. Time for a light stroll and then to bed.' He glanced Ella's way, his gaze a caress across her entire body.

Ella stood. 'I might join you.'

'Shall we all go, then?' Vera asked.

Ella's stomach lurched, and with it, the now-familiar pressure built behind her eyes. *Gods, no, don't let the prickling start...* 'Actually, I think I should head straight to bed after all. I feel my headache returning.'

Lynden frowned. 'That's a shame, Ella, my sweet. You look pale.'

'Yes, you do.' Jonas was watching her again, eyes narrowed.

'My thanks for a pleasant evening. Enjoy your walk.' Ella avoided looking at Jonas and fled before anyone could reply.

The next morning, Ella woke to find a note pushed beneath her barred door. She opened it and read. *Meet me in the stables after breakfast.* The note wasn't signed, but it had to be from Jonas. Her entire body liquefied. His words echoed in her mind. *There's no shame in following your desires, El...*

As soon as she finished breakfast, Ella hid in her room until she could be certain the others were occupied, and then she slipped back down the stairs and outside. She wished she knew how to make herself invisible, so she could move about unseen, but thankfully, none of the servants paid her much mind as she crossed the grounds towards the stables.

When she entered, she saw Jonas leaning lazily against a stall, a self-satisfied grin creeping across his features. He was enjoying this, seeing her sneak around after him. She almost turned and fled, but her hunger for him urged her onward.

Jonas didn't move. He was waiting for her to come to him. *Curse him!*

And yet, she did it. Slowly at first, her steps hesitant, but then she could smell him, almost taste him, was already imagining his lips pressed to hers. And then he was there, right in front of her, his arms around her, his hand gripping her nape, tugging gently at her hair, his other hand finding her back, her legs, her buttocks, as he pressed her up against the stall's post.

'We don't have long,' he whispered. His kisses were soft yet insistent against hers, his tongue teasing. 'I won't do anything you don't want me to.' His lips trailed her neck as he unlaced her bodice. 'Is this all fine?'

She nodded, biting her lip, urging him on.

He loosened her bodice, his fingers tracing as his eyes drank her in, admiring the tender skin of her waist and torso, the arc of her breasts, to where her complexion darkened around her hardened nipples. He cupped her breasts, and she stifled a moan. The sounds of his pleasure, of his need, echoed hers.

He brought his mouth back to her lips, pulled her even closer. She returned his kisses as her hands explored the hardness of his chest, his torso, the play of muscles beneath his shirt, now untucked. She could feel his arousal beneath his trousers and part of her wanted to explore even further.

'I wish we had more time...' he said, pulling away.

Ella came to her senses, hearing the distant sounds as someone approached.

Jonas hastily tucked in his shirt and helped Ella relace her bodice. They scrambled to tidy their hair and smooth out their clothes. Ella tried to force her breathing to slow, will her heartbeat to ease into a more natural rhythm, as though anyone who saw her right now would hear it as clearly as she felt it.

'There you are, my lord!' It was a servant. 'Lady Vera is ready to head out when you are.'

'Wait—you're riding with Vera today?' Ella stepped away as though Jonas had slapped her.

Jonas addressed the lad. 'You have my thanks. Please tell the lovely lady I will meet her shortly.'

The servant tried to hide his curiosity as he nodded and scurried away.

Once they were alone again, Jonas turned his attention to the stalls.

'Jonas—I—' Her voice cut off. She didn't know what to say. She was so confused. After what they had just shared... 'This was foolish. I don't know what I was thinking... I—I shouldn't have come here.'

Fussing at a bridle, Jonas gave Ella a wry smile. 'It's like I said last night, El. I play the hand that's dealt me.' He stopped what he was doing, took both her hands in his and held her gaze. 'El, this is what I want. *You* are what I want. Never forget that.'

Ella stood, unmoving, as Jonas prepared for his ride. She wanted to flee, but Lynden or Vera might see her if she left now. Better to wait until Jonas and Vera were gone, then slip back inside.

Eventually, Jonas exited the stables, pressing one last kiss to Ella's lips as he went to find Vera.

Ella slumped against a nearby wall. What had just happened? Was Jonas trying to tell her it was his duty to court Vera? Venn's words from all those moons ago echoed in her mind. *It's my duty to Nedran...* First Venn, and now Jonas. But then, where did that leave her?

She sighed. Lynden had warned her. Gods, she had warned herself! Yet she refused to give up. Venn had not declared for her sister, and Jonas had just said himself he wanted her.

*He'd bed half the women in Ycelt if he could,* Lynden had said.

She wanted to shout, to scream.

The bridles on the wall beside her rattled. Steeds whinnied, tossing their manes, stomping their hooves.

A sharp inhale. Thank every god and demon she was alone. She could not have explained this away.

She let out a slow breath. That background hum was now abuzz, coursing through every inch of her. Where was it supposed to go? What was she supposed to do with it? Why had Amber never taught her how to manage all this pent-up energy with no outlet? She had learned the myriad ways *not* to use her magic, sources of power that were forbidden, but nothing that could help her now—with this.

A familiar mind touched hers. *Amber.* Ella closed off her thoughts like a door slamming shut. If she let Amber in now, she might be tempted to flee to Aryon after all, and all of this would have been for nothing.

Voices approached. She straightened up and took a few deliberate breaths. A moment later, the servant who had interrupted her and Jonas earlier re-entered the stable. Another lad was with him. Both carried pails and brooms. When they saw her, they halted.

'Your Highness.' They bowed, equipment dangling as they watched her inquisitively.

She was about to offer some excuse for why she was still there, but paused. She didn't owe them anything. Instead, she smiled, forcing her tone to remain calm and even. 'Good day to you both.'

At her words, her smile, their faces softened, jaws slack. They watched her dreamily, almost as though they were smitten.

She swallowed and stood even taller, letting warmth flow outward, like a valve releasing water, and with it, the pressure that had been thrumming through her eased.

'Can we help with anything, Your Highness? Is there anything you need?' They stood poised to do her bidding.

'Nothing, my thanks.' She left them to their chores, feeling their adoring eyes follow her back towards the main keep.

Afterwards, she would wish she had asked them for their silence.

# Forty

'Oh! Lyn, I'm so excited, but I can hardly breathe in this dress!' Vera said.

Ella hated to admit it, but Vera looked exquisite. Her luscious crimson gown complemented her flaxen hair and bright eyes.

'If you'll hold still a moment, I can adjust these laces,' Lynden said. 'Ella, my sweet, could I trouble you to take this side?'

Ella took the laces from Lynden, resisting the urge to cinch them in tighter until they pinched Vera's fair skin.

Alongside Lynden and Vera's sophisticated gowns, Ella's dress looked plain and shabby. She had done her best to alter the cut to flatter her shape, but nothing could disguise the worn fabric and dated style. She'd only used a few simple pins to hold up her hair, too, with Bess and Lynden both fussing over Vera.

Still, when the guests arrived that evening for Vera's birthday ball, Ella could sense appreciative eyes on her. Appreciative and inquisitive.

She heard murmurings, and caught the undercurrent of thoughts upon her, their words and wonderings toppling over one another, until she couldn't follow a single thread. 'She's still here...', 'Why not her sisters?', 'She and the king were always together...', 'He still hasn't taken a wife...', 'As lovely as her mother...'

Ella kept her breath steady, focusing on the smoothness of the wine glass in her hands, the smell, taste, and texture of each mouthful, as she tried to force their unwelcome gossip from her mind.

From the other side of the room, Jonas caught her gaze and smiled archly, sipping his wine. Over the rim of his glass, he took in her hair, her eyes, her lips, as though it was Ella he consumed in his mind. Heat rising, she felt her skin flush, and her legs turn to water.

'What do you think, Jonas?' Vera's question cut across the space between them, drawing him into her conversation.

Jonas turned towards her. 'My apologies. What did you say?' He flashed a smile.

Ella watched Vera regress into a girlish puddle. Is that how Ella appeared when Jonas smiled at her? She sighed inwardly. Wasn't that what happened to every woman around him?

As usual, Venn did not dance, but attended to business with the various guests. Jonas, too, was subdued, barely dancing as he worked the room, for once charming the husbands as much as the wives when he wasn't by Vera's side.

Ella's stomach sank when she spotted Lord Kerr of Rynwood among the guests. Determined to hover around her like a mosquito, the lord fetched her wine and begged for her hand on the dance floor. She took it, but only because it was better than sitting around, waiting for either brother to notice her.

Across the room, Venn whispered something in Jonas's ear. A moment later, Jonas made his way to Vera's side, offering her his hand. Vera's entire face lit up as he led her to the dance floor. Arms poised, they stepped in time with the music. Jonas ran his hand along Vera's arm, bringing it to her low-cut bodice to admire what had once been Ella's sapphire, which glimmered under the light of the candelabra.

Ella wanted to knock his hand off, to shove Vera aside. Before she was even aware of it, a surge of power coursed through her and a nearby servant tripped, knocking Jonas's hand away and spilling the contents of a wine carafe right across Vera's chest. The corners of Ella's lips curved before she pulled herself together and gasped, along with the other guests.

A minor commotion erupted before Lynden and Venn rushed to Vera's side. Jonas stood by Vera, but he was watching Ella. Vera followed Jonas's gaze, her venomous eyes landing upon Ella. She drew Jonas's attention back to her and her decolletage, as she used a cloth to absorb the spilled liquid from her crimson dress, though a blood-like stain remained.

The days grew longer and warmer as the weeks passed. With Jonas now helping Venn with his duties, the dryhten could attend more to his family and guests, joining them at mealtimes and some evenings, though Ella noticed he still seemed preoccupied. The men stepped up their training, which gave Ella a good excuse to avoid Vera and Lynden as she took to her old habit of watching the men out in the field.

Now, however, she felt the urge to join in, though she realised what Jonas had taught her would be next to useless on a battlefield. Their complex manoeuvres were a world apart from the defensive strategies she had learned. She understood why, of course. She wasn't about to become a warrior and join a troupe of any kind. Rather, he had given her the tools to defend herself should their army ever fail, and an enemy breached the city walls. Or worse, the castle keep.

Then, on a day when thick clouds forced Ella indoors, she arrived in the women's hall only to have the room fall silent. Lynden and Vera huddled together. Vera's eyes were red and puffy. The serving women eyed Ella as though she were a stranger—or worse, a traitor. Had word of her and Jonas that day in the stables made its way back to Vera?

Ella's instinct told her to turn and flee, yet another part urged her to stay. She drew a breath, sucking up the surrounding warmth, wrapping it around her to steady her nerves. A preternatural calm soothed her, leaving a chill in the air. Head held high, she eyed each of the women and strode into the room, sinking into a nearby chair with a sigh. With deliberate casualness, she took out her needlework.

'The weather looks to be changing outside,' she said. 'There's quite a bluster building up. It wouldn't surprise me if there's a storm by nightfall. Oh—Bess, do you have any more of this green thread? I want to finish this section. I think I'm almost ready to start work on a wedding shirt for my dower chest.'

Bess curtsied. 'I'll have a look for you, Your Highness.'

The other women joined the search and rifled through their baskets, relieved to have an excuse to avoid meeting her gaze.

'I think I found some.' Lynden held it out. 'Oh, it doesn't quite match, does it? Never mind, I'm sure we can fetch you some from town in the morning. Shall we play a game of tiles instead?'

Vera sniffed and cleared her throat. 'What a lovely idea, Lyn. And then I'd best pack before supper.'

'Oh, you're leaving?' Ella's tone was as sweet as honey. 'I'm sorry to hear that.'

Vera's expression hardened, but she remained silent.

Ella was relieved when they settled into their game, but more so when the next day the servants loaded Vera's trunk onto her waiting carriage.

# FORTY-ONE

In the weeks following Vera's departure, an eerie calm replaced the tension and urgency Ella felt surrounding every interaction during her stay, like the aftermath of a storm. The peace was a relief, yet Ella was suddenly aware of what she had been doing, sneaking around with Jonas, railing against her rival. She had acted like a captive feline rattling around in her cage, goaded into snapping at shadows, while distracting herself with a shiny toy.

Lynden was gracious enough not to mention the tension between Ella and Vera, and the women settled back into the easy intimacy of their friendship as though Vera had never intruded upon their world.

Venn and Jonas were now in the thick of their training and duties. When either or both saw her, they were as cordial as ever. Jonas's smile still turned her entire body molten, and she was careful to avoid being left alone with him.

Then there was Venn. From time to time, as she watched him train, she sensed his eyes on her and his attention sent a warm glow through her entire being. Why was she still so drawn to him? She thought she had hardened her heart to him. But when he looked at her... Among this sea of bodies, if Jonas shone like the brightest star, Venn was the entire moon. She wanted Jonas. Every part of her craved him. But if she had the chance to marry Venn, her heart's first love, a man she knew was honourable beyond measure, she would do so in a heartbeat.

As everyone settled into their more usual routines, Ella could almost forget the past few moons ever happened. And when her newfound calm persisted, she hoped it would stay this way evermore.

But then one morning as she and Lynden were finishing breakfast, a young page arrived carrying a letter from her brother that threatened to upheave her world once more.

Ella took the letter. Cold rippled down her spine as she ran her fingers over the seal.

The boy held a second letter, addressed to Venn.

'News from the king?' Lynden asked. 'Lord Venn should be in his study.'

'My lady.' The page bowed and retreated.

Ella broke the seal. A sharp pounding behind her eyes. She squinted, queasy.

'Ella?' Lynden squeezed Ella's arm. 'You look pale. Another headache?'

She nodded as the parchment blurred out of focus. The pressure built as though a blacksmith had taken a hammer to her skull. She steadied her hands and tried again to read.

'Gohran writes Venn will visit soon and asks if I wish to join him for my sixteenth birthday,' she said, her words landing like stones.

Her birthday. Solstice.

Had it been a full year since she had left Erldan? Since Gohran had betrayed and murdered their mother? As if she wished to go home to commemorate that! She tossed the letter aside, pressing her fingers to her temples. The tension behind her eyes was like the static of a storm building.

Ella pictured her home—a world away—and wondered how her sisters fared. Did she even miss them? If she were honest, not truly. She worried for them and pondered about them, but despite everything, her time at Nedran had been some of the happiest of her life.

Lynden reached out to take Ella's hand. 'Should I ask the servants to help you pack?'

Lynden's kindness and concern were a stark reminder of what she'd missed growing up. Lynden had taken Ella under her wing as her sisters never had. Only her father and some servants had shown her any kind of warmth, but they hadn't been her friends. Gohran was the closest person she'd had to a friend, and magic had robbed her of that. *Odd little Ella. A witch.* She never felt like that here. At Nedran, she felt *wanted*. At ease. She only wished it had not come at such a cost.

Ella picked the letter back up and read it over. Even if Gohran only meant for her to visit, not stay, she wasn't ready to give this up. She scrunched up the letter. *Curse Gohran to every hell and back.*

'Ella?'

'Have your courier inform the king I will not be returning with Lord Venn,' she said. If her brother wanted her back at Erldan, he would have to drag her there.

Thunder rumbled through her entire body. *An omen.* It had to be.

Ella steadied her breath. *What use were the god's messages to her?* When she and Amber had tried to uncover their meaning back at Erldan, it had changed nothing. They had murdered her mother, her world turned upside down, and there was not one cursed thing she could do to stop it.

On the morning Venn was due to leave for Erldan, he asked Ella if he could take her riding before he headed out. For a moment, time all but ceased. It had been so long since they had ridden together, just the two of them, and she realised how much she had missed it. Missed him. She also felt a wave of guilt—shame, even—as though by acting on her desire for Jonas, she had betrayed him. Yet another part of her felt justified in having done so. Venn had discarded her at every turn, while Jonas was...*Jonas.* She sighed.

Venn guided them to the place where they'd ridden on their first outing at Nedran, and Ella tried to put everything else out of her mind. She breathed in the summer grass, grown tall after the spring rains, basked in the warmth on her skin, savouring these precious moments.

They dismounted and strolled arm in arm along the banks of the river towards the weeping willow. Though it was still early, cicadas thrummed, promising a scorching day. Ella leaned into Venn, the shape of his body comforting, familiar. Once he had felt solid and safe, and their conversation flowed, but on this day, he was subdued, barely speaking for the entire ride. Ella wasn't sure if the stiltedness was coming from her or him.

She studied his demeanour. 'Something troubles you, my lord.'

Venn turned to face her, clasping her hands in his. For a long moment, he stared into her eyes, studying her face as though to etch her image into his memory the way a scribe carves onto stone. Ella sensed in him a mixture of sorrow, guilt, fear, and some emotion she couldn't quite place. Anger, almost. No—resentment. She longed to take that pain away.

With a sigh, he released her hands and moved closer to the water's edge. Another moment passed, and he shrugged as if to shake off his solemn mood. 'Did your brother ever play a game called Foresight?' he asked, his voice tight.

'Not that I recall.'

'Father often used to make me play. It was supposed to be fun. There were all these elaborate rules about which pieces could make what moves and how those moves influenced the other pieces. If you made the wrong move, you could cut yourself off entirely. I struggle to remember it now. In any case, it was never fun.'

Ella placed her arms upon his elbows, coaxing him back towards her. She drew him close, capturing his hands in hers. He pulled her into his chest. She drank in the comfort of his sandalwood scent, the reassuring shape of his torso, his chest. His soothing arms wrapped around her, and she longed to lose herself in this moment forever.

Venn let out a slow breath. He stroked Ella's hair and kissed her forehead, lingering, a deep ache behind every heartbeat, and then he released her.

In the void of that touch, Ella's world felt cold and empty.

Later, as she watched Venn depart, Ella was sorry she hadn't agreed to go with him. The pressure she'd felt the day her brother's letter arrived was back, like the uneasiness of a storm brewing inside her. Outside, the cicadas' singing had grown more intense and urgent, building to a frantic crescendo that throbbed through her mind.

Much as she tried, she couldn't shake the feeling. *Venn will only be gone for a few days. A week at most,* she told herself. So why did he look at her as though he were saying goodbye?

Ella summoned just enough power to ease the pressure behind her eyes and push through the discomfort, but remnants of danger prickled the back of her neck, urging caution. She just didn't know about what.

After dinner, she suggested playing tiles before Jonas could propose a walk in the grounds. In fact, for the next few days, she tried to avoid Jonas altogether. But after a few evenings like this, Lynden declined Ella's invitation.

'I'm so sleepy, Ella, my sweet. If I play tiles tonight, I think I'll fall asleep at the table. Why don't you and Jonas take one of your walks?'

Jonas sat across the room, reading by lantern light. Upon this cue, he put his book and drink down, and stood to join them, offering his arm to Ella.

Memories of his hands roaming, his lips trailing, his entire body pressed against hers pulsed through her. Yet she hesitated. The prickle at her nape travelled the length of her spine. She should make some excuse. Flee.

But then he smiled, brow arched, lips curled, and every ounce of her resistance dissolved.

Jonas guided her out into the night air, his touch like static against her skin. She couldn't tell if it was from fear or anticipation.

As soon as they were out of sight of the main keep, he slid his hand from her arm to her waist, drawing her to him. 'It's been too long...' he whispered, kissing her neck, his hands moving along her body, cupping her breasts through the fabric of her dress, rubbing his thumbs over her nipples. She let out a small moan. 'I love the sounds you make.' He drew her even closer. She could feel every part of him, his need rising to match hers.

Again, that hammering behind her eyes, sharper now. A jagged inhale. Pulling away, she slid out of his grip and turned to face him.

'El? What is it?'

She hesitated, chewing her lip, not knowing where to begin. The pressure increased. Images of Venn and the way he had looked at her before he rode to Erldan crowded her mind. She cleared her throat. Swallowed. Finally, she found her voice and her words escaped her lips, unfiltered. 'Do you know why Venn was so... Sad... Before he left for Erldan?'

'You're asking me about Venn?' Jonas looked incredulous.

'He wasn't himself, and I wondered if it had something to do with us...'

Jonas looked heavenward, palms to the sky as if pleading with the gods to recognise his plight.

'Please, Jonas. I've never seen him like that.'

He met her gaze, slipped his arms back around her, and brought her in close. He ran his nose along hers, his lips brushing against her cheek as he said in a hot whisper, 'Well, it wouldn't occur to Venn that anything too scandalous could go on between his princess and scoundrel brother. I've the utmost respect for him, and wouldn't abuse his trust, would I? Not with sweet, innocent Ella...' His timbre tied her stomach into knots.

She stepped back, disentangling herself. 'This was a bad idea. I think we should head inside.'

He drew her back towards him. 'We could take things upstairs, but I don't think the servants could pretend to be blind as they do now.'

That hammering again. 'I didn't mean for *that!*' His breath was acrid with cloves and cinnamon. 'You've been drinking!'

One hand slipped around her waist, the other traced the back of her neck. 'I've missed you...' He pressed his wet mouth onto hers.

She shoved him away. 'You're drunk!'

Mouth set in a line, he nodded. 'Perhaps I have had a little too much. What about tomorrow night, then? I promise I won't touch a drop.'

'I don't think it's a good idea, Jonas. Not while Venn is away.'

'You don't want to spend this time, just the two of us?'

*Curse those hazel eyes, those lips!* The memory of their heat echoed along her neck, drowning out the hammering, as his desire fed hers. Ella sighed. 'Tomorrow, then.'

# Forty-Two

The following morning, Lynden's cousin Moyra arrived to visit, joining Lynden, Ella, and the serving women in the women's hall for most of the day. An elderly widow, Moyra seemed content to witter away as if silence made her uncomfortable.

'When my Rorn passed on, this one's mother took me in,' she told Ella, gesturing towards Lynden. 'Rorn's overlord at the time made such a fuss about keeping me on. Said he'd servants enough already, as if that's all I'd be! The shame of it is that the widow of a retired captain is no one, no matter how well-connected by birth, if she has no holding of her own.'

'How dreadful for you,' Ella said with genuine sympathy, thankful for the distraction, as Moyra monopolised their conversation.

'Thank you, dear. Such a love, aren't you?' Moyra reached over and petted Ella's cheeks. 'My! Skin as soft as a butterfly's wing, too. You are helping her find a suitable husband, aren't you, Lynnie? I mean no disrespect to your brother, Your Highness. And in fact, I have the utmost respect for such a great, great man. But man, he is, and you can't trust men in these matters, believe me.' She nodded conspiratorially at Ella.

'Oh! That reminds me—did you hear about that poor lass in the next town?' Without waiting for a response, Moyra went on. 'Scandalous, I tell you. Falls pregnant and the old beast she's burdened with swears it's not his. Which makes me wonder if he can still pull the cart, if you take my meaning. She's certainly something to look at from all accounts. Anyway, the old ox says it can't be his, and when he beats it out of her, she claims the father is of noble birth. Which just goes to prove my point—you can't trust men one iota.'

'Come now, Mirrie, you can't say that about every man,' Lynden said.

'Maybe not, but there's few like our Venn. I prefer not to leave these things to chance. Just mention a suitable name here and there, and they'll think it was their idea. Isn't that right, Bessie?'

Bess smiled and continued her work.

'Speaking of your brother, Your Highness, is there any news of a future queen? A king should always think of his heirs, especially being an only son.'

'I believe he's wanting to settle me and my sisters first,' Ella said.

Moyra frowned. 'How odd. You would think he'd want to sort out his own pen first, but there you are. Even more reason to get onto steering him in the right direction for you, Your Highness. I hear he's very fond of you, but I wouldn't want to rely on that...'

Lynden rolled her eyes. 'Enough, Mirrie! Leave her be.'

'Oh, very well. Just promise me you'll keep it in mind.'

'*Yes*, Mirrie. Now, you haven't told me a thing about my other cousins...'

That night at supper, Lynden was late arriving, which forced Ella to sit on her own opposite Jonas. Uneasy silence pressed in on them.

'Moyra's quite a character, isn't she?' Jonas finally offered.

'Yes, she's very... Lively,' Ella responded, keeping a keen lookout for either the woman in question or Lynden.

When Lynden eventually bustled in, her words toppled over each other as she plonked herself down at the table. 'Oh Ella, I'm so sorry. Moyra was only in town for the day, and she couldn't help but play matchmaker. I tell you, she never changes. I had to hear yet another round of look-after-Ella before she left.'

'She won't be joining us this evening, then?' Ella ventured.

'No, you're safe,' Lynden promised.

'Oh.'

'Ella, my sweet, you look disappointed!'

'Yes, El, you do.' Jonas's tone was flat.

Unflinching, Ella said, 'I feel dreadfully rude. I should have bid farewell.'

'Oh, I wouldn't worry.' Lynden waved her hand for emphasis. 'She'll be back in a week to see Venn, I guarantee it. She really comes to see our brother, or rather, to be seen by him.'

'*It pays to be seen by the important people, Lynnie. You can't leave these things to chance,*' Jonas mimicked.

'Stop!' Lynden laughed. 'She means well, I suppose. And she passed on her apologies to you, Ella dearest. But she couldn't possibly impose.'

'In other words, she was disappointed not to find the dryhten of the house in residence,' Jonas said. 'And there's nothing a dryhten's younger brother can do for her...'

The pair continued to mock their poorer cousin over dinner.

As soon as the servants cleared their dishes, Lynden stood to leave. 'You'll have to excuse me this evening. I have letters to write,' she said.

Ella was about to follow when Jonas caught her arm. 'As you saw, I've not touched a drop of wine, nor mead, nor ale.' He raised a brow, his lips teasing.

Ella hesitated.

His fingers stroked her arm and a lightning thrill travelled through her, goose-pimpling her flesh. *That molten smile...* She took his arm and let him lead her outside.

Once they were away from the main keep, he said, 'You seem a little out of sorts.' An arch sneer. 'You can't tell me Moyra's absence irks you that much. Or is it the sour aftertaste of her attempt at matchmaking dampening your spirits?'

'Not at all, I assure you.'

'Then what? El, you've been avoiding me for weeks... And again last night.'

She wanted to deny it, but he was right.

'If this is about Vera—'

'It's not,' she blurted, though it was a lie. Something was off. Jonas wasn't himself. Pressure was building behind her eyes again, that pounding warning her... Of what? He was waiting for her to say something. She could hardly tell him the god was trying to warn her that something was awry, but she had to tell him something. Something true. 'Jonas, I can't let you bed me, and I'm not sure I can trust myself when I'm with you.'

A bitter smirk. 'Oh, of course. We can't have you spoiled now, can we? Not when we must return you to your brother, your oh-so-caring brother, who must look after his precious little sister. So precious that no one can touch her. Someone should tell miserable Moyra she's wasting her time trying to set you up with anyone.'

'What are you insinuating?'

'Don't you think it's strange that Gohran threw your sisters to the wolves, but protected you?'

Ella trembled, flames pirouetting in her mind's eye. *If people suspected the truth about her...*

Jonas continued. 'Think about it. After birthing Sheevan's bastard, Jaydyn is comfortably housed at Erldan. Gohran couldn't care less for her precious honour. And what about Raeyn? Gohran knows how Venn feels about you. By every god and goddess, the entire kingdom can see the way he makes those big bovine eyes at you. Do you think it would matter strategically which sister Venn married? So why is Gohran so insistent on making him choose Raeyn?'

Ella stepped back, but Jonas grabbed her wrists.

'El, look at me.' She did, but tears welled. 'Haven't you ever wondered why the gloriously handsome king with everything in the world to offer still won't take a wife? I can assure you the rest of the Cursed kingdom has.'

She shook her head back and forth. It couldn't be true. Yet hadn't Vera and even Moyra implied the same thing?

He let go of her wrists and paced before her. 'You can't see it, can you? Venn would marry you, *spoiled* or otherwise. He wouldn't throw a copper over us, so long as he gets you in the end. His loyalty to your brother is the only thing that keeps him by Raeyn's side. He's still hoping he can earn your brother's esteem and ask for your hand instead of Raeyn's. Do you know what the real shame of that is? He's just as blind as you. Gohran will never let you marry. He wants you chaste, untouched. Because if he can't have you, no one will.'

If what Jonas was suggesting was true… Is that what people believed? Her stomach lurched. 'This kingdom is fetid with ugly, misguided rumours,' she threw back. 'People should tend to their own fields, instead of tilling the soil of others.'

He turned to face her, arms crossed. 'Maybe so. But even if your maidenhead wasn't worth a copper to your brother, that doesn't change the fact that I'll never have you. This isn't about bedding you. I could have any other woman, if that's all I wanted. It's that you don't love me. I thought maybe, before last night, but when we finally had a moment alone together, you asked about *him*. How did you imagine I'd be, every day, watching you pine after my brother, boring old perfect Venn? You don't think I know that you'd rather be with him when you're with me?'

'No, Jonas, it's not like that…' She thought it had been, but now, seeing Jonas like this… There was a hardness in his jaw, behind his eyes, like stones. First the strangeness in Venn, and now Jonas. 'Why are you being like this? Has something happened? Has someone said something?' She reached out for him, but he shrugged away.

'You'll know soon enough.'

'Please—I can't bear seeing you like this.' He shook his head, turning back to face her, and she felt his pain as though it was her own, a curse of her magic that she still couldn't suppress.

Jonas swallowed. Evenly, he said, 'Venn has gone to deliver an ultimatum to your brother. Either Gohran allows him to marry you, or he will sever all ties between our cities. It's been damaging enough for Nedran to be associated with a witch queen's family. But it's a risk worth taking for the prize that you are. Gohran wasn't asking you to return with Venn to visit. He wants you to go home. And when Venn returns without Gohran's permission, he will send you packing.'

Ella's breath caught. *How had she not realised?* She'd been so wrapped up in her machinations, she'd missed what was right under her nose.

She realised Jonas was still speaking. 'I had wanted us to spend our last nights together as we haven't before. Let us do what we want for once. But you ran from me as soon as Venn was out of sight. By the goddess, you might admit it's not your respect for him that keeps us apart. It's that you don't love me. Not the way you love him. And this is our last night together, El. Ever.'

Ella stared at the scar near Jonas's eye and watched it twitch to avoid seeing the pleading in his gaze. 'You know we can't.' She held up her hands to stop him from interrupting. 'What chance will I have at making a decent match if you leave me with child? I'll not ruin myself like Jaydyn.'

'We'll be careful,' he insisted. He watched her, arms folded over his chest.

The pounding pressure was still there, but if Jonas was right and this was their last night together... She drew just enough power to shove the feeling aside.

Reaching up, Ella tugged at his wrists and peeled them away. She ran her palms along his chest to twine around his neck and drew his mouth to hers. Pent-up longing pulsed through her—and through him. 'I do care for you, Jonas—deeply. I've relished these past moons. You make me laugh, make me feel wanted. You've shown me a kind of passion I never knew existed. Please, don't bed me. Just...'

He silenced her with his lips, slipping his arms around her. She met his kisses, gentle, then insistent as he pressed her to the grass. She could sense him memorising the rise and fall of her body against his, yielding and unyielding as she memorised him. He could taste her mouth as she tasted his, the smell of her hair, the smell of him. He drew her against him, and she felt every inch of his need for her, for what they were doing. Her need rose to meet his. He did not enter her, but touched and explored, their bodies finding and fuelling one another. Waves of pleasure pulsed through her, over and again. Just when she thought she couldn't take any more, he pulled her to rest across his chest, his cheeks wet with tears.

# FORTY-THREE

When Erldan's royal carriage pulled up at Nedran's gates, the sun was just cresting the horizon. A footman swung the door open with a flourish and Gohran stepped out, closely followed by Venn.

Gohran tossed his cloak over one shoulder, and Venn saw the king's eyes narrow as he surveyed the city that would soon be bound to his.

Venn signalled to Mykan to prepare for their guest. 'Fetch Lord Jonas, will you? He should be here to greet the king.'

When the steward hesitated, casting a nervous glance in Gohran's direction, Venn hung back to put some distance between himself and the king. 'What is it?' he whispered.

'My lord, I've not seen your brother since supper last night.'

Venn groaned. 'Is Lady Lynden about?'

'I'll find her right away, my lord.' Mykan scurried towards the main keep.

By the time they reached the great hall, Lynden was waiting for them. Once the formalities were out of the way, Gohran asked after Ella.

'I've not seen her since last night, Your Highness. She isn't in her room. I presumed she was getting some air before breakfast...' Lynden's voice trailed off as she watched the king's handsome face grow frighteningly pale.

'She often liked to ride in the mornings, Your Highness,' Venn said. 'She won't have gone out alone. Jonas is probably with her.'

'Then they've gone on foot. I already checked the stables, and all the horses are there.' Lynden said.

A crimson flush made its way up the king's neck, setting his cheeks alight. Venn looked over at his sister and saw her biting her lip anxiously. His stomach sank. He headed towards the water garden, half expecting to find the pair standing there, mocking him, but the courtyard was blessedly empty. Venn let his breath out in a long puff.

'Lyn, where else do they usually go walking?'

'Along the western meadow—but let me go.'

Before they could stop him, Gohran was striding toward the field.

'Lyn, wait here in case they come back,' Venn commanded as he trailed after the king.

He was only a few steps behind Gohran when they reached the couple, still curled up together in the grass, fast asleep.

'**E**lla!' Gohran barked.

Ella jerked awake and sat up. A huge black silhouette towered over her like a stone pillar, backlit by a halo of morning sun. To the side hovered another shadow—Venn. By every god and demon, she knew how this must look. She edged away from Jonas, one hand shielding her eyes. Beside her, Jonas stirred.

'So, Venn, do you still want her?' Gohran's words like lead.

Through the shadows, Ella could just make out Venn's features, the twist of his mouth, the slump of his eyes. Not that she needed to see it. She felt that hurt, sharp and keen, as though she had ripped his heart from his chest, chewed it up, spat it out and trod upon it.

She looked at Jonas, propped on one elbow, his other arm raised to block out Elnora's glare. With a sinking feeling, Ella saw his mouth twist into a bitter smirk. In fact, he looked as though he were about to throw his head back with sardonic laughter.

'Ella, get your things.' Gohran's tone was like ice.

'Please, it's not what you think, I swear.'

Venn turned to his brother. 'Jonas?'

Eyes cold, mouth tight, Jonas shrugged. 'Would it matter what I said at this point? Has it ever mattered?'

Venn's voice cracked. 'Ella, Gohran had given us permission to marry.'

'*Had*, yes. But you see now that Raeyn is the more suitable choice.' Gohran almost sounded pleased. 'I'll not tell you again, Ella. Straighten yourself up. You're coming back home with me. Now!' He turned to Venn. 'Have my sister's belongings brought to the carriage immediately. I never should have left her here so long unsupervised.'

How could she have been such a fool? Jonas had said Venn didn't care, but he was wrong. So wrong. Worst of all, she couldn't even blame him. It had been her choice.

# PART THREE: CASTIGATION

## THE KINGDOM OF ERLDAN, YCELT

**Year: 796 A.S.**

# FORTY-FOUR

Upstairs in her old tower room at Erldan, Ella picked at her supper. The stone walls loomed around her like a prison. What she would give to turn back the hours, to take that wounded look away from Venn, to have Gohran see her as he had before, untainted. And if she ever saw Jonas again, she would scourge his very soul.

Her mind replayed the same events. She recalled the pressure of a storm building, a static charge thundering through her limbs. The god had tried to warn her, as it had about her mother, and she had ignored Him. Now she had lost Venn and Jonas while destroying the last of her brother's esteem.

Why hadn't she trusted her instincts, her abilities? She had wanted to quash her magic, ignore it. Even when it kept spilling out, overflowing, she had refused to make use of it. As if she could *will* herself to be other than she was. Her mother's magic had cost Prya her life. Ella would not let that happen to her. Nor would she continue to pretend. Her magic might be a curse, but by every god and demon, she would make of it what she could. To think she might have spied upon Venn, upon her brother, persuaded them to secure her future, or meditated on what the gods had in store. Made a different choice.

She closed her eyes and opened her mind, reaching for the far stretches of her perception. *Nothing.* Now when she wanted to know what waited for her, the god chose silence. Amber's voice echoed in her memory. *It's forbidden to search for omens not freely revealed.* Yet, what was to stop her? Who would ever know? Then she heard her mother's voice. *You must use everything Amber taught you to protect yourself. Use every tool at your disposal—regardless of the cost. Promise me.*

Through a blur of hot tears, Ella stared at the dust-coated floor. She swiped the moisture from her cheeks and crouched to roll back her rug. Dust swirled and resettled. She picked up a hunk of old charcoal from the hearth and took a deep breath. *Forbidden.* Again, she saw Venn's wounded eyes and her brother's reproach. What more had she to lose?

Ella drew the charcoal across the floor, tracing the sigils Amber had shown her upon the exposed boards. With a sure hand, she mapped out the grey arcs and peaks, her memory picture-perfect. Once complete, she stood back, hands on hips, a brazen smirk upon her lips. There was no going back now.

She lit some incense and waited until the room filled with smoke, growing more daring with each breath. She glanced at the unbarred door, then back at her drawing. With a toss of her head, she lay down in the centre of the markings and closed her eyes. Through each inhale, she imagined drawing the tension from her body, allowing each exhale to relax her muscles and steady her mind. After a few moments, she felt a shift and pull as the currents of space and time tugged her mind this way and that. With an even breath, she cast her focus outwards.

For a long time, nothing happened. Then, finally, an image emerged in her mind's eye. Blurry at first, the edges soon sharpened as it came into focus. Before her, she saw Gohran, his face hovering above hers. For a moment, she thought he was there in the room with her. Her arms shot forward to push him away, trying to squirm out from under him. Instead of connecting with flesh, her palms passed straight through. She lay back, exhaling, studying Gohran's face. His flushed features appeared contorted in a way Ella had never seen. When she looked more closely, she saw his puffed and swollen eyes, his wet cheeks. *Why?* she thought into the void. An anxious, agonising wait, met by silence.

The image in her mind muddied like liquid, then stilled, and the scene changed. Now she saw Venn, felt his arms circle around her. Head tilted upward, Ella sensed his lips pressing against hers, warmer than her kisses with Jonas had been, yet she felt hollow. Empty. No—guilty!

Again, her vision distorted before resolving. This time she saw two sweaty figures, bare flesh, naked limbs, moving rhythmically. Jonas, entwined with some woman she didn't recognise. Ella's heart lurched.

Her body grew heavy, the floor frosty beneath her, like a nagging hunger tugging at her mind. Part of her wanted to stay, to uncover still more. Laughter rang out—not hers—an eerie taunt, daring her to follow. Terror shot through her. She needed to return to consciousness now!

She sat up, swiping at the air. The room appeared solid before her. She took in her wine-coloured bedclothes, the cracks between the stones of her hearth, and the stale odour of cold ash. Shivering, she grabbed her blanket and hugged it around her shoulders, then unrolled her carpet and collapsed atop it. For a long time, she lay trembling. Every muscle burned as if she'd just run for miles.

Her visions echoed in her mind, but she could make no sense of them. If this was a preview of her future, it was useless to her!

Chill bored into her bones. She wrapped her blanket around tighter and surrendered her consciousness to the dark of exhausted sleep, with the memory of Venn's lips still upon hers.

Ella woke the next morning to a fist pounding on her door. 'Princess Ella! Wake up, Princess!' It was Lyrra.

Rubbing her eyes, Ella pulled back her blanket. Every limb felt like it had been dipped in lead. 'I'm coming. You don't have to shout.' Ella hefted herself up and stumbled to open the door.

Lyrra looked her up and down. 'What have you done to your dress?' Lyrra tugged at Ella's skirt, smoothing the wrinkles. 'Here, let me fix up your hair, but then we must go. We're already late.'

Ella fly-swatted Lyrra's hands away. 'Late for what?'

'The daily worship.'

'Daily?' Too weary to protest, Ella allowed Lyrra to tidy her up and usher her towards the temple in the centre of town.

She and Lyrra weren't the only ones hurrying to make the service. Feet scurried along the streets, peasants in proper shirts and pinafores, a few in full dresses. Some of them nodded her way in recognition before hastening on. As they passed weathered shop fronts with patched roofs, picking their footing to avoid potholes and cracks, Ella wondered if Erldan had always looked so shabby. Compared with vibrant, modern Nedran, it seemed like a poorly mended shirt.

In stark contrast, the once dreary chapel was now brim-full of light and worshippers both. The temple must have undergone a complete refurbishment—and not just with a coat of whitewash, but with freshly painted frescos and gold-leaf mosaics. The roof was no longer a mess of thatch, but sealed with elegant ceramic tiles. Even the windows seemed larger than Ella remembered, fitted with proper stained glass, fiery colours from the morning light playing over the congregation.

By the time they arrived, the service was already underway. They squeezed through the crowd to get to their positions in the front row. Gohran glanced their way, his mouth a grim line, then turned his attention back to Davith, the priest. Dotted here and there, Ella counted a handful of well-groomed men who didn't quite blend in with the general mill of bodies. Her stomach clenched. *Henads.*

Most of the service comprised the usual feast day chants and prayers, which Ella knew, along with familiar hymns. She drifted into her thoughts, not realising she was weeping until she put her hand to her cheeks to find them wet.

'Vigilance,' Davith's words reverberated to the far corners of the room. 'Our Lady reigns triumphant over all other gods, yet heretics walk among us. Though She exiled the false god Xenon, He sends his followers to perpetuate the Curse.' Davith searched the faces of the crowd. 'And why are these heretics so dangerous? Because they use magic to tempt us, to manipulate. Because they can get inside our minds and force us to defy Elnora's will.' He touched his temples with both hands theatrically.

Ella clamped down on her thoughts, but weakly—she was so weary!

Davith peered into the crowd, catching and holding as many pairs of eyes as he could. 'Even those closest to you. Mothers, daughters, sisters, brothers, those we cherish—no one is immune to their influence. And what can you do? You can stop them. It is within your power. Choose to follow the path of the light. Be on your guard, ready to denounce.'

Heat writhed deep in Ella's core. She imagined growing talons to tear out Davith's throat. Gohran spun her way. She willed a veneer of calm, locking her feelings up tight. Gohran turned back to face the front. Thank every god her working the previous night had left her depleted, keeping her anger from spilling beyond her control.

Later, she would wonder at herself, that for the better part of a year, she had put aside her fury over the injustice done to her mother, taking strolls, shopping for dresses, and playing at seduction, while these monsters infiltrated and poisoned her home.

# Forty-Five

It had been some moons since Amber had spied upon Ella. Her time in Ycelt felt like another lifetime. She had watched Ella settle into Nedran and assumed she was tucked away, safe in that city. Then one summer evening she felt something pinch at her mind. Though Elnora's light had sunk beneath the horizon, the heat of the day lingered. She and Nykki were scrubbing dinner pots together, shoulder to shoulder over the sink, seeking comfort in one of the few forms of permitted touch.

Amber willed Nykki to be still so she could use the wash water's reflection to answer the call. Ella's image sharpened into focus. Ella was inside her old tower room, brushing out her hair in her mirror. Her face looked wan, eyelids puffed and swollen. What was she doing back at Erldan?

Ella's thoughts toppled over one another. Images of Erldan's temple flooded with light, bodies crammed in together, faceless stiff-postured men among them, the head priest gesturing before the altar.

Amber exhaled slowly. *Ella, it's Amber. I'm here,* she thought.

Ella's thoughts slammed shut, leaving Amber staring at the ceramic pots bobbing in the soapy water before her.

Ella had not meant to contact her. This was a panicked cry, not aimed at Amber or anyone.

*What is it?* Nykki queried, mind-to-mind.

*Ella is back at Erldan, and the kingdom is crawling with henads,* Amber thought back. The rest she slipped wordlessly into Nykki's mind, sharing the images she'd witnessed.

Nykki drew a breath and returned a soothing flow. Grateful, Amber did not dare meet Nykki's gaze as she reinforced the mental shield around them both.

Should she tell Breeyan, or would the High Priestess have her own means of watching over the kingdom? It occurred to Amber that with her sister gone, the High Priestess might be blind to the goings-on inside Erldan. Unless she had seen at least one person from Erldan in the flesh and could recognise the pattern of their mind or their physical form, there was no way to spy on them from afar.

She pictured Breeyan's pursed lips, the crinkles around her eyes and forehead deepening and hardening as her mind lashed out. If she admitted Ella had ended up back in harm's way at Erldan, she would remind the High Priestess that Amber was the one who had left her behind.

Nykki's mind caressed hers.

What could the High Priestess do about it, anyway? It's not like she could send Amber or anyone else back to fetch Ella. Not while henads crawled the kingdom like flies upon a carcass.

If only Ella wouldn't shut her out, Amber could talk to her and convince her to plan her escape.

*She's not ready, my love, and no one can change that. Not the god, not anyone.*

She squeezed Nykki's hand beneath the wash water with a sigh. Nykki was right. Amber could only watch and wait to see how the fates unfolded.

The summer sun was beating down upon their backs. Venn's sweat-soaked shirt clung and chafed beneath his leather vest. He wiped the moisture from his forehead with his sleeve and swung his sword back and forth in a few practice strokes. His stance was wide and as elegant as a troupe dancer. He fronted his opponent, stocky, sun-kissed Harn. Facing away, he swiped at the air before turning a semi-circle and striking his man's outstretched blade so hard the sword flew from his hands and thudded on the coarse brown grass a few feet away.

'My lord!' Harn yelped, leaping back.

Venn retrieved the sword. 'My apologies.' Blade trailing along the ground, he handed the sword back hilt first. At that moment, he didn't trust himself with steel in his hand.

Gohran had written almost immediately after returning to Erldan with his sister to indicate he was still open to negotiations and declared that, while disappointed in his friend, he did not hold the actions of one brother against the other. He also hinted at a full reconciliation, which could mean he was prepared to consider a betrothal for one of his sisters, even now. What Gohran didn't make clear was which one. Worse, Venn didn't know which he wanted it to be. The king also implied they would need to renegotiate the terms of any such arrangement. A blood price, Venn thought, for Ella's dishonour.

Venn dried his palms on his trousers and called out to his men. 'Shuffle your positions!' Heightened tensions between Nedran and Erldan put Nedran in a precarious position. His men had best get used to making order out of chaos.

The riders jostled into formation. There was a notable gap where Jonas should have stood. Venn swore under his breath.

Earlier, in the wake of Gohran and Ella's exodus, Jonas had pursued his brother to the great hall. 'If you'll just let me, I can explain...'

Venn confronted his brother square-on, palms raised. 'What could you possibly say that would make this better, Jonas? Can you erase the memory of the two of you together from my mind? Can you erase it from the mind of the king?' Venn kicked a nearby chair, which toppled over, picked up another and threw it against a wall. The chair's legs splintered with a loud crack.

Jonas ran his fingers through his hair, letting out a slow breath, then strode toward the door, head shaking.

Stone-faced, Venn watched his brother depart.

Later that evening, Lynden found him. With hands on hips, she shook her head. 'I wish you two would stop behaving like a pair of rams rutting over a ewe in season. I've lost a friend over this too, you know.'

Venn grunted. 'It could have cost us all much more.'

'You know, Jonas packed his belongings when he left,' Lynden said.

'Good riddance!'

Lynden softened her stance and her voice, resting her hand on her brother's shoulder. 'Venn, you don't know what really happened. Ella felt for you deeply. She confessed as much to me herself.'

'That may be the case, Lyn, but I judge a person by their actions.'

Venn pulled himself away from his reverie and took his attention back to his men and paced, examining their form. 'Baillee, Rhyder, fall into line. Maynard, you take the rear.' Venn stomped through a gap in the formation. 'Not like that.' He slapped his men's laxly held weapons aside. 'How is this slop supposed to keep our enemies out? Tighten up.' Some more jostling until the men stood alert and ready to storm. Venn pictured his brother's face. Fist raised, he yelled, 'Charge!'

Silken and soft, Leesa's hair smelled sweetly of jasmine. *Like Ella's.* Jonas wrapped his arm around the gentle curve of her waist, which had grown a little thicker since their last tryst. Grall had gone to Herron on business, leaving The Riverside Tavern in his wife's hands. It was the first time Jonas and Leesa had spent an entire night together.

With Ella gone, Jonas reverted to his old ways to escape his brother's disapproval, meandering east to see Leesa in Rassit before veering back northwards to Lichen. It didn't matter what he did. It was never good enough for Venn. Why bother trying to be anything other than what his flawless brother assumed him to be? A simple philanderer. He didn't regret pursuing Ella, or any moment they had spent together. She flooded his senses every waking and sleeping moment. He regretted bringing her dishonour, however. It wasn't fair to punish women for acting on their natural desires. He cursed Gohran and Venn both for casting judgement upon her, for wanting to control her. In his ideal world, men and women would be free to engage wherever their hearts and bodies took them.

Leesa was a case in point. Another woman traded off at the whim of men. Each time they took their pleasure together, Leesa was asserting her defiance, claiming her body for her own.

Leesa stirred. She rolled over to face him. He kissed her forehead.

'I should let you get to work,' he said, climbing out of bed to dress.

With the covers pulled back, he admired her loveliness. In the morning light, he noticed bluish-yellow shadows upon her limbs.

'Leese, what happened?' he motioned to her bruises.

She looked down. 'I had to shift all those barrels of ale that came in the other day. You know how clumsy I can be,' she added.

Jonas narrowed his eyes. 'I can't say I've ever noticed that about you.'

'That's because you only see the best in people,' she said, with a dismissive wave, pulling the covers back over herself.

He leaned down to kiss her. 'I see people exactly as they are.'

She placed a finger across his lips. 'It's probably best if you don't come back for a while.'

He pulled back.

'It's Grall. He knows I've been seeing someone.'

'Leese—'

'He doesn't know who.'

'Curse him to every hell and back!'

She silenced him with a kiss, and Jonas tasted the salt of tears.

'Please. Just go.'

He did, but not before he caught her running her hand across her belly.

# Forty-Six

Alone in her tower room, Ella threw herself back into her studies, drilling the skills Amber taught her, which she had allowed to wither over the past year at Nedran.

She tried to avoid her brother as much as possible, which was easy enough when nearly every time she entered a room, he stood to leave. When forced together, he wore a pained expression, almost as though he couldn't stand to look at her. She recoiled. Did she disgust him that much?

Whenever she sat with her sisters in the women's quarters, she made polite, meaningless conversation as they worked on the never-ending task of stitching the wretched shirts and smocks that were owed to each person in Erldan's service. She kept waiting for Raeyn's hurt at her betrayal to land, but she soon realised Gohran hadn't told her sisters anything about the planned betrothal. All they knew was Ella had returned home in disgrace after a tryst with Venn's younger brother. Still, she felt guilty whenever she saw Raeyn and awkward when she saw Jaydyn. In the end, her sisters' lives epitomised the despair and bitterness of dreams lost, promises broken, and possibilities stolen.

One afternoon Jaydyn arrived in the women's hall after Ella, baby Serrah at her breast. Jaydyn looked pale, her hair thinner than Ella remembered. Both her face and baby Serrah's were blotchy with blemishes. Milk pimples, Jaydyn called them. 'They'll be gone when Serrah's weaned,' she said. 'Or so the midwife tells me.'

'Jay, why didn't Gohran hire a wetnurse?'

Jaydyn smirked. 'He says we can't spare the coin.'

Ella frowned. 'I know Erldan isn't a great kingdom, but we're hardly poor!'

'By the goddess, baby sister, they really didn't tell you anything, did they?' Jaydyn shook her head. 'Why do you think we're still picking away at these goddess-forsaken shirts?'

For the first time, Ella inspected the cloth she held. It wasn't new, but repurposed linen and mended silk that had been bleached and starched.

'Jay, please. Tell me what's been happening.'

With a sigh, Jaydyn shifted Serrah to her other breast. 'It began shortly after mother's trial when the priests arrived. They started showing up everywhere, urging folk to attend worship, which they were only too eager to do.' Jaydyn rolled her eyes. 'You should have seen how many people turned up to mother's trial, too, as pious as you please. No one wanted to find themselves beside our mother on that pyre. And when the priests passed their urn around, peasants piled money into it, money they didn't have to spare. Some gave up bovine, fertile ilaks, fowl and swine.'

A creeping sensation crossed Ella's flesh.

'Davith started accompanying Gohran in his official duties. He said it was just until they invested Gohran as king. But it didn't stop. Then, after Gohran's coronation, the raids began.'

'Raids?' Ella's stomach churned.

'You've seen the henads hanging around?' Ella nodded. 'They searched houses and hovels alike. Ella, they raided this house.'

Ella pictured the memories behind her sister's words. Henads thundering through the halls in the early hours of Elnora's light, forcing every member of the household out of bed, examining them one by one. Jaydyn trying to cover herself as they forced her to strip naked so they could look for marks of heresy. Henads firing questions, twisting responses, trying to trip them into saying they knew about mother, that she was a witch, that they were all witches like her.

'They wanted me to tell them Xenon was the father of my babe, that I'd bewitched Sheevan. It got so I didn't know my head from my feet.' Jaydyn placed Serrah so that her belly lay across her mother's chest. 'This went on for weeks. Finally, Gohran tired of it. He pleaded with Davith to make it stop. Davith agreed, but only after Gohran vouched for Erldan's ongoing piety—and her financial support. Worship is no longer a matter of faith here—it is law.'

It seemed Ella's world lurched and crumbled. 'I had no idea.'

'Of course not. Gohran wanted to protect his precious baby sister.'

The bitter crack in Jaydyn's voice reminded Ella of Jonas on that last night.

'The henads still hang around, just to remind Gohran of his promise. And as though that hadn't cost us enough, Sheevan's family severed ties with Erldan, so we've lost the income from Creywmm's taxes, too.'

Ella realised the severed ties must be why Vera could finally visit Nedran while she was still there. 'But what about Serrah? By every god, she is their granddaughter.'

'After mother's execution, Sheevan's family appealed to the priests to break the treaty between Creywmm and Erldan. A contract dissolved by priests is incontrovertible. With the betrothal broken, Serrah remains illegitimate and no responsibility of theirs.'

'Surely Creywmm needs Erldan's protection?'

'Creywmm still has ties to the king in Herron, and from what I hear, Herron's army is almost as large as ours. Gohran says they see being stained by heresy as a greater risk than losing a powerful ally.'

Herron was in a part of Ycelt that was strongly influenced by the priests. 'It all seems too much.'

Jaydyn didn't reply.

Ella looked down at her niece. She reached out a finger to touch Serrah's pink skin. Serrah gripped her finger in her tiny hand. Such an innocent life caught up in ruthless politicking. Ella shuddered, an omen-like sensation crawling down her spine. 'Can I hold her?'

'Of course. You'll need as much practice as you can get, and sooner rather than later.' Jaydyn passed Serrah to her sister.

'He didn't bed me, Jay.'

Jaydyn looked incredulous. 'Well, Gohran's convinced he did, so all I can say is you'll have all the misfortune with none of the benefits.'

Ella winced.

Serrah gurgled and nestled against her. Everything else melted away as Ella took in those cheeks like silk, that crown of soft fuzz atop her head, chubby fists flailing.

Raeyn entered and took her usual chair by the window. 'A letter just arrived from Nedran.' She studied Ella's expression. 'Gohran sent me away while he read it.'

'Tell me you at least tried to hear his reaction from outside the door?' Jaydyn wore a salacious grin.

'With Gohran wearing his murderous face?'

Ella was aware of her sisters' eyes on her, but she continued to fuss over her niece. That letter could contain almost anything. She didn't dare hope, and yet, in her vision, she had seen herself with Venn.

At supper, all three girls were eager for news from their brother. He sighed. 'You can stop fencing around the topic. All you are doing is reminding me how much each of you lacks in subtlety. Lord Venn wanted to offer his continued friendship and support. Satisfied?'

The girls fell silent.

Almost unconsciously, Ella tried to sense whether there was more to the letter. Her mind met a stone-like wall of resistance. She pulled back.

Straight after supper, Ella ran upstairs to her room and barred the door, for once leaving before Gohran could make his escape. Although mid-summer, the evening was chilly enough that the servants had laid her hearth. With a wave of her hand, Ella set it alight, flames catching and sparking. She knelt, hungry to see Venn again. Her skills were rusty, but with her desire strong behind the working, his image appeared almost instantly.

There he sat, drink in one hand, the other marking a place in a ledger. Ella noticed a livid bruise up the side of one cheek. He glanced up from his books, seeming to look straight at her. He wore the expression of a dog kicked by its master. She longed to reach out to him, to take back that kick.

Ella erased the vision and thought of Jonas. When his image came into focus, Ella didn't recognise his lavish surroundings. Sitting opposite was Vera of Lichen. Jonas brought a honey-coated almond to her lips, which curved into a welcoming *ooh*. Ella scrubbed at the air to banish the picture. She trembled, on the verge of tears.

She considered spying on Lynden next, but couldn't face seeing her friend. With an exhale, she extinguished the fire and crawled into bed.

Alone in his chamber, Gohran read and re-read Venn's letter. How had things come to this? Erldan's ledgers were stark, her coffers barren, yet Davith assured him Erldan grew rich with Elnora's souls.

Gohran knelt at the small altar he had assembled in the centre of the room—the only modification he had made to the chamber that once belonged to his father. Atop it sat a statue of Elnora, basking in the permanent rays of the sun, represented by the candlelight he kept burning day and night.

It seemed his days would forever involve mopping up the messes of the women in his life. It was mother's fault. As Davith often reminded him, Queen Prya had been lax with her daughters. She had not schooled them in Elnora's ways.

Raeyn lingered in the shadows of her sisters, while Jaydyn displayed such a lack of sense that what should have been justified, royal confidence came across as brash and foolish. He didn't blame Ella for what happened to her at Nedran. Venn's brother was a renowned philanderer, and she was naïve. No, he blamed Jonas, and more so himself. It was selfish to keep her away for so long. As he'd told his mother when she insisted on introducing Ella into society, Ella belonged at Aryon. He couldn't let her marry Venn. Not now. And it would be a miracle of the sun if Venn was still prepared to entertain a betrothal with Raeyn, given his family's tainted honour.

The memory of Ella's startled face, her crumpled dress and mussed-up hair, limbs wound around Venn's younger brother, slipped unbidden into his mind. A deep seething beneath his ribcage.

He picked up a waiting candle and held it over the dying flame of its fellow. It blazed and settled into a steady flicker. Gohran held it over the exposed skin of his opposite wrist and let the wax drip. He flinched as each drop landed. Sharp, then smooth. Soothing calm stilled his heart and quietened his mind. He placed the candle on the altar.

'Goddess, forgive me...'

# FORTY-SEVEN

Breeyan lounged before her private hearth, sipping fortified wine from one of Aryon's aged barrels—one of the few comforts her privilege afforded her. In her other hand, she stroked a small, threadbare blanket, yellowed with age. She brought it to her face and inhaled. Even after all these years, she fancied she could still smell him, the inimitable perfume of her flesh, her blood. Her belly and breasts ached to think of him, longed to feel his heartbeat against her chest.

Her sister may have stolen her lover and her rightful place as queen, but Breeyan had taken her revenge. She recalled the intoxicating thrill of luring King Rohan to her bed. And then the agony of handing over her newborn son, still smelling of her womb, her milk. The price she paid for defying Xenon's laws.

It was with sour gratification that Breeyan watched from afar as her sister raised her husband's bastard—a daily reminder of his betrayal. Had Breeyan's envy, her resentment, somehow manifested her sister's downfall, and at her son Gohran's hands? She downed her wine and poured another. A shudder. Prya's death was not a thing she would wish upon anyone.

Clutching Gohran's blanket, she let her focus drift as she stared into the dancing flames of her hearth. His outline came into focus, eyes closed, mouthing in silence. He must be praying. Breeyan widened the vision to take in his surroundings. He was in Rohan's old room. A sharp twinge in her abdomen.

She sensed power flowing from him and onto the altar. The candlelight flared and flickered, growing taller and fatter. Was this the outlet he had found for his magic, worshipping a god that loathed and feared his very existence?

He turned and looked aside. Someone had entered. She couldn't make out any details through the fire, yet she recognised the pattern of the intruder through Gohran's mind. Davith.

She had watched the head priest leech his way into Gohran's esteem upon Rohan's death. In his father's absence, Gohran had no patriarch, no one to mentor or nurture him, for the gods knew Prya could never be that for him. It stung to think of the years she could have raised him, guided him. Loved him.

A surge of warmth surrounded Gohran as Davith neared, which Breeyan perceived as a halo of blue light around them both. The priest rested a hand on Gohran's shoulder. Gohran peered up, adoring. Waves of reassuring light lulled and mollified.

She sensed in him a desperate thirst for Davith's approval. Had she created that need in him when she handed him over to the prying arms of her younger sister, who could never love him as a mother should?

Another pour. The decanter was almost empty.

The flames of her fire dimmed. She struggled to make out what they were saying, their voices muffled. Something about Ella being back at Erldan. When had that happened?

She waved her hand and blinked to clear her vision. Wine had spilled on the blanket, now wet with her tears.

She took a moment to compose herself, stowed the blanket beneath her robe, and summoned Amber.

After some minutes, Amber arrived, sleepy-eyed.

'Your Holiness?' A curtsy.

She didn't offer the novice a seat.

'Ella is back at Erldan. How?'

'I—I don't know...'

'You knew she was back.'

Amber remained silent while Breeyan ravaged her thoughts. Amber winced, but Breeyan ignored her discomfort and pushed on, viewing Ella's fears as seen through Amber's eyes.

Breeyan scowled. 'The king must honour the treaty and send her here.' *But we may need to remind him of his duty.* She slipped the thought directly into Amber's mind. 'Leave it with me,' she said aloud.

She dismissed Amber with a wave. She needed time to meditate on this.

# Forty-Eight

A full two cycles of the moon had passed since Ella's return, and she was still being confronted by all that had changed while she was away. The outline of her life looked much as it had before her sojourn at Nedran, but all the details had changed. Each morning, she accompanied her sisters to the temple under duress. Gohran often left ahead of them to confer with Davith before the service. Then they would return to breakfast, and she would shuffle to the women's quarters with her sisters until the noon tea. The afternoons afforded her some time to practise her skills, though her sisters often requested she stay to help them work through the mound of sewing, with fewer serving women to assist.

Then, on a morning when the leaves were turning burnt umber, as Ella ascended the steps of the temple alongside her sisters, she heard a commotion on the street behind her. Through the bustling crowd came a sound like the squalling of a tortured cat. She peered through the onlookers, and saw the crowd part to let that someone through—a shabbily dressed girl, heavy with child, hair hanging loose about her shoulders. Two puffed-up fellows gripped her arms. Ella recognised them as henads. The girl continued wailing, kicking the air as they dragged her along the street.

'That's Shiana, the miller's lass,' Ella heard a woman whisper nearby.

'Who's the father?' said her companion.

'Leon, one of the king's riders, though a few of the other lads claim they've taken a tumble with her, too.'

The henads carried Shiana inside the temple and restrained her while the surrounding pews filled with worshippers, Ella and her sisters among them. Shiana writhed and screamed. Davith faced her square-on and grasped her jaw so that she couldn't look away. She kicked at him until one of the henads grabbed her legs.

'Do you understand the charge made against you?'

Shiana whimpered.

Davith stepped back, turned towards the now silent crowd, and boomed, 'Let the accuser come forward.'

There was a shuffle in the far corner of the room, which rippled with hushed whispers before someone shoved a youthful rider forward. Ella didn't recognise him.

'Come here, Child of the Sun,' Davith beckoned.

The lad trembled. Tall but not yet filled out, he was handsome, with dark hair and eyes and ruddy skin. His comrades nudged him forward, and he shuffled towards the altar. He stared down at his feet, refusing to meet anyone's gaze. When he neared Shiana, she renewed her efforts to break free and hurled a gob of spit his way. He jerked aside, and it spattered on the ground. One of the henads slapped her. Once, twice, thrice. She stilled.

'Leon, loyal servant of Elnora, you have accused this woman of heresy and witchcraft. Do you bear witness to this charge?'

Leon glanced up at Shiana, then back at the floor, nodding. His shoulders shook, mouth quivering.

Ella's nails dug into her palms. Her jaw ached, teeth grinding. She sensed Gohran watching her and bound her emotions up.

Davith addressed Shiana. 'Your accuser has spoken. I have no choice but to arrest you, Shiana, for using witchcraft as a weapon of seduction. Your hearing is set for first light tomorrow.' With a wave of his hand, the matter was closed.

Shiana's entire body sagged, and her captors escorted her limp body out to the holding cell. Behind them, the congregation erupted in a buzz of nervous whispers.

Ella felt the entire temple was closing in around her. Her throat was dry, her chest tight. She couldn't get enough air. She sat, forcing her heart to still, drawing deep belly breaths.

Half-heard murmurs among the crowd. 'Her first one…', 'Poor lass. Must remind her of her mother…'

A hand rested upon her shoulder. Gohran's. A comforting squeeze, and with it, the stroke of a sympathetic mind, quickly withdrawn. Turning his back, he stepped forward to assist Davith in officiating the service.

As soon as the service was over, Ella hurried back to the main keep. After breakfast, she excused herself and slipped back outside. The air was cold and the sky grey. She hugged her arms across her chest and trudged towards the barracks where a group of riders were betting on tiles. When she entered, they looked up, nudging one another, appraising. Did they not realise who she was?

She straightened to her full height, head raised, standing as her mother had once stood. 'I wish to speak with Leon of the Fox Clan.'

Two men wearing sly grins elbowed each other.

One of them sniggered. 'I wager you do.'

Ella spun and faced him with all the hauteur she could muster. 'Is this the proper way to address royalty?' She held his gaze, unblinking, unflinching, until he squirmed and shifted, and finally looked away, dropping to one knee.

'He's out back, *Your Highness*.' The rider nodded toward the stables.

Ella found Leon huddled on the floor, hiding his face in his hands, shoulders shaking. 'Leon?'

Startled, he looked up, eyes red, cheeks swollen. Up close he appeared even younger than Ella had first estimated, his acne-pocked skin pink and inflamed from weeping. Ella almost pitied him. 'Leon, I know you're afraid.' She crouched beside him. 'You don't want to be a father. Not now. And that is understandable. But can you knowingly put an innocent girl—and your unborn child—to death?'

He shook his head, eyes cast downward. 'She—she bewitched me...' He sounded like a petulant child.

'You don't need to be bewitched to want to bed someone against your better judgement, Leon.'

'I swear it!'

'Do you know what they do to heretics?' Her voice was still soft.

He wiped his nose upon his sleeve.

Her tone grew bitter. 'They burn them.' She paused, waiting for her words to land. 'While they are still alive.'

He shook his head, mouthing, *'No'*.

'Yes, Leon. They tie them up and let the fire eat their flesh. They feel every flame, every inch of their bodies being tortured. And then their ashes are tossed away. Shiana won't receive a proper burial with the gods' blessing. She will be condemned for eternity.'

He covered his face with his hands. 'Stop it! Stop! She used me... She lied...'

*To get away from her father.* The thought slipped into her mind. Ella pictured it then, Shiana cowering from her father's red and bloated face as he screamed in hers, spittle flying. His arm raised, knuckles white, gripping a ladle above her, ready to strike again.

Leon's voice was plaintive. 'The Cleansing will save her soul. She will be reborn, clean.'

'No, Leon...' *You know that's not true*, she thought, not daring to speak such heresy aloud, yet hoping it would reach him.

He shook his head, back and forth. 'I already tried to talk to the head priest, I swear! His Holiness said the henads must investigate, anyway. He said if she's innocent, they'll see that...'

Ella rested her hands upon Leon's, peeling them away from his face. She caught his gaze and held it. His mind lay open to her. Part of him believed Shiana bewitched him, couldn't understand how else he had found himself fenced in. Mixed up with his guilt were his wounded pride, and buried deep, the pain of a torn heart, for he had truly loved her. Ella withdrew her mind and left him alone with his grief.

That evening, Ella sought Gohran, who, as usual, had locked himself away in his private study.

As she approached, a page stepped in front of the door. 'His Royal Highness does not wish to be disturbed.'

Cursed if she would cower and grovel like one of Gohran's subjects! 'This cannot wait.' Ella shoved the page aside and pushed open the door.

Gohran looked up. 'Ella! You shouldn't be here. I've much to tend to.'

The page bustled in behind her. 'My apologies, Your Highness, the princess, she—'

Gohran held up his palm. 'It's fine, Ferros. Leave us.' The page bowed. 'Close the door behind you.'

'Your Highness.' Another bow.

Ella plonked herself down on the chair opposite and met her brother's gaze straight on.

Gohran waited until the door latched shut. He lowered his hand and stood to pace the room. 'If you have come about the young witch, you are wasting your time, Ella. I haven't that sort of influence over the priests.'

'Davith listens to you.'

'I didn't accuse the girl, so it's none of my affair.'

Ella stood and stepped towards her brother. 'Leon has already tried to recant, but Davith told him the henads must investigate. Even if Davith won't listen to you, the riders will. They are your men. Tell them there is no shame in confessing the truth. If you promise to make provision for Shiana, to give her a place in the household, they have no reason to lie. We could use another pair of hands to get these wretched shirts sewn, and she will be too grateful to have any qualms about the terms of her keep.'

Gohran watched his sister, a strange expression playing over his face. Ella couldn't tell if it was resentment or admiration. After a moment, he looked away. 'And how would it seem if I gave a place in my very own retinue to a girl accused of heresy?'

Ella snapped. 'By the time you give her a position, Shiana's charge will be proved false.' Soft and imploring, 'Please, Gon, you know as well as I do there isn't a magical bone in that girl's body.'

That strange expression was there again.

Gohran sighed. 'As you wish. I'll let word get out that I'll make provision for the girl. But Ella, that is all I can do. The rest is in the hands of the priests and the goddess.'

# FORTY-NINE

That night, Ella's nightmares were worse than ever. Wherever she turned, she had to wade through smoke and ash. She wandered the cindered streets where stone buildings bore the black stains of fire. She kept her eyes straight ahead, refusing to look too closely, knowing if she did, she would see those remnants weren't inanimate rock and timber, but charred corpses of man and animal alike. In the distance, an infant wailed, lost, afraid, alone. *Make it stop! Why couldn't she wake?*

She forced her eyes open and sat up. Chill air struck her exposed skin. The wailing continued. It wasn't from her dream. It was coming from inside the keep. *Serrah?*

Ella pushed back her bedclothes and made her way over to the dresser. No washbasin. Where was Lyrra? She picked up her hand mirror and looked at her reflection. Over her shoulder hovered a charred and sunken face, flesh melted, mouthing silently. She squealed and turned, dropping the mirror. Nothing there. Glass hit the floor and shattered.

Serrah's sobs grew louder. Ella knelt to scoop up the glass, gingerly collecting the larger pieces in her cupped palm.

Footfalls clambered up the stairs, and a chambermaid pushed open her door. 'Here, Your Highness, let me clear that.' The maid brushed the fragments to one side.

When she crouched to roll up Ella's rug, Ella grasped her shoulders. 'Leave it! Go see to my sister and niece. Can you not hear Serrah wailing?'

'Of course, Your Highness. My apologies.' The maid curtsied and scurried back out.

Ella closed and bolted the door behind her. She turned and let out her breath, then hurried back to the rug and stooped to roll it back. The reckless sigils she had drawn beneath taunted her. She scrubbed at the charcoal, using spit upon a corner of her underskirt to shift the more stubborn lines until the floor was bare and clean.

Sweat pricked at her armpits and across her forehead. Lyrra still hadn't arrived with her wash water. With a frown, she hefted the rug back into place, swept up the last of the broken glass, and headed out towards the communal washroom.

Out in the corridor, she bumped into Raeyn. 'Where have you been? Gohran's furious,' she said.

'Where's Lyrra? What's going on?'

'The trial has started. Lyrra's had to head home.'

'What do you mean?'

'I thought you knew. Shiana is Lyrra's cousin.'

It took a moment for Raeyn's words to sink in. The trial was going ahead. Gohran may not have had the chance to intervene. All at once, her dream made sense.

'Ella? Ella, are you even listening?'

'Yes, yes, of course. My apologies. I hadn't realised that. Poor Lyrra.'

'Don't waste your pity. It won't change anything.' Raeyn's face scrunched and her eyes welled with tears.

Ella felt Raeyn's bitterness and resignation, as if it were her own. Ella wanted to sink into the darkest pit of the last hell. Her siblings hadn't abandoned her this past year. They had been fending off henads and raids and interrogations. And what had she been doing? Frittering away her time in faraway Nedran feeling pity for herself. She swallowed the charcoal lump in her throat and followed Raeyn to the temple.

They struggled to push their way through the crowd to get inside. The acrid odour of anxious sweat, unwashed hair, and clothing surrounded them. Ella tried not to gag. She peered around the backs of people's heads and in between their shoulders to spot Davith at the helm. Shiana stood shackled beside him, deathly pale, immobile and defeated. Three henads sat in a solemn row nearby, watching, waiting to pass judgement. Before them perched a stool where various witnesses testified, and further along sat a scribe, furiously recording every word.

Leon stared at the floor with shoulders slumped. His timid replies barely travelled beyond the first few rows, so the herald had to repeat his words to the spectators. Ella and Raeyn had missed the start of Leon's testimony, but it was clear he had come as close to recanting as he could. He told the court he was no longer sure of what had happened, that he could have been mistaken, that he was confused.

Davith's response boomed across the hall. 'Does not Our Lady of the Dark Sun tell us to be wary of the moon, for just as it tugs upon water, it can tug upon men's hearts and minds, causing them to sway against their right judgement. We see that very confusion in this child of the sun. Can we not also attribute what Leon of the Fox described to the work of evil? Was it not an unwanted and unperceived influence over him? And now that we have apprehended the culprit, can we not see Leon's senses have returned? The influence broken by the intervention of all that is righteous and holy.'

The henads nodded sagely to one another.

'Now I call forward those who witnessed the atrocity...'

One by one, Leon's comrades testified. Where before they were howling Shiana down as a witch, each claiming to have bedded her, no one was prepared to back that claim in the henads' court. Ella wondered if it was Gohran's intervention or fear that kept them quiet. Every time one of them mentioned how besotted Leon had been with the accused, Davith held this up as evidence of Shiana using magic.

'Does not Our Lady tell us that heretics will poison the minds of the weak-willed and unwary? For guile and wiles are the weapons of the unholy.'

*Hopeless*, Ella thought, as this back and forth continued. It didn't matter what a witness argued. Davith manipulated their words until they appeared to support the original accusation. If Leon had been willing, it was Shiana's influence. If he was unwilling, then the same reasoning applied.

Eventually, the interrogation dwindled to a halt. The henads withdrew to deliberate, and the temple erupted in a wave of whispers. The undercurrent of eagerness all around clawed at Ella. Was the horror of Shiana's fate nothing more than a spectacle? Ella sensed it wasn't so much that people wanted the trial to end in a conviction, but they would feel disappointed if it didn't. Like the expectation that builds when lightning courses the sky, without the clap of thunder that follows. Was this how it had been for her mother? Had she been aware of the morbid hunger in all those minds?

By the time the henads returned, that awe-filled anticipation had escalated, resembling a true blood thirst, which would have been as apparent to Shiana as it was to Ella.

The henads approached the king first, who sat in his usual place in the front row. He stood to greet them, and a stir went through the crowd. With an almost imperceptible bow, one of them passed the wax tablet to Gohran. Ella sensed the temperature in the room rising as Gohran read the ruling.

Her brother's mind touched hers, a moment of recognition and accord, though his expression was a mask of stone. *Her efforts to intervene had failed.* Ella's entire body sagged.

Gohran bowed deeply. 'Your Holiness,' he said slowly, evenly, handing the tablet to Davith. 'Before you pronounce judgement, let me ask you to consider the innocent and unborn soul that resides within the accused. I would beg you to consider exile as an alternative to Cleansing in this case, a sentence which considers its life as well as hers.'

Ella's breath caught.

Davith stroked his chin. 'Sentiment worthy of a great king.' A sage nod. 'While I see your reasoning, Your Highness, I fear it is flawed. The unborn monster carried by a heretic is as unclean as its mother. Conceived of witchcraft, we cannot even consider it to have a soul. Rather, it is an abomination. The only way we can save it is in the same way as its mother. The Cleansing of the soul by fire.' He turned towards the crowd. 'Thus, I pronounce my sentence. The flames of our goddess are all that can help them and us now.'

Shiana let out a piercing wail, matched by Leon, who leapt onto the dais, grasping for her.

Flames filled Ella's sight, hair smoking, skin melting, dirt thrown upon ashes, voices jeering, spit flying. Her entire body shook.

She breathed and focused on the wood beneath her feet, the touch of fabric against her skin. *It wasn't real. Just a vision.* She blinked, sensing Leon's thoughts upon her. Not her vision, but his, a projection of the horrors playing in his mind's eye.

She pushed and shoved her way through the milling bodies, abuzz with the thrill of anticipation. In a perverse empathy, Ella understood their panicked and sickened hearts pounding in mock excitement. But why were the priests so hungry for bloodshed? Did they keep the people afraid merely to maintain control? The thought rang true, and with it, the realisation that this case set an ugly precedent. These riders had proved anyone could wield the law as a weapon to rid them of unwanted burdens, jealousies, and rivalries. They could settle gripes against a neighbour with a story here, a rumour there, and there was no way to refute it.

As soon as she was free from the hordes, Ella fled to the main keep. She had her maid draw her a bath, and then peeled off her dress and underclothes, relishing the prickle of cool air against her skin. She dipped a toe into the water. 'It needs more heat.' She stood, arms loose by her sides. Her skin tightened and contracted, nipples hardening, the tiny hairs upon her flesh standing upright as she waited for the maid to return with more hot water. Once steam rose steadily, she climbed into the tub and sank beneath the water's surface. Her skin puckered and blushed. Soon she was pink all over and her flesh tingled.

Ella picked up her grey pumice stone. She scoured her skin with vigour, sloughing away sweat and tears, until her abraded skin flamed scarlet.

'Your Highness, stop!'

Ella kept scrubbing. The horrid stench of charred flesh clung to her, the sour taste of guilt upon her tongue.

'You're red raw, Princess!'

She didn't stop. 'Leave me.'

What she would have given to take back her words to Leon the previous day. She had wanted to shame him into action, not torment him! With a clammy shudder, Ella realised his torment would be short indeed. He wouldn't do anything so unclean as to take his own life, but she could see him place himself in risky situations over and again, until fate took pity on him. And he hadn't understood what he was doing when he accused Shiana, not truly.

It was noon tea when the others returned. A sombre silence had settled over everyone, even Serrah, who lay awake but subdued in her mother's arms. Food was served, but no one ate much of anything.

Finally, Gohran stood. 'I'll be in my study,' he said, his stride as close to fleeing as dignity allowed. Soon after, Raeyn and Jaydyn headed up to the women's hall. Ella stood to follow, but then changed her mind, and detoured via Gohran's study.

Gohran hunched over his desk, head in his hands, fingers clutching his thick hair.

He glanced up. 'What is it, El?'

Eyes soft, she reached for him, resting a gentle hand upon his shoulder. He flinched, and she pulled her hand away. She swallowed. 'What will happen to Lyrra, Gon?'

'She'll return when she's ready, I suppose.'

Lyrra's leaving had been a mercy, not condemnation, she realised.

Gohran started to speak and then stopped, running his hands through his hair. He let out a sigh before trying again, selecting his words carefully. 'This morning's trial wasn't the first, Ella. It wasn't the first and it won't be the last.'

It was a warning, a caution. Ella nodded. She wanted to speak up, to acknowledge she understood, but she caught herself. She reached out to him once more.

This time, Gohran clasped her hand in his, then pulled her into an embrace. His body felt taller, more muscled than she remembered, yet his smell was just like always. Her old Gon. She could feel his heart thudding, shoulders trembling, breath warm against her neck. When he released her, his eyes were shadowed.

'I need to be alone.' His voice caught, and the moment was over.

# Fifty

Echoes of Shiana's trial haunted Ella's dreams. Night after night, she pictured Shiana struggle, kick, scream, and spit. Then, as Davith pronounced his verdict, Shiana would fall silent and crumple, as limp as Ella's doll made of rags. Ella would let out a battle cry, claw her way through the crowds and howl the henads down. Onlookers would tackle her as she wrestled her way free, just as Jonas had taught her, arms swinging, grabbing anything she could to fend them off.

In her dreams, Gohran would watch on, eyes like motionless sapphires, and she would fight her way to stand before him. Each time, he would raise his arm, pointing to her as he had their mother at Ella's birthday ball, mouthing, *Witch!* Then she would rouse, drenched in sweat, Gohran's words echoing in her mind. *It wasn't the first, and it won't be the last.*

In the wake of these nightmares, for the next few weeks, Ella attempted to appear as amenable as possible. Much as it pained her, she attended Shiana's Cleansing and was punctual for all of Davith's services. By day, she shadowed her sisters, and in the evenings, she stopped by Gohran's study to ask about his day, using her magic to swallow her anger, to stuff it down deeper than she thought imaginable, quietening her fear and her fury.

Then came a night when Ella regained control in her dream. Before her brother could point to her, she rose, standing upright. Energy surged around her. Through the god-sight, she pictured all that fear, hatred, and blood thirst, as pockets of raw power. She sucked the energy into her, allowed it to feed every morsel of her being. It churned and spun until the surrounding pews in the temple trembled, the windows shuddered, and the floor beneath her shook.

Ella continued to draw power into her, condensing it into a sphere of pure force. She raised her palms, and the sphere rose with them. She held the light force above the congregation, above the holy men, above her brother, and with a roar, let it loose. Azure light flashed, blinding. The stained glass shattered, walls crumbled, and the roof toppled. Beams and tiles thundered down, covering them all with dust and debris until Ella was the only person standing.

A moment later, Gohran crawled out from beneath the rubble and knelt at her feet. *Forgive me*, he whispered, climbing to stand beside her. When he reached his full height, he drew her to him as he had in his study after Shiana's trial. She sank into his embrace. *Her old Gon.*

Ella woke, her cheeks wet, but she wore a satisfied smile. She recalled not just Gohran's warning, but the embrace that followed, sensing echoes of Gohran's regard for her and his former affection. In that touch, she felt hope. For the first time, she saw how she might restore her image in his eyes and amend their fractured relationship. She had tried to deny and shut her magic down, but what if she could wield it as a weapon?

Ella looked at her palms. She could still feel that sphere of pure force between them. This kind of power might only exist in fantasy, but it wasn't her only weapon. Ella could persuade when she put her mind to it. She recalled wanting the tower room, her very own palfrey, a new dress, and smiling at her father, seeing his will melt and bend to hers. *And the chill that followed.* She shuddered. She'd witnessed the same power when Amber had calmed her, slipping thoughts into her mind. It was the magic she'd seen her mother use, warping Gohran's will to hers, and then Sheevan's... Another shudder rippled through her. She shoved the memories down. *She wasn't like them. Couldn't be.*

Yet she had to be.

Ella sensed bugs crawling, saw flames pirouette, smelled charred remains, and gagged. Her mother's fate, Shiana's fate, would not be hers.

Nor did she want to end up trapped at Aryon like her aunt, like Amber, celibate slaves to a heretical god, locked away from civilisation, from everyone and everything she had ever known.

Her mother's voice echoed in her mind. *Use every tool at your disposal.*

Could she use her magic to persuade Gohran that he was wrong about her? And if she could, might she have a viable future here in Ycelt? And if Gohran could forgive her, might Venn, too? She had to win Gohran over. Her entire future depended on it.

That evening, Ella brought a decanter of distilled spirits with her when she stopped by Gohran's study. Where before she had braced herself and stuffed her anger and magic down with it, now she suppressed her fury but allowed her power to flow.

She sensed Gohran's thoughts on her, and met them with a smile, willing him to see her as he had when they were playmates and confidantes. She served him a glass and watched him take a sip. His skin flushed, and he nodded appreciatively. 'I asked the chamberlain to source this one especially.'

Ella sat facing him, pouring warmth into her smile the way she had once smiled at their father. She felt it flowing, the telltale tingle coursing from her core to her limbs and out beyond her fingertips, recognising it now for what it was. Power to warp and bend, to ingratiate and beguile, just as the priests described.

She watched Gohran's features relax as if he'd drunk the entire carafe. 'I know it's not been easy for you, El, but you've settled back in well.'

A flutter in her belly. 'Thank you, Your Highness.' If he believed she was settling in, avoiding drawing the henads' attention, he had no reason to send her away.

'I was worried we might have to consider alternative arrangements.'

Her grip stiffened around the carafe, knuckles whitening. She reached over and refilled her brother's glass.

'I'm sure your sisters are grateful that you are back. They've had much to tend to between them.'

Ella exhaled. Her brother still watched her. She studied the play of light upon the liquid. She didn't dare meet those eyes, so like their mother's, so like hers.

'I'm glad you're back,' his voice was low.

'Thank you, Your Highness.' She cleared her throat. 'What are you working on?'

'Just scribing from today's people's court.'

'Scribing?'

Gohran rubbed his temples. 'We've had to let my page Ferros go.'

'I see.'

'I'm hoping to renegotiate the hallit trade, which will bring in a bit more income, but meantime, we all have to do our part.'

Ella knew the priests never had to scribe for themselves.

'I can scribe for you, Your Highness. And run errands. When my sisters don't need me...' She smiled again, warmth filled with hope.

He looked her up, then down, head tilted, rubbing his chin. He was softening towards her. She could feel it. 'It would be a better use of your time. My thanks.'

From that day, Ella joined the king in his official duties. She fetched his papers, maintained his ledgers, served refreshments, took notes from official proceedings, anything she could to be useful to him. At first, the remaining servants cast her curious glances, but ultimately, they accepted her help. Any pair of hands was welcome.

When Gohran didn't need her, she continued to assist her sisters in the women's hall. They scarcely noticed her comings and goings, save to query her on news that might affect them. Ella shared what she could, but it was mostly administrative matters, neighbours' gripes to be settled, taxes to be collected, and betrothals to be approved.

Equinox came and went, marked only by the priests' midday ritual. As the days grew shorter, the trees shed their leaves, but Elnora's rays still carried warmth that year.

On a morning when the air was still and the sun shining, Gohran asked Ella to accompany him to survey the city walls.

As they set out, Ella was aware of Gohran's eyes on her as often as the terrain in front of them. Eventually, they slowed, and their steeds ambled side by side.

'You ride exceptionally well.' There was a hint of pride in Gohran's tone.

'I had ample opportunity to practise all those moons I was away.'

Gohran's smile grew tight, and Ella wished she had kept her mouth shut.

Once they reached the western archway that led to the old glade where she and Gohran used to play, Gohran helped her down from her steed. She looked up, shading her eyes, breathing the fecund scent of moist grass, and fallen leaves.

'Remember how we used to make daisy chains out here?' she said, picturing with warmth how it had been between them, hoping to evoke those same fond memories in him, the pair of them loafing in the long summer grass, playing with her old dolls.

A wry twist to his mouth. 'We'll have to close this archway off before the next equinox.' He sighed. Still watching her, Gohran looked years younger, more vulnerable somehow. 'I'll be sad to see it blocked off, but it's a weakness in our defences.'

Ella ran her hand along the jagged stones. Imagining it sealed up was like placing a lid over her entire childhood, and yet it seemed fitting somehow. 'Truly, it would be better to board it up.'

'I'm thinking of taking on more men, too. It will make things that bit tighter, but I'm still hopeful of securing a new trade agreement with Nedran. In fact, with Lord Venn so keen to restore goodwill, he has offered to amend the terms of the contract in Erldan's favour.'

'That is good news.'

'Not as good as it might have been. A business arrangement signed in blood wouldn't hold the way a marriage contract binds.'

A chill wind rustled the surrounding leaves. The hairs at Ella's nape twinged, and a shiver ran the length of her spine. 'Not for any other lord, perhaps.' The irony did not escape Ella that while Venn's sense of honour held him loyal to her brother and that agreement, it had done her no favours.

Gohran seemed to wait for her to say something. 'I appreciate all you've done for me, Gon.' She smiled up at him, resting her hand upon his arm, trying to recapture his softness, his warmth. Through that touch, she felt his coldness melting. He returned her smile.

'Come, let's finish this side, and then we should head back.'

It took some weeks for Gohran and Ella to complete the survey in between their other duties. Various tradespeople, such as carpenters, masons, and smiths, accompanied them on occasion to offer advice. Ella recorded all the weak points indicated by Gohran or his advisers and noted any recommendations and estimated costs. Then in the evenings, she would join him to go through the ledgers, alone, or with Gohran's trusted financial advisers. It seemed Erldan hadn't maintained their defences adequately for over a generation. Repair works would cost them, but Gohran was determined to make fortifying the city a priority.

When the head of the mason's guild arrived with a sample of building materials and a construction plan, Ella wrinkled her nose and narrowed her eyes the way Lynden had done in the marketplace at Nedran.

'Is this the best you can offer?' She turned to Gohran. 'I wonder if we might be better off sourcing masonry from the guild in Myan. I hear they specialise in buttressing, too.'

'Your Highness, I assure you we can meet your requirements in a fraction of the time.'

Ella shrugged and crossed her arms over her chest. 'It still seems costly for what you're offering.'

'You will save on transportation costs, Your Highness.'

She turned to Gohran, and said in a low voice, 'I'm certain we can do better. Let me write to the Myan guild master.' Then to the mason, 'You have our thanks, but we won't waste any more of your time.' Ella motioned towards the door.

The mason looked to Gohran, who mirrored Ella's stance.

Stricken, the mason knelt. 'Your Highness, I guarantee my guild can make your city the most defensible in this entire region. We ask only that you cover the cost of raw materials and provide our men and their families with their keep for the duration. We do not stand to profit from anything more than your good esteem.'

Gohran held out his hand. 'Then I think we can come to an arrangement.'

The mason kissed the sapphire ring once worn by Queen Prya and swore to make good on his pledge.

# Fifty-One

It did not surprise Amber when Breeyan requested she head back to Ycelt to remind King Gohran of his obligations under the treaty. She only hoped the risky trip would help restore the High Priestess's opinion of her.

Between them, they decided the safest way to reach the king was to send word via the township of Harnal, rather than venturing back into Erldan. Dressed in a plain smock, her un-braided hair pinned back, Amber set out at dawn. Breeyan had furnished her with a purse of silver and a sealed scroll addressed to the king. The seal was fake, the coded message purportedly from a cousin, but Gohran would have to be a fool to mistake its meaning.

Alone on the road, Amber was more afraid of bandits, thieves, and opportunistic predators than henads. So, when nightfall came, she camped some distance from the road, laying with her back to her fire, her senses alert to signs of danger.

After a restless night, she packed her belongings at first light and rode towards Harnal. She circled east before joining the west-running road, the way she and Prya had ridden years earlier. Guided by memory and the sun's path across the sky, it was only as she joined the main road that Amber encountered other travellers, and by the time she arrived at her destination, the sky was awash with blushing hues as Elnora sank towards the horizon.

Harnal was much as Amber remembered, unbothered by the henads she knew combed nearby Erldan. When she arrived, the town was quiet, most people having already packed up for the day. She hurried towards the inn where she recalled meeting up with Queen Prya's serving women.

The door groaned as Amber entered. The dining hall smelled of sweat, sour hops, and boiled fowl. She shuffled over to the bar and waved a coin at the attendant. She wrapped her thoughts up and made herself appear as bland as possible in the minds of anyone she encountered. After arranging lodging for the night, she took a seat near the far wall where she could monitor the door while eating her supper.

A copper-haired woman arrived to top up her ale. Her pale skin and freckles reminded Amber of Ella's sisters.

'What brings you to Harnal?' she asked.

Amber took a sip of ale. 'I'm headed to Erldan to deliver a message for my mistress, but if I can find a reliable courier, it would save me a night's travel. The trip took longer than I expected, and I don't want my mistress to take it amiss.' Amber set her heavy purse atop the table beside her.

The serving woman smiled. 'Well now, you can trust my son, Stevyn. He's as honest as they come. I'll be sure to send him your way.'

The woman turned to leave, then paused, frowning as she looked Amber over. 'Have you been this way before? You look familiar...'

'Not for some time.' Amber kept her breathing steady.

The serving woman rested her hands on her hips, lips puckered. 'I do know you! You used to work at the palace. I recognise those gingery-blonde locks. Weren't you a handmaid or a chambermaid or such?'

'A tutor. But I had to head back home, and now my mistress wants the dues still owed me.'

She snorted. 'Your mistress will have to get in line! King Gohran owes a lot of dues from what I hear, and I hear more than my share.'

Amber caught the woman's gaze and let her power flow. 'Then I'd best get my letter off quickly.'

The serving woman's mouth slackened, her focus soft. 'Of course. I'll have my Stevyn come see you at first light.'

'My thanks.' Amber released her.

Amber used her influence again in the morning when handing over the scroll to the courier. She wanted to be certain Breeyan's message arrived without tampering.

That night, she set up camp just a short distance from Harnal. She stared into the flames of her campfire and drew power, letting her mind drift to the king. She would not return to Aryon until she saw the letter in his hands. As the image built up, she realised she had never tried to spy on Gohran before. With her god-sight, she pictured his gait, his voice, his raven hair and brilliant blue eyes, everything she could recall of him. His outline came into focus. He was as handsome as Ella was lovely, but there was an edge to his manner, a pent-up force that roiled beneath the surface, ready to erupt.

He crouched before what appeared to be a cobbled-together altar, blue light emanating from him and wrapping around it, as though he were pouring latent energy into his worship. A hot-cold quiver crossed Amber's flesh. *Was he even aware of what he was doing?*

She widened her vision. The letter was there, looking as though someone had tossed it to one side.

She was about to shut the working down, but curiosity nagged at her. She drew more power and studied Gohran's simulacrum. Through the god-sight, his aura appeared warped, twisted back on itself. She had seen nothing like it.

Jaw tight, he picked up a ceremonial knife and trimmed an unused candle. He lit the wick and held it over his outstretched arm until the hot wax dripped over the tender skin of the inside of his wrist. His simulacrum juddered. He placed the candle on the altar. The knife was halfway to the bench top when he paused, then brought it to the same portion of skin and pressed down. The blade bit through his flesh and thick blood welled along the cut.

Amber's vision blazed white-hot. Heart racing, power thrummed through every morsel of her. She craved that heat the way a long-parched desert thirsts for rain.

Amber wrenched herself away from the fire, grabbed her canteen, and splashed cold water over her face. She threw dirt on the flames and stomped out the last of the cinders until she lay sweat-drenched and trembling.

She hadn't felt that lustful thirst since being forced to draw power directly from Ella. Its memory echoed through her flesh, through her very soul. She longed to relight her fire, to draw still more. The power was intoxicating. She could see why it was forbidden.

Amber stared into the dark, panting. She steadied her breath and watched the stars wink in and out behind the clouds, noticing the chill against her skin, smelling the earth beneath her torso and limbs until she felt embodied and grounded once more, her heart beating in a steady rhythm.

At least she could assure Breeyan that Gohran had received the letter. But what had she just witnessed? Did she dare consult the High Priestess? If not, who else could help her make sense of it? Why did everything have to be cloaked in secrecy? She hated this feeling of isolation, and once again cursed Prya and Breeyan for putting her in this position. She rolled over, pulled her blanket around her, and allowed herself the luxury of weeping alone in the dark of night.

'**G**on, what is it?' That evening, as Ella kept Gohran's glass filled, her brother rubbed his temples, frowning. She sensed a turbulent undercurrent gnawing at him.

Gohran drained his glass. 'You've been a great help to me these past few moons, El.' He fingered the corner of a letter that bore a seal Ella didn't recognise. 'However, I'm reminded that I still need to make good on all of Erldan's commitments.'

*The treaty.*

Ella swallowed, the familiar feeling of bugs crawling.

'I'm still hopeful of reaching an agreement with Nedran. And while several lords have expressed interest in forging ties, despite Erldan's reduced circumstances, I need to weigh all the options. It's down to me to decide what is best for Erldan.'

'That must be a heavy burden, Gon.'

A twist to his mouth.

Ella's heart thudded in her chest. She couldn't take her eyes off that letter. One daughter from Erldan—any daughter—could fulfil the treaty. Gohran was unlikely to sacrifice Raeyn and forfeit her advantage as Princess Elder, nor could she imagine Gohran sending Jaydyn with a babe in arms. But he might consider their middle sister unmarriageable for the same reason, which could only strengthen Ella's position. Unless Ella's dishonour with Jonas became more widely known, Gohran could still make her a worthy match. So, what could be done about Serrah?

Ella thought back to the many conversations she'd had with Lynden, trying to still her heart, to ease the crawling. She recalled gossip overheard at the Red Rose, whisperings from Vera and even Lynden's cousin Moyra. Deals done to hide dishonour and to save bloodlines.

She reached across to refill Gohran's glass. 'You know,' she said slowly, 'It might please a wealthy widower to take on a younger wife with a small child...'

Gohran paused, his glass halfway to his mouth. 'Go on.'

'It takes the burden off him to... Well, to uphold all his commitments, you could say.' Ella frowned, rubbing her chin. 'Though it might not be to Erldan's greatest advantage to be burdened with a less virile ally...' She studied her brother. The next seed she planted had to take root. It was her or it was Jaydyn. She recalled her vision, seeing a future with Venn, and steeled herself for what she was about to do. She took a deep breath. 'There are also respectable women who would be content to foster or adopt a noble-born child for the same reason. Some will even pay for a young child with the right bloodlines.' A stone-like weight in her chest. 'It would certainly provide additional options to consider...'

'Will they indeed?' Gohran downed the rest of that glass and started on another. He picked up the letter, crumpled it in one palm, and tossed it into the fire.

Later in her room, as Ella recalled planting her seed with icy, deliberate intent, she heaved the contents of her stomach into her chamber pot. She pushed back sweaty strands of hair from around her face and recalled her consternation at the thought of baby Serrah being caught up in ruthless politicking. Never did she think it would be at her instigation.

She climbed into her evening bath. How had she become this person? What had happened to her? Almost pleading with herself, she thought, *it wasn't the only option I gave him, not even the first...*

Yet she had given it to him.

Ella sank beneath the water's surface, allowing the last of her breath bubbles to float upward and burst free. She ran her nails along her thighs, across her arms, driving them deeper, leaving reddened welts. Hair wafted in front of her face, dark tendrils tangling around her nose and throat. Her chest burned. She dug her nails in harder. What if she never surfaced again, and just allowed the empty void to take her...?

'Princess!'

Hands grasped and thrust Ella upward towards the crisp air. She gasped and spluttered. Blessed air filled her lungs over and again.

'By the goddess, what were you thinking?' A maid held Ella to her warm chest, squeezing her tight. Ella sagged against that warmth. 'Hush, Your Highness,' the maid soothed. 'All will be well. All will be right...'

Ella shuddered and wept, crying in ugly, juddering gasps. She knew nothing would ever be right again.

# Fifty-Two

'You know I have always valued your guidance.' Gohran stayed back after the service the following morning to confer with Davith. He had dismissed Davith's neophytes so they could be alone and lent a hand to straighten pews, polish, and stow candelabra in their stead.

Davith rested a hand upon the king's shoulder. 'As I have valued yours, Your Highness.' Light streamed through the stained glass, playing upon Davith's features like an ethereal glow.

'I am aware time is passing, and I still have no firm arrangements in place for my sisters.' Gohran's face was half in shadow.

'Or for yourself,' Davith said pointedly.

Gohran shooed his concern away. 'I need to settle them first.'

'As you have said.'

'I had assumed no one would take Jaydyn on, given her circumstances, but Ella says otherwise.'

'Ella, the youngest princess?'

Gohran nodded. 'She has been accompanying me, giving me counsel.'

'I see.'

'You don't approve.'

'It is... Unusual.'

'No more so than a younger son acting as a page,' Gohran said hastily. 'In fact, she has served me better than any page before now. She offers me a perspective I may not have access to if I relied solely on the minds of men.' He heard the defensiveness in his voice.

'Oh? How so?'

'She offers a point of view that I find... Unique.'

A sour twist to Davith's mouth.

'In any case, I value her opinion. It seems she has much matured during her time at Nedran.' *Why should he have to justify himself?*

'And you want what from me, Your Highness?'

'I suppose I'm just thinking aloud...'

Davith waited for him to continue.

'I'm still hoping Venn will overlook the events of this summer and rekindle his bond with Raeyn. If I arrange an adoption for Serrah, I can honour my mother's wishes and place Jaydyn with her relations...' He hated lying to Davith, but he saw no other way to explain the dilemma posed by Erldan's treaty with Aryon.

Davith continued stacking volumes of scripture. 'And your youngest sister? Where will you match her?'

'I was thinking she could stay here, with me, as my second.'

Davith halted and faced him.

'At least until I marry. And then we will have plenty of options for her.'

'I see.'

'As I said, I'm just thinking aloud.'

Davith's eyes narrowed. 'You might do well to consider a match for her further afield. To the far north or further east, for instance. Or even Rynwood, which would position Erldan with ties between Herron and the High Realm in Galliarn.'

'I had contemplated Rynwood. If Venn won't consider a betrothal with Raeyn after everything that has transpired, Lord Kerr might be a prudent match for her. I know Kerr had set his sights on Ella, but with no other commitments to consider, I might persuade him to make an offer for the Princess Elder.'

'But not Ella?'

'Not just yet.'

Davith's expression tightened. 'I'm sure His Highness knows best...'

Gohran finished up in silence and headed back to the keep. Davith's disapproval gnawed at him. For a time, he tried to focus on his work, but eventually he gave up and went hunting. Blood sport would soothe him. It always did.

Ella knew her suggestions had taken hold when Gohran arranged for Raeyn and Jaydyn to visit Kerr of Rynwood's sister, Layla. The trio had become friends when Kerr and Layla had stayed at Erldan the previous year, while Ella was at Nedran. A widow at just nineteen, Layla had a small daughter, and she had written to say she would appreciate the company of the girls and baby Serrah. Ella was to stay behind at Erldan. She had no connection to Layla, and Gohran had become quite reliant on her.

Ella had mixed feelings about the visit. Trepidation. Hope. Guilt. The visit would position Ella's sisters in fresh company, including that of Lord Kerr himself. Ella knew firsthand the interest Kerr had shown in forging a bond with her family. Beyond that, she dared not speculate.

For the first few days while her sisters were away, Ella only saw Gohran at breakfast and supper. They spoke of the weather, the hallit trade, administrative household matters, nothing more. Gohran spent most of his time out riding and hunting for what little game was left as the chill of winter set in, leaving Ella alone with her shadowed thoughts.

Then one morning as Ella pushed her barely touched food around her plate, Gohran said with some concern, 'You really need to eat properly, El. Your face looks drawn.'

'Yes, Your Highness,' she said, though she had no appetite.

Gohran frowned. 'Would it help if you had something nicer to wear?' He draped his napkin across his emptied plate and gestured to a nearby servant.

Ella looked down at her re-purposed dress.

'Didn't you mention as much to me in your letters while you were away? That you had to borrow all your dresses?'

'Yes, but how can we—?'

Gohran held up his hand. 'One of my vassals sent some cloth with their last instalment of taxes. It's from Myan, I'm told. There was only enough for one dress, so I wanted to wait until your sisters were gone to give it to you.'

The servant brought over a length of fabric, a luscious cream and gold weave.

'It's beautiful,' Ella breathed.

Gohran grinned. 'Look inside.'

Ella peeled back the centre fold of the material to reveal a string of white pearls.

'You'll still need to forage for all the trimmings, but I'm sure you'll make something of it.'

Open-mouthed, she stared at the fine cloth and creamy pearls.

He fixed his eyes back on her plate. 'Now you've no reason not to eat up.'

A new dress seemed so trivial considering all that had transpired and what she now knew of Erldan's circumstances. Yet she could not overlook the significance of such a gift.

Gohran placed a warm hand over hers. 'Why don't we take a ride together after breakfast?'

'Your Highness?'

'El, you don't need to call me that.' He looked at her so earnestly, with genuine warmth.

This is what she had longed for, to win him over, for him to see her as he once had. She longed to soak up that warmth, yet a cold creeping dread seeped into her belly.

Oblivious, Gohran continued with enthusiasm. 'Eat up, and then let's get some colour back in those cheeks.'

Frost coated much of the landscape as Ella and Gohran set out atop their steeds. Crisp air filled their lungs and their breath formed vaporous puffs.

Despite herself, the ride lifted Ella's spirits. The masonry works were underway, the hallit trade was being renegotiated, and she could simply relax and enjoy her steed's rhythmic motion, taking in the changing landscape of her home as the winter solstice approached.

They rode towards Gohran's hunting preserve and Gohran kicked his steed into a gallop. Ella followed, with the crackle and thud of underbrush beneath them. Eventually, they slowed, nearing a creek that was coated with a layer of ice.

Gohran dismounted and tethered his steed, then helped Ella down and tethered hers. 'Shall we cross over?' He grinned slyly, the way he had when they used to sneak out as children, disappearing for hours as they explored the grounds beyond Erldan's walls.

Ella hesitated when she saw the edges of the ice. 'Is it safe?' She couldn't tell how thick it was.

'Just tread carefully and follow my lead.' Gohran held out his hand.

She squeezed his hand in hers and leaned against him for balance, placing her feet gingerly in his stead. His breath was slow and deliberate as he strategically selected each step. When he reached the other side, he lifted her off the ice and onto the grassy bank. She moved aside to shake out her dress.

'Let's keep going. I found some chestnuts growing through here the other day.' Gohran trod animatedly through the undergrowth. He seemed so at ease out here, as if they had slipped back through time. Her old Gon.

Ella hitched up her skirts and trailed after. She tried to keep up, but her cumbersome layers kept catching on bare branches and twigs. A corner of her cloak snagged on a protruding bough. She yanked it loose and felt a sharp stab in her forearm. With a grimace, she pulled herself free, brushed her hair from her face and reached down to smooth out her skirt and sleeves. She pressed on.

Gohran was quite a way ahead now. Picking up speed, the ground was slippery from the frost. Another step and Ella lost her footing and toppled over. She landed on the hard ground with a thwack.

Gohran turned around. 'Ella!' He rushed back to where she had fallen and crouched over her. 'Are you hurt?'

'My pride hurts more than anything,' she said, pushing herself back up to her feet.

Gohran rocked back on his heels, relieved. Then his face froze. Red smeared Ella's cheeks and dress. 'El, you're bleeding...' Bright crimson liquid soaked through her sleeve. He pushed the fabric up her arm to reveal an ugly gash.

Gohran's pupils enlarged as his skin flushed.

'I struck my arm against that cursed tree back there...' her voice trailed off.

Power surged, coursing through and around them. It was shifting between them. Everything felt hazy and warm. Sounds thickened, as though they stood underwater.

Ella heard Gohran's heartbeat. Saw it. Felt it as if it were her own, thudding, pounding. The edges of the trees and the surrounding grass appeared soft and blurred. She met Gohran's gaze. Saw his entire body as a cluster of tiny crystals, and saw herself reflected the same way through his eyes. She was melting into him. He was dissolving into her.

*We are alike. A matched pair.* Ella heard Gohran's innermost thoughts as though he had spoken aloud.

She looked down at her symmetrical form, then across at his. Gohran's crystalline body warped and shuddered. Something wasn't right.

*Matched, but mismatched.*

Gohran tugged at his shirttails, placed a corner between his teeth, and tore away a strip of cloth. He wound it over and around the gash, then tied it off and wiped his bloodied hands upon the nearby grass.

'Better?' he asked, over-loudly, breaking the strange spell that had come over them.

Ella nodded, struggling to speak. 'My thanks.' She blinked to restore her vision until her surroundings appeared solid and bland.

Yet the channel that had opened between them remained. The entire journey back, every glance they shared, every touch, felt like her mind blended into his, their thoughts coinciding without a sound passing through their lips.

And it didn't stop. That evening in the parlour, as Ella read from a book of old war stories and Gohran inked out a series of letters beside her, their thoughts kept intermingling.

Gohran looked up from his work as though he could sense Ella's thoughts on him. 'It's been good to spend this time together, just the two of us.' *Like the old days...*

His expression was tender, but there was some undercurrent Ella didn't understand. The candelabra cast odd flickering shadows that turned his eyes into dark pools. Ella caught her breath and hugged her arms across her chest. The movement put pressure on her injured arm, and she winced.

'How is your wound?' Gohran asked aloud.

'A little sore, but nothing sinister.' She pushed up her sleeve to show Gohran the makeshift bandage.

He took her arm in his hands, frowning. 'We should change that dressing.' He unwound the cloth and peeled it back to expose her flesh. The wound bled a little and heat flowed between them.

Through that touch, Ella felt the full weight of the kingdom pressing in on them, the priests and their henads draining Erldan dry, always fearful. So many secrets... But right then, with her arm in Gohran's, those burdens seemed far away.

*Wait—were these her thoughts, or his?* His perspective was bleeding into hers.

A snap of her mind. She pulled her hands away. *You brought this on yourself... On us.* Her deepest under-thoughts slipped out, the anger and resentment she had tried to bury lay exposed.

The hurt behind his eyes was like a stab through her chest. She couldn't breathe. *She couldn't lose him, lose this, not now.*

She slid her hands back in his, aching to take that pain away, to heal this rift. She sent her longing for them to be as they once were through the strange channel now open between them. Power surged through her, soothing and wrapping around him, yearning for warmth, for affection. *He was her Gon.*

She felt it then, her warmth reflected in him, washing over and through her.

And beneath, she sensed his deeper thoughts, his memories. Of Ella being warm and kind where their mother had been cold and remote, of Ella loving him as no one else could. She looked up to him, nurtured him, and saw him not as a future king, a disappointing son, or an overbearing brother, but as he was. Who he was at his core.

Aloud, he said, 'El, you know I only want what's best for you and your sisters, for Erldan...'

His thoughts kept bleeding into hers. How could he ever explain why he had to denounce their mother? That people were growing suspicious and distrustful. That it was the only way to protect them. To protect her.

In that moment, she knew it as she knew her own heart. His concern for her. Especially her. He cared for her and wanted to keep her safe. *She was his El.*

When their eyes met, she sensed longing for understanding, acceptance, and forgiveness, but it was tangled up in something else, some deep wound that perhaps not even he understood. Then the moment was over, Gohran's emotional fortress firmly back in place.

# FIFTY-THREE

Amber traced Nykki's neck with her fingertips, drawing back her hair. An electric thrill travelled the length of her body. How she savoured that touch! She breathed in Nykki's scent, lingering as, strand by silken strand, she braided her beloved's hair. The pair huddled together as they did most mornings to prepare for the day ahead. The priestess's garb was simple, but the elaborate rituals surrounding it formed part of their worship.

Amber caught Nykki's gaze and stroked her lover's mind. Imagined it was her body in all the places they were forbidden to touch. She relished the sensations her mind's manoeuvrings evoked as Nykki's mind and body responded to her touch. Amber sensed her struggling to keep her expression neutral and her thoughts shielded from anyone except the two of them. She drank in Nykki's experience of the exquisite moisture between her thighs, heat rising through her core, her hastened breath, her throbbing heart. She channelled her body's responses back into Nykki's mind to amplify and heighten their pleasure.

It had been this way between them since Amber returned to Aryon after delivering Gohran's letter. Where once she felt deep love and affection for Nykki, she now experienced a kind of animal hunger. She ached to be near her and was acutely aware of each sensation of their incidental touch. Even then, it wasn't enough. Like a thirst she couldn't slake, Amber orchestrated opportunities for the two of them to make contact.

Tasting pure power for a second time had awakened something raw and carnal within her. Not just a desire to draw more power—and at the intensity derived from forbidden sources—but for desire itself.

Without uttering a word or thought, she and Nykki understood the danger-ous line they walked. To shield their secret from curious and watchful minds, they drew upon the charge of energy their lust generated and created a mental cocoon.

Yet as their charade progressed, Amber noticed herself becoming as curious and watchful as she feared her companions to be. She and Nykki couldn't be the only priestesses to explore in this way. Regardless of what the Elders and Wise taught, the women at Aryon were not automatons. Their flesh experienced the same natural and physical urges as those without magic. And Xenon had not always forbidden lust among his followers. Amber knew there was some important piece of lore that explained why this had changed, but she had not located it.

She was eager for the cooler months to arrive when everything slowed down at Aryon. Winters this far west and south of the Cursed land were mild. Yet they afforded the women time to rest, to check upon their stores, to study and scribe. Amber hoped to use this time to find that missing piece of lore.

She also wanted to meditate. She still had so many unanswered questions about the strangeness she had observed through the god-sight in both Ella and Gohran. Over and again, she considered going to the High Priestess. But when-ever she pictured the peculiar power emanating from the princess or the king's warped aura, she hesitated, a cold god-sent warning rippling down her spine. She would bide her time to put the pieces together and keep her observations and questions to herself.

Finally, Amber had time to pull out an old copy of her favourite manuscript, *The Lost Warriors*. The volume recorded annals from the old war between the god Xenon and the former High King. These ancient sagas depicted the strong women who followed and fought for the moon god and included the decrees Xenon made following the war that formed part of the Curse. Among them, she hoped to find an explanation for Xenon's ruling on lust.

Back then, before Xenon had laid His Curse, and before his followers were exiled, people openly used magical influence to gain power. Some priestesses had troupes of worshippers. Others took up arms and joined the war alongside the men. Many of the stories within the manuscript followed these lost warriors. But the stories Amber loved best described women who were free to love and lust as they pleased. Many took multiple lovers and lived lascivious lives. *The Lost Warriors* was one of the few sources where she had found evidence that priestesses were once permitted a more carnal way of life.

As she read, Amber imagined she and Nykki were the figures she read about. It was the closest she would ever get to the life that was stolen from her before she was even born. What the covert caresses of her mind could barely approximate. The priestesses taught her that when Xenon and his followers lost the war, they were forced from their homeland and into hiding. But Amber realised what they had truly lost was their freedom to live a whole and fulfilling life.

Amber opened the volume to a passage that told the story of a warrior priestess, Xarion. Xarion was one of her favourite figures from the sagas. The warrior priestess had used her powerful magic to infiltrate the High King's men, but had fallen in love with the king's captain. Amber relished the early parts of the story, when Xarion and the captain were falling in love. Before everything took a tragic turn, for all these stories had some message or moral embedded in them. It was the message of this story that she was certain contained the missing piece of lore that might go some way to answering Amber's questions.

But as she read, she found the story was incomplete. One passage finished mid-sentence, and when Amber flipped the page over, it continued at an entirely different point in the story. Whole chunks of text were missing. Where was the rest of the story? Had some priestess been too lazy to transcribe the entire thing, or were the passages deliberately omitted? Amber had left her copy of the book back at Erldan, so she couldn't compare the two. Did Ella have it still?

Once her thoughts landed on the princess, Amber felt a telltale god-sent nagging at her mind. She needed to know why. She wrapped a shield around her thoughts and shuffled to the kitchen under the guise of offering to help prepare the evening meal. Once there, she set about slicing vegetables into chunks that she tossed into waiting pots, munching a few edible pieces as she waited for her moment to scry unobserved.

Eventually, she found an opening, offering to watch over the stove while her sisters fetched more produce from the cellar. The moment she was alone, she let her gaze blur out of focus and peered into the stove's flames, drawing upon its heat to build and sustain her vision. She pictured Ella and imagined seeing her through the flames until her vision became reality.

The princess sat with her brother, King Gohran. If Ella had been on her own, Amber would have called to her, mind to mind. Instead, she drew additional heat and concentrated on Ella's simulacrum. *Why the nagging?* she thought, waiting for the god to guide her vision. *What did He want her to see?*

When there was no obvious answer, Amber watched and waited. The same blue force she had seen through the god-sight previously was swirling around the princess, only now it buckled and shifted, as though it struggled to remain contained. It appeared more like the strange shifts and currents she had seen when she spied upon Gohran. Wait, was she seeing Ella's simulacrum or his? The pair of auras seemed to be entwined or entangled somehow. What was she looking at? Why, by every god, was Ella's aura tangled up with her brother's? And what by every demon was wrong with his?

Amber could hear her sisters returning and blinked to restore her natural focus before they caught her scrying. She took in the pots that sat over the stove, bringing her awareness to the small knife in one hand and the rough tuber in the other. She put both aside and reached for another hunk of wood to stoke the fire, which had died down from her working.

A creeping dread made its way into Amber's stomach. The blue force swirling around Ella—there was something about it. Something linked to that very story of the warrior priestess, the text that was missing.

From what she recalled, when Xarion had used her gifts to infiltrate the king's men, she had manipulated and seduced. At first, it aided the god and his followers, but over time had tragic consequences, leading to death and destruction. This was the story used to warn against the dangers of carnal desire, to justify Xenon's decree that no priestess be touched with lust, but Amber could not remember why.

She had first seen the force emanating from Ella when she had scried upon her back at Nedran. Ella hadn't needed to do anything. The force just swirled around her and Venn. Something about that force had reminded Amber of Xarion's story, of that important piece of lore...

*That force... not something she was doing, but something about her...*

That was it. It was the same power described in the story of the warrior priestess. Xarion couldn't just influence the thoughts of others, which many priestesses could do. She could alter the way others felt about her. That was what she had observed in Ella through the god-sight, what enchanted her every time she laid eyes on the princess. Beguilement. The rarest and most perilous of Xenon's gifts.

Amber drew a breath.

The story's tragic ending flooded back to her. Though it had not been her intention, Xarion had destroyed the lives of every person she loved. That was the message of the story. Beguilement was not safe for Xarion or anyone in the warrior priestess's orbit. And if Ella could beguile to that degree, she should be here, at Aryon. Not only for her safety, but for the safety of those around her.

# Fifty-Four

In the weeks leading up to the winter solstice, Ella felt Gohran continue to soften towards her. They spent their mornings together, either riding or with Ella watching him practise sword craft. The rest of the time, Ella helped Gohran with his duties or worked on sewing her new dress, which was almost finished. The peculiar blending of their minds kept happening, usually when she and Gohran were in contact or connected, such as when their eyes met, or when Gohran helped Ella on or off her steed.

In those moments, she knew he cared for her and wanted her to be happy. He continued to confide in her about matters of state, treating her as his trusted advisor. And when he smiled, she could almost ignore the shadowy undercurrent running beneath, that coldness that made him pull away, putting distance between them. Almost as though he feared her, feared being close to her.

When the winter solstice arrived, Gohran announced over breakfast he had important news. 'It appears we will have the funds to finish the city walls sooner than expected.'

'Good news about the trade agreement, then?' Ella asked.

'Better than that. We might be celebrating soon enough.'

Ella felt her heart skip. Almost fearfully, she looked across at her brother. He had to mean a betrothal. But whose?

'Celebrating what, Gon? Tell me.' Her heart was in her throat. She drew breath, waiting, a tingle creeping along her arms.

'You'll have to wait until this evening,' he said.

'Gon, please...'

Gohran stood, stooped to kiss her forehead, and strode out of the room.

Ella stared after him, breath held until she thought her chest might burst. Did she dare hope she could be with Venn after all?

That evening, Ella examined her cream dress. She wanted to present it finished, to show off her hard work and appreciation. Have Gohran realise it would be a waste to send her to Aryon to become a sworn priestess, have him see she was a catch worthy of a mighty dryhten.

Ella slipped it on. At sixteen and a half summers, she was no longer the scrawny girl she had been. Borrowing makeup from her sister's dresser, she applied kohl to her eyes, rouged her cheekbones and painted her lips a luscious scarlet. Her hair she styled and pinned, finishing her look by adorning her neck with the pearls Gohran gifted her.

Satisfied with her reflection, Ella ambled downstairs towards the dining hall, anticipating the look on her brother's face.

His reaction did not disappoint.

Gohran stood when she entered, mouth agape.

She grinned and gave a little twirl. 'I hope this will suffice for these mysterious celebrations. Will Lord Venn approve, do you think?'

Panic caught in Gohran's throat. He couldn't speak.

Ella saw it then. Read the excruciatingly clear thought behind his eyes as the colour drained from his cheeks. 'By every demon, I'm a fool,' she whispered. The news was about a betrothal, but not for her. It was for Raeyn.

Ella felt her world lurch and crumble. These past moons had been for nothing. She had swallowed her anger and stuffed it down, used her magic to ingratiate herself, to win Gohran over, and for what? His will on this matter was intractable.

And if Venn married her sister after all, what would become of her? Even if Gohran sent Jaydyn to Aryon and allowed her to stay in Ycelt, what then? Would Gohran force her to play handmaid to Raeyn or his future wife? Would she play nursemaid to their hordes of children, fear always at her heels in case one of them noticed something unusual about her? What kind of life was that? Or would she be married off to someone as loathsome as Lord Kerr after all?

Power surged through her as she met her brother square-on. All her hatred, her resentment, everything she had quashed these past moons, lay open to him. Memories flashed in her mind of Gohran's enormous eyes that day in the glade as he mouthed, 'Witch!' His raised hand slapping their pregnant sister. Gohran's booming voice denouncing their mother. His hovering silhouette dragging her back to Erldan. *Let him read her contempt. What more had she to lose?*

Upon the table, a carafe of wine rattled. Panicked, Ella reached for it and grasped it with both hands. It trembled against her hold. She had to make it stop. The cutlery and crockery shook, too.

Gohran's eyes widened, then narrowed. Ella felt more than saw it. She picked up the carafe and splashed its contents full in Gohran's face, then smashed the glass upon the floor. She turned and marched upstairs before the servants came running.

Gohran swore under his breath. 'Ella!' he growled, wiping his face on his sleeve as he stomped after her.

Ella braced herself. At least her brother's temper was honest and familiar.

He followed her to her room and barred the door behind them. For a time, he paced the floor. When he finally turned to face her, Ella flinched in anticipation. Instead of striking her, he cupped her cheeks in his hands, eyes beseeching.

Ella fought the haziness caused by that touch, as for a long moment he stared. She felt as though bugs crawled along her limbs.

'Why? Why do you do this to me?' His voice cracked.

Ella felt icy all over, yet Gohran's grip was like fire on her skin.

'I risked everything for you, and now you do this!' He pointed to her dress and make-up. 'Are you trying to torment me?'

She could only shake her head feebly.

'What am I supposed to do, El? What am I supposed to think, to feel? You see this?' He pinched his face, his arm, his leg. 'This is the flesh the goddess gave me. But to test me, She made it weak.'

Ella trembled. She had never—ever—seen Gohran like this. Finally, she found her voice. 'Then punish Her, not me.'

'Is that what you think? That I'm trying to punish you?'

'Aren't you? Haven't you taken away the one thing I ever truly wanted?' Her mind lay open to him as she pictured Venn with her sister.

Gohran laughed, but there was no mirth in it. 'No, Ella, you did that. I was ready to give you up, to give you to my best friend in the world. But what did you do? Debased yourself with that—*nobody*!' She sensed him picturing her as he'd found her with Jonas the last solstice morning.

She shook her head back and forth.

'I could live with Venn having you, but not *him*.' His arms clasped her shoulders so hard they ached. Sweat across his forehead mingled with the moisture of spilled wine.

'What are you saying?' Her voice was barely audible.

He pulled her close, held her against his chest, and breathed her name.

Ella felt his heart vibrate against hers as he buried his face in her hair, all the while fighting the subsuming of her will within his as power seeped out of his very skin.

'These last few weeks—I know you felt it, too. We *are* a matched pair. We can be to each other what no one else can ever be to us.'

'Gohran, no...' All those filthy words Jonas had thrown at her echoed in her mind. *Gohran will never let you marry. He wants you chaste, untouched. Because if he can't have you, no one will.* She felt the colour leave her face as dread filled her belly.

'Our Lady of the Dark Sun is cruel, Ella. She has tested my flesh, but to test you, She poisoned my heart.' Again, his voice cracked as he caught her wrists in his.

Ella trembled as Gohran's eyes glazed over. His thoughts bled into hers and she experienced a twisted, fractured lust that he honestly believed she shared. Every time she had reached out to him, longed for his good opinion, his forgiveness, for them to be as they once were, she was pouring oil onto the flames of a fire he tried to extinguish over and again. In her, he saw an echo of his own power that beguiled beyond all reason. With her alone, he could be his true self—a truth reflected that he couldn't bear to see.

He drew her to him, pressing her down onto her bed, climbing on top of her, trapping her under his weight. By every god and demon, he had grown in this past year and a half. His arms pinned her down, his legs wedged against hers. She went limp as her doll made of rags. A part of her felt his breath, damp against her neck, and the sudden cold of air against skin as he tugged at her dress. Another part of her was somewhere else entirely, watching them both from the outside, struggling to fend off the worse horror that was the melding of their minds.

Jonas had taught her how to fend off an intruder, an enemy, a stranger. Nothing could have prepared her for this.

When Gohran was finally done, Ella wriggled out from beneath him. Above, she saw his frightened, tear-stained face—the exact expression she had seen in her vision. Choking, she pushed him away. This time, he let her go.

'Forgive me...' he whispered, covering his face with his hands.

Ella thought she had felt numbness before, but not like this.

Gohran had retreated away and into himself and was rocking back and forth.

Ella tossed the pearls at his feet and turned away.

She pulled on an old ugly dress and her winter cloak, grabbed Amber's book, and fled to the stables.

'Princess Ella!' a servant called as she brushed past. Other servants stood, staring. She ignored them all.

Saddling one of the tamer steeds, her body quivered as she mounted and rode towards the city gates. The streets were almost empty. The few stragglers moved about their business as though nothing was amiss. Her vision was blurred, but not by tears. She couldn't cry. She felt like an empty shell, as though she was broken inside. Everything danced before her, as bright as daylight, and she realised it was her power, bleeding around her, too much for her to contain.

Ella knew she should ride west to Aryon, that it was the only place she would ever be truly safe, but if this much of her vision had come true, there must still be hope. She needed to see Venn. She veered north and kicked her steed to a gallop.

# PART FOUR: INDOMITABLE

## NEDRAN PROVINCE, YCELT

**Year: 796 A.S.**

# FIFTY-FIVE

Much of the trip to Nedran was a blur. The world around Ella refused to sit still, colours blending and merging, only to separate once more, as her weary mind clutched at each image and sensation. Every jig of the horse jolted through her body, her palms rubbed raw from clinging to the reins. Twigs breaking underfoot resounded like the thwack of snapped tree branches. Hooves clomped as pounding drums. The odour of sweat, earth, and blood infused her senses, while the stars appeared as spheres of luminescence that bloated and contracted with no mercy for her tired eyes.

At some point, Ella must have dismounted. She recalled hobbling through the inner-city gates and up to the main keep. Lightning sheeted the sky in an eerie reverse-light before thunder growled. Air thick with moisture crackled, eager to shed. The first oversized flakes of thunder snow fell as she felt an arm slip around her, propping her up before her unsteady legs gave out.

After that, there was nakedness, warm water, scrubbing, and more scrubbing. Next, a poultice soothed her bruises, while a comforting hand brushed her hair and another rested upon her back. She hugged her legs to her chest, merciful darkness hiding blood-tinged water.

All the while came questions. So many questions.

Later she remembered being patted dry with something soft, swallowing bitter herbs, sinking into a pillowy bed, until finally the shifting calmed, and she fell deep, deep into the darkness.

'Please,' Ella stammered, 'I don't want anyone to know I'm here.'

When Bess came running to tell Lynden her old friend was back, and apparently hurt, Lynden hurried to meet her. She helped Ella inside and got her cleaned up. Ella shook all over and bruises stained her skin.

Every time Lynden tried to ask what had happened, Ella tensed like a wounded animal. 'You can see it, can't you? Smell it on me?'

'Ella, my sweet, you're not making any sense.'

Ella's eyes darted, following things that weren't there. 'Make it stop,' she kept saying. 'Why won't anything stay still?'

That was when Lynden had asked Bess to fetch a sleeping draught.

Childlike, Ella allowed Lynden to dress her, raising and lowering her limbs when prompted, shuffling wordlessly into Lynden's bed.

When Ella allowed, Lynden held her as a mother would a frightened child, rocking her back and forth. Eventually, Ella met her gaze. In that moment, Lynden did see something. Or rather, felt it. Everything wavered erratically, the sizzle and crackle of Ella's touch upon hers. Warmth oozed between them. It leaked from Ella's eyes, her skin where Lynden's hands rested upon her, and slipped around her like bath water.

*Finally, an outlet.*

The thought wasn't Lynden's, and yet she heard it as a voice inside her head. Her mouth tried to form words, questions, but her tongue had grown gluggy, and her mind fogged. The warmth was melting and melding into her, her curiosity dissolving. As it did so, her vision—or was it Ella's?—calmed. Her body no longer jolted with every contact. Whatever had happened, it was none of her concern—Ella was safe now.

Ella stayed tucked in Lynden's chamber for over a week. Bess arrived periodically with meals, sometimes staying to keep Ella company when Lynden's duties kept her away. Ella didn't have to worry about Bess asking questions—Bess knew better than to say a word to anyone. Occasionally she sensed curiosity nagging at Lynden, but every time her friend came close to asking Ella what had happened, her gaze fogged over as the impulse evaporated. And each day Ella woke to the memory of Gohran's enormous face hovering above hers. His eyes were like looking in a mirror, cheeks polluted with tears as his body rocked back and forth, his intolerable weight bearing down, trapping her.

One morning Lynden caught Ella shoving at the air, pushing away the bed-clothes, squirming, before leaning over the bed's edge, dry retching. Ella's eyes watered as her stomach went into spasm, but she couldn't cry. Lynden's hands rested upon her shoulders, rubbed her back and her arms. She straightened up and leaned into Lynden's chest, breathing, breathing, taking some excess energy into herself as she built a chamber within her mind to lock the images away. Coddled within this artificial calm, the shaking stilled, and she could ignore the memories shoving themselves at her—for a time.

When Ella mustered the courage to look at her reflection in Lynden's dresser mirror, she saw a face that could be anyone's. It certainly wasn't hers. Eyes dead, mouth rigid, it belonged to someone wooden. Someone hollow. She traced her fingers along her arms where purple and blue blotches had yellowed, the pale of her neck still circled with the darker red of Gohran's mouth. Her hair was dull and greasy, the fur of a sick cat.

She bathed repeatedly, sliding down into scalding water as if she could scrub not only her skin but the deeper stain that marred her soul. She drew upon the water's heat to renew the steel-like chamber of her mind. To lock, store, and hide what no one could erase. The thought of anyone knowing the truth... Bile filled the back of her throat.

Out of her bath, she pulled on her dress, staring at the bruises still visible along her exposed flesh. Without Ella needing to utter a word, Lynden offered her a shawl, tenderly covering her. Hair combed, cheeks pinched to imitate the inner fire now smothered and extinguished, Ella examined the mirror-stranger of her reflection once more, knowing this shell of a being couldn't hide forever.

# Fifty-Six

Gohran didn't know how long he stayed huddled on Ella's bedroom floor. Consummating the connection between them was a breaking dam. A buildup of pressure, of need, suppressed for so long, finally bursting free. But like a dam, it released not only water. It carried debris with it. Anger, hurt, and betrayal, dumping all over its surrounds to pierce and maim. He kept seeing Ella's fear, her revulsion. Yet hadn't she wanted it—needed it—too? Everything she had said and done since her return from Nedran affirmed it. And yet when it happened... By the goddess, was he some kind of monster?

His own sister.

He meant what he had said. This was his punishment, his burden for being born Cursed.

Worst of all, what he would scarce admit to himself, was that he ached for her, even now.

He closed his eyes and breathed in the silence where she had been, the echo of her that remained in the smell of her bedclothes, her dresser, even the walls that bore witness to his shame—a secret he would carry to his grave. The connection was still there. He could feel it taunting him. Reassuring him.

*Gods, what if she were to tell someone...? What would become of him? Of them?* He steadied his breath and pulled himself together and up off the floor, emerging into the shadowy corridor. The surrounding walls, ceiling, and floor seemed to keel, as though the world itself was unstable. His legs wobbled, and he leant against the wall to find his bearings.

Teeth gritted, he barked at the first servant he encountered. 'Go clean up the tower room before the princess returns.'

The servant curtsied. 'Your Highness.' Head bowed, she hovered, hesitating.

'Well?'

'Your Highness, the princess... She's gone.'

His vision flashed red. 'What do you mean, she's gone?'

'She rode out before—'

'Rode out?' he thundered.

'Yes, Your Highness. No one realised what she intended until it was too late...'

Gohran grabbed the servant by the yoke. 'You mean to tell me the princess just took a steed and exited the city? Where were the guards?'

'The watch was just changing over, Your Highness, and with fewer men—'

'Lazy, drunken fools, all of them! Did no one think to go after her?'

'They assumed you knew...'

'As if I would allow the princess to leave the city unaccompanied, let alone at night! Fetch the guards. I'll have the skin off their backs for this.' He thrust the servant aside, and she scurried away.

Gohran took a deep breath and closed his eyes. He could sense her still, the connection strong between them. She would ride to Nedran, he was certain. She had nowhere else to go. And Venn would turn her back around and send her home again. With winter closing in, it would only be a question of when, and he could live with that. It would give her time to accept the truth that she wasn't yet ready to face—they were two halves of a fractured whole.

In the days that followed, Gohran kept to himself as much as possible. He attended the morning worship but did not linger to confer with Davith. 'I have much to oversee and no page,' he explained.

'I thought your youngest sister was fulfilling that... Need...' Davith said with a sour twist to his mouth.

Gohran inhaled sharply. 'She was acting as my page, however—'

Davith held up his hand. 'No need to explain yourself to me, Your Highness,' he said in a way that implied he expected that very thing.

Gohran turned to leave.

'Always have I advised you to take a firmer hand with the princesses, Your Highness. You allow them to live like falcons when they are mere sparrows, and they repay you by taking liberties with your generosity.'

Gohran pivoted sharply. 'Did I seek your counsel just now, Your Holiness?'

'You did not, Highness,' Davith nodded sagely, that sour twist there again. 'Nonetheless, it is my duty as High Priest to provide it.' He rested a heavy hand on Gohran's shoulder. 'And when you decide you've had enough of your flock flouting your authority, my priests will be only too happy to remind them of the goddess's supremacy.'

Gohran shrugged Davith's hand away, straightened, and spoke through gritted teeth. 'This is my kingdom, and these are my subjects. When I require assistance with matters of the spirit, not the state, I'll let you know.' Turning his back once more, he strode away.

Alone in his room, Gohran's altar taunted him. His flame for the goddess was burning low. He crouched to rekindle it. Hands trembling, he hesitated. Why had She done this to him? Made him the very thing She despised, then punished him in the most heinous way. Ella was his castigation.

And he was hers.

Gohran choked back his tears and grabbed the makeshift altar with both hands, hefted it upside down and hurled it. Its wooden frame splintered. He retrieved a broken plank of timber, raised it above his head, and then thwacked it down, again and again. His statue of Elnora shattered, the sound reverberating through his core as something broke inside him.

He smelled smoke. The diminished flame remained alive. Wood and cloth smouldered as the flames caught and grew. Gohran dropped to his knees, sobbing. Fire blazed and smoke thickened all around, choking him. He coughed, heat searing his flesh, and he inched closer. Let the flames lick him, taste him, devour him as they had his mother.

The edges of his bed, his dresser, and his tapestries smouldered, igniting. Soon flames surrounded him. He closed his eyes. Felt the heat closing in. At last, he could surrender to Her and end his torment.

Thundering outside. Servants clambered as they burst through the door and into his chamber to find him kneeling, fire singeing his hair and catching the corners of his clothes.

'By the goddess!'

'Highness!'

Voices yelling, calling, grabbing him, pulling him away, smothering him and his half-Cleansed altar in thick blankets.

Someone arrived with pails of water to douse and extinguish the last of the flames.

Gohran's vision blurred with tears as he sat staring at the remains of his charred altar. She would not allow him to be Cleansed. Not yet. He reached for the fragments of Elnora's statue, held them in his palm and whispered, 'Forgive me.'

# FIFTY-SEVEN

Venn sifted through the various parchments on his desk, cross-checking figures against notations on his ledger. He rested his fingers on his temples and let out a frustrated sigh. This debacle with Ella and Jonas was costing Nedran dearly. But if Gohran agreed to the betrothal he had proposed between him and Raeyn—what the king had wanted all along—Venn might renegotiate their trade agreement once they smoothed relations between their provinces.

He hadn't yet approached the Princess Elder to ask if she even wanted to marry. There was no point in raising her hopes, given how volatile the situation was. And as it would not be a love match, he saw no reason to court Raeyn beyond what custom and courtesy demanded to make their union civil. To do otherwise would be a cruel fiction.

A knock at the door. Venn's steward, Mykan, entered. 'A visitor, my lord.' He bowed, then stood aside to let them through.

There Ella stood, with a shawl drawn about her shoulders and neck like a commoner. Venn had never seen her look so pitiful. He stepped out from behind his desk and signalled for Mykan to leave them.

'My lord,' Ella curtsied.

'You waste your time, Your Highness. My brother isn't here.' He heard the chill of winter in his voice.

'It was you I came to see.' Ella edged closer. 'It was always you.'

Venn flinched. Ella's voice was soft as spring grass, yet within it, he imagined prickles of deceit.

'Please, hear me out.'

She moved nearer, her pleading eyes the outer edges of a sunset, where violet turns to blue. Eyes he'd adored once. He tried without success to look away. Her gaze had captured his. He felt oddly weightless, as though he might follow those eyes into the night sky. Her fingers brushed his face, honey-warm and endless. Her longing tugged at him, palpable. In that moment, it was his. It became harder to concentrate, to follow a train of thought. He would scoop her into his arms, take her far from here, forget he'd ever seen her with…

He shuddered, caught her hands, and turned her away.

Ella winced and stumbled, her shawl falling from her shoulders. Green and purple smeared her arms and magenta stained her neck.

'By Our Lady! Ella, what happened?'

She lowered her eyes. 'My brother's temper got the better of him,' she explained, though it was no explanation at all. 'He's still angry over what he thinks happened here. But my lord, nothing happened, I swear to you.'

'It didn't look like *nothing*.'

'Please, my lord, I can't go back there.'

'I am honour-bound to offer refuge to all who ask, but to harbour you here would offend His Highness. Is there somewhere else you can stay? I'll have my men escort you there, of course, but—'

'I've nowhere else to go.' Ella fell upon Venn's chest, shaking. 'Please, Venn.'

For a moment, Venn remained stiffly upright, tempted to shrug her away once more. Yet a more powerful sensation churned around him. The honey-warmth was back, a reverie, an exquisite tenderness he could drown in. He could feel his outer shell cracking, and a moment later, the withering of his hard-fought negotiations.

She leaned further into him, and he hooked his arms around her, drawing her close as if he could absorb her warmth into his skin, and deeper, into his soul. Maybe he could forget the last few moons, forget he'd ever…

When he spoke, his voice was syrupy. 'Perhaps we can give your brother time to calm down. See if we can talk things through.' His eyes grew soft, almost sleepy. The smell of her hair was all around as he kissed her forehead. He reached for remnants of resentment, but they kept slipping away like snow melting on warm fingertips.

'I should never have left you alone with him.'

Days stretched into weeks as Gohran rattled around inside the walls of the castle keep, barking out orders and flying into rages. Though he felt entirely disconnected from his actions, he performed his duties with diligence. Servants shuffled meekly around him, ducking to avoid hurled furniture and smashed crockery. The more they cowered, the more he despised them, letting loose with even greater force.

Up in his chamber, he stared at the scorched floor where his altar had stood. Without his worship and the comfort of his priest, he felt hollow. Empty. The only person who could fill that void, the only person who could ever understand, was the one he had hurt most. *He could feel her still.* Through their connection, he drank her in, allowing her essence to fill his hollow soul where once the goddess had placated and soothed, quieting his rage and agitation, though the feeling didn't last. He needed her by his side.

A knock at his door. 'A letter from Nedran, Your Highness.'

Gohran did not need to open the letter to know what it contained. Still, he took it and closed the door to read. Ella was exactly where he knew she would be, and as he expected, Venn judged the season unfit to send her back to Erldan right away. The only surprise was Venn requesting that Gohran defer all discussions of his pending proposal to Raeyn. He wished to break the news to Ella himself when the moment was fitting. Gohran wrote back, agreeing, but added, 'Surely it would be better to douse the princess's hopes right away?' He did not tell Venn that Ella already knew he intended to marry Raeyn.

At least Venn would not want Ella now. And when he sent her back home, Gohran could instate her as his official adviser. Even now—especially now—he saw that his plan to keep her by his side was the only way for them to be who they truly were. Eventually, he would need to settle her, but that was a problem for the future.

He was just about to head out when someone else stopped him, this time one of his riders.

'What is it?' he snapped, irritated.

'Your Highness, there's been word of some disturbance in the villages near the northeastern border.'

'Disturbance?'

'Yes, Your Highness. Some outlaws raided a homestead. There have been reports of kidnappings and... And rituals.'

Gohran's eyes narrowed. 'Send an escort to fetch the elder princesses home from Rynwood as soon as the weather permits. Then we will conduct a patrol and sort this out.'

# FIFTY-EIGHT

For stretches at a time, Ella pushed what had happened to the farthest reaches of her mind. Being back at Nedran helped. She could pretend to herself she had never left, that her return to Erldan had been a horrible dream. It was only the thrumming through her body, abuzz with overflowing energy, startling at the least noise or touch, and the nightmare flashes that came unbidden, that would not let her forget.

She spent what time she could with Venn, who had holed up over the coldest parts of winter. She found her power flowed easily through their physical contact. Whenever she gently touched his arm, she could feel it pouring out of her and wrapping around him, and the buzzing stilled for a time.

Venn told her he had written to Gohran to say the roads were too icy now to travel by carriage, and he would not send the princess away on horseback, so she could breathe for a few weeks more.

But on a day when the first blossoms of spring were budding, Venn raised the question of Ella's return. They were out walking by the Leaping Lake. Shallow water murmured over jagged rocks, waiting for the snowmelt to swell it back to its usual flow.

Venn rested his arm around Ella's shoulder. 'I have to write to your brother again soon.'

Ice in her veins and lead in her stomach. 'I can't go back, my lord. I won't. What if he hurts me again, or sends me to a temple? I couldn't live like that. Please, Venn.' Eyes wide, her lip quivered.

Venn drew her close and cradled her against his chest. She trembled like a frightened cat. 'He won't send you to a temple, Ella. You're his sister. A princess.'

'You don't know him, Venn. You think you do, but you don't. He will hurt me, he will—' Panic rose in her throat.

'Hush, now...' he breathed into her hair. 'I'll do what I can to protect you, you know that, but he is your overlord.'

Ella pulled away. Even now, knowing Gohran had hurt her, and how she feared him, he put her brother's wishes above hers, above his own. 'He doesn't have to be.'

Her meaning was not lost on him. Venn took her hands in his, eyes pleading. 'I would marry you in a second, Ella, if Gohran would allow it.'

She had to stop herself from screaming that he wouldn't even try. She understood all too well what her rash behaviour had cost Nedran in renegotiating the hallit agreement. He wouldn't dare risk the remnants of his relationship with Gohran—it was his duty to Nedran. Yet she wondered if he would have been willing to risk even that if it wasn't for Jonas. Part of him still doubted her, doubted her love for him. His anger and hurt at her betrayal lurked behind every thought.

Ella could read Venn so easily now. She wasn't sure if it was from embracing her power where once she had tried to suppress it, or because there was so much more of it surging through her.

She drew upon that excess power now to soothe Venn's pain. But as she did so, she saw his thoughts reflected clearly. He was picturing her brother. She froze, immobilised. If Venn forced her to return... Everything pressed in on her. Gohran's hateful, tear-stained face above hers. Rocking. Grasping. She couldn't breathe.

She shoved Venn's hands away, pushed past him, and ran back along the river's edge. The ground was uneven, and though she stumbled, she did not stop. She heard Venn call her name, but it sounded muffled and dreamlike. She kept running, jumping over stones, and darting between branches. He called out again, but she pressed on. Another leap and her foot rolled over a loose rock. It shifted and toppled. She was falling, down, down towards the running water, her body colliding with rock and dry-packed earth, until she landed at the bottom of the creek bed. Ella scrambled to her feet.

Venn had caught up with her and hovered above, arms outstretched.

She ignored him, grasped the rocky embankment, and tried to climb. She kept slipping, her dresses weighed down with water and mud from the shallow creek.

Venn grasped her torso and lifted her back up towards him. He drew her away from the water's edge and onto the nearby grass. Her wet dress soaked him. 'Hush, Ella, my love. I won't make you leave.' He wrapped his cloak around her, and she sagged against him, shivering. 'We'll find a way through this, I promise you.'

'There is no other way.' She wept and shuddered with hiccup breaths. 'You can't risk Nedran, I understand that, and Gohran will never let me marry. You said it yourself. He is my overlord. To defy him would be treason. Me being here... I know I can't stay. I *know* that.' Hair stuck to her cheeks. Tenderly, Venn brushed it aside. When he looked at her, his will was hers. She could feel it.

An orb of fairy-grass tumbled through the air beside them. With cupped hands, Ella trapped it. 'This is me, Venn.'

Venn wrapped his large hands around hers. 'It's *us*.' He opened her palms and freed the grass fairy with a puff of breath. It circled and danced. 'We will find a way, Ella.'

She shook her head, fire in her chest. 'I don't see how if you won't become my overlord...' She watched the fairy grass tumble.

'El...'

'Remember when we first walked together beside the tombs of the Ancients?'

Venn nodded and swallowed the lump in his throat. 'Like it was yesterday.'

'What if we were to pledge ourselves to one another before the gods, the way the Ancients did?'

'Come now, Ella, this isn't a game.'

She faced him, her expression anything but playful. 'Not even Gohran would defy a god-sworn oath.'

'And then what—you would be my mistress? I would never make you live like that.'

'Even if it's my choice?'

'I have Nedran to think of.'

'So, you'll take a legal wife and she'll birth your heirs. What is a betrothal but a contract, a treaty? It's not about love.'

'Even if that wife is your sister?'

'I can help raise my nieces and nephews.'

'Ella, please. You might think you could live that way, but I couldn't. It wouldn't be fair to anyone.'

She waved away his objections. 'Then abdicate. You still have a successor.'

'Jonas.'

'Exactly. He can marry for duty and keep as many mistresses as he cares to. We both know he has no lust for politicking, so he would be ruler in name only. A figurehead. Nedran would still be yours.'

'You're grasping.'

She ran her hands across his chest. 'It could work, Venn. You'll make it work.'

'Ella—'

She stifled his words with a kiss.

Ella's honey-warmth became a fiery insistence, nagging. All over, Venn tingled, his mind mead-muddled. He could feel the swell of her breasts through the wet fabric, the slope of her waist and belly. Ella unlaced her soggy bodice. The animal lust he'd staved off for the entire year she was at Nedran was omnipresent. The desire he had pushed aside and fled from, only for his brother to sweep in and—

'No,' he whispered. He stayed her hands. 'Not like this.'

Ella pulled away and knelt at Venn's feet. 'I will never love another as I love you. Make me your mistress or not, I will still pledge myself to you.' Head bowed, voice slow and deliberate, she intoned her vows before the gods, promising to love and honour him, just like in an Ancient's betrothal ritual.

When she stood back up and met Venn's gaze, he ached for her warmth, the exquisite thrill that coursed through his body whenever she touched him. He could have that forever, truly be with her. He just had to utter the words. Reaching out a finger to her lips, he kissed her gingerly and then pulled back.

This was ludicrous. What she was suggesting—it was absurd. This wasn't some whimsical saga. They both had responsibilities and owed their families and their provinces loyalty, duty, and accountability.

The need tugged and pulled. His entire body might have been made from iron filings, and hers a sailor's point.

An image flashed before him then, of Gohran the day they had pledged and sealed their friendship before the gods. The life force that had surged between them and through him was what he felt now, flowing from Ella and wrapping around him. He had felt the goddess that day. He felt her now.

After another moment, he knelt, mirroring Ella's pose of moments before, and pledged his life to her. Around them, the wind whispered through the trees and Venn imagined it was the sound of the gods answering. This time when they kissed and Ella urged him towards the grass, he didn't hold back.

# Fifty-Nine

Gohran welcomed the return of his older sisters from Rynwood. With Raeyn appointed as regent, he could head out to conduct the patrol of greater Erldan. By right of fealty, Erldan's army was free to roam any of the king's vassal's lands. A law created for times of war, when there would be no moment to gather proper letters of passage. But this was a technicality, for any challenge in times of peace would bring war soon enough. Gohran took advantage of that law now to survey the farthest reaches of his vassal's lands, almost into the neighbouring kingdom of Herron.

While Gohran exchanged their horses at every other stop, his men got no relief. Burning muscles, blisters and chafing were all he heard about for a time until he bid them cease their whining.

'How do you expect to cope in a true battle?'

True battle. Head tipped back towards Elnora, Gohran closed his eyes and smelled the grass and dirt, letting the sun etch into his cheeks. In battle he might honour Her, send Her souls of sacrifice. Or be sacrificed himself, Cleansed finally in death. Yet as they crested each hill, pressed into every valley, with not so much as a bandit to challenge them, Gohran grew despondent. He dug nails into blisters and left his shirt damp with sweat to abrade him still more, revelling in each fiery sting.

A caw interrupted Gohran's musings. He looked up to see a portent of ravens circling beyond the next hillcrest. Blood pumped at his temples. With a signal, his men pulled up, falling into line around him. Chances were, it was only a fallen animal, but Gohran dared not risk it, not when corruption clung to the air, making his skin pucker like a fowl's flesh.

'You smell that?' he asked Tarraen, who pulled up nearby.

'I don't smell a thing, Your Highness.'

'Gods, it's enough to rot a man's lungs.'

Turning in his saddle, Gohran singled out four of the men to scout ahead with him. The youngest, Ganno, galloped to the lead with an eager salute. Gohran followed at the rear, the reek settling in his gut, urging him onwards. Forest stretched to the west and south, while to the north lay the first of Creywmm's farmsteads, land now forbidden to them. Straight ahead, the grass grew wild, pasture for wandering herds. The five set out at a canter.

'Your Highness, I see something,' Ganno called as he crested the hill ahead of the others. 'Shall I go on?'

It was more than a stench now. It was a clammy hand down Gohran's spine, the taste of bile at the back of his throat. 'No, Ganno. Wait here—all of you.'

'But—'

One hand went up, and the men fell silent. Gohran dismounted and threw his horse's reigns to the tallest lad, standing beside Ganno. He covered his nose and mouth with one hand and trudged through the long grass.

His nose told him it would not be pleasant, but nothing could have prepared him for what he next saw. A wooden platform stood amid a field. Poles on either side formed a large frame around it. At first, he thought it might have been an old well or gallows, but instead of a drawdown or noose, the dais supported a tilted cross, like a giant 'X'. Attached to the cross was what must be a human. A peasant woman, judging by the remnants of cloth, for nothing else could have distinguished her. Most of the flesh was eaten away. What remained was home to hordes of insects. Ravens kept diving to pick at the choicest carrion and their feasting had exposed the worst of the horror. It was almost as though someone had tried to mimic a Cleansing but without fire. Whoever had done this hadn't tied or nailed the victim to wood, as people still did in parts of Ycelt. Instead, they had skewered her with spear-thin pikes, like a boar. The corners of the cross splintered the bone of her wrists and ankles. The shivery damp of a fever drenched Gohran with sweat.

Something near the feet of the corpse moved. For a moment, Gohran could have sworn he heard a child wailing, but it was only a raven. He braced himself and clutched at a piece of torn dress. It came away but pulled some flesh with it. He let go of the fabric, sure he would vomit. From beneath his shirt, he pulled out a kerchief to wave at the smaller bundle, urging the insects away. Enough of them shunned his swats to let him see what lay beneath. An infant, tied to its mother's feet and left to die. Something at its neck glittered. Gohran drew his sword. Gingerly, he hooked the object—a chain—onto the end of his blade. With a tug, it came free and thudded onto the grass. He knelt to get a closer look. The chain circled a metal disc, roughly coin-sized, and graved with a large 'X'. Using his kerchief, he picked it up. It felt hot, for a moment, aglow, a fiery silver blue.

'Your Highness—Gods, Your Highness!'

Gohran slipped the chain beneath his shirt. Turning back, he held his arms out to stop the men from coming closer. Too late. He heard someone vomiting onto the nearby grass. Ganno, no doubt.

'Why? Why would anyone...?'

*Heretics.* The word stuck in Gohran's throat. 'These poor souls deserve a proper burial, but I'm not about to make any of you cut them down. We'll cremate the bodies where they stand.' Well, they were half Cleansed, anyway, he thought, though this barbarism was no true Cleansing at all.

Gohran could have sworn a raven turned and looked straight at him, before gliding on, its beak gorged with rotting meat. He felt shivery all over. Something had changed, shifted. He could feel it in his blood. The feeling stayed with him long after they burnt the bodies until he wondered whether burning the corpses had been the right thing to do.

That night, they made camp well to the north. No one wanted to eat much of anything, agreeing that what they'd seen was enough to curdle any man's stomach. The drink flowed freely, however, as the men passed skins of ale back and forth, taking up a chorus as they drank. The singing dragged on until the songs ran out and the men bastardised the lyrics from one to fit the tune of another.

For once, Gohran had no desire to be on his own. The unease still nagged, creeping. Someone started up a ballad from the old war about a heretic who seduced the king's captain. The captain was the tale's hero, betraying the witch and winning them the war. For this lament, they borrowed from a light-hearted jig, the effect all the better for its absurdity.

*And then she came a-canting,*

*A-chanting,*

*A-courting.*

*And so, he bid her*

*Calling,*

*To mourning,*

*Till dawning.*

*Until he rode to greet her,*

*To meet her,*

*Betray her.*

*With sword in hand, he called her,*

*He trawled her,*

*And mauled her.*

*By morn, she would be beaten,*

*Her people all retreatin'*

*Before they could be eaten...*

This line brought the clinging unease to the fore. It must be the horror of what he'd seen that lingered, he thought. And yet it was more than that. No—*other* than that. That woman could have been him, his mother, his sister...

Ella.

That was it! Until this afternoon, his connection to Ella had been strong, pulsing. He had felt her presence as though she rode beside him. He knew their bond still gripped her as it did him. Now that feeling tugged and gnawed, a rope pulled too tight. Not broken, but strained. There could only be one cause.

'Venn.'

# SIXTY

Venn lazed naked in the grass, utterly intoxicated by their lovemaking, before drifting to sleep. As Ella leaned on one elbow watching him, she felt a wave of relief, and yet she also felt hollow, dirty, tasting bitter tears of guilt and remorse.

When Venn eventually woke, a contented smile played on his lips. Ella stroked his dark hair and tried to return his smile.

Venn sat up. 'What is it, my love?'

'I was just wondering what will happen when Gohran finds out.'

Venn pulled her to his chest. 'When I spoke my vows, I meant them. We are as good as married in my eyes and the eyes of the gods, if not the priests or the law.'

Ella's eyes lit up, and she sensed Venn sliding along her joy. He wanted to please her so badly it hurt.

When she kissed him in gratitude, he took her in his arms once more. Harsh realities could wait a while longer.

From that night, Venn had Ella sit beside him at meals as though she truly was his wife. To all who saw them, they appeared as besotted with one another as new lovers could be, sharing their supper and wine, always touching.

For almost a week they spent every moment together, culminating in Venn presenting Ella with a betrothal brooch.

'It was my mother's,' he said as he pinned it to her dress.

Ella threw her arms around his neck and kissed him. Could this truly be happening?

'We'll have to write to your brother now.'

Footsteps approached. Someone cleared their throat.

'My lord?' Mykan stood in the doorway, waving a parchment.

'What is it?' Venn continued to admire Ella's brooch, running his fingers through her hair.

'Trouble to the south.'

'Mmm?'

'My lord, this is important.'

Venn looked over, annoyed. 'Then give it to my captain. Make him earn his keep.' He waved the steward away.

Mykan again cleared his throat. 'There's also the matter of your court, my lord. I turned another score of complainants away this morning, but several matters await your jurisdiction.'

Ella's stomach clenched.

'Where is my goddess-forsaken brother? Can't he see to them?'

'Venn.' Ella rested her hand on his arm.

Venn was about to continue his rant when Ella sensed his mind sway and skip in a drift akin to drunkenness. After a moment, the feeling passed.

'Forgive me, my love? I'd best see to this,' Venn said, and stood to accompany his steward.

As soon as they were gone, Ella sank back into her chair. *By every god and demon. What had she done?*

Gohran was still on patrol when confirmation of Ella's situation reached him from a most unexpected quarter. His troop had stopped outside the town of Rynwood to make camp and change their horses. They were just setting up when an escort greeted them, Lord Kerr at its head.

'Can't have you staying out here with trouble afoot, Your Highness,' the lord said with a low bow.

'Indeed?'

The escort led Gohran and a small honour guard inside the city while the rest of the men remained at the camp. When they reached the inner gates, Kerr dismounted and took the king's reigns.

Upon the walls of the main keep, Gohran saw someone had raised the royal standard alongside that of Rynwood.

'No harm in letting people know you've royalty in residence,' Kerr said when he caught Gohran staring upwards.

A servant arrived with sweet wine, and ushered them through to a parlour where a small feast of smoked meats, cheeses and preserved fruit awaited.

Gohran took a raisin from an offered plate and swallowed it with a mouthful of wine. 'You mentioned there's been trouble. We may have come across some of it on our way here.'

'Oh? It could well be. We've had some—undesirables—skirting around near the border.' Kerr signalled to a servant.

'Undesirables?'

'You know, bandits and the like.' Kerr's eyes followed the servant to the doorway.

'When was the last time you heard of bandits stringing up women and children?' Gohran could have sworn Kerr paled. 'If ever you need the loan of my men...'

'Ah, here's my sister.' Kerr turned to greet a young woman wearing a widow's cowl.

'Did I hear someone mention bandits?' Lady Layla dropped a fine curtsy, and Gohran took her hand stiffly.

Fortunately for the lass, many a man would forgive the shortness of stature in a woman, and while her brother's stockiness made him appear portly, Layla's resulted in a pleasant plumpness about her breasts and hips, aided by the corsetry that cinched in her waist. Despite her bland blue eyes, pale skin and dull yellow hair peeking through her cowl, she was not unpleasant to look at.

'I was just about to say that if your brother can furnish me and my men with fresh steeds, we can make a swift strike around the forest's edge, as far as Creywmm and Herron. If any bandits are hiding thereabouts, they'd be wise to evacuate before we arrive.'

'How generous of you, Your Highness. I would have thought such a minor concern would be beneath your notice. Can I offer more wine?' Layla held up a carafe.

Gohran nodded. 'Sometimes it is best to take a firmer hand.' As she filled his glass, he noticed her peering up at him coyly, her inner arms pressing against her breasts to create a pillowy cleft. 'The royal guard is always ready to help stamp out *undesirables*. And my head priest has given his assurance that he and his fellows are available to any of my vassals.' Gohran felt the disc beneath his shirt grow hot.

'Your priest?' Layla put the carafe back down and pushed a lock of fallen hair behind her cowl.

Kerr wiped his brow with a kerchief. 'My humble thanks for your generous offer, but we have the matter in hand, I assure you.'

'As you please. As much as I do not share my late mother's penchant for the Moon god, I see no need for honest citizens to take matters of heresy into their own hands. I would as soon see those who consider themselves above Our Lady's servants put down.' Having said his piece, Gohran moved the conversation on, for which Kerr looked immensely grateful.

After supper, the family again retired to the parlour. Kerr sat in the corner, leaving the only vacant seat for his sister beside the king. Layla took it upon herself to keep Gohran's glass filled, and before long, Kerr mumbled something about needing to fetch a book from his study and left the pair alone.

'It was so lovely to have your sisters stay, Your Highness.' Layla twirled a locket that sat low on her neck, just above her bodice. 'I was quite hoping to see more of them, but now with no hope for Kerr and Ella...'

Gohran stiffened. 'I told your brother he was welcome to any of my sisters, provided he chose Jaydyn. Raeyn has been all but promised to my closest friend, and Ella shall not marry before her older sisters.'

'So, it's not true, then? Is she not soon to be wed?'

'Pardon?'

'I heard Ella was back at Nedran, that she and the dryhten were... Well, I just assumed...'

'Kindly don't.'

'My sincerest apologies, Your Highness. I meant no offence.' After a moment, Layla's hand made its way back to her locket. 'Perhaps then, you might mention me to Raeyn and Jaydyn? It would be lovely to visit again soon. It gets lonely out here with no husband to keep me warm.'

Gohran was aware of Layla's hand upon his knee. He stood to leave. 'Excuse me. I need to be fresh for the morning's journey.'

# SIXTY-ONE

It was a mild evening when Jonas finally arrived back at Nedran, having wintered with Vera and her family at Lichen. Venn was fussing over Ella, brushing a stray lock of hair from her cheek as they made their way to the dining hall for supper. When they entered, Jonas glanced up, looking as though he'd swallowed a mouthful of flies. Venn rested his hands upon Ella's shoulders, and escorted her to the chair beside his, all the while fending off his brother's glare.

'Princess Ella, I didn't expect to see you back.' Jonas's tone was flat.

He looked at her as if he could see her shame as clearly as the dress she wore. Ella flinched, wanting to sink beneath the earth to the deepest pit of the last hell.

'I heard your brother has been making a tour of greater Erldan.' Jonas passed her a dish piled with meat and vegetables. He looked at Venn. 'I assume you're acting as nursemaid again?'

'The princess is here under my protection,' Venn said.

'Protection?'

Ella steeled herself and ignored his question. She took the offered dish and passed it on to Venn. 'How were your hearings this morning, my love?'

Jonas nearly spit his mouthful across the room.

'Nothing out of the ordinary. Except for one matter on which I would like your opinion. I have asked the complainant—Sammyn, I think his name was—to return for judgement in the morning.'

Jonas narrowed his gaze. 'Is that mother's brooch I see pinned to your dress, El?' He turned to Venn. 'Did I miss a proclamation?'

Venn put out his hand to stop Ella from responding. He straightened up and faced his brother square-on. 'Ella and I have made a pledge to one another, and for as long as I am lord here, I expect you to treat the princess as you would my legal wife. We have only to await King Gohran's return and we will have the priests bless our union.'

Jonas threw up his hands, eyes to the heavens. 'You'll need the blessing of the gods themselves to sway the king at this point.' He stabbed a hunk of meat and dropped it onto his plate before turning his attention to his sister. 'Vera sends her warmest regards, Lyn. I was thinking I might have overstayed my welcome, but her parents seemed quite genuine when they said they hoped I would be back soon.'

Even now, hearing about Jonas and Vera stabbed at Ella the way Jonas stabbed at his meat. She sank back into her chair, pushing food around her plate.

For the rest of the meal, Jonas conversed with his sister, leaving Venn and Ella to talk amongst themselves. Beneath the table, Venn squeezed Ella's hand, his eyes full of concern. Occasionally he shot his brother a glance as murderous as Gohran's could be, and as soon as she was able, Ella excused herself and slipped away.

Venn stood to follow, but she stopped him. 'You stay, my love. I just need to lie down for a moment.'

Ella hadn't realised how much it would pain her to see Jonas again. She couldn't seem to use her sway on him as she had on Lynden and Venn. When he looked at her, she felt naked, her soul stripped bare.

Later, as she lay with Venn in his oversized bed, her lover was restless. Jonas was right. Whatever childish rites they had carried out, swearing themselves directly to the gods, Gohran might still deny them. And while Venn feared the loss of an alliance, Gohran might consider Ella's actions treasonous.

Ella bent across to kiss Venn, trying to soothe herself as much as him. 'Please, my love, let it go. Jonas only said what he did to get a rise. It must hurt him to see us together.'

'You are right, of course.' Venn's shoulders relaxed, and he took her in his arms, melting into her warmth.

Given the regularity of their lovemaking, Ella no longer had to use conscious magic to influence Venn. Instead, whatever she willed, he complied.

Afterwards, Ella watched Venn with a creeping dread settling in her belly. Since the beginning of their affair, or perhaps from the first moment Ella had used her powers on him, Venn had changed. No longer the honourable leader she had admired, he was like an extension of herself. Whatever she asked of him, he did without question, often without her even having to voice her wishes. She found she had to prompt him to attend to his army and his people, whom he'd once placed above everything. Often, he wanted to confer with her on matters of state. But what did she know about any of that? Only the little she had observed while acting as Gohran's page. There was none of the thrill and hunger she'd felt with Jonas—that she felt still if she were honest. And when she looked at Venn and saw a mere shell of the man with whom she'd fallen in love, it reminded her of her hollow mirror-image, that nothing-person staring back, now a carapace for shame and guilt.

And each night, alone in the dark, as Venn slept soundly beside her, she cried herself to sleep.

# Sixty-Two

Gohran's journey back from Rynwood was swift. They passed several other vigilante Cleansings along the way, but none so gruesome as the first. Now, safe in his private study, Gohran emptied his pouch onto his desk. A pile of coins and gems spilled out. Among them were the pearls he'd gifted to Ella and the metal disc he'd found upon the child-corpse. He couldn't say why, but he had so far avoided mentioning the Cleansings and disc to Davith. Perhaps it was for the same reason Kerr had shied away from discussing the undesirable element under his jurisdiction. Stamping out vigilantes was no simple task. It wasn't like putting down a rebellion, making a conquest, or even ridding a territory of bandits. It required the type of concerted effort henads used to uncover heretics, which could take years or even decades. And it could prove unpopular if the people saw the vigilantes as doing the job of their overlords.

Gohran ran his fingers along the smooth surface of Ella's pearls. With his other hand, he rubbed the disc between thumb and forefinger. When he'd found the disc, he'd assumed the sunlight had caused it to glow, but when he placed it under the light of his lantern, it stayed stubbornly dull. He tossed the pearls aside and picked up his wine glass, a delicate blown goblet, doubtless from the far eastern sea, a parting gift from his hosts at Rynwood. He would have said a courting gift, but Kerr couldn't possibly expect Gohran to consort with Layla, though she'd obviously been offering herself to him. Perhaps she hoped to become his mistress? An affair was one way to forge a connection, he supposed, if Kerr could not have the princess he preferred. Tilting the glass,

Gohran watched the line of liquid slosh from one side to the other, before consuming the entire contents in one swallow.

'I heard Ella was back at Nedran, that she and the dryhten were...'

Venn and Ella.

The disc fired up, luminous. Gohran had assumed Venn would not want Ella now. Was the dryhten as powerless around her as Gohran was? And if people were gossiping... He had to take the matter in hand.

Pressure built behind Gohran's temples as a painful ache throbbed through his limbs and loins.

The tension intensified until he thought his head and body might explode. Beneath his grip, the goblet shattered. Bloody fragments littered the desk and blood dripped down his arm.

Gohran stared at it, a cold grin spreading across his face. He closed his eyes, leaned back in his chair, and exhaled slowly as the pressure eased. *Relief.*

As the days grew longer and warmer, Ella found that by suppertime each evening, she could barely keep her eyes open. When she could, she napped in the warm afternoons, and she would have slept late, too, if it hadn't been for the churning in her stomach waking her. At first, she assumed her nightmares induced it, but when she felt nauseous yet hungry all at once, she counted the turnings of the moon. *How long had it been? Far too long.* It should have been her moon-time when she first saw Venn in his study after returning to Nedran. Why hadn't she realised then?

Images flashed behind her eyes. Swords clashing, arrows flying, blood flowing. With an icy shiver of foresight, Ella knew Venn must believe the babe to be his. Not for her sake, but because the truth could only lead to bloodshed.

That morning, Ella followed Venn out to watch him train. She silently thanked the gods that whatever change her magic had brought about, he hadn't lost his skills on the field. Jonas was there too, staring insolently at his brother as the riders went around the circle, sparring with wooden swords.

When the brothers finally faced off, Jonas slashed his wooden sword down, powerful and fast, scoring the final touch to win the set, though he would never be a match for Venn.

From time to time, Ella noticed Jonas glance first at her and then back to Venn. Something in his expression gave Ella pause. She stood and brushed the grass from her skirts and hurried back inside, the sound of blood pumping in her ears.

When suppertime came around, Ella cried off sick. The thought of facing the two brothers was overwhelming. She had just laid down when there was a knock at the door. Ella thought it might be Venn, but a moment later Lynden appeared carrying her supper.

'I hope those two sort things out soon.' Lynden put the tray down and sat on the bed beside Ella. 'This looks worse than your usual headaches. Shall I fetch a medic?'

Ella propped herself up and brushed her hair back from her face. 'Don't trouble yourself. I'm just overtired.'

'Are you worried about your brother? I heard he's back at Erldan. Vera mentioned it to Jonas.'

'Is there anything Vera doesn't hear?'

Eyes soft, Lynden reached for Ella's hand. 'You'll have to ask for the king's blessing soon, my sweet.' Ella sensed her wanting to say more, but that desire kept slipping away.

Ella shuddered. She recalled a conversation between some women at the Red Rose about a herbalist in the town who, for an exorbitant fee, would rid women of their troubles. They'd described the process as barbaric. If she took that risk and survived, and someone found out, under the laws of the priests, abortions carried the death penalty. Ella shuddered again.

'Let me fetch you another blanket.' Before she left, Lynden tucked Ella under the covers and set the supper tray within easy reach without Ella needing to utter a word. Where Lynden had always been warm and caring, there was something wooden about her actions now.

As soon as she was gone, Ella pushed the tray aside, trying not to weep. *Her magic had altered Lynden, too.*

As it transpired, Ella and Venn did not need to write to Gohran. A letter from the king himself arrived the next morning.

'What does it say?' Ella asked as Venn read the small parchment, shaking his head. Finally, he handed the scroll over. With nail-bitten fingers, Ella took it and read.

*To my so-called friend,*

*I am told you intend to seal your family's betrayal with a treaty of marriage, so write to congratulate you on your forthcoming nuptials. Whether by your doing or your brother's, my sister is spoiled for any other, so you can have her or not, as you please. Know that the alliance which ensues thereby is a lawful one, but not one of my heart or willingness to keep.*

*No longer yours, Gohran.*

'Why? Why write such a hateful letter, yet give us what we want?'

Venn sighed and shrugged. 'He speaks the truth, Ella, my love. Your brother gets his precious alliance, and the marriage contract will keep him loyal where he no longer honours me.'

Ella reached out to him. Venn had loved Gohran like a brother. Pulling him close, she sucked up his empty ache and drew it into herself. If she could do nothing else, she could help ease this pain for him.

By afternoon it seemed news of Gohran's letter had spread. Ella was heading towards the stables when Jonas caught her arm.

'What do you want?' She recoiled away from him.

Jonas stood so that she couldn't pass. 'Answer me this. Do you honestly think marrying Venn is the right thing to do?'

'Do you honestly think it's any of your business at this point?' She folded her arms across her chest and faced him square-on.

'The decisions you make affect all of us, El. Your brother might have agreed to it, but have you stopped to think what it will mean for Nedran, for Erldan? The way Gohran sees things now...'

'He was willing to let us marry before—no thanks to you. Why should it be any different now?'

'Because everything is different now.'

'It doesn't have to be,' she threw back.

Jonas looked her up and down, his gaze lingering over her fuller breasts and slimmer face, and she felt he could read her very soul.

'What really happened at Erldan, Ella?'

His eyes, so full of concern, not influenced by her, but genuine. A part of her she'd almost forgotten longed to melt. She shoved the longing down beneath the hard casing she now wore, alongside the many memories she wished she could erase. 'I've already said—Gohran lost his temper and threatened to send me away.'

'And he beat you,' Jonas prompted.

'Yes.'

'He beat you *now*. Because of what happened between us back *then*.' Incredulous.

'Nothing happened between us.' *Why did she find it so hard to lock her thoughts up?*

'It wasn't nothing to me.' Jonas ran his fingers along the outside of her arms, the barest caress. 'I am sorry he hurt you, but I'm not sorry we spent that night or any other moment together.' He leaned in closer, whispering. 'Maybe you are right. Maybe it doesn't have to be any different now.'

She clamped down on her emotions and stepped back. 'No, Jonas. You were right before. Everything is different now.'

Jonas cocked his head, studying her, as though he were trying to solve a riddle. 'Perhaps you're right... Something is undoubtedly different about you.'

She froze.

He rubbed his chin in a mockery of contemplation. 'And Venn. I never thought I'd see my perfect, upright brother so lust-addled. You've certainly worked your magic on him, haven't you?'

Ella's body tensed like a startled game. Bile in her throat, she thought she might faint.

Something in her stance seemed to give Jonas pause. His eyes softened. 'A poor choice of words, my apologies.'

Ella exhaled, fear morphing into anger as she found her voice. 'Venn's not been himself since *you* let him think you bed me. And of course, I've changed, Jonas. How did you think it would be for me after being dragged home in disgrace?'

'I am sorry, El. Truly. I didn't mean for things to turn out that way.' Beseeching. 'But you made your choice, too.'

'I did, and I paid a price you'll never have to experience.'

He nodded, mouth set in a grim line. 'You're right. It is different for me. I wish it weren't, and I would sell my soul to change it.'

'Don't, Jonas. Don't make promises like that. Not even in jest. You don't know what the gods will make of it.'

'Okay, then.' He gestured heavenward. 'I wish I could change the plight of women in this cursed land,' he boomed.

The distant bustle of townsfolk and the occasional whinny of a horse were all that answered.

Jonas moved close once more, his gentle hands stroking. 'I mean it, El. I wish I could change what happened, for all our sakes.'

'Well, you can't, and neither can I.'

He reached for her cheek, her hair, his eyes searching, longing.

Her body stiffened. 'I think it would be best if you weren't here when Gohran arrived.' Her brother would be present for the sealing of the betrothal.

'You don't have to worry yourself on that score. I have no desire to see the king ever again. Not unless he's at the other end of my sword.'

'Hush, Jonas! That's treason.'

'He's not my king. I've sworn no vows of fealty.'

'But once my betrothal is sealed, you will have to.'

'El, you don't have to marry Venn. I know I can't offer you much, but it's got to be better than this charade.' His hazel eyes yearning.

Her limbs turned to water. In that moment, she felt herself waver. She closed her eyes and exhaled. Opening them again, she met his gaze, head shaking. 'No Jonas. If we were to elope... The damage to Nedran is already done. This is the only way to repair relations between our provinces. And I still love Venn. I do...' Her voice sounded weak, even to her.

He swallowed, voice cracking. 'El...' A deep breath. He cleared his throat. 'I'll support whatever you decide, and I'll be gone before Gohran arrives, but I want you to know that whatever happens, you can always come to me.'

She looked down.

He lifted her chin to face him. Eyes locked. 'El, swear to me that if ever you need, you'll come to me. Promise?'

She nodded, not trusting herself to speak, breaking away before he could see her tears.

# SIXTY-THREE

Venn had written his thanks to Gohran and invited him to Nedran to finalise the betrothal. Ella knew it was what protocol demanded, regardless of anyone's feelings on the matter. So, each day she meditated, locking away her memories and purging her emotions in anticipation of seeing him again. Her future depended on it.

But when Gohran arrived a few days later, Ella's chainmail of calm might have been made from ilak's wool. When she saw his and Venn's stiff greeting, she hung back, body trembling. It was like ice and flame polluted her veins. Images of that day flashed behind her mind's eye, and she willed a veneer of calm. She sensed Gohran's fiery eyes stalking her. She now recognised his pained expression for what it was—suppressed desire, anguish, and self-loathing, projected onto her.

With sickening dread, she also realised his every emotion now lay open to her, and likely he could read hers just as easily. In the same way that making love to Venn had bonded them, Gohran forcing himself on Ella had wedged a channel between them. Yet unlike with Venn, where the energy flowed in one direction, Ella could feel Gohran passing power back to her in a horrifying kind of equilibrium.

As soon as she could, she escaped Gohran's hot stare and headed to her room. She sent the maid away, barred the door, and slumped to the floor. Gohran was here to seal her betrothal to Venn—the very thing she'd longed for, yet it seemed a punishment. Why? Why did it have to be like this? Was Gohran right? Was this castigation of the gods? But for what? For being born with powers she never asked for? Or for trying to carve out her future, instead of subjugating herself to the whims of others?

Eyes closed, Ella steadied her breath. She just needed to get through this visit and then she would be pledged to Venn and free of *him*.

Yet even as this thought arose, she could feel his presence, inextricably bound to her. She ran one hand along the small of her belly and the other over her swollen breasts. She wanted to believe this baby was Venn's. Needed something to give her hope, even if it was a lie. She swallowed the sour taste of bile that rose in her throat.

She would never be free.

Protocol demanded Ella attend their dinner that evening, so she sucked up as much power as she could to shield herself from the inevitable fear that would hijack her mind and body the instant she saw her brother.

When Lynden and Gohran arrived together, Ella could see from the easy way they chatted they must have spent the afternoon with one another. Now and then, Ella caught Lynden smiling shyly at her brother. Gohran responded with more warmth than she had ever seen him show, their hands touching as he passed platters and offered wine. Once, this might have warmed Ella's heart. But seeing her friend so relaxed around Gohran, knowing how damaged he was inside, what he was capable of as a result, felt as sharp as a switch across her naked back.

After a time, Gohran signalled to a nearby servant. As if by some pre-arranged signal, the servant carried a long wooden box and presented it to Ella. 'Your betrothal gift,' Gohran said. 'Unfortunately, it isn't anything you haven't seen before, but a gift is a gift, and it seemed a shame to have it go to waste.'

Ella's stomach sank through the floor. She took the box and opened it. Inside sat her cream dress, laundered and pressed, the string of pearls she had thrown at Gohran's feet nestled on top. 'Excuse me.' She set the box aside and hurried out of the room. Rushing past the servants, she didn't stop until she reached the water garden. Cold air hit her burning cheeks as her stomach convulsed repeatedly. She only returned to the hall once her insides were empty, and she could keep her shaking under control.

As she took her place, Gohran watched her with narrow eyes. He tore at a chunk of bread and used it to sop up his gravy. To Venn, he said, 'I had hoped your brother would be here.'

His tone was perfectly indifferent, but Ella's jaw stiffened.

'I trust you will forgive Lord Jonas's absence, Your Highness. He could not delay his duties in the north.' Venn's reply was as courteous as if he'd been truly ignorant of Gohran's intent.

Bloody juices soaked into Gohran's bread. 'You're looking awfully pale, Ella. I hope you're not *ill*.'

Had she imagined the emphasis? No, not with Gohran.

'So, Lord Venn.' He paused, waiting until he had everyone's full attention. 'When were you planning on announcing your news?' He popped the blood-soaked bread into his mouth, sucking at his fingers.

Ella nearly choked on her wine. Beside her, Venn turned sheet white.

In the end, it was Lynden who broke the silence. 'Ella, my sweet, you're with child?' She smiled what seemed to be a genuine smile. 'Venn, that's wonderful!'

Venn didn't look pleased, however. 'Ella?'

'You're going to be a father, Venn,' she said hopefully.

Venn shifted in his seat and cleared his throat into his wine glass.

'Oh, I hope it's a girl!' Lynden exclaimed. 'Though a boy would be better for the realm.'

Ella shrank into her chair and watched from her mental cocoon. She realised she had begun to resent Venn and Lynden, existing so loosely within themselves that it was impossible to know where their wills ended and hers began. More and more she understood her mother's coldness, forced to manipulate even those dearest to her. She shivered, causing Venn to circle his arms about her protectively. Where there should have been warmth, the action felt wooden and forced, reminding Ella of Sheevan, a marionette under her mother's control.

And all the while, across the table, Gohran stared and chewed.

Gohran had just lowered his lantern's wick when there was a quiet knock at the door. A moment later, it opened and Gohran saw Lynden's silhouette in the doorway. She looked beautiful, standing there in her nightdress.

'Your Highness.' She stepped inside.

'I was just on my way to bed.' There was a catch in his voice.

Moonlight from the window cast a glow along the edge of Lynden's hair, which fell in waves down her back as she tiptoed over to his chair. She stood above him, running her hands across his shoulders. He leaned in, burying his face. His shoulders shook, arms gripping her waist.

Lynden's fingers found his neck, his hair, as Gohran's hand moved towards her buttocks, the other tracing her back. His breath grew hot, and he stood, tugging at the ties of her nightdress, peeling the fabric away. Gohran gripped her back until his knuckles paled. He kissed her neck, her breasts, and she pressed against him. He caught her wrists in his hands and nudged her towards the rug, pushing her dress up above her thighs as he knelt before her. She bit her lip, back arching.

Gohran dared not close his eyes. He knew he would see the red of Ella's lips bitten through, the terror in her azure eyes. Lynden moved feverishly, limbs clutching him, pulling him deeper. Her half-closed eyes stopped seeing, but they could have reflected Ella's, wincing. She cried out, and he smothered her mouth with his. She whimpered still more, her nails biting into his back.

His vision turned black and shimmery and he rolled off her. Breathing hard, the rug's fibres prickled as he stared at the ceiling. A nighthawk's squawk disguised the rusty sound of his tears.

Later, when he was alone again, Gohran barred his door. What should have been a release left him restless, like trying to quench a thirst with saltwater. He sat naked on the bed, his hands upon his thighs. The crackle of static before a storm thundered through his limbs. He struggled to follow any single thought as he noticed a distant ache in his legs. Where his hands rested, he was gripping, blunt nails digging in. Instead of letting go, he grabbed more tightly, driving his nails into his flesh. He ran both hands along the length of his thighs and waited for the waves of soothing solace. They did not come. After a moment, he dug still harder. Again—nothing. Where his nails had just clawed, he saw raised welts. His throat was bone-dry. He gripped harder, ramming his nails into exposed flesh. It was not enough. Bare leg taunted him.

*Breathe. Breathe.*

His eyes searched the room, landing on a small penknife that rested on the writing table. A knife that was sharp enough to cut quills. Sharp enough to cut. And he needed more.

He shrugged the thought away. Not again. This vile impurity, impiety, that would not leave him be.

He wiped the sweat from his forehead. His shaking worsened, as though an excess of—something—filled him. He dragged his moist palms along his shirtfront, then grabbed the knife and gripped it crossways above his thigh, the blade just touching his skin. His knuckles had turned ghost-white. From here, there was no turning back. With a jagged breath, he drew the blade across his flesh. Biting pain as blood welled.

The cut was only an inch across, but it was enough. Relief ebbed and pulsed. What he had craved since destroying his altar, the only thing that could soothe him apart from *her*. He moaned softly... *Finally!*

# Sixty-Four

For appearances' sake, Ella spent that night in her old guest room. She lay awake a long time before sleep took her. When it did, she dreamed of her mother, stake-bound and charred, but still alive. Prya's head lolled atop her body as she mouthed Gohran's name over and again. Afterwards, Ella saw herself screaming and sweating. Something inside her writhed. She shoved and pushed to get it out, to be rid of it. It wriggled and squirmed as though trapped inside a cocoon.

Ella looked up. A robed woman with black hair and blue eyes stood over her. For a moment she thought it was her mother, but the woman's features were harder, weather worn. She handed Ella a knife hilt first. 'You must,' she whispered. 'Do it now or there will be no end.'

Ella swallowed, taking the knife in both hands. She turned it towards the giant bulge that was her pregnant belly. The blade glowed. She bit down on her lip, closed her eyes, and cut.

'Do not stop. Set it free. Free us...'

Ella winced in anticipation, but there was no pain. Instead, as she sliced clean across, she felt an intense relief, like water bursting through a dam. The release came in waves, and she lay back, watching the priestess's eyes glow, only now they weren't the woman's eyes, but Gohran's.

He watched the creature climb out of Ella's womb. 'The cut wasn't deep enough. You see—it lives,' he said.

Already it was growing, in a few quick seconds becoming a young girl. The likeness to herself was so strong Ella might have been looking at a mirror that saw into the past.

After a moment, the girl turned away and began skipping into the distance. Ella tried to follow, but always the child was just beyond her grasp. When she reached a pair of castle gates that bore Nedran's emblem, the girl passed through, but by the time Ella arrived, the gates had slammed shut, forever closed to her.

She called out to the girl-child, who stopped and turned, staring down at Ella's middle. Ella followed her frown to see the gash in her stomach still open. She was bleeding. So much blood! Ella called out once more, begging, but it was too late. The girl wept, shaking her head back and forth. After a moment, she turned away and continued, her dying mother looking on.

Ella woke to pain, sudden and biting in her abdomen, like the worst bout of moon-time. She edged her fingers between her damp thighs, then peered at them. Blood. Her heart thudded. She braced herself for the next cramp. It never came. She pressed upon her belly, smudging crimson fingers across her nightshirt, but all was still. Tentative fingers slipped below. Nothing. She shoved, and she pressed, howling silently through the ceiling at the gods.

It seemed Ella lay half-hunched, half-sprawled in a tangle of sheets for hours before Lynden found her. When she did, Lynden pulled her close and called for help.

Moments later, Bess arrived, panting from the stairs.

'Fetch His Royal Highness, Bess.' Lynden didn't take her eyes off Ella.

'Not Gohran. Please...' Ella whimpered.

'Princess Ella needs a medic.'

Bess hovered in the doorway.

'Go, Bess.'

'There's no pain now. I'm well. Please.' Ella's mind reached and stretched, grasping for her power to make them stop, but she found nothing.

'Ella,' Lynden pointed to Ella's blood-smeared nightgown. 'That's Nedran's heir you're carrying.'

Lynden's voice held the command of a chamberlain's strap and Ella felt the last of her will slither away. She tried to sit up. *Nedran's heir.* Too heavy. Lightning forks behind her eyes. Bedclothes wrapped her up and carried her into the dark.

Ella woke sometime later to the lurch and shift of a moving carriage. Erldan's carriage. Gohran sat watching her with a twist to his mouth. She shrank away from him, wishing she could claw her way out through the seat.

'Where are you taking me?'

Eyes straight, his voice an adder's tongue. 'Somewhere you'll be looked after. Somewhere safe.'

Ella reached for her power, but again found nothing. What had flowed so readily in the preceding weeks quivered, stifled by crowded memories, edging, shoving, to blind, to silence, to immobilise.

The carriage bumped back and forth, jerked by pits and potholes.

'Gohran. Gohran, I'm going to be sick.'

Gohran whistled for the driver to stop. He helped Ella down onto the grass, but kept a hold of one arm. With the other, he drew her hair back from her wan face. When Ella was done, he offered her his kerchief to wipe her mouth.

'We'd best keep on. Elnora's setting.'

Gohran was right. The sun was sinking ahead of them. Ella examined their surrounds. No wonder the road was so rough. It was no more than a deer trail. They were not heading back to Erldan, or to any sizable town or village. She couldn't even see signs of nearby farmsteads. Was he taking her to a remote herbalist who trafficked in poisons?

Gohran caught her looking around. 'There is nowhere to run, Ella.' He ushered her back into the carriage. 'I assure you, I only want to keep you safe.' Another whistle and they were again on their way.

Eventually, Elnora grappled at their backs, spreading the grey light of pre-dawn before cresting the horizon. Ahead, Ella saw the outline of a citadel.

*Aryon.*

Ella knew it instinctively. She choked back a bitter laugh. Of course! Why wouldn't Gohran send her to live with the witches? She was a witch, after all. No wonder he hadn't laid a lustful finger on her—he didn't need to. By locking Ella away in a celibate religious order, he could be certain no man would have her ever again. Jonas's words echoed in her mind once more. *If he can't have you, no one will.*

Two priestesses met the carriage, a blonde lass and an older woman with grey-streaked raven hair. The older one watched them with hard but familiar eyes—azure blue, the colour reflected every time she looked at her brother, at her mother, or in a mirror. The eyes from her dream. Aunt Bree, it must be. The fair-haired woman wore a plain robe, while Breeyan's robe was laden with sigils. Not much taller than Ella, Breeyan held herself with an air of command, as Prya had once done, as Gohran did now. Perhaps she was someone high up, maybe even their leader. When she stared at Ella, Ella felt as though Breeyan had turned her soul inside out.

Gohran stepped out of the carriage. He latched the door from the outside and ushered Breeyan away. Ella tried to watch through the carriage's small window, to hear through the walls, but Gohran led them out of sight and hearing. Still peering at the window, Ella tried to scry them out, letting her eyes go out of focus against the reflective glass. Now and then she could make out two silhouettes huddled together to form a shadowy orb, but the picture kept fogging over, slipping away. Exhausted, she gave up.

Breeyan sucked in her breath. Gohran. Here. How many years had it been? Gods, he walked just like his father. And he was tall, almost a man. He looked at her without recognition. She might have been one of his vassals. She let her eyes go out of focus to examine his aura. Instead of hugging his physical form, it shrank and swelled, buckling and shifting unlike anything she'd ever seen.

As soon as they were far enough away, Breeyan hissed, 'It's a bit late to be bringing her now.'

'Will you take her or not?'

'You know she's with child?'

'I'm not blind.'

It was early days, judging by Ella's aura. She wouldn't show through her dress for some moons. 'Why would you think a celibate order of sworn priestesses would take in a pregnant girl?'

'Because if you refuse her, Aunt, I might be forced to denounce her, as I did her mother.'

His words fell like a blow. Breeyan tightened her thought-shield. 'Who is the father? Is he likely to come looking for her?'

'Only Ella can answer that.'

'And her dowry?'

'I can offer you five warhorses, or their equivalent value in farm stock, if that should please you more, plus twenty silvers.'

Breeyan pretended to weigh his offer. He reeked of guilt. 'I'll take her for two horses and the rest in stock—breeding stock, plus twenty-five silvers.'

Breeyan watched as her priestesses ushered her niece towards the citadel. Ella peered back at them and Breeyan felt an odd hollowness, some emotion she couldn't quite place. It was almost like looking at her sister Prya but seeing her own reflection staring back. Resentment simmered beneath Ella's facade and Breeyan sensed scars marring her aura. She recalled arriving at the order all those years ago. She had cried for days on end. Finally, the High Priestess had pulled her aside and had words with her. After that, she'd buckled down, striving to become powerful, substituting one set of aspirations for another. It worked, too. Before completing her term as a novice, Breeyan had earned her place as Her Holiness' apprentice. She hoped the same would happen for Ella. It would be difficult, with Ella raising a child, but they could manage.

Breeyan turned her attention back to the king—her Gohran. She sensed his blanket still hidden beneath her robe where she kept it pressed against her heart. She could not hold him to her. Could not reveal the truth, for he must believe himself to be the true heir to Erldan.

A wry twist to Breeyan's mouth as she considered that without Rohan's betrayal and her sacrifice, Prya might have been cast aside, her womb capable of only carrying and bearing daughters. Had that occurred, Breeyan might have taken her rightful place after all, and she and Rohan could have raised their son together...

Breeyan brushed her pathetic fantasy aside, bringing her attention back to the grown man who stood before her, handsome and haughty. She inhaled and steeled herself, heart hardening. She could not even offer him shelter, the laws of the order preventing any unsworn male from stepping across Aryon's threshold. Instead, their interactions would be brief and perfunctory, the contract drawn up and brought out to them to seal.

Afterwards, as Gohran's carriage sank below the distant valley, the sealed contract in her hand, Breeyan noticed an unfamiliar wetness upon her cheeks. She brushed the tears away. At least she had Ella now, and with such a dowry.

# SIXTY-FIVE

When Lynden had woken Venn with news of Ella, Gohran had already taken her to fetch help.

'By the goddess. Lyn, why didn't you wake me? I would have gone with them.' Venn was almost in tears, running his hands through his hair as he paced.

'There wasn't time. Once Bess woke Gohran—'

Venn erupted. 'She should have woken *me*!' Then his voice cracked, and he repeated softly, 'She should have woken me...' Face in his hands, his shoulders shook. He couldn't lose her, not now. She was his sun, his soul, his everything.

Lynden rested an arm upon his shoulder. 'I'm so sorry, Venn. Gohran was the first person I thought of...'

With a deep inhale, Venn pulled himself together. 'It's not your fault, Lyn.'

'Gohran will take her to a medic, and all will be well. You'll see.'

Yet Venn couldn't shake the feeling that Lynden was mistaken. That something was very wrong.

Hunger, exhaustion, and fear of the horses pulling up lame forced Gohran and his driver Jarrod to stop when they came upon a small village on the way back from Aryon. The village sat on the outer fringes of habitable territory and appeared to belong to nomads rather than farmers, filled mostly with makeshift huts, the herd beasts free-roaming. A few of the structures were more substantial, but they seemed as old as time itself.

They pulled the carriage up beside the road. Long, straw-like grass whipped at their thighs as they walked towards the largest farmstead. A farmer leading ill-fed herd beasts by the tether stooped to kneel as they passed. He was as poorly nourished as his beasts, all jutting bones and sunken flesh, clothes hanging loosely around him.

Gohran barely acknowledged the gesture. His legs wobbled as though he'd been on horseback for seven days together. In the wind, the grass rippled like water. He stared at it rather than at the peasants who continued to mill. To Gohran they resembled a blur of brownish grey, possessing an overabundance of curious eyes. He wanted to scream at them to stop watching him, to leave him be. They kept bowing to him—to *him.* He gripped his hilt to steady his hands. He had the distinct sense of another set of eyes, ones he could not see, spying on him. Not Ella's. He shuddered.

Gohran went in search of a bath, leaving Jarrod to enlist a couple of dirt-encrusted youths to help build a fire and erect their tents. Someone pointed the king towards a stream. A heated tub was apparently too much to hope for. As he approached, it surprised him to find the water flowing strong. He kicked off his boots, unbuckled his scabbard, and plunged in.

On the surface, the water still held the day's warmth. Lower down, where his toes sludged between mud and vegetation it was wintry. He ducked beneath the surface for as long as he could stand and then climbed back out. He sat wet and shivering upon the bank. His neck still crawled with the feeling of being watched. It was hard to breathe. Cold air assaulted his skin. He'd had the taste of violence in his throat and the cries of hunger in his ears when he agreed to his aunt's terms, but what choice did he have? He felt for the pendant still tucked beneath his clinging shirt. His hands shook. Being so near Ella again had stirred him in ways that did not bear thinking about. What he had done, and now, knowing she was with child... What if it was—? *Oh, by the goddess!*

His stomach went into spasm. Saliva filled his mouth. He rolled over, perched on hands and knees, and heaved. Water from his hair ran off his brow and into his eyes. He blinked it away and spat onto the grass.

From behind came a child's voice, a girl. 'Pardon, my lord. Are you well?' Dark blue eyes peered at him.

Everything shifted and blurred. With a spray of water, Gohran got to his feet. He gripped the small girl by her shoulders. Her eyes bulged and her mouth quivered. Her frame was so delicate it might break—*like Ella's*. She struggled at first and then went limp, as Ella had under him. His fingers dug into her arms. 'I am so sorry,' he mouthed, head shaking back and forth. He blinked again, water covering his tears.

'Your Highness!' Jarrod stood over them.

*Not Ella. Not Ella. Just a child, a dark-haired little girl.* He let her go. A peasant woman snatched the child away. Arms blanketed and ushered her safely from him.

'That was King Gohran,' someone whispered.

Browns and greys, watching, watching. Gohran took a step back, smoothed his shirt and stood, palms out. 'I am sorry—I have just lost... So sorry...'

'Forgive His Highness,' Jarrod called to the gathered crowd. 'The king is not himself.' Jarrod's arm slid around his shoulder and drew him back towards camp and the warmth of the fire. Jarrod offered a skin of mead, presumably acquired from the villagers. Hands still trembling, Gohran sipped and then gulped, liquid spilling over and running down his cheeks, down his neck. There was food, too, but Gohran waved it away. A haze bubbled around him. The world would not sit still. It was like he hovered just outside his body. He took the next skin of mead that was offered to his tent and tied the flaps tight behind him.

In the morning, Jarrod found Gohran sprawled on the tent floor, the half-drunk skin draped beside him like a disembodied liver. More food arrived from the villagers—eggs, salted meat, and bread. 'It is quite good, Your Highness. It will help settle your stomach.'

This time, Gohran ate. Once finished, Jarrod took the empty wooden plate and watched him push the tent flap open and climb out into the glare of daylight. Jarrod crawled after to see him heading towards a copse, presumably to relieve himself, and set about dismantling the tent. No one offered to help pack up their gear and Jarrod did not ask.

As he hauled the rolled-up tent onto the carriage, Jarrod noticed an oversized cart laden with goods nearby. The cart contained mostly farm produce, and sacks of grain, all bundled and ready for transport. It was from this pile that the villagers had provided for the king. A woman hovered beside it, facing away, as though on guard.

'Excuse me,' he called. She ignored him, swaying slightly from foot to foot. 'Good lady.' Louder this time.

Jolting, she looked Jarrod's way, no longer swaying. Her eyes were a startling aquamarine, her hair so pale it was almost indistinguishable from her white skin.

'These goods here—' He pointed. 'Haven't your taxes already been collected?'

'Yes, sir.' She pulled her shawl up to cover her hair. 'Tithes. That there are tithes.'

He threw her a copper for her trouble, and then a few more. 'For the food,' he said. She scrambled to secret them away beneath her dress and resumed her post.

As soon as Gohran returned, they drove out, the vast wilderness jogging past. Jarrod wondered at the people living out here. Great expanses appeared completely parched, the earth orange and cracked. Those villagers had settled where there was water aplenty, but they were hardly fat from their bounty. Were the priests' tithes as much, if not more, than their lord's taxes? And that woman with her peculiar eyes... They were enough to pimple your flesh. She reminded him of those priestesses, an odd-looking bunch, all of them.

Jarrod had learned to be blind, deaf, and dumb as his king's service required, but taking Princess Ella to that place was certainly one of the more unusual things he'd witnessed. What happened next, however, was more so.

A couple of hours out of Nedran, Gohran ordered Jarrod to steer off the main road and unhitch a horse. Saddled with what might have been an overnight pack, Gohran left him waiting while he rode towards a nearby hillcrest. When Gohran returned several hours later, he was covered in mud, but no longer as jittery.

'We'll head straight for Nedran,' he said as he climbed aboard the carriage.

'Yes, Your Highness.'

Gohran did not know what had possessed him to bury the talisman beside his sister's mock grave. He had finished filling the hole back in, just deep enough to look convincing, and was placing the last of the gathered stones upon her counterfeit cairn when he felt it fire against his chest. He pulled it out and watched it blaze. It had glowed that way when he pulled Ella close during their carriage ride, too. He'd pictured its owner, that infant child, left to die, clinging to its skewered mother's skirts. It was that image more than any other urging him towards Aryon. That woman might have been Ella, the infant, her unborn child.

The child.

*It couldn't be...*

Standing over the mock grave, staring at the disc sitting in his open palm, remembering, it was all he could do not to lose the contents of his stomach. He had the peculiar sensation then that it was not his nausea, but Ella's. His shaking grew while the disc burned, taunting him. It slipped from his hand and landed beside the cairn. And then it came to him, what he needed to do. Bury it, like her. And so, he'd picked the shovel back up and started digging.

With all their stop-starting, it was twilight before Gohran reached the dryhten's great city. Venn ran to meet the carriage, Lynden trailing behind. Venn's hair stuck out in all directions, as though he'd been tugging on it. He looked as though he had not shaved, nor slept.

Gohran stepped out of the carriage, dirt crusting his clothes, his hair, his skin.

'What news?', 'How is Ella?', 'Where is she?', they bombarded him.

'The babe—she—I'm so sorry...' Gohran's voice cracked.

Lynden pushed her way to the front and reached for Gohran's elbows. 'Your Highness...?'

He shook his head. 'Gone. Ella's gone.' She had to be. From him. From everyone.

# THE LOST WARRIORS CONTINUES...

### *Ella's Curse, Book Two of The Lost Warriors*

**Cursed. Forbidden. Betrayed.**

*'The Curse hurts not only the violator—it touches those around them. It's said to bring horror thrice over.'*

All Ella's life, the threat of Xenon's Curse has loomed. The Curse of War and the Curse of Death. But when forced to live alongside the Sworn Priestesses of the Black Moon while carrying her forbidden child, she discovers the Curse is not all it seems.

Back in Ycelt, Gohran redoubles his efforts to stamp out heresy under the guiding hand of his head priest as the tendrils of Ella's power wrap themselves tighter around the lives of everyone she holds dear, threatening to tear them apart.

Venn, her erstwhile betrothed, risks the prosperity of his lands in his grief. Jonas, unmoored by Ella's apparent passing, finds himself tangled in a larger web of political intrigue and religious conspiracy than he could have imagined.

Will Gohran's rash behaviour and Ella's yearning for freedom lead them all down a path of darkness not seen since the time of the Ancients?

**Get your copy: https://mybook.to/EllasCurse**

# THANK YOU

## Thank you for joining me on this journey

**Need more?**

Dive deeper into the world you love with this bonus prequel novella

### *Breeyan's Betrayal*
### *A Lost Warriors Novella*

**'*...He could never give her the thing she craved most: his heart.*'**

*Forced from her home, a sworn priestess of the Black Moon, Breeyan seizes the chance to revisit her former life and the throne her sister stole. But while Queen Prya recovers from yet another miscarriage, she leaves Breeyan to entertain her first love: the king. A novice priestess, Breeyan should pose no threat. After all, King Rohan belongs to her sister, and she to the god. But can you ever trust someone you once betrayed?*

Subscribe to receive your exclusive prequel novella FREE:

christinepriestly.com/newsletter/

**Loving the series so far?**

Rate and review Christine's work wherever you get your books and book recommendations. Your support helps bring this work to new readers.

**Follow and connect**

Subscribe to Christine's newsletter for new releases, bonus content, and more:

christinepriestly.com/newsletter/

Website: christinepriestly.com

Connect: linktr.ee/christinepriestly

A full colour version of the map of Ycelt is available from:

christinepriestly.com/map/

# ACKNOWLEDGEMENTS

A tremendous shout out to the enthusiastic guides and helpful NPCs who made this journey through the tangled depths of my creative psyche possible:

To my muse, who occasionally showed up fashionably late but always brought the best ideas to the party, often at 3 AM (who needs sleep, anyway?)

To my furry companions: Ra, who insisted my glasses be on the floor (my face is for HIS face, thank you very much!); Luna, who pushed me off HER chair; and Loki, who demanded (loudly) that I write in bed so he could snuggle my feet.

To the friends who patiently listened to my plot ramblings and offered insightful advice, even though you probably had no idea what I was talking about.

To my family who know this has always been my dream (but it's okay, I got a 'real job' first!)

To my editor, whose enthusiasm, eye for detail, and patience with all my newbie publishing questions got this beast over the line.

To the fictional characters who refused to cooperate and constantly threw unexpected plot twists my way, keeping me on my toes and providing ample opportunities for character development (both theirs and mine).

To my alpha and beta readers: Imogen Reed, Kelly Richter, Lisa Witten, Courtney Gillespie, Samantha Starling, and Rebecca Ciezarek, who gave up their precious time, and expertly navigated the treacherous waters of my creative brain to point out gaping plot holes, inadvertent character flaws and important details like Jonas still being on his horse while inside a tavern, and seeming to teleport around (why do fictional characters need to follow the laws of physics, anyway?) I hope you're not too scarred! And most of all, for being my cheer squad and forcing me to keep writing so we can all find out what happens next.

And finally, to you, esteemed reader, for embarking on this wild ride with me. Whether you laughed, cried, or rolled your eyes at my attempts, your support means the world to me. Without you, this book would be nothing more than words on a page.

Thank you, from the bottom of my caffeine-fuelled and purr-filled heart.

With love and endless gratitude,

Christine Priestly

# ABOUT THE AUTHOR

**Christine Priestly** is an Australian author with a penchant for sipping tea, cuddling cats, and spinning stories (and poles!) in her spare time. By day, she's unravelling the mysteries of human desire as a sexologist and hypnotherapist, but by night, she's weaving tales that will leave you breathless and entertained. Her work has appeared in magazines and anthologies over the years, adding a dash of darkness and a pinch of spice to the literary world. So, grab a cuppa, pet your feline friend, and get ready to dive into Christine's world of words—it's one wild ride!

Follow Christine's journey and see upcoming titles:

christinepriestly.com

9 781763 512306